CAPTIVE DREAMS

CAPTIVE DREAMS

MICHAEL FLYNN

an imprint of

ARC
MANOR
Rockville, Maryland

ISBN: 978-1-61242-059-2

www.PhoenixPick.com
Sign Up for Free Ebooks

Copyright Acknowledgements (Original Publications):

Melodies of the Heart, copyright © 1994 by Michael Flynn. Originally appeared in *Analog Science Fiction and Fact*, January 1994.

Captive Dreams, copyright © 1992 by Michael Flynn. Originally appeared in *Analog Science Fiction and Fact*, August 1992.

Hopeful Monsters, copyright © 2012 by Michael Flynn. Original (First) Publication.

Places Where the Roads Don't Go, copyright © 2012 by Michael Flynn. Original (First) Publication.

Remember'd Kisses, copyright © 1988 by Michael Flynn. Originally appeared in *Analog Science Fiction and Fact*, December 1988.

Buried Hopes, copyright © 2012 by Michael Flynn. Original (First) Publication.

Library of Congress Cataloging-in-Publication Data

Flynn, Michael (Michael F.)
  Captive dreams / Michael Flynn.
    p. cm.
  ISBN 978-1-61242-059-2 (alk. paper) -- ISBN 978-1-61242-060-8 (e-book)
  I. Title.
PS3556.L89C37 2012
813'.54--dc23
                          2012025714

Published by Phoenix Pick
an imprint of Arc Manor
P. O. Box 10339
Rockville, MD 20849-0339
www.ArcManor.com

CONTENTS

INTRODUCTION

While writing the story "Remember'd Kisses" in 1988, I whimsically added a bit of color to one scene, in which the protagonist, Henry Norris Carter, looks out his back window.

> *The kitchen faced on a woods protected by "greenbelt" legislation from development. No danger of ticky-tacky working class homes depressing the property values. The canopy of the trees looked like a silhouette cut from black construction paper, the false dawn providing an eerie backlighting.*

Now, that described the scene outside the back window of the house where I was then living and in which by no coincidence I was writing the story. Two roads in the township fish-hooked into each other to form a rough oval, and the houses around the inside of the oval enclosed this bit of woodland, making it undevelopable. Write what you know, right? The intent was to induce something of a melancholy mood: the black silhouettes of the trees in the eerie lighting of the false dawn. It was a throwaway detail, no more.

A year or so later, I was writing the story "Melodies of the Heart" and because of a passing reference, I wrote a scene in which the character Dr. Wilkes walks through those woods and visits briefly with Henry and Barbry Carter. So arose the idea that the two otherwise unconnected stories took place in the same neighborhood.

Dr. Wilkes also meets with Charles Singer of "Soul of the City" and "The Washer at the Ford," but before he had become SingerLabs. In "Remember'd Kisses," Henry Carter had been described as working at SingerLabs sometime after the death of Charles Singer. So both stories were imagined in the milieu of *The Nanotech Chronicles*.

Concurrently with "Melodies…," I was working on the novelette "Captive Dreams" and had decided by then to place it too in the same neighborhood; and so little Ethan visits briefly with the now elderly Dr. Wilkes.

At this point I had the notion of writing stand-alone stories for each house in the neighborhood, with casual handshakes among them.

This was a curse. No further stories suggested themselves. Or more precisely, they wanted to be set elsewhere (or elsewhen) and I was disinclined to force a story into the neighborhood. I began to write *Firestar*, shorter fiction became less frequent, and eventually I dropped the idea.

Fast forward seventeen years. Shahid Mahmud of Phoenix Pick/Arc Manor, while producing an ebook of my collection *The Forest of Time*, asked me if I had any uncollected stories. Quite a few actually; but a rather eclectic mix. But one of them was "Captive Dreams," and I recalled my earlier intention. Shahid was intrigued, but "Melodies of the Heart" had already appeared several times, including in the just re-issued *The Forest of Time*. "Remember'd Kisses" had not appeared recently, but had been included in *The Nanotech Chronicles*. And the total word count of the three stories was not quite enough.

"Why not write a couple of new stories to sweeten the pot for readers?" he asked.

And that was how "Places Where the Roads Don't Go," "Hopeful Monsters," and "Buried Hopes" came into being during early-to-mid 2011. The three were pretty much written concurrently: When I got stuck on one story, I would flip over to one of the others. But if I had to give them an order, it would be the one just given, except that "Places…" received an extensive rewrite after the other two were finished.

And so we have here six stories: three old, three new; two novella-length, two novelettes, and two short stories.

The sequence used in this book is according to the implicit internal chronology of the story matter. However, some readers, interested for some reason in the development of my writing, may prefer to read them in the order of composition, which I have spelled out above.

A story should not need a spokesman, not even its author. It should speak for itself. But sometimes curious readers may be interested in the circumstances of the writing or in the speculative science involved. I have added a short afterword to each story, but you may prefer to skip those until you have read the entire set, or skip them entirely.

MELODIES OF THE HEART

I have never been to visit in the gardens of my youth. They are dim and faded memories, brittle with time: A small river town stretched across stony bluffs and hills. Cliffside stairs switchbacking to a downtown of marvels and magical stores. A little frame house nestled in a spot of green, with marigolds tracing its bounds. Men wore hats. Cars gleamed with chrome and sported tail-fins enough to take flight. Grown-ups were very tall and mysterious. Sometimes, if you were good, they gave you a nickel, which you could rush to the corner grocery and buy red hot dollars and jawbreakers and licorice whips.

I don't remember the music, though. I know I should; but I don't. I even know what the tunes must have been; I've heard them often enough on Classic Rock and Golden Oldy shows. But that is now; my memories are silent.

I don't go back; I have never gone back. The town would all be all different—grimier and dirtier and twenty years more run down. The house I grew up in was sold, and then sold again. Strangers live there now. The cliffside stairs have fallen into disrepair, and half the downtown stores are boarded up and silent. The corner groceries are gone, and a nickel won't buy you squat. Grown-ups are not so tall.

They are still a mystery, though. Some things never change.

> *The music is dreamy,*
> *It's peaches and creamy,*
> *Oh! don't let my feet touch the ground...*

I remember her as I always remember her: sitting against the wall in the garden sunshine, eyes closed, humming to herself.

9

The first time I saw Mae Holloway was my first day at Sunny Dale. On a tour of the grounds, before being shown to my office, the director pointed out a shrunken and bent old woman shrouded in a shapeless, pale-hued gown. "Our Oldest Resident." I smiled and acted as if I cared. What was she to me? Nothing, then.

The resident doctor program was new then. A conservative looking for a penny to pinch and a liberal looking for a middle-class professional to kick had gotten drunk together one night and come up with the notion that, if you misunderstood the tax code, your professional services could be extorted by the state. My sentence was to provide on-site medical care at the Home three days a week. Dr. Khan, who kept an office five miles away, remained the "primary care provider."

The Home had set aside a little room that I could use for a clinic. I had a metal desk, an old battered filing cabinet, a chair with a bad caster that caused the wheel to seize up—as if there were a Rule that the furniture there be as old and as worn as the inhabitants. For supplies, I had the usual medicines for aches and pains. Some digitalis. Ointments of one sort or another. Splints and bandages. Not much else. The residents were not ill, only old and tired. First aid and mortuaries covered most of their medical needs.

The second time I saw Mae Holloway was later that same first day. The knock on the door was so light and tentative that at first I was unsure I had heard it. I paused, glanced at the door, then bent again over my medical journal. A moment later, the knock came again. Loud! As if someone had attacked the door with a hammer. I turned the journal down open to the page I had been reading and called out an invitation.

The door opened and I waited patiently while she shuffled across the room. Hobble, hobble, hobble. You would think old folks would move faster. It wasn't as though they had a lot of time to waste.

When she had settled into the hard plastic seat opposite my desk, she leaned forward, cupping both her hands over the knob of an old black-thorn walking stick. Her face was as wrinkled as that East Tennessee hill country she had once called home. "You know," she said—loudly, as the slightly deaf often do, "you oughtn't leave your door shut like that. Folks see it, they think you have someone in here, so they jes' mosey on."

That notion had been in the back of my mind, too. I had thought to use this time to keep up with my professional reading. "What may I do for you, Mrs. Holloway?" I said.

She looked away momentarily. "I think—" Her jaw worked. She took a breath. "I think I am going insane."

I stared at her for a moment. Just my luck. A nut case right off the bat. Then I nodded. "I see. And why do you say that?"

"I hear music. In my head."

"Music?"

"Yes. You know. Like this." And she hummed a few bars of a nondescript tune.

"I see—"

"That was *One O'Clock Jump*!" she said, nearly shouting now. "I used to listen to Benny Goodman's band on *Let's Dance*! Of course, I was younger then!"

"I'm sure you were."

"What did you say?"

"I said, 'I'm sure you were'!" I shouted at her across the desk.

"Oh. Yes," she said in a slightly softer voice. "I'm sorry, but it's sometimes hard for me to hear over the music. It grows loud, then soft." The old woman puckered her face and her eyes drifted, becoming distanced. "Right now, it's *King Porter*. A few minutes ago it was—"

"Yes, I'm sure," I said. Old folks are slow and rambling and forgetful; a trial to talk with. I rose, hooking my stethoscope into my ears, and circled the desk. Might as well get it over with. Mrs. Holloway, recognizing the routine, unfastened the top buttons of her gown.

Old folks have a certain smell to them, like babies; only not so pleasant. It is a sour, dusty smell, like an attic in the summer heat. Their skin is dry, spotted parchment, repulsive to the touch. When I placed the diaphragm against her chest, she smiled nervously. "I don't think you'll hear my music that way," she said.

"Of course not," I told her. "Did you think I would?"

She rapped the floor with her walking stick. Once, very sharp. "I'm no child, Doctor Wilkes! I have not been a child for a long, long time; so, don't treat me like one." She waved her hand up and down her body. "How many children do you know who look like me?"

"Just one," I snapped back. And instantly regretted the remark. There was no point in being rude; and it was none of her business anyway. "Tell me about your music," I said, unhooking my stethoscope and stepping away.

She worked her lips and glared at me for a while before she made up her mind to cooperate. Finally, she looked down at the floor. "It was one, two nights ago," she whispered. Her hands gripped her walking stick so tightly that the knuckles stood out large and white. She twisted it as if screwing it into the floor. "I dreamed I was dancing in the Roseland Ballroom, like I used to do years and years ago. Oh, I was once so light on my feet! I was dancing with Ben Wickham—he's dead now, of course; but he was one smooth apple and sure knew how to pitch woo. The band was a swing band—I was a swinger, did you know?—and they were playing Goodman tunes. *Sing, Sing, Sing. Stardust.* But it was so loud, I woke up. I thought I was still dreaming for a while, because I could still hear the music. Then I got riled. I thought, who could be playing their radio so loud in the middle of the night? So I took myself down the hall, room by room, and listened at each door. But the music stayed the same, no matter where I went. That's when I knowed..." She paused, swallowed hard, looked into the corner. "That's when I knowed, knew, it was all in my head."

I opened the sphygmomanometer on my desk. Mae Holloway was over a hundred years old, according to the Home's director; well past her time to shuffle off. If her mind was playing tricks on her in her last years, well, that's what old minds did. Yet, I had read of similar cases of "head" music. "There are several possibilities, Mrs. Holloway," I said, speaking loudly and distinctly while I fastened the pressure cuff to her arm, "but the best bet is that the music really *is* all in your head."

I smiled at the *bon mot*, but all the wire went out of her and she sagged shapelessly in her chair. Her right hand went to her forehead and squeezed. Her eyes twisted tight shut. "Oh, no," she muttered. "Oh, dear God, no. It's finally happened."

Mossbacks have no sense of humor. "Please, Mrs. Holloway! I didn't mean 'in your head' like that. I meant the fillings in your teeth. A pun. Fillings sometimes act like crystal radios and pick up broadcast signals, vibrating the small bones of the middle ear. You are most likely picking up a local radio station. Perhaps a dentist could..."

She looked up at me and her eyes burned. "That was a wicked joke to pull, boy. It was cruel."

"I didn't mean it that way—"

"And I know all about fillings and radios and such," she snapped. "Will Hickey had that problem here five years ago. But that can't be why I hear music." And she extruded a ghastly set of false teeth.

"Well, then—"

"And what sort of radio station could it be? Swing tunes all the time, and only those that I know? Over and over, all night long, with no interruptions. No commercials. No announcements of song titles or performers." She raised her free hand to block her ear, a futile gesture, because the music was on the other side.

On the other side of the ear...? I recalled certain case studies from medical school. Odd cases. "There are other possibilities," I said. "Neuro-logical problems…" I pumped the bulb and she winced as the cuff tight-ened. She lowered her hand slowly and looked at me.

"Neuro…?" Her voice trembled.

"Fossil memories," I said.

She shook her head. "I ain't—I'm not rememberin'. I'm hearin'. I know the difference."

I let the air out of the cuff and unfastened it. "I will explain as simply as I can. Hearing occurs in the brain, not the ear. Sound waves vibrate certain bones in your middle ear. These vibrations are converted into neural im-pulses and conveyed to the auditory cortex by the eighth cranial nerve. It is the auditory cortex that creates 'sound.' If the nerve were connected to the brain's olfactory region, instead, you would 'smell' music."

She grunted. "Quite a bit of it smells, these days."

Hah, hah. "The point is that the sensory cortices can be stimulated without external input. Severe migraines, for example, often cause people to 'see' visions or 'hear' voices. And sometimes the stimulus reactivates so-called 'fossil' memories, which your mind interprets as contemporary. That may be what you are experiencing."

She looked a little to the side, not saying anything. I listened to her wheezy breath. Then she gave me a glance, quick, almost shy. "Then, you don't think I'm…You know…Crazy?" Have you ever heard hope and fear fused into a single question? I don't know. At her age, I think I might prefer a pleasant fantasy world over the dingy real one.

"It's unlikely," I told her. "Such people usually hear voices, not music. If you were going insane, you wouldn't hear Benny Goodman tunes; you would hear Benny Goodman—probably giving you important instruc-tions."

A smile twitched her lips and she seemed calmer, though still uneasy. "It's always been a bother to me," she said quietly, looking past me, "the notion that I might be—well, you know. All my life, it seems, as far back as I can remember."

Which was not that far, the director had told me that morning. "All your life. Why is that?"

She looked away and did not speak for a moment. When she did, she said, "I haven't had no, any, headaches, doc. And I don't have any now. If that's what did it, how come I can still hear the music?"

If she did not want to talk about her fears, that was fine with me. I was no psychiatrist, anyway. "I can't be sure without further tests, but a trigger event—possibly even a mild stroke—could have initiated the process." I had been carefully observing her motor functions, but I could detect none of the slackness or slurring of the voice typical of severe hemiplegia. "Dr. Wing is the resident neurologist at the hospital," I said. "I'll consult with him."

She looked suddenly alarmed, and shook her head. "No hospitals," she said firmly. "Folks go to hospitals, they die."

At her age, that was largely true. I sighed. "Perhaps at Khan's clinic, then. There really are some tests we should run."

That seemed to calm her somewhat, for she closed her eyes and her lips moved slightly.

"Have you experienced any loss of appetite, or episodes of drowsiness?" I asked. "Have you become irritable, forgetful, less alert?" Useless questions. What geezer did not have those symptoms? I would have to inquire among the staff to find out if there had been a recent change in her behavior.

And she wasn't listening anymore. At least, not to me. "Thank you, Doctor Wilkes. I was so afraid…That music…But only a stroke, only a stroke. It's such a relief. Thank you. Such a relief."

A relief? Compared to madness, I suppose it was. She struggled to her feet, still babbling. When she left my office, hobbling once more over her walking stick, she was humming to herself again. I didn't know the tune.

> *Even though we're drifting down life's stream apart,*
> *Your face I still can see in dream's domain;*
> *I know that it would ease my breaking heart*
> *To hold you in my arms just once again.*

It was dark when I arrived home. As I turned into the driveway, I hit the dashboard remote, and the garage door rose up like a welcoming lover. I slid into the left-hand slot without slowing, easing the Lincoln to a halt just as the tennis ball, hanging by a string from the ceiling, touched the windshield. Brenda never understood that. Brenda always came to a complete stop in the driveway before raising the garage door.

I could see without looking that I had beaten her home again. And they said doctors kept long hours…When I stepped from the car, I turned my back on the empty slot.

I stood for some moments at the door to the kitchen, jiggling the car keys in my hand. Then, instead of entering the house, I turned and left the garage through the back-yard door. I had seen the second-story light on as I came down the street. Deirdre's room. Tonight, for some reason, I couldn't face going inside just yet.

The back yard was a gloom of emerald and jade. The house blocked the glare of the street lamps, conceding just enough light to tease shape from shadow. I walked slowly through the damp grass toward the back of the lot. Glowing clouds undulated in the water of the swimming pool, as if the ground had opened up and swallowed the night sky. Only a few stars poked through the overcast. Polaris? Sirius? I had no way of knowing. I doubted that half a dozen people in the township knew the stars by name; or perhaps even that they had names. We have become strangers to our skies.

At the back of the lot, the property met a patch of woodland—a bit of unofficial greenbelt, undeveloped because it was inaccessible from the road. Squirrels lived there, and blue jays and cardinals. And possum and skunk, too. I listened to the rustle of the night dwellers passing through the carpet of dead leaves. Through the trees I could make out the lights of the house opposite. Distant music and muffled voices. Henry and Barbara Carter were throwing a party.

That damned old woman…Damn all of them. Shambling, crackling, brittle, dried-out old husks, clinging fingernail-tight to what was left of life…

I jammed my hands in my pockets and stood there. For how long, I do not know. It might have been five minutes or half an hour. Finally the light on the second floor went out. Then I turned back to the house and re-entered through the garage. The right-hand stall was still empty.

Consuela sat at the kitchen table near the French doors, cradling a ceramic mug shaped like an Olmec head. Half the live-in nurses in the country are Latin; and half of those are named Consuela. The odor of cocoa filled the room, and the steam from the cup wreathed her broad, flat face, lending it a sheen. More *Indio* than *Ladino*, her complexion contrasted starkly with her nurse's whites. Her jet black hair was pulled severely back, and was held in place with a plain, wooden pin.

"Good evening, Nurse," I said. "Is Dee-dee down for the night?"

"Yes, Doctor. She is."

I glanced up at the ceiling. "I usually tuck her in."

She gave me an odd look. "Yes, you do."

"Well. I was running a little late today. Did she miss me?"

Consuela looked through the French doors at the back yard. "She did."

"I'll make it up to her tomorrow."

She nodded. "I'm sure she would like that."

I shed my coat and carried it to the hall closet. A dim night-light glowed at the top of the stairwell. "Has Mrs. Wilkes called?"

"An hour ago." Consuela's voice drifted down the hallway from the kitchen. "She has a big case to prepare for tomorrow. She will be late."

I hung the coat on the closet rack and stood quietly still for a moment before closing the door. Another big case. I studied the stairs to the upper floor. Brenda had begun getting the big cases when Deirdre was eighteen months and alopecia had set in. Brenda never tucked Dee-dee into bed after that.

Consuela was washing her cup at the sink when I returned to the kitchen. She was short and dark and stocky. Not quite chubby, but with a roundness that scorned New York and Paris fashion. I rummaged in the freezer for a frozen dinner. Brenda had picked Consuela from among a dozen applicants. Brenda was tall and thin and blonde.

I put the dinner in the microwave and started the radiation. "I met an interesting woman today," I said.

Consuela dried her cup and hung it on the rack. "All women are interesting," she said.

"This one hears music in her head." I saw how that piqued her interest.

"We all do," she said, half-turned to go.

I carried my microwaved meal and sat at the table. "Not like this. Not like hearing a radio at top volume."

She hesitated a moment longer; then she shrugged and sat across the table from me. "Tell me of this woman."

I moved the macaroni and cheese around on my plate. "I spoke with Dr. Wing over the car phone. He believes it may be a case of 'incontinent nostalgia,' or Jackson's Syndrome."

I explained how trauma to the temporal lobe sometimes caused spontaneous upwellings of memory, often accompanied by "dreamy states" and feelings of profound and poignant joy. Oliver Sacks had written about it in one of his best sellers. "Shostakovich had a splinter in his left temporal lobe," I said. "When he cocked his head, he heard melodies. And there have been other cases. Stephen Foster, perhaps." I took a bite of my meal. "Odd, isn't it, how often the memories are musical."

Consuela nodded. "Sometimes the music is enough."

"Other memories may follow, though."

"Sometimes the music is enough," she repeated enigmatically.

"It should make the old lady happy, at least."

Consuela gave me a curious look. "Why should it make her happy?" she asked.

"She has forgotten her early years completely. This condition may help her remember." An old lady reliving her childhood. Suddenly there was bitterness in my mouth. I dropped my fork into the serving tray.

Consuela shook her head. "Why should it make her happy?" she asked again.

> *That little bird knew lots of things,*
> *It did, upon my word…*

✦

The universe balances. For every Consuela Montejo there is a Noor Khan.

Dr. Noor Khan was a crane, all bones and joints. She was tall, almost as tall as I, but thin to the point of gauntness. She cocked her head habitually from side to side. That, the bulging eyes, and the hooked nose accentuated her bird-like appearance. A good run, a flapping of the arms, and she might take squawking flight—and perhaps appear more graceful.

"Mae Holloway. Oh, my, yes. She is a feisty one, is she not?" Khan rooted in her filing cabinet, her head bobbing as she talked. "Does she have a problem?"

"Incontinent nostalgia, it's sometimes called," I said. "She is experiencing spontaneous, musical recollections, possibly triggered by a mild stroke to the temporal lobes." I told her about the music and Wing's theories.

She bobbed her head. "Curious. Like *déjà vu*, only different." Then, more sternly. "If she has had a stroke, even a mild one, I must see her at once."

"I've told her that, but she's stubborn. I thought since you knew her better…"

Noor Khan sighed. "Yes. Well, the older we grow, the more set in our ways we become. Mae must be set in concrete."

It was a joke and I gave it a thin smile. *The older we grow…*

The file she finally pulled was a thick one. I took the folder from her and carried it to her desk. I had nothing in particular in mind, just a review of Holloway's medical history. I began paging through the records. In addition to Dr. Khan's notes, there were copies of records from other doctors. I looked up at Khan. "Don't you have patients waiting?"

She raised an eyebrow. "My office hours start at ten, so I have no patients at the moment. You need not worry that I am neglecting them."

If it was a reproof, it was a mild one, and couched in face-saving Oriental terms. I hate it when people watch me read. I always feel as if they were reading over my shoulder. I wanted to tell Khan that I would call her if I needed her; but it was, after all, her office and I was sitting at her desk, so I don't know what I expected her to do. "Sorry," I said. "I didn't mean to ruffle your feathers."

Holloway was in unusually good health for a woman her age. Her bones had grown brittle and her eyes nearsighted—but no glaucoma; and very little osteoporosis. She had gotten a hearing aid at an age when most people were already either stone deaf or stone dead. Clinical evidence showed that she had once given birth, and that an anciently broken leg had not healed entirely straight. What right had she to enjoy such good health?

Khan had been on the phone. "Mae has agreed to come in," she told me as she hung up. "I will send the van to pick her up on Tuesday. I wish I could do a CAT scan here. I would hate to force her into hospital."

"It's a waste, anyway," I muttered.

"What?"

I clamped my jaw shut. All that high technology, and for what? To add a few miserable months to lives already years too long? How many dollars per day of life was that? How much of it was productively returned? That governor, years ago. What was his name? Lamm? He said that the old had a duty to die and make room for the young. "Nothing," I said.

"What is wrong?" asked Khan.

"There's nothing wrong with me."

"That wasn't what I asked."

I turned my attention to the folder and squinted at the spidery, illegible handwriting on the oldest record: 1962, if the date was really what it looked like. Why did so many doctors have poor handwriting? Holloway's estimated age looked more like an 85 than a 65. I waved the sheet of stationery at her. "Look at the handwriting on this," I complained. "It's like reading Sanskrit."

Khan took the letter. "I can read Sanskrit, a little," she said with a smile. "It's Doctor Bench's memo, isn't it? Yes, I thought so. I found it when I assumed Dr. Rosenblum's practice a few years ago. Dr. Bench promised he would send Mrs. Holloway's older records, but he never did, so Howard had to start a medical history almost from scratch, with only this capsule summary."

I took the sheet back from her. "Why didn't Bench follow through?"

She shrugged. "Who knows? He put it off. Then one of those California brush fires destroyed his office. Medically, Mae is a blank before 1962."

Just like her mind, I thought. Just like her mind.

> *For the joy of eye and ear*
> *For the heart and mind's delight*
> *For the mystic harmony*
> *Linking sense to sound and sight...*

✦

The third time I saw Mae Holloway, she was waiting by the clinic door when I arrived to open it. Eyes closed, propped against the wall by her walking stick, she hummed an obscure melody. "Good morning, Mrs. Holloway," I said. "Feeling better today?"

She opened her eyes and squeezed her face into a ghastly pucker. "Consarn music kept me awake again last night."

I gave her a pleasant smile. "Too bad you don't hear Easy Listening." I stepped through the door ahead of her. I heard her cane tap-tap-tapping behind me and wondered if a practiced ear could identify an oldster by her distinctive cane tap. I could imagine Tonto, ear pressed to the ground. "Many geezer come this way, *kemo sabe.*"

Snapping open my briefcase, I extracted my journals and stacked them on the desk. Mae lowered herself into the visitor's chair. "Jimmy Kovacs will be coming in to see you later today. He threw his back out again."

I opened the issue of the *Brain* that Dr. Wing had lent me. "Never throw anything out that you might need again later," I said, running my eye down the table of contents.

"You do study on those books, doctor."

"I like to keep up on things."

I flipped the journal open to the article I had been seeking and began to read. After a few minutes, she spoke again. "If you spent half the time studying on people as you do studying on books, you'd be better at doctorin'."

I looked up scowling. Who was she to judge? A bent-up, shriveled old woman who had seen more years than she had a right to. "The body is an intricate machine," I told her. "The more thoroughly I understand its mechanisms, the better able I am to repair it."

"A machine," she repeated.

"Like an automobile."

"And you're jest an auto mechanic." She shook her head.

I smiled, but without humor. "Yes, I am. Maybe that's less glamorous than being a godlike healer, but I think it's closer to the truth." An auto mechanic. And some cars were old jalopies destined for the junk heap; so why put more work into them? I did not tell her that. And others were not built right to begin with. I did not tell her that, either. It was a cold vision, but in its way, comforting. Helplessness is greater solace than failure.

Mae grunted. "Mostly milk sours 'cause it's old."

I scowled again. More hillbilly philosophy? Or simply an addled mind unable to hold to a topic? "Does it," I said.

She studied me for a long while without speaking. Finally, she shook her head. "Most car accidents are caused by the driver."

"I'll pass that along to the National Transportation Safety Board."

"What I mean is, you might pay as much attention to the driver as to the automobile."

I sighed and laid the journal aside. "I take it that you want to tell me what is playing on your personal Top 40 today."

She snorted, but I could see that she really did. I leaned back in my chair and linked my hands behind my head. "So, tell me, Mrs. Holloway, what is 'shaking'?"

She made fish faces with her lips. Mentally, I had dubbed her Granny Guppy when she did that. It was as if she had to flex her lips first to ready them for the arduous task of flapping.

"*Does Your Mother Know You're Out, Cecelia?*"

"What?" It took a moment. Then I realized that it must have been a song title. Some popular ditty now thankfully forgotten by everyone save this one old lady. "Was that a favorite song of yours?" I asked.

She shook her head. "Oh, mercy, no; but there was a year when you couldn't hardly avoid it."

"I see."

"And, let's see…" She stopped and cocked her head. The Listening Look, I called it. "Now it's *The Red, Red Robin*—"

"Comes bob-bob-bobbing along?"

"Yes, that's the one. And already today I've heard *Don't Bring Lulu* and *Side by Side* and *Kitten on the Keys* and *Bye-bye Blackbird*." She made a pout with her lips. "I do wish the songs would play out entirely."

"You told me they weren't your favorite songs."

"Some are, some aren't. They're just songs I once heard. Sometimes they remind me of things. Sometimes it seems as if they *almost* remind me of things. Things long forgotten, but waiting for me, just around a corner somewhere." She shook herself suddenly. "Tin Pan Alley wasn't my favorite, though," she went on. "I was a sheba. I went for the wild stuff. The Charleston; the Black Bottom. All those side kicks…I was a little old for that, but…Those were wild days, I tell you. Hip flasks and stockings rolled down and toss away the corset." She gave me a wink.

This…*prune* had gone for the wild stuff? Though, grant her, she had had her youth once. It didn't seem fair that she should have it twice. "Sheba?" I asked.

"A sheba," she said. "A flapper. The men were sheiks. Because of that… What was his name?" She tapped her cane staccato on the floor. "Valentino, that was it. Valentino. Oh, those eyes of his! All the younger girls dreamed about having him; and I wouldn't have minded one bit, myself. He had It."

"It?"

"It. Valentino drove the girls wild, he did. And a few boys, too. Clara Bow had It, too."

"Sex appeal?"

"Pshaw. Sex appeal is for snugglepups. A gal didn't have It unless both sexes felt something. Women, too. Women were coming out back then. We could smoke, pet, put a bun on if we wanted to—least, 'til the dries put on the kabosh. We had the vote. Why we even had a governor, back in Wyoming, where I once lived. Nellie Taylor Ross. I met her once, did I tell you? Why I remember—"

Her sudden silence piqued me. "You remember what?"

"Doc?" Her voice quavered and her eyes looked right past me, wide as tunnels.

"What is it?"

"Doc? I can see 'em. Plain as day."

"See whom, Mrs. Holloway?" Was the old biddy having a seizure right there in my office?

She looked to her left, then her right. "We're sitting in the gallery," she announced. "All of us wearing pants, too, 'stead o' dresses. And down there…Down there…" She aimed a shaking finger at a point somewhere below my desk. "That's Alice with the gavel. Law's sake! They're ghosts, Doc. They're ghosts all around me!"

"Mrs. Holloway," I said. "Mrs. Holloway, close your eyes."

She turned to me. "What?"

"Close your eyes."

She did. "I can still see 'em," she said, with a wonder that was close to terror. "I can still see 'em. Like my eyes were still open." She raised a shaking hand to her mouth. Her ragged breath slowly calmed and, more quietly, she repeated, "I can still see 'em." A heartbeat went by, then she sighed. "They're fading, now," she said. "Fading." Finally, she opened her eyes. She looked troubled. "Doc, what happened to me? Was it a hallucy-nation?"

I leaned back in my chair and folded my hands under my chin. "Not quite. Simply a non-musical memory."

"But…It was so *real*, like I done traveled back in time."

"You were here the whole time," I assured her with a grin.

She struck the floor with her cane. "I know that. I could see you just as plain as I could see Alice and the others."

I sighed. Her sense of humor had dried out along with the rest of her. "Patients with your condition sometimes fall into 'dreamy states,'" I explained. "They see or hear their present and their remembered surroundings simultaneously, like a film that has been double-exposed. Hughlings Jackson described the symptom in 1880. He called it a 'doubling of consciousness.'" I smiled and tapped the journal Wing had given me. "Comes from studying on books," I said.

But she wasn't paying me attention. "I remember it all so clearly now. I'd forgotten. Alice Robertson of Oklahoma was the first woman to preside over the House of Representatives. June 20, 1921, it was. Temporary Speaker. Oh, those were a fine fifteen minutes, I tell you." She sighed and shook her head. "I wonder," she said. "I wonder if I might remember my Ma and Pa and my little brother. Zach…? Was that his name? It's always been a trouble to me that I've forgotten. It don't seem right to forget your own kin."

An inverse square law, I suppose. Memories dim and blur with age, their strength depending on distance and mass. Too many of Mae's memories were too distant. They had passed beyond the horizon of her mind, and had faded like an old photograph left too long in the sun. And yet sometimes, near the end, like ashes collapsing in a dying fire, the past can become brighter than the present.

"No," I said. "It don't seem right."

"And Mister…Haven't thought on that man in donkey's years," she said. "Green Holloway was my man. I always called him Mister. He called me his Lorena."

"Lorena?"

Mae shrugged. "I don't remember why. There was a song…He took the name from that. It was real popular, so I suppose I'll recollect it bye and bye. He was an older man, was Mister. I remember him striding up through Black's hell; gray and grizzled, but strong as splo. All brass and buckles in his state militia uniform. Company H, 5th Tennessee. Just that one scene has stayed with me all my life, like an old brown photograph. Dear Lord, but that man had arms like cooper's bands. I can close my eyes and feel them around me sometimes, even today." She shivered and looked down.

"Splo?" I prompted.

"Splo," she repeated in a distracted voice. Then, more strongly, as if shoving some memory aside, "Angel teat. We called it apple john back then. Mister kept a still out behind the joe. Whenever he run off a batch, he'd invite the spear-side over and we'd all get screwed."

I bet. Whatever she had said. "Apple john was moonshine?" *High tail it, Luke. The revenooers are a-coming.* What kind of Barney Google life had she led up in those Tennessee hills? "So when you say you got screwed, you mean you got drunk, not, uh…"

Mae sucked in her lips and gnawed on them. "It was good whilst we were together," she said at last. "Right good." Her lips thinned. "But Mister, he lit a shuck on me, just like all the others." She gave me a look, half angry, half wary; and I could almost see the shutter come down behind her eyes. "Ain't no use getting close to nobody," she said. "They're always gone when you need them. Why, I ain't, haven't seen Little Zach nigh unto…" She looked momentarily confused. "Not for years and years. I loved that boy like he was more'n a brother; but he yondered off and never come back." She creaked to her feet. "So, I'll just twenty-three skidoo, Jack. You got things to do; so do I."

I watched her go, thinking she was right about one thing. Old milk does go sour.

> *There will I find a settled rest*
> *While others go and come.*
> *No more a stranger or a guest*
> *But like a child at home.*

Brenda's silver Beemer was parked in the garage when I got home. I pulled up beside it and contemplated its shiny perfection as I turned my engine off. Brenda was home. How long had it been, now? Three weeks? Four? It was hard to remember. Leave early; back late. That was our life. A quick peck in the morning and no-time-for-breakfast-dear. Tiptoes late at night; and the sheets rustle and the mattress sags; and it was hardly

MICHAEL FLYNN: CAPTIVE DREAMS

enough even to ruffle your sleep. Always on the run; always working late. One of us would have to slow down, or we might never meet at all.

My first thought was that I might give Consuela the night off. It had been so long since Brenda and I had been alone together. My second thought was that she had gotten in trouble at the office and had lost her job.

Doctors make good money. Lawyers make good money. Doctors married to lawyers make *very* good money. It was not enough.

"Brenda?" I called as I entered the kitchen from the garage. "I'm home!" There was no one in the kitchen; though something tangy with orange and sage was baking in the oven. "Brenda?" I called again as I reached the hall closet.

A squeal from upstairs. "Daddy's home!"

I hung up my overcoat. "Hello, Dee-dee. Is Mommy with you?" Unlikely, but possible. Stranger things have happened.

"No." Followed by a long silence. "Connie is telling me a story, about a mule and an ox."

Another silence; then footsteps on the stairs. Consuela looked at me over the banister as she descended.

"The mule and the ox?" I said.

"Nothing," she replied curtly. "An old Mayan folk tale."

"Where's Brenda?" I asked her. "I know she's home; her car is in the garage." Maybe she was in the back yard; by the pool or in the woods.

No, she didn't like the woods; she was afraid of deer ticks.

"Mrs. Wilkes came home early," Consuela said, "and packed a bag—"

Mentally, I froze. Not *this*. Not *now*. Without Brenda's income… "Packed a bag? Why?"

"She said she must go to Washington for a few days, to assist in an argument before the Supreme Court."

"Oh." Sudden relief coupled with sudden irritation. She could have phoned. At the Home. In my car. I showed Consuela my teeth. "The Supreme Court, you say. Well. That's quite a feather in her cap."

"Were she an Indio, a feather in the cap might mean something."

"Consuela. A joke? Did Brenda say when she would be back?"

Consuela hesitated, then shook her head. "She came home; packed her bag; gave me instructions. When the car arrived, she left."

And never said good-bye to Dee-dee. Maybe a wave from the doorway, a crueler good-bye than none at all. "What sort of instructions?" That wasn't the question I wanted to ask. I wanted to ask whose car had picked her up. Whom she was assisting in Washington? Walther Crowe, the steel-eyed senior partner with the smooth, European mannerisms? Fitz-Patrick, the young comer who figured so often on the society pages? But Consuela would not know; or, if she did, she would not say. There were some places where an outsider did not deliberately set herself.

"The sort of instructions," she replied, "that are unnecessary to give a professional. But they were only to let me know that I was her employee."

"You're angry." I received no answer. Then I asked, "Have you and Dee-dee eaten yet?"

"No." A short answer, not quite a retort.

"I didn't pull rank on you. Brenda did."

She shrugged and looked up at me with her head cocked to the side. "You are a doctor; I am a nurse. We have a professional relationship. Mrs. Wilkes is only an employer."

She was in a bad mood. I had never seen her angry before. I wondered what patronizing tone Brenda had used with her. I always made the effort to treat Consuela as an equal; but Brenda seldom did. Sometimes I thought Brenda was half-afraid of our Deirdre's nurse; though for what reason, I could not say. I glanced at the overcoat in the closet. "Would you and Dee-dee like to go out to eat?"

She gave me a thoughtful look; then shook her head. "She will not leave the house."

I glanced at the stairs. "No, she'll not budge, will she?" It was an old argument, never won. "She can play outside. She can go to school with the other children. There is no medical reason to stay in her—"

"There is something wrong with her heart."

"No, it's too soon for—"

"There is something wrong with her heart," she repeated.

"Oh." I looked away. "But…We'll eat in the dining room today. The three of us. Whatever that is you have in the oven. I'll set the table with the good dinnerware."

"A special occasion?"

I shook my head. "No. Only maybe we each have a reason to be unhappy just now." I wondered if Brenda had left a message in the bedroom. Some hint as to when she'd return. I headed toward the dining room.

"The ox was weary of plowing," Consuela said.

"Eh?" I turned and looked back at her. "What was that?"

"The ox was weary of plowing. All day, up the field and down, while the farmer cracked the whip behind him. Each night in the barn, when the ox complained, the mule would laugh. 'If you detest the plowing so much, why do it?' 'It is my job, señor mule,' the ox would reply. 'Then do it and don't complain. Otherwise, refuse. Go on strike.' The ox thought about this and, several days later, when the farmer came to him with the harness, the ox would not budge. 'What is wrong, señor ox?' the farmer asked him. 'I am on strike,' the ox replied. 'All day I plow with no rest. I deserve a rest.' The farmer nodded. 'There is justice in what you say. You have worked hard. Yet the fields must be plowed before the rains come.' And so he hitched the mule to the plow and cracked the whip over him and worked him for many weeks until the plowing was done."

Consuela stopped and with a slight gesture of the head turned for the kitchen.

Although entitled to two evenings a week off, Consuela seldom took them, preferring the solitude of her own room. She lived there quietly, usually with the hall door closed; always with the connecting door to Dee-dee's room open. Once a month, she sent a check to Guatemala. She read books. Sometimes she played softly on a sort of flute: weird, serpentine melodies that she had brought with her from the jungle. More than once, the strange notes had caused Brenda to stop whatever she was doing, whether mending or reading law or even making love, and listen with her head cocked until the music stopped. Then she would shiver slightly, and resume whatever she had been doing as though nothing had happened.

Consuela had furnished her room with Meso-American bric-a-brac. Colorful, twisty things. Statuettes, wall hangings, a window treatment. Squat little figurines with secretive, knowing smiles. A garland of fabric flowers. An obsidian carving that suggested a panther in mid-leap. Brenda found it all vaguely disturbing, as if she expected chittering monkeys swinging from the bookshelves and curtains; as if Consuela had brought a part of the jungle with her into Brenda's clear, ordered, rational world. It wasn't proper, at all. It was somehow out of control.

"Did you like having dinner downstairs today?" I asked Dee-dee as I studied Consuela's room through the connecting door. The flute lay silent on Consuela's dresser top. It was the kind you blew straight into, with two rows of holes, one for each hand.

"It was okay, I guess." A weak voice, steady but faint.

I turned around. "Only okay?" There was an odd contrast here, a paradox. Although it was evening and Deirdre's room was shrouded in darkness, Consuela's room had seemed bright with rioting colors.

"Did I leave any toys downstairs?" A worried voice in the darkness. Anxious.

"No, I checked." I resolved to check again, just in case we had overlooked something that had rolled under the sofa. Brenda detested disorder. She did not like finding things out of place.

"Mommy won't mind, will she? That I ate downstairs."

I turned. "Not if we don't tell her. Mommy will be at the Supreme Court for a few days."

Dee-dee made a sound in her throat. No sorrow, no joy. Just acknowledgment. Mommy might never come home at all for all the difference it made in Dee-dee's life. "Ready to be tucked in?"

Dee-dee grinned a delicious smile and snuggled deeper into the sheets. It was a heartbreaking smile. I gave her back the best one I could muster, and took a long, slow step toward her bed. She shrieked and ducked under the covers. I waited until she peeked out and took another step. It was a game we played, every move as encrusted with ritual as a Roman Mass.

Hutchinson-Gilford Syndrome. Dee-dee's smile was snaggle-toothed. Her hair, sparse; her skin, thin and yellow.

*Manifestations: Alopecia, onset at birth to eighteen months, with degeneration of hair follicles. Thin skin. Hypoplasia of the nails…*I had read the entry in *Smith's* over and over, looking for the one item I had missed, the loophole I had overlooked. It was committed to memory now; like a mantra. *Periarticular fibrosis; stiff or partially flexed prominent joints. Skeletal hypoplasia, dysphasia and degeneration.*

Dee-dee had weighed 2.7 kilos at birth. Her fontanel had ossified late, but the slowness of her growth had not become apparent until seven months. She lagged the normal growth charts by one-third. When she lost hair, it did not grow back. Her skin had brownish-yellow "liver" spots.

Natural history: Deficit of growth becomes severe after one year. The tendency to fatigue easily may limit participation in childhood activities. Intelligence and brain development are unimpaired.

Deirdre Wilkes was an alert, active mind trapped in a body aging far too quickly. A shrunken little gnome of a ten-year-old. *Etiology: Unknown.* I hugged her and kissed her on the cheek. Then I tucked the sheets tightly under the mattress.

Prognosis: The life span is shortened by relentless arterial atheromatosis. Death usually occurs at puberty.

There were no papers delivered on Hutchinson-Gilford that I had not crawled through word after word, searching for the slightest whisper of a breakthrough. Some sign along the horizon of research. But there were no hints. There were no loopholes.

Prognosis: death.

There were no exceptions.

Deirdre could smile because she was only a child and could not comprehend what was happening to her body. She knew she would have to "go away" someday, but she didn't know what that really meant.

Smiling was the hardest part of the game.

> *Come along, Josephine, In my flying machine.*
> *We'll go up in the air...*

How can I explain the feelings of dread and depression that enveloped me every time I entered Sunny Dale? I was surrounded by ancients. Bent, gray, hobbling creatures forever muttering over events long forgotten or families never seen. And always repeating their statements, always repeating their statements, as if it were I who were hard of hearing and not they. The Home was a waiting room for Death. Waiting and waiting, until they had done with waiting. Here is where the yellowed skin and the liver spots belonged. Here! Not on the frame of a ten-year-old.

The fourth time I saw Mae Holloway, she crept up behind me as I opened the door to the clinic. "Morning, doc," I heard her say.

"Good morning, Mrs. H.," I replied without turning around. I opened the door and stepped through. Inevitably, she followed, humming. I wondered if this was going to become a daily ritual. She planted herself in the visitor's chair. Somehow, it had become her own. "The show just ended," she announced. "Oh, it was a peach." She waved a hand at my desk. "Go on, set down. Make yourself pleasant."

It was my own fault, really. I had shown an interest in her tiresome recollections, and now she felt she had to share everything with me, as if I were one of her batty, old cronies. No good deed goes unpunished. Perhaps I was the only one who put up with her.

But I did have a notion that could wring a little use out of my sentence. I could write a book about Mae Holloway and her musical memories. People were fascinated with how the mind worked; or rather with how it failed to work. Sacks had described similar cases of incontinent nostalgia in one of his books; and if he could make the best-seller lists with a collection of neurological case studies, why not I? With fame, came money; and the things money could buy.

But my book would have to be something new, something different; not just a retelling of the same neurological tales. The teleology, perhaps. Sacks had failed to discover any meaning to the music his patients had heard, any reason *why* this tune or that was rememb-heard. If I kept a record, I might discover enough of a pattern to form the basis of a book. I rummaged in my desk drawer and took out a set of file cards that I had bought to make notes on my patients. Might as well get started. I poised my pen over a card. "What show was that?" I asked.

"*Girl of the Golden West*. David Belasco's new stage play." She shook her head. "I first seen it, oh, years and years ago, in Pittsburgh; before they made it a highfalutin' opera. That final scene, where Dick Johnson is hiding in the attic, and his blood drips through the ceiling onto the sheriff… That was taken from real life, you know."

"Was it." I wrote *Girl of the Golden West* and *doubling episode* and made a note to look it up. Then I poised my pen over a fresh card. "I'd like to ask you a few questions about your music, Mrs. Holloway. That is, if you don't mind."

She gave me a surprised glance and looked secretly pleased. She fussed with her gown and settled herself into her seat. "You may fire when ready, Gridley."

"You *are* still hearing the music, aren't you, Mrs. Holloway?"

"Well, the songs aren't so loud as they were. They don't keep me awake anymore; but if I concentrate, I can hear 'em."

I made a note. "You've learned to filter them out, that's all."

"*If You Talk in Your Sleep, Don't Mention My Name*."

"What?"

"*If You Talk in Your Sleep, Don't Mention My Name*. That was one of 'em. The tunes I been hearing. Go on, write that down. Songs were getting real speedy in those days. There was *Mary Took the Calves to the Dairy Show* and *This is No Place for a Minister's Son*. Heh-heh. The blues was all in a lather over 'em. That, and actor-folks actually kissing each other in the moving picture shows. They tried to get that banned. And the animal dances, too."

"Animal dances?"

"Oh, there were a passel of 'em," she said. "There was the kangaroo dip, the crab step, the fox trot, the fish walk, the bunny hug, the lame duck…I don't remember them all."

"The fox trot," I offered. "I think people still dance that."

Mae snorted. "All the fire's out of it. You should have read what the preachers and the newspapers had to say about it back then. They sure were peeved; but the kids thought it was flossy. It was a way to get their parents' goat. 'Bug them,' I guess you say now."

"Kids? Isn't the fox trot a ballroom dance for, well, you know—mature people?"

She made her sour lemon face. "Sure. Now. But today's old folks were

29

yesterday's kids. And they still like the music they liked when they were young. Heh-heh. When you're ninety or a hundred, sonny, you'll be a-listening to that acid rock stuff and telling your grandkids what hell-raisers you used to be. And they won't believe you, either. We tote the same bags with us all our lives, doc. The same interests; the same likes and dislikes. Those older'n us and those younger'n us, why, they have their own bags." A sudden scowl, halfway between fright and puzzlement, passed across her face like the shadow of a cloud. Then she hunched her shoulders. "Me, I've got too many bags."

She'd get no argument from me on that. "Have you heard any other songs?" I asked.

She folded her hands over the knob of her walking stick and rested her chin on them. "Let's see…Yesterday, I heared, heard *Waiting for the Robert E. Lee* and *A Perfect Day.* Those were real popular, once. And lots of Cohan songs. 'Oh, it was Mary, Mary, long before the fashion changed…' And *Rosie O'Grady.* Then there was *Memphis Blues.* Young folks thought it was 'hep.' Even better than ragtime."

She shook her head. "I never cottoned too well to those kids, though," she said. "They remind me of the kids nowadays. A little too…What do they say now? 'Close to the edge.' Ran wild when they were young 'uns, they did. Hung around barbershops. Hawked papers as newsies. Worked the growler for their old man."

I looked up from my notes. "Worked the growler?"

"Took the beer bucket to the saloon to get it filled. Imagine sending a child—even girls!—into a saloon! No wonder Carrie and the others wanted to close 'em up. Maybe folks my age were a little too stuck on ourselves, like the younger folks said; but at least we had principles. With us, it wasn't all just to have a good time. We fought for things worth fighting for. Suffrage. Prohibition. Birth control. Oh, those were times, I tell you. Maggie, making those speeches about birth control and standing up there on the stage that one time with the tape over her mouth, because they wouldn't let her talk. I helped her open that clinic of hers over in Brooklyn, though I never did care for her attitude about Jews and coloreds. Controlling 'undesirables' wasn't the real reason for birth control, anyway."

"Mrs. Holloway!"

She looked at me and laughed. "Now, don't tell me your generation is shocked at such talk!"

"It's not that. It's…"

"That old folks wrangled over it, too? Well, folks aren't born old. We were young, too; and as full of piss and vinegar as anyone else. I read *Moral*

Physiology when it first come out; though Mister did try mightily to discourage me. And, later, there was *The Unwelcomed Child*. Doc, if men had babies, birth control would never have been a crime."

*Folks aren't born old...*I squared off my deck of index cards. "I suppose not." My generation had been as strong as any for civil rights and feminism. Certainly stronger than the hard-edged, cynics coming up behind us. It sounded as if Mae had had a similar generational experience. Though, that would put her in the generation *before* the hell-raising Lost Generation. What was it called? The Missionary Generation? Maybe she was older than she looked; though that hardly seemed possible. "Let's get back to the songs—" I suggested.

"Yes, the songs," she said. "The songs. Why, I recollect a man had a right good voice...Now what was his name...? A wonderful dancer, too."

"Ben Wickham?" I suggested.

"No. No, Ben was later. This was out Pittsburgh way. Joe Paxton. That was it." She tilted her head back. "He was a barnstormer, Joe was. He knew 'em all. Calbraith Rodgers, Glenn Curtiss, Pancho Barnes, even Wilbur Wright. Took me up oncet, through the Alleghenies. Oh, my, that was something, let me tell you. The wind in your face and the ground drifting by beneath you, and the golden sun peeking between the shoulders of the hills...And you felt you were dancing with the clouds." She sighed, and the light in her eyes slowly faded. "But he was like all the rest." Her face closed up; became hard. "I come on him one day packing his valise, and when I asked him why he was cutting out, all he would say was, 'How old is Ann?'"

"What?"

She blinked and focused moistened eyes on me. Slowly, before they could even fall, her tears vanished into the sand of her soul. "Oh, that's what everyone said back then. 'How old is Ann?' It meant 'Who knows?' Came from one of those brain teasers that ran in the *New York Press*. You know. 'If Mary is twice as old as Ann was when Mary...' And it goes through all sorts of contortions and ends up 'How old is Ann?' Most folks hadn't the foggiest notion and didn't care, so they started saying 'How old is Ann?' when they didn't know the answer to something." She pushed down on her walking stick and started to rise.

"Wait. I still have a few questions."

"Well, I don't have any more answers. Joe...Well, he turned out worthless in the end; but we had some high times together." Then she sighed and looked off into the distance. "And he did take me flying, once, when flying was more than just a ride."

As I was walking down the street, down the street, down the street,
A handsome gal I chanced to meet. Oh, she was fair to view.
Lovely Fan', won't you come out tonight, come out tonight, come out
tonight?
Lovely Fan', won't you come out tonight, and dance by the light of the
moon?

It was late in the evening—midnight, perhaps—and, dressed in house-coat and slippers, I was frowning over a legal pad and a few dozen index cards, a cup of cold coffee beside me on the kitchen table. I was surrounded by small, sourceless sounds. If you have been in a sleeping building at night, you know what I mean. Creaks and rustlings and the sighs of… What? Spirits? Air circulation vents? The soft groan of settling timbers. The breath of the wind against the windows. The staccato scritching of tiny night creatures dancing across the roof shingles. The distant rumble of a red-eye flight making its descent into the metropolitan area. Among such confused, muttering sounds, who can distinguish the pad of bare feet on the floor?

A gasp, and I turned.

I had never seen Consuela when she was not wearing nurse's whites. Perhaps once or twice, bundled in a coat as she sought one of her rare nights out; but never in a red and yellow flowing flowered robe. Never with her black hair unfastened and sweeping around her like a raven-feather cape. She stood in the kitchen doorway, clenching the collar in her fist.

"Consuela," I said.

"I—saw the light on. I thought you had already gone to sleep. So I—" Consuela flustered was a new sight, too. She turned to go. "I did not mean to disturb you."

"No, no. Stay a while." I laid my pen down and stretched. "I couldn't get to sleep, so I came down here to work a while." When she hesitated, I stood and pulled a chair out for her. She gave me a sidelong look, then bobbed her head once and took a seat. I wondered if she thought I might "try something." Late at night; wife away; both of us in pajamas, thoughts of bed in our minds. Hell, *I* wondered if I might try something. Brenda had grown more distant each year since Deirdre's birth.

But Consuela was not my type. She was too short, too wide, too dark. I studied her covertly while I handled her chair. Well, perhaps not "too." And she did have a liquid grace to her, like a panther striding through the jungle. Brenda's grace was of a different sort. Brenda was fireworks arcing and bursting across the night sky. You might get burnt, but never bitten.

"Would you like something to drink?" I asked when she had gotten settled. "Apple juice, orange juice." Too late for coffee; and a liqueur would have been inappropriate.

"Orange juice would be fine, thank you," she said.

I went to the refrigerator and removed the carafe. Like everyone else, we buy our OJ in wax-coated paperboard containers; but Brenda transferred the milk, the juices, and half a dozen other articles into carafes and canisters and other more appropriate receptacles. Most people shelved their groceries. We repackaged ours.

"Do you remember the old woman I told you about last week?"

"The one who hears music? Yes."

I brought the glasses to the table. "She's starting to remember other things, now." I told her about Mae's recollections, her consciousness doubling. "I've started to keep track of what she sees and hears," I said, indicating the papers on the table. "And I've sent to the military archives to see if they could locate Green Holloway's service records. Later this week, I plan to go into the City to check the census records at the National Archives."

Consuela picked up the legal pad and glanced at it. "Why are you doing this thing?"

"For verification. I'm thinking I might write a book."

She looked at me. "About Mrs. Holloway?"

"Yes. And I think I may have found an angle, too." I pointed to the pad she held. "That is a list of the songs and events Holloway has rememb-heard."

After a moment's hesitation, Consuela read through the list. She shook her head. "You are looking for meaning in this?" Her voice held a twist of skepticism in it. For a moment, I saw how my activities might look from her perspective. Searching for meaning in the remembered songs of a half-senile old woman. What should that be called, senemancy? Melodimancy? What sort of auguries did High Priest Wilkes find, eviscerating this morning's ditties?

"Not meaning," I said. "Pattern. Explanation. Some way to make sense of what she is going through."

Consuela gave me that blank look she liked to affect. "It may not make sense."

"But it almost does." I riffed the stack of index cards. Each card held information about a song Mae had heard. The composer, songwriter, performer; the date, the topic, the genre. Whether Mae had liked it or not.

"The first time she came to me," I said, "she was 'rememb-hearing' swing tunes from the 1930s. A few days later, it was music of the 'Roaring Twenties.' Then the jazz gave way to George M. Cohan and the 'animal dance' music of the Mauve Decade. Do you see? The songs keep coming from earlier in her life."

Memphis Blues, 1912. *A Perfect Day*, 1910. *Mary Took the Calves to the Dairy Show*, 1909. *Rosie O Grady*, 1906. Songs my grandparents heard as children. "East side, west side, All around the town…" I remembered how Granny used to sit my brother and me on her lap, one on each knee, and rock us back and forth while she sang that. I paused and cocked my head, listening into the silence of the night.

But I could hear nothing. I could remember *that* she sang it; but I could not remember the singing.

"It is a voyage," I said, loudly, to cover the silence. "A voyage of discovery up the stream of time."

Consuela shook her head. "Rivers have rapids," she said, "and falls."

> *Hello, my baby, hello, my honey, hello, my ragtime gal…*
> *Send me a kiss by wire,*
> *Baby, my heart's on fire.*

Mae's morning visits fell into a routine. She settled herself into her chair with an air of proprietorship and croaked out snatches of tunes while I wrote down what I could, recording the rest on a cheap pocket tape recorder I had purchased. She hummed *The Maple Leaf Rag* and *Grace and Beauty* and the *St. Louis Tickle*. I suffered through her renditions of *My Gal Sal* and *The Rosary*. ("A big hit," she assured me, "for over twenty-five years.") She remem-heard the bawdy *Hot Time in the Old Town Tonight* (sounding grotesque on her ancient lips), the raggy *You've Been a Good Old Wagon, But You've Done Broke Down*, and the poignant *Good-bye, Dolly Gray*.

She frowned for a moment. "Or was that 'Nellie Gray'?" Then she shrugged. "Those were happy songs, mostly," she said. "Oh, they were such good songs back then. Not like today, all angry and shouting. Even the sad songs were sweet. Like *Tell Them That You Saw Me* or *She's Only a Bird in a Gilded Cage*. And Mister taught me *Lorena*, once. I wish I could recollect that 'un. And *Barbry Ellen*. I learned me that 'un when I was knee-high to a grasshopper. Pa told me it was the President's favorite song. The old President, from when his Pappy fought in the War. I haven't heard those yet. Or—" She cocked her head to the side. "Well, dad-blast it!"

"What's wrong, Mrs. Holloway?"

"I'm starting to hear coon songs."

"Coon songs!"

She shook her head. "Coon songs. They was—were—all the rage. *Coon, Coon, Coon* and *All Coons Look Alike to Me* and *If the Man in the Moon Were a Coon*. Some of them songs were writ by coloreds themselves, because they had to write what was popular if they wanted to make any money."

"Mrs. Holloway…!"

"Never said I liked 'em," she snapped back. "I met plenty of coloreds in my time, and there's some good and some bad, just like any other folks. Will Biddle, he farmed two hollers over from my Pa when I was a sprout, and he worked as hard as any man-jack in the hills, and carried water for no man. My Pa said—My Pa…" She paused, frowned and shook her head.

"Pa?"

"What is it?"

"Oh."

"Mrs. Holloway?"

She spoke in a whisper, not looking at me, not looking at anything I could see. "I remember when my Pa died. Him a-laying on the bed, all wore out by life. Gray and wrinkled and toothless. And, dear Lord, how that ached me. I remember thinking how he'd been such a strong man. Such a strong man." She sighed. "It's an old apartment, and the wallpaper is peeling off'n the walls. There's a big, dark water stain on one wall and the steam radiator is hissing like a cat."

"You don't remember where you were…are?" I asked, jotting a few quick notes.

She shook her head. "No. I'm humming *In the Good Old Summertime*. Or maybe the tune is just running through my head. Pa, he…" A tear formed in the corner of her eye. "He wants me to sing him the song."

"The song? What song is that?"

"An old, old song he used to love. 'Sing it to me one last time,' he says. And I can't sing at all because my throat's clenched up so tight. But he asks me again, and…Those eyes of his! How I loved that old man." Mae's own eyes had glazed over as she lived the scene again in her mind. She reached out as if clasping another pair of hands in her own and croaked haltingly:

> "*I gaze on the moon as I tread the drear wild,*
> *And feel that my mother now thinks of her child…*
> *Be it ever so humble…*"

She could not finish. For a time, she sobbed softly. Then she brushed her eye with her sleeve and looked past me. "I never knew, doc. I never knew at all what a blessing it was to forget."

> *Come and sit by my side if you love me.*
> *Do not hasten to bid me adieu,*
> *But remember the bright Mohawk Valley*
> *And the girl that has loved you so true.*

Later that day, as I was leaving the Home, I noticed Mae sitting in the common room and paused a moment to eavesdrop. There were a handful of other residents mouldering in chairs and rockers; but Mae sat singing quietly to herself and I thought what the hell, and pulled out my pocket tape recorder and stepped up quietly beside her.

It was a patriotic hymn. *America, the Beautiful.* I'm sure you've heard it. Even I know the words to that one. Enough to know that Mae had them all wrong. *Oh beautiful for halcyon skies? Above the enameled plain?* And the choruses…The way Mae sang it, "God shed his grace for thee" sounded more like a plea than a statement.

> *America! America! God shed his grace for thee*
> *Till selfish gain no longer stain The banner of the free!*

The faulty recollection disturbed me. If Mae's memories were unreliable, then what of my book? What if my whole rationale turned out wrong?

Her croakings died away and she opened her eyes and spotted me. "Heading home, doc?"

"It's been a long day," I said. There was no sign on her face of her earlier melancholy, except that maybe her cheeks sagged a little lower than before, her eyes gazed a little more sadly. She seemed older, somehow; if such a thing were possible.

She patted the chair next to her. "Hot foot it on over," she said. "You're just in time for the slapstick."

She was obviously having another doubling episode and, in some odd way, I was being asked to participate. I looked at my watch, but decided that since our morning session had been cut short, I might as well make the time up now. My next visit was not until Friday. If I waited until then, these memories could be lost.

"Slapstick?" I asked, taking the seat she had offered.

"You never been to the Shows?" She tsk-ed and shook her head. "Well,

Jee-whiskers. They been the place to go ever since Tony Pastor got rid of the cootchee-cootchee and cleaned up his acts. A young man can take his steady there now and make goo-goo eyes." She nudged me with her elbow. "A fellow can be gay with his fairy up in the balcony."

I pulled away from her. "I beg your pardon?"

"Don't you want to be gay?" she asked.

"I should hope not! I have a wife, a dau…"

Mae laughed suddenly and capped a gnarled hand over her mouth. So help me, she blushed. "Oh, my goodness, me! I didn't mean were you a *cake-eater*. I got all mixed up. I was sitting down front at the burly-Q and I was sitting here in the TV room with you. When we said, 'be gay,' we meant let your hair down and relax. And a 'fairy' was your girl friend, what they used to call a chicken when I was younger. All the boys wanted to be gay blades, with their starched collars and straw hats and spats. And their moustaches! You never saw such moustaches! Waxed and curled and bar-bered." She chuckled to herself. "I was a regular daisy, myself." She closed her eyes and leaned back.

"A regular daisy?"

"A daisy," she repeated. "Like in the song. Gals was going out to work in them days. So they made a song about it. Now, let me see…" She pouted and stared closed-eyed at the sky. "How did that go?" She began to sing in a cracked, quavery voice.

> *"My daughter's as fine a young girl as you'll meet*
> *In your travels day in and day out;*
> *But she's getting high-toned and she's putting on airs*
> *Since she has been working about…*
>
> *When she comes home at night from her office,*
> *She walks in with a swag like a fighter;*
> *And she says to her ma, 'Look at elegant me!'*
> *Since my daughter plays on the typewriter.*
>
> *She says she's a 'regular daisy,'*
> *Uses slang 'til my poor heart is sore;*
> *She now warbles snatches from operas*
> *Where she used to sing 'Peggy O Moore.'*
>
> *Now the red on her nails looks ignited;*
> *She's bleached her hair 'til it's lighter.*

Now perhaps I should always be mad at the man
That taught her to play the typewriter.

She cries in her sleep, 'Your letter's to hand.'
She calls her old father, 'esquire';
And the neighbors they shout
When my daughter turns out,
'There goes Bridget Typewriter Maguire.'"

When Mae was done, she laughed again and wiped tears from her eyes. "Law's sake," she said. "Girls a-working in the offices. I remember what a stir-up that was. Folks said secretarial was man's work, and women couldn't be good typewriters, no how. There was another song, *Everybody Works But Father*, about how if women was to go to work, all the men would be out of jobs. Heh-heh. I swan! It weren't long afore one gal in four had herself a 'position,' like they used to say; and folks my age complained how the youngsters were 'going to pot.'" She shook her head and chuckled.

"I always did find those kids more to my taste," she went on. "There was something about 'em; some spark that I liked. They knew how to have fun without that ragged edge that the next batch had. And they had, I don't know, call it a dream. They were out to change the world. They sure weren't wishy-washy like the other folks my age. 'Middle aged,' that's what the kids back then called us. We were 'Professor Tweetzers' and 'Miss Nancys' and 'goo-goos'. And to tell you the truth, Doc, I thought they pegged it right. People my age grew up trying to imitate their parents; until they saw how much more fun the kids were having. Then they tried to be just like their kids. Heh-heh."

I grunted something noncommittal. Middle-aged crazy, just like my uncle Larry. "I suppose there were a lot of 'mid-life crises' back then, too," I ventured. Uncle Larry had gone heavy into love beads and incense, radical politics. He grew a moustache and wore bell-bottoms. The whole hippie scene. Walked out on his wife for a young "chick" and thought it was all "groovy." I remember how pathetic those thirtysomething wannabes seemed to us in college.

Dad, now, he never had an "identity crisis." He always knew exactly who he was. He had gone off to Europe and saved the world and then came back home and rebuilt it. Uncle Larry was too young to save the world in the Forties, and too old to save it in the Sixties. He was part of that bewildered, silent generation sandwiched between the heroes and the prophets.

"Neurasthenia," Mae said. "We called it neurasthenia back then. Seems everyone I knew was getting divorced or having an attack of 'the nerves.' Even the president was down in the mullygrubs when he was younger. Nervous breakdown. That's what you call it nowadays, isn't it? Now, T. R. There was a man with sand in him. Him and that 'strenuous life' he always preached about. Why, he'd fight a circle saw. Saw him that time in Milwaukee. Shot in the chest, and he still gave a stem-winder of a speech before he let them take him off. Did you know he got me in trouble one time?"

"Who, Teddy Roosevelt? How?"

"T.R., he was a-hunting and come on a bear cub; but he wouldn't shoot the poor thing because it wasn't the manly thing to do. So, some sharper started making stuffed animal dolls and called 'em Teddy's Bear. I given one to my neighbor child as a present." Mae slapped her knee. "Well, her ma had herself a conniption fit, 'cause the experts all said how animal dolls would give young 'uns the nightmares. And the other president who had the neurasthenia." Mae scowled and waved a hand in front of her face. "Oh, I know who it was," she said in an irritated voice. "That college professor. What was his name?"

"Wilson," I suggested, "Woodrow Wilson."

"That's the one. I think he was always jealous of T.R. He wouldn't let him take the Rough Riders into the Great War."

I started to make some comment, but Mae's mouth dropped open. "The war…?" she whispered. "The war! Oh, Mister…" Her face crumpled. "Oh, Mister! You're too old!" She covered her face and began to weep.

She felt in her sleeves for a handkerchief; then wiped her eyes and looked at me. "I forgot," she said. "I forgot. It was the war. Mister went away to the war. That's why he never come back. He never run out on me, at all. He would have come back after it was over, if he'd still been alive. He would have."

"I'm sure he would have," I said awkwardly.

"I told him he was too old for that sort of thing; but he just laughed and said it was a good cause and they needed men like him to spunk up the young 'uns. So he marched away one day and someone he never met before shot him dead and I don't even know when and where it happened."

"I'm sorry," I said, at a loss for anything else to say. A good cause? The War to End All Wars, nearly forgotten now; its players, comic-opera Ruritanians on herky-jerky black and white newsreels. The last war begun in innocence.

Her hands had twisted the handkerchief into a knot. She fussed with it, straightened it out on her lap, smoothed it with her hand. In a quiet voice, she said, "Tell me, doc. Tell me. Why do they have wars?"

I shook my head. Was there ever a good reason? To make the world safe for democracy? To stop the death camps? To free the slaves? Maybe. Those were better reasons than cheap oil. But up close, no matter what the reason, it was husbands and sons and brothers who never came home.

> *Oh, them golden slippers, Oh, them golden slippers,*
> *Golden slippers I'm gonna wear, Because they look so neat;*
> *Oh, them golden slippers, Oh, them golden slippers,*
> *Golden slippers I'm gonna wear To walk them golden streets.*

✦

Ever since our late evening encounter, Consuela had begun wearing blouses, skirts and robes around the house instead of her nurse's whites. The colors were bright, even garish; the patterns, blocky and intricate. The costumes made the woman more open, less mysterious. It was as if, having once seen her *deshabille*, a barrier had come down. She had begun teaching Dee-dee to play the cane flute. Sometimes I heard them in the evening, the notes drifting down from above stairs, lingering in the air. Was it a signal, I wondered? I sensed that the relationship between Consuela and myself had changed; but in what direction, I did not know.

Dee-dee should have been in school. She should have been in fifth grade; and she should have come home on the school bus, full of laughter and bursting to tell us what she had learned that day. Brenda and I should have helped her with her homework, nursed her bruises, and hugged her when she cried. That was the natural order of things.

But Dee-dee lived in her room; played in the dark. She studied at home, tutored by Consuela or myself or by private instructors we sometimes hired. School and other children were far away. She was a prisoner, half of her mother's strained disapproval, half of her own withdrawal. Save for Consuela and myself and a few, brief contacts with Brenda, she had no other person in her short, bounded life. Who could dream what scenarios her dolls performed in the silence of her room?

I found the two of them at the kitchen table, Consuela with her inevitable cocoa, Dee-dee with a glass of milk and a stack of Graham crackers. There were cracker crumbs scattered across the Formica and a ring of white across Dee-dee's lip.

I beamed at her. "The princess has come down from her tower once more!"

She tucked her head in a little. "It's all right, isn't it?"

I kissed her on the forehead. How sparse her hair had grown! "Of course, it is!"

I settled myself across the table from Consuela. She was wearing an ivory blouse with a square-cut neck bordered by red stitching in the shape of flowers. "Thank you, nurse," I said. "She should be downstairs more often."

"Yes, I know."

Was there a hint of disapproval there? A slight drawing together of the lips? I wanted to make excuses for Brenda. It was not that Brenda made Dee-dee stay in her room, but that she never made her leave. It was Deirdre who stayed always by herself. "So, what did you do today, Dee-dee?"

"Oh, nothing. I read my schoolbooks. Watched TV. I helped Connie bake a cake."

"Did you? Sounds like a pretty busy day to me."

She and Consuela shared a grin with each other. "We played ball, a little, until I got tired. And then we played word games. I see something... blue! What is it?"

"The sky?"

"I can't see the sky from here. It's long and thin."

"Hmm. Long, thin and blue. Spaghetti with blueberry sauce?"

Dee-dee laughed. "No, silly. It has a knot in it."

"Hmm. I can't imagine what it could be." I straightened my tie and Dee-dee laughed again. I looked down at the tie and gave a mock start. "Wait! Long, thin, blue and a knot...It's my belt!"

"No! It's your tie!"

"My tie? Why..." I gave her a look of total amazement. "Why, you're absolutely, positively right. Now, why didn't I see that. It was right under my nose. Imagine missing something right under your nose!"

We played a few more rounds of "I see something" and then Dee-dee wandered back to the family room and settled on the floor in front of the TV. I watched her for a while as she stared at the pictures flickering there. I thought of how little time was left before cartoons would play unwatched.

Consuela placed a cup of coffee in front of me. I sipped from it absently while I sorted through the day's mail stacked on the table. "Brenda will be coming home on Monday," I said. Consuela already knew that and I knew that she knew, so I don't know why I said it.

But why Monday? Why not Friday? Why spend another weekend in Washington with Walther Crowe? I could think of any number of reasons, I could.

"Deirdre will be happy to have her mother back," Consuela said in flat tones. I was looking at the envelopes, so I did not see her face. I knew what she meant, though. No more flute lessons; no more games downstairs. I reached across the table and placed my hand atop one of hers. It was warm, probably from holding the cocoa mug.

"Deirdre's mother never left," I said.

Consuela looked away. "I am only her nurse."

"You take care of her. That's more…" I caught myself. I had started to say that that was more than Brenda did; but there were some things that husbands did not say about their wives to other women. I noticed, however, that Consuela had not pulled her hand away from mine.

I released her hand. "Say, here's a letter from the National Archives." I said with forced heartiness, dancing away from the sudden abyss that had yawned open before me. Too many lives had been ruined by reading invitations where none were written.

Consuela stood and turned away, taking her cup to the sink. I slit the envelope open with my index finger and pulled out the yellow flimsy. *Veteran: Holloway, Green. Branch of Service: Infantry (Co. H, 5th Tennessee). Years of Service: 1918 or 1919*. It was the order form I had sent to the Military Service Records department after Mae's earlier recollection of her husband. As I unfolded it, Consuela came and stood beside me, reading over my shoulder. Somehow, it was not uncomfortable.

> ☑ *We were unable to complete your request as written.*
> ☑ *We found additional pension and military service files of the same name (or similar variations).*
> ☑ *The enclosed records are those which best match the information provided. Please resubmit, if these are not the desired files.*

I grunted and paged through the sheets. Company muster rolls. A Memorandum of Prisoner of War Records: *Paroled and exchanged at Cumberland Gap, Sept. 5/62.*

The last page was a white photocopy of a form printed in an old-fashioned typeface. **Casualty Sheet.** The blanks were penned in by an elegant Spencerian hand. Name, *Green Holloway*. Rank, *Private*. Company *"H"*, Regiment *5"*. Division, *3"*. Corps, *23"*. Arm, *Inf.* State, *Tenn.*

Nature of casualty, *Bullet wound of chest (fatal).*
Place of casualty, *Resaca, Ga.*
Date of casualty, *May 14, 1864, the regiment being in action that date.*
Jno. T. Henry, Clerk.

I tossed the sheets to the kitchen table. "These can't be right," I said.

Consuela picked them up. "What is wrong?"

"Right name, wrong war. These are for a Green Holloway who died in the Civil War."

Consuela raised an eyebrow. "And who served in the same company as your patient's husband?"

"State militia regiments were raised locally, and the same families served in them, generation after generation. Green here was probably 'Mister's' grandfather. Back then children were often given their parents' or grandparents' names." I took the photocopies from Consuela and stuffed them back in the envelope. "Well, there was a waste of ten dollars." I dropped the envelope on the table.

Dee-dee called from the family room. "What's this big book you brought home?"

"*The Encyclopedia of Song,*" I said over my shoulder. "It's to help me with a patient I have."

"The old lady who hears music?"

I turned in my chair. "Yes. Did Connie tell you about her?"

Dee-dee nodded. "I wish I could hear music like that. You wouldn't need headphones or a Walkman, would you?"

I remembered that Mae had had two very unhappy recollections in one day. "No," I said, "but you don't get to pick the station, either."

Later that evening, after Dee-dee had been tucked away, I spread my index cards and sheets of paper over the kitchen table, and arranged the tape recorder on my left where I could replay it as needed. The song encyclopedia lay in front of me, open to its index. A pot of coffee stood ready on my right.

Consuela no longer retreated to her own room after dinner. When I looked up from my work I could see her, relaxed on the sofa in the family room, quietly reading a book. Her shoes off, her legs tucked up underneath her, the way some women sit curled up. I watched her silently for a while. So serene, like a jaguar indolent upon a tree limb. She appeared unaware of my regard, and I bent again over my work before she looked up.

I soon verified that Mae's latest recollections were from the Gay Nineties. The earliest one, *Ta-Ra-Ra Boom-der-ay*, had been written in 1890, and the others dated from the same era. *Good-bye, Dolly Gray* had been a favorite of the soldiers going off to fight in the Philippine "insurrection," while *Hot Time in the Old Town* had been the Rough Riders' "theme song." Mae's version of *America the Beautiful*, I discovered, was the original 1895 lyrics. Apparently, Katherine Lee Bates had written the song as much for protest as for patriotism.

When I had finished the cataloguing, I closed the songbook, leaned back in my chair and stretched my arms over my head. Consuela looked up at the motion and I smiled at her and she smiled back. I checked my watch. "Almost bedtime," I said. Consuela said nothing, but nodded slightly.

Middle-aged?

The thought struck me like a discordant note and I turned back to my work. I ran the tape back and forth until I found what I was looking for. Yes. Mae had said that the "young folks" at the turn of the century had called her age-mates "middle-aged." So Mae must have already been mature by then. How was that possible? At most, she might have been a teenager, one of the "young folks," herself.

Unless she had looked old for her age.

God! I stabbed the shut-off button with my forefinger.

After a moment, I ran the tape through again, listening for Mae's descriptions of her peers and her younger contemporaries. "Wishy-washy." Folks her age had been wishy-washy. Yet, in an earlier session, she had described her age-mates as moralistic. I flipped through my written notes until I found it.

Yes, just as I remembered. But, psychologically, that made no sense. Irresolute twenty-somethings do not mature into forty-something moralists. The irresolute become the two-sides-to-every-question types; the mediators, the compromisers, the peace-makers. The ones both sides despise—and miss desperately when they are gone. The moralists are no-compromise world-savers. They preach "prohibition," not "temperance."

The wild youth Mae remembered from the Ragtime Era and the Mauve Decade—the hard-edged "newsies"—those were the young Hemingways, Bogies and Mae Wests; the "Blood-and-Guts" Pattons and the "Give-'em-Hell" Harrys. The Lost Generation, they had been called. The idealistic, young teeners and twentysomethings of the Gay Nineties that Mae found so simpatico were the young FDR, W.E.B. DuBois and Jane Addams. The generation of "missionaries" out to save the world. They had all been "the kids" to her. But that would put Mae into the even older,

Progressive Generation, a contemporary of T.R. and Edison and Booker T. Washington.

I drummed my pencil against the tabletop. That would make her a hundred and twenty years old, or thereabout. That wasn't possible, was it? I pushed myself from the table and went to the bookcase in the family room.

The Guinness Book of Records sat next to the dictionary, the thesaurus, the atlas and the almanac, all neatly racked together. Sometimes, Brenda's obsessive organizing paid off. I noticed that Dee-dee had left one of her own books, *The Boxcar Children*, on the shelf and made a mental note to return it to her room later.

According to Guinness, the oldest human being whose birth could be authenticated was Shigechiyo Izumi of Japan, who had died in 1986 at the ripe age of 120 years and 237 days. So, a few wheezing, stumbling geezers did manage to hang around that long. But not many. Actuarial tables suggested one life in two billion. So, with nearly six billion of us snorting and breathing and poking each other with our elbows, two or three such ancients were possible. Maybe, just maybe, Mae could match Izumi's record. The last surviving Progressive.

The oldest human being.

The oldest human being remembers.

The oldest human being remembers pop music of the last hundred years.

A Hundred-and-Twentysomething. Great book title. It had "best seller" written all over it.

> *'Neath the chestnut tree, where the wild flow'rs grow,*
> *And the stream ripples forth through the vale,*
> *Where the birds shall warble their songs in spring,*
> *There lay poor Lilly Dale.*

On my next visit, Mae was not waiting by the office door for me to unlock it. So, after I had set my desk in order, I hung the "Back in a Minute" sign on the door knob and went to look for her. Not that I was concerned. It was just that I had grown used to her garrulous presence.

I found Jimmy Kovacs in the common room watching one of those inane morning "news" shows. "Good morning, Jimmy. How's your back?"

He grinned at me. "Oh, I can't complain." He waited a beat. "They won't let me."

I smiled briefly. "Glad to hear it. Have you seen—"

"First hurt my back, oh, it must have been sixty-six, sixty-seven. Lifting forms."

"I know. You told me already. I'm looking for—"

"Not forms like paperwork. Though nowadays you could strain your back lifting them, too." He cackled at his feeble joke. It hadn't been funny the first two times, either. "No, I'm talking about those 600-pound forms we used to use on the old flat-bed perfectors. Hot type. Blocks of lead quoined into big iron frames. Those days, printing magazines was a *job*, I tell you. You could smell the ink; you could feel the presses pounding through the floor and the heat from the molten lead in the linotypes." He shook his head. "I saw the old place once a few years back. A couple of prissy kids going ticky-ticky on those computer keyboards…" He made typing motions with his two index fingers.

I interrupted before he could give me another disquisition on the decadence of the printing industry. I could just imagine the noise, the lead vapors, the heavy weight-lifting. Some people have odd notions about the Good Old Days. "Have you seen Mae this morning, Jimmy?"

"Who? Mae? Sure, I saw the old gal. She was headed for the gardens." He pointed vaguely.

Old gal? I chuckled at the pot calling the kettle black. But then I realized with a sudden shock that there were more years between Mae and Jimmy than there were between Jimmy and me. There was old, and then there was *old*. Perhaps we should distinguish more carefully among them… say "fogies," "mossbacks" and "geezers."

Mae was sitting in the garden sunshine, against the red brick back wall, upon a stone settee. I watched her for a few moments from behind the large plate glass window. The sun was from her right, illuminating the red and yellow blossoms around her and sparkling the morning dew like diamonds strewn across the grass. The dewdrops were matched by those on her cheeks. She wore a green print dress with flowers, so that the dress, the grass and the flower beds; the tears and the dew, all blended together, like old ladies' garden camouflage.

She did not see me coming. Her eyes were closed tight, looking upon another, different world. I stood beside her, unsure whether to rouse her. Were those tears of joy or tears of sorrow? Would it be right to interrupt either? I compromised by placing my hand on her shoulder. Her dry, bird-like claw reached up and pressed itself against mine.

"Is that you, Doctor Wilkes?" I don't know how she knew that. Perhaps her eyes had not been entirely closed. She opened them and looked at me, and I could see that her regurgitated memories had been sorrowful ones. That is the problem with Jackson's syndrome. You remember. You can't help remembering. "Oh, Doctor Wilkes. My mama. My sweet, sweet mama. She's dead."

The announcement did not astonish me. Had either of Mae Holloway's parents been alive I would have been astonished. I started to tell her that, but my words came out surprisingly gentle. "It happened a long time ago," I told her. "It's a hurt long over."

She shook her head. "No. It happened this morning. I saw Pa leaning over my bed. Oh, such a strong, young man he was! But he'd been crying. His eyes were red and his beard and hair weren't combed. He told me that my mama was dead at last and she weren't a-hurtin' no more."

Mae Holloway pulled me down to sit beside her on the hard, cold bench, and she curled against me for all the world like a little girl. I hesitated and almost pulled away; but I am not without pity, even for an old woman who half-thought she was a child.

"He told me it was my fault."

"What?" Her voice had been muffled against my jacket.

"He told me it was my fault."

"Who? Your father told you that? That was…cruel."

She spoke in a high-pitched, childish voice. "He tol' me that mama never gotten well since I was borned. There was something about my birthin' that hurt her inside. I was six and I never seen my mama when she weren't a-bed…"

She couldn't finish. Awkwardly, I put an arm around her shoulder. A husband who lost his wife to childbirth would blame the child, whether consciously or not. Especially a husband in the full flush of youth. Worse still, if it was a lingering death. If for years the juices of life had drained away, leaving a gasping, joyless husk behind.

If for years the juices of life had drained away, leaving a gasping, joyless husk behind.

"I have to get back to my office," I said, standing abruptly. "There may be a patient waiting. Is there anything I can get you? A sedative?"

She shook her head slowly back and forth several times. When she spoke, she sounded more like the adult Mae. "No. No, thank you. I ain't— haven't had these memories for so long that I got to feel them now, even when it pains me. There'll be worse coming back to me, by and by. And better, too. The Good Man'll help me bear it."

It wasn't until I was back behind my desk and had made some notes about her recollection for my projected book that I was struck with an annoying inconsistency. If Mae's mother had died from complications of childbirth, where did her "little brother Zach" come from?

Step-brother, probably. A young man like her father would have sought a new bride before too long. Eventually, we put tragedy behind us and get on with life. But if I was going to analyze the progress of Mae's condition, I would need to confirm her recollections. After all, memories are tricky things. The memories of the old, trickier than most.

> *Peaches in the summertime,*
> *Apples in the fall;*
> *If I can't have the girl I love,*
> *I won't have none at all.*

There was music in the air when I returned home, and I followed the thread of it through the garage and into the back yard, where I found Consuela sitting on a blanket of red, orange and brown, swathed in a flowing, pale green muumuu, and Deirdre beside her playing on the cane flute. Dee-dee's thin, knobby fingers moved haltingly and the notes were flat, but I actually recognized the tune. Something about a spider and a waterspout.

"Hello, Dee-dee. Hello, Consuela."

Deirdre turned. "Daddy!" she said. She pulled herself erect on Consuela's gown and hobbled across the grass to me. I crouched down and hugged her. "Dee-dee, you're outside playing."

"Connie said it was all right."

"Of course, it's all right. I wish you would come out more often."

A cloud passed across the sunshine. "Connie said no one can see me in the yard." A hesitation. "And Mommy's not home."

No one to tell her how awful she looked. No cruel, taunting children. No thoughtlessly sympathetic adults offering useless condolences. Nothing but Connie, and me, and the afternoon sun. I looked over Dee-dee's shoulder. "Thank you, nur— Thank you, Connie."

She blinked at my use of her familiar name, but made no comment. "The sunshine is good for her."

"She *is* my sunshine. Aren't you, Dee-dee?" *You are my sunshine, my only sunshine.* A fragment of tune. Only, how did the rest of it go?

"Oh, Daddy…"

"So, has Connie been teaching you to play the flute?"

"Yes. And she showed me lots of things. Did you know there are zillions of different bugs in our grass?"

"Are there?" *You make me happy when skies are grey.*

"Yeah. There's ants and centipedes and…and mites? And honey bees. Honey bees like these little white flowers." And she showed me a ball of clover she had tucked behind her ear.

"You better watch that," I said, "or the bees will come after you, too."

"Oh, Daddy…"

"Because you're so sweet." *You'll never know, dear, how much I love you.*

"Daaaddyyy. I saw some spiders, too."

"Going up the waterspout?"

She giggled. "There are different kinds of spiders, too. They're like eensy-weensy tigers, Connie says. They eat flies and other bugs. Yuck! I wouldn't want to be a spider, would you?"

"No."

"But you are!" Secret triumph in her voice. She had just tricked me, somehow. "There was this spider that was nothing but a little brown ball with legs *this* long!" She held her arms far enough apart to cause horror movie buffs to blanch. "They named it after you," she added with another giggle. "They call it a Daddy-long-legs. You're a daddy and you have long legs, so you must be a spider, too."

"Then…I've got you in my web!" I grabbed her and she squealed. "And now I'm going to gobble you up!" I started kissing her on the cheeks. She giggled and made a pretense of escape. I held her all the tighter. *Please don't take my sunshine away.*

We sat for a while on the blanket, just the three of us. Consuela told us stories from Guatemala. How a rabbit had gotten deeply into debt and then tricked his creditors into eating one another. How a disobedient child was turned into a monkey. Dee-dee giggled at that and said she would *like* to be a monkey. I told them about Mae Holloway.

"She didn't give me any new songs today," I said, "but she finally remembered something from her childhood." I explained how her mother had died and her father had blamed her for it.

"Poor girl!" Consuela said, looking past me. "It's not right for a little girl to grow up without a mother."

"Deirdre Wilkes! What on *earth* are you doing out*side* in the *dirt*?"

Dee-dee stiffened in my arms. I turned and saw Brenda in the open garage door, straight as a rod. A navy blue business suit with white ruffled blouse. Matching overcoat, hanging open. A suitbag slung from one shoulder; a briefcase clenched in the other hand. "Brenda," I said, standing up with Dee-dee in my arm. "We didn't expect you until Monday."

She looked at each of us. "Evidently not."

"Dee-dee was just getting a little sunshine."

Brenda stepped close and whispered. "The neighbors might see."

I wanted to say, So what? But I held my peace. You learn there are times when it is best to say nothing at all. You learn.

"Nurse." She spoke to Consuela. "Aren't you dressed a bit casually?"

"Yes, señora. It is after five." When she had to, Consuela could remember what was in her contract.

"A professional does not watch the clock. And a professional dresses appropriately for her practice. How do you think it would look if I went to the office in blouse and skirt instead of a suit? Take Deirdre inside. Don't you know there are all sorts of bugs and dirt out here? What if she were stung by a bee? Or bitten by a deer tick?"

"Brenda," I said, "I don't think—"

She turned to me. "Yes, exactly. You didn't think. How could you have allowed this, Paul? Look, in her hand. That's Nurse's whistle, or whatever it is. Has Deirdre been playing it? Putting it in her mouth. How unsanitary! And there are weeds in her hair. For God's sake, Paul, you're a doctor. You should have said something."

Sometimes I thought Brenda had been raised in a sterile bubble. The least little thing out of place, the least little thing done wrong, was enough to set her off. Dust was a hanging offense. She hadn't always been that way. At school, she'd been reasonably tidy, but not obsessed. It had only been in the last few years that cleanliness and order had begun to consume her life. Each year, I could see the watchspring wound tighter and tighter.

Consuela bundled up flute, blanket and Dee-dee and took them inside, leaving me alone with Brenda. I tried to give her a hug, and she endured it briefly. "Welcome home."

"Christ, Paul. I go away for two weeks and everything is falling apart."

"No, Nurse was right to bring her outside. Deirdre should have as much normal activity as possible. There is nothing wrong with her mind. It's just her body aging too fast." That wasn't strictly true. Hutchinson-Gilford was sometimes called *progeria*, but it differed in some of its particulars from normal senile aging.

Brenda swatted at a swarm of midges. "There are too many bugs out here," she said. "Let's go inside. Carry my suitbag for me."

I took it from her and followed her inside the house. She dropped her briefcase on the sofa in the living room and continued to the hall closet, where she shed her overcoat. "You're home early," I said again.

"That's right. Surprised?" She draped her overcoat carefully across a hanger.

"Well…" *Yes, I was.* "Did Crowe drop you off?"

She shoved the other coats aside with a hard swipe. "Yes." Then she turned and started up the stairs. I closed the closet door for her.

"How was Washington?" I asked. "Did you impress the Supremes?"

She didn't answer and I followed her up the stairs. I found her in our bedroom, shedding her travel clothes. I hung the suit bag on the closet door. "Did you hear me? I asked how—"

"I heard you." She dropped her skirt to the floor and sent it in the direction of the hamper with a flick of her foot. "Walther offered me a partnership."

"Did he?" I retrieved her skirt and put it in the hamper. "That's great news!" It was. Partners made a bundle. They took a cut of the fees the associates charged. "It opens up all sorts of opportunities."

Brenda gave me a funny look. "Yes," she said. "It does." If I hadn't known better, I would have said she looked distressed. It was hard to imagine Brenda being unsure.

"What's wrong?" I said.

"Nothing. It's just that there are conditions attached."

"What conditions? A probationary period? You've been an associate there for seven years. They should know your work by now."

"It isn't that."

"Then, what…"

Deirdre interrupted us. She stood in the doorway of our bedroom, one foot crossed pigeon-toed over the other, a gnarled finger tucked in one shrunken cheek. "Mommy?"

Brenda looked at a point on the door jamb a quarter inch above Dee-dee's head. "What is it, honey."

"I should tell you 'welcome home' and 'I missed you.'"

I could almost hear *Connie said…* in front of that statement and I wondered if Brenda could hear it, too.

"I missed you, too, honey," Brenda told the door knob.

"I've got to take my bath, now."

"Good. Be sure to get all that dirt washed off."

"Okay, Mommy." A brief catch, and then, "I love you, Mommy."

Brenda nodded. "Yes."

Dee-dee waited a moment longer, then turned and bolted for the bathroom. I could hear Connie already running the water. I waited until the bathroom door closed before I turned to Brenda. "You could have told her that you loved her, too."

"I do," she said, pulling on a pair of slacks. "She knows I do."

"Not unless you tell her once in a while."

She flashed me an irritated look, but made no reply. She took a blouse from her closet and held it in front of her while she stood before the mirror. "Let's go out to eat tonight."

"Go out? Well, you know that Dee-dee doesn't like to leave the house, but…"

"Take Deirdre with us? Whatever are you thinking of, Paul? She would be horribly embarrassed. Think of the stares she'd get! No, Consuela can feed her that Mexican goulash she's cooking."

"Guatemalan."

"What?"

"It's Guatemalan, whatever it is."

"Do you have to argue with everything I say?"

"I thought, with you being just back and all, that the three of us—" *The four of us.* "—could eat dinner together, for a change."

"I won't expose Deirdre to the rudeness of strangers."

"No, not when she can get it at home." I don't know why I said that. It just came out.

Brenda stiffened. "What does that crack mean?"

I turned away. "Nothing."

"No, tell me!"

I turned back and faced her. "All right. You treat Dee-dee like a nonperson. She's sick, Brenda, and it's not contagious and it's not her fault."

"Then whose fault is it?"

"That's lawyer talk. It's no one's fault. It just happens. We've been over that and over that. There is no treatment for progeria."

"And, oh, how it gnaws at you! *You can't cure her!*"

"No one can!"

"But especially you."

No one could cure Dee-dee. I knew that. It was helplessness, not failure. I had accepted that long ago. "And *you're* angry and bitter," I replied, "because there's nobody you can sue!"

She flung her blouse aside and it landed in a wad in the corner. "Maybe," she said through clenched teeth, "Maybe I'll take that partnership offer, after all."

✦

It was not until much later that evening, as I lay awake in bed, Brenda a thousand miles away on the other side, that I remembered Consuela's remark. *It's not right for a little girl to grow up without a mother.* I wondered. Had she been making a comment, or making an offer?

> *I don't want to play in your yard.*
> *I don't like you anymore.*
> *You'll be sorry when you see me*
> *Sliding down our cellar door.*

The next time I saw Mae Holloway, we quarreled.

Perhaps it was her own constant sourness coming to the fore; or perhaps it was her fear of insanity returning. But it may have been a bad humor that I carried with me from Brenda's homecoming. We had smoothed things out, Brenda and I, but it was a fragile repair, the cracks plastered over with I-was-tired and I-didn't-mean-it, and we both feared to press too hard, lest it buckle on us. At dinner, she had told me about the case she had helped argue, and I told her about Mae Holloway and we both pretended to care. But it was all monologue. Listening holds fewer risks than response; and an attentive smile, less peril than engagement.

Mae wouldn't look at me when I greeted her. She stared resolutely at the floor, at the medicine cabinet, out the window. Sometimes, she stared into another world. I noticed how she gnawed on her lips.

"We have a couple of days to catch up on, Mrs. Holloway," I said. "I hope you've been making notes, like I asked."

She shook her head slowly, but in a distracted way. She was not responding to my statement, but to some inner reality. "I just keep remembering and remembering, doc. There's music all the time, and that double vision—"

"Consciousness doubling."

"It's like I'm in two places at once. Sometimes, I forget which is which and I try to step around things only I cain't, because they're only ghosts, only ghosts. And sometimes, I recollect things that couldn't have…"

The "dreamy states" of Jackson patients often grow deeper and more frequent. In one woman, they had occupied nearly her entire day; and, in the end, they had crowded out her normal consciousness entirely. "I could prescribe something, if you like," I said. "These spells of yours are similar to epileptic seizures. So, there are drugs that…"

She shook her head again. "No. I won't take drugs." She looked directly at me at last. "Don't you understand? I've got to know. It's always been bits and pieces. Just flashes. A jimble-jamble that never made sense. Now…" She paused and took a deep breath. "Now, at least, I'll know."

"Know what, Mrs. Holloway."

"About…Everything." She looked away again. Talking with her today was like pulling teeth.

"What about the songs, Mae? We didn't get anything useful on Wednesday and I wasn't here Tuesday or yesterday, so that's three days we have to catch up on."

Mae turned and studied me with lips as thin as broth. "You don't care about any of this, do you? It's all professional; not like you and I are friends. You don't care if'n I live or die; and I don't care if'n you do."

"Mrs. Holloway, I…"

"Good." She gave a sharp nod of her head. "That's jake with me. Because I don't like having friends," she said. "I decided a long time ago if'n I don't have 'em, I won't miss 'em when they cut out. So let's just keep this doc and old lady." Her stare was half admonition, half challenge, as if she dared me to leap the barriers she had set down around her.

I shrugged. Keep things professional. That was fine with me, too. A crabby old lady like her, it was no wonder they all ran out on her.

She handed over a crumpled, yellow sheet of lined paper, which I flattened out on my desk. She had written in a soft pencil, so I smeared some of the writing and smudged my palm. I set a stack of fresh index cards by and began to copy the song titles for later research. *Where Did You Get That Hat? Comrades. The Fountain in the Park. Love's Old Sweet Song.* While I worked, I could hear Mae humming to herself. I knew without looking that she had her eyes closed, that she was living more and more in another world, gradually leaving this one behind. *White Wings. Walking for That Cake. My Grandfather's Clock. In the Gloaming. Silver Threads Among the Gold. The Mulligan Guard.* Mae was her own Hit Parade. Though if the music did play continually, as she said, this list could only be a sample of what she had heard over the last three days. *The Man on the Flying Trapeze. Sweet Genevieve. Champagne Charlie. You Naughty, Naughty Men. When You and I Were Young, Maggie. Beautiful Dreamer.* Three days' worth of unclaimed memories.

I noticed that she had recorded no doubling episodes, this time. Because she had not had any? It seemed doubtful, considering. But one entry had been crossed out; rubbed over with the pencil until there was nothing but a black smear and a small hole in the paper where the pencil point had worn through. I held it up to the light, but could make out nothing.

I heard Mae draw in her breath and looked up in time to see a mien on her face almost of ecstasy. "What is it?"

"I'm standing out in a meadow. There's a sparkling stream meandering through it, and great, grey, rocky mountains rearing all around. Yellow flowers shivering in the breeze and I think how awful purty and peaceful it is." She sighed. "Oh, doc, sometimes, just for a second, we can be so happy."

Jackson had often described his patients' "dreamy states" as being accompanied by intense feelings of euphoria; sudden bursts of child-like joy. No doubt some endorphin released in the brain.

"There's a fellow coming up toward me from the ranch," she continued, trepidation edging into her voice. "My age, maybe a little older. Might be Mister's younger brother, because he favors him some. He's a-weeping something awful. I reach out to him and he puts his head on my shoulder and says…" Mae stopped and winced in pain. She sucked in her breath and held it. Then she let it out slowly. "And he says how Sweet Annie is dead and the baby, too; and there was nothing the sawbones could do. Nothing at all. And I think, *Thank you, Goodman Lord. Thank you, that she won't suffer the way that Ma did.* And then a mockingbird takes wing from the aspen tree right in front of me and I think how awful peaceful the meadow is now that the screaming has stopped."

She wiped at her nose with her sleeve. "Listen to it. Can you hear it, doc? There ain't a sound but for the breeze and that old mockingbird." The look on her face changed somehow, changed subtly. "Listen to the mockingbird," she croaked. "Listen to the mockingbird. Oh, the mockingbird still singing o'er her grave…"

Then she looked about in sudden surprise. "Land's sake! Now, how did I get here? Why, everybody's so happy; singing the mockingbird song and dancing all over the lawn and a-hugging each other." A smile slowly came over her face. She had apparently tripped from one doubling episode directly into another, due to some association with the song, and the imprinted emotions were playing back with it, overwriting the melancholy of the first episode. Or else she had seized on the remembered joy herself, and had wrapped herself in it against the cold.

"I'm a-wearing my Sanitary Commission uniform," she went on, preening her shabby, faded gown. She shot her cuffs, straightened something at her throat that wasn't there. "I was a nurse, you know; and when the news come that the war was finally over we all hied over to the White House and had ourselves a party on the lawn, the whole kit 'n boodle of us. Then the President his-self come out and joined us." She turned in her seat and pointed toward the medicine cabinet. "Here he comes now!"

And in that instant, her joy became absolute terror. "Him?" Her smile stretched to a ghastly rictus and she cowered into her chair, covering her eyes with her hand. But you can't close your eyes to memory. You can't. "No! I kin still see him!" she said.

What was so terrifying about seeing president Wilson close up? "What's wrong, Mrs. Holloway?"

"They shot him."

"What, on the White House lawn? No president has been shot there…" And certainly not Wilson.

She took her hands away from her eyes, glanced warily left, then right. Slowly, she relaxed, though her hands continued to tremble. Then, she looked at me. "No, the shooting happened later," she snapped, anger blossoming from her fear. Then she closed up and her eyes took on a haunted look. "I'm taking up too much of your time, doc," she said, creaking to her feet.

"No, you're not. Really," I told her.

"Then you're taking up too much of mine." I thought her blackthorn stick would punch holes in the floor tiles as she left.

After a moment's hesitation, I followed. She had recalled her father's death. She had remembered that her birth had killed her mother and that her father had blamed her for it. She had remembered her husband going off to war, never to return. Sad memories, sorrowful memories; but there was something about this new recollection that terrified her.

She thought she was going crazy.

It was easy to track her through the garden. Deep holes punched into the sod marked her trail among the flower beds. When I caught up with her, she was leaning over a plot of gold and crimson marigolds. "You know, I remember exactly where I was when President Kennedy was shot," I said by way of easing her into conversation.

Mae Holloway scowled and bent over the flower bed. "Don't make no difference no-how," she said. "He's dead either way, ain't he?" She turned her back on me.

"No particular reason." I had figured it out. She had seen McKinley, not Wilson; and her husband had fought in the Spanish-American War, not World War I.

She turned her dried-out old face to me. "Think I'm getting senile, doc? Why aren't you back in your office reading on your books? You might have a patient to ignore."

"They'll find me if they need me."

"I tol' you the songs I been remembering. Why did you follow me out here, anyway?"

I had better things to do than have a bitter old woman berate me. "If you feel in a friendlier mood later," I said, "you know where to find me."

Back in my office, I began checking the latest tunes against the song encyclopedia. The mindless transcription kept me busy, so that I did not dwell on Mae's intransigence. Let her stew in her own sour juices.

But I soon noticed a disturbing trend in the data. *Champagne Charlie* was written in 1868. *You Naughty, Naughty Men* ("When married how you treat us and of each fond hope defeat us, and there's some will even beat us...") had created a scandal at Niblo's Gardens in 1866. And *Beautiful Dreamer* dated from *1864*. Mae could not have heard those songs when they were new. Born in the early seventies at best, tucked away back in the hills of Tennessee—"So far back in the hollers," she had said one time, "that they had to pipe in the daylight."—She must have heard them later.

And if a little bit later, why not a whole lot later?

And there went the whole rationale for my book.

The problem with assigning dates to Mae's neurological hootenanny was that she could have heard the songs at any time. A melody written in the Twenties, like *The Red, Red Robin*, is heard and sung by millions of children today. Scott Joplin created his piano rags at the turn of the century; yet most people knew them from *The Sting*, a movie made in the Seventies and set in the Thirties, an era when ragtime had been long out of fashion.

(The telescoping effect of distance. From this far down the river of years, who can distinguish the Mauve Decade from the Thirties? Henry James and Upton Sinclair and Ernest Hemingway came of age in very different worlds; but they seem alike to us because they are just dead people in funny clothing, singing quaint, antique songs. "Old-fashioned" is enough to blur them together.)

Face it. Many of those old songs were still being sung and record-ed when *I* was young. Lawrence Welk. Mitch Miller. Preservation Hall. Leon Redbone had warbled *Champagne Charlie* on the Tonight Show in front of God and everybody. Wasn't it far more likely that Mae had heard it then, than that she had heard it in 1868?

A Hundred and Twentysomething. I had deduced a remarkable age for Mae from the dates of the songs she remembered. If that was a will-o'-the wisp, what was the point? There was no teleology to interest the profes-sionals; no hook to grab the public. How many people would care about an old woman's recollections? Not enough to make a best seller.

And what right had that old bat, what right had anyone, to live so long when *children* were dying? What use were a few extra years remembering the past when there were others who would never have a future?

Damn! I saw that I had torn the index card. I rummaged in the drawer for tape, found none, and wondered if it made any sense to bother recopying the information. The whole effort was a waste of time. I picked up the deck of index cards and threw them. I missed the wastebasket and they fluttered like dead leaves across the room.

> *Oh, how old is she, Billy Boy, Billy Boy?*
> *Oh, how old is she, charming Billy?*
> *She's twice six and she's twice seven,*
> *Forty-eight and eleven.*
> *She's a young thing that cannot leave her mother.*

I could have gone home, instead, and gotten an early start on the weekend.

I had planned to visit the National Archives today, but to continue the book project now seemed pointless. The whole rationale had collapsed; and Mae had withdrawn into that fearful isolation in which I had found her. There was no reason not to go home. Brenda had taken the day off to recuperate from her trip. She was probably waiting for me. So, I closed the clinic at noon and took the Transit to Newark's Penn Station, where I transferred to the PATH train into the World Trade Center. From there a cab dropped me at Varick and Houston in lower Manhattan.

If we did not meet, we could not quarrel.

The young woman behind the information desk was a pixie: short, with serious bangs and serious, round glasses. Her name tag read Sara. "Green?" she said when I had explained my mission. "What an odd name. It might be a nickname. You know, like 'Red.' One of my grandfathers was called 'Blackie' because his family name was White. She took out a sheet of scratch paper and made some notes on it. "I'd suggest you start with the 1910 Census and look for Green Holloway in the Soundex."

"Soundex?" I said. "What is that?"

"It's like an Index, but it's based on sounds, not spelling. Which is good, since the enumerators didn't always spell the names right. Holloway might have been recorded as, oh, H-a-l-i-w-a-y, for example, or even H-a-l-l-w-a-y; but the Soundex code would be the same."

"I see. Clever."

She took out a brochure and jotted another note on the scratch pad. "Holloway would be...H. Then L is a 4, and the W and Y don't count. That's H400. There will be a lot of other names listed under H400, like Holly and Hall, but that should narrow your search." She filled out a request voucher for me. "Even with the Soundex," she said as she wrote, "there are no guarantees. There are all sorts of omissions, duplicates, wrong names, wrong ages. Dad missed his great-grandmother in the 1900 Census, because she was living with her son-in-law and the enumerator had listed her with the son-in-law's family name. One of my great-great-grandfathers 'aged' fourteen years between the 1870 and 1880 censuses; and his wife-to-be was listed twice in 1860. People weren't always home; so, the enumerator would try to get the information from a neighbor, who didn't always know. So you should always cross-check your information."

She directed me to an empty carrel, and shortly after, an older man delivered the 1910 Soundex for Blount County, Tennessee. I threaded the microfilm spool into the viewer and spun forward, looking for H400. Each frame was an index card with the head of household on top and everyone else listed below with their ages and relationships.

I slowed when I started to see first names starting with G: Gary... George...Gerhard...Glenn...Granville...Gretchen...Gus...No Green. I backed up and checked each of the G's, one by one, thinking Green might be out of sequence.

Still, no luck. And I couldn't think of any other way "Green" might be spelled. Unless it was a nickname, in which case, forget it. I scrolled ahead to the M's. If the census taker had interviewed Mae, Green might be listed as "Mister."

But...No "Mister." Then I checked the M's again, this time searching for "Mae" or "May," because if Mister had died in the Spanish-American War rather than World War I, Mae herself would have been listed as head-of-household in 1910.

Still nothing. It was a fool's errand, anyway. For all I knew, Mae was really Anna-Mae or Lulu-Mae or some other such Appalachianism, which would make finding her close to impossible.

I tried the 1900 Soundex next. But I came up dry on that, too. No Green, no Mister, no Mae. Eventually, I gave up.

I leaned back in the chair and stretched my arms over my head. Now what? *We lived so far back in the hollers they had to pipe in the daylight.* It could be that the census takers had flat out missed her. Or she had already left the hills by 1900. In which case, I did not know where to search. She had gone to Cincinnati, I remembered. And to California. At one time or another, she had mentioned San Francisco, and Chicago, and Wyoming, and even New York City. The old bag had a lot of travel stickers on her.

I took a walk to stretch my legs. If I left now, and the trains were on time, and the traffic was light, I could still be home in time to tuck Dee-dee in. But a check of the sidewalk outside the building showed the crowds running thick. The Financial District was getting an early start on the weekend. Not a good time to be leaving the City. Not a good time at all. Traffic heading for the tunnels sat at a standstill. Tightly-packed herds of humans trampled the sidewalks. I would have likened them to sheep, but for the in-your-face single-mindedness with which they marched toward their parking lots and subway entrances.

The trains would be SRO, packed in with tired, sweaty office workers chattering about Fashion Statements or Sunday's Big Game; or (the occasional Type A personality) hunched over their laptops, working feverishly on their next deal or their next angina, whichever came first.

Was there ever a time when the New York crowds thinned out? Perhaps there was a continual stream of drones flowing through the streets of Manhattan twenty-four hours a day. Or maybe they were simply walking around and around this one block just to fool me. A Potemkin Crowd.

I returned to the information desk. "I guess as long as I'm stuck here I'll check 1890." That would be before the Spanish-American War, so Green might be alive and listed.

"I'm sorry," Sara told me. "The 1890 Census was destroyed in a fire in 1921, and only a few fragments survived."

I sighed. "Dead end, I guess. I'm sorry I took up so much of your time."

"That's what I'm here for. You could try 1880, though, and look for the parents. There's a partial Soundex for households with children aged ten and under. If the woman was born in the 1870s like you think…"

I shook my head. "No. I know she was born a Murray, but I don't know her father's name." Checking each and every M600 for a young child named Mae was not an appealing task. I might only be killing time; but I had no intention of bludgeoning it to death. I'd have a better chance hunting Holloways, because Green's name was so out of the ordinary. But I'd have to go frame-by-frame there, too, since I didn't know his parents' names, either. That sort of painstaking research was the reason why God invented professionals.

Sara pointed to a row of shelves near the carrels. "There is one other option. There are printed indices of Heads of Households for 1870 and earlier."

I shook my head. "The grandparents? I don't know their names, either."

"Did she have a brother?"

"Zach," I said. "Just the two of them, as far as I know. At least, she's never mentioned any other siblings."

"Children sometimes were given their grandparents' names. Maybe her father's parents were Zach and Mae Murray. It's a shot in the dark, but what do you have to lose? If you don't look, you'll never find anything."

"Okay, thanks." I wandered over to the row of index volumes and studied them. I was blowing off the time now and I knew it. Still, I could always strike it lucky.

The indices for Tennessee ran from 1820 through 1860. Thick, bound volumes on heavy paper. No Soundex here. I'd have to remember to check alternate spellings. I pulled out the volume for 1860 and flipped through the pages until I found Murray. Murrays were "thick as ticks on a hound dog's hide," but none of them were named Zach. However, when I checked *H*, I did find a "Green Holloway" in District 2, Greenback, Tennessee. Mister's grandfather? How many Green Holloways could there be? I copied the information and put in a request for the spool; then, just for luck, I checked 1850, as well.

The 1850 Census listed a "Greenberry Hollaway," also in District 2, Greenback P.O. I chuckled. Greenberry? Imagine sending a kid to school with a name like Greenberry!

Green appeared in the 1840 and 1830 indices, too. And 1830 listed a "Josh Murry" in the same census district as Green. Mae's great-grandfather? Worth a look, anyway.

The trail ended there. The Blount County returns for 1820 were lost, and all the earlier censuses had all been destroyed when the British burned Washington in 1814.

I put the volumes back on the shelf. There was a thick atlas on a reading stand next to the indices and, out of curiosity, I turned it open to Tennessee. It took me a while to find Greenback. When I finally did, I saw that it lay in Loudon County, not Blount.

"That doesn't make any sense," I muttered.

"What doesn't?" A shriveled, dried-up old man with wire-frame glasses was standing by my elbow waiting to use the atlas.

"The indices all say Blount County, but the town is in Loudon." I didn't bother to explain. It wasn't any of his business. There could be any number of reasons for the discrepancy. The Greenback post office could have serviced parts of Blount County.

The man adjusted his glasses and peered at the map. I stepped aside. "It's all yours," I said.

"Now, hold on, sonny." He opened his satchel, something halfway between a purse and a briefcase, and pulled out a dog-eared, soft-bound red book. He licked his forefinger and rubbed pages aside. He hummed and nodded as he read. "Here's your answer," he said, jabbing a finger at a table. "Loudon County was erected in 1870 from parts of Blount and neighboring counties. Greenback was in the part that became Loudon County. See?" He closed the book one-handed with a snap. "It's simple."

I guess if hanging around musty old records is your whole life, it's easy to sound like an expert. He looked like something the Archives would have in storage anyway. "Thanks," I said.

The whole afternoon had been a waste of time. I had been searching in the wrong county. Blast the forgetfulness of age! Mae had said she had been born in Blount County, so I had looked in Blount County. And all the while, the records were tucked safely away under Loudon.

I checked the clock on the wall. Four-thirty? Too late to start over. Time to pack it in and catch the train.

When I returned to my carrel, however, I found the spool for 1860 Blount County had already been delivered. I considered sending it back, but decided to give it a fast read before leaving. I mounted the spool and spun the fast forward, slowing when I reached District 2. About a third of the way through, I stopped.

NAMES	AGE	SEX	COLOR	OCCUPATION, ETC.	VALUE OF REAL ESTATE	VALUE OF PERSONAL PROPERTY	BIRTH-PLACE
Holloway, Green	56	M	W	Farmer	$800	$100	Tenn
" Mabel	37	F	"				"
" Zachary	22	M	"				"

Hah! There it was. Success—of sorts—at last! This Green Holloway must have been the same one whose Civil War records I had gotten. Green and Mabel Holloway begat Zach Holloway, who must have begat Green "Mister" Holloway. Jesus. If those ages were correct, Mabel was only 15 when she did her begatting. Who said babies having babies was a modern thing? But, kids grew up faster back then. They took on a lot of adult responsibilities at fifteen or sixteen. Today, they behave like juveniles into their late twenties.

Now that I knew what I was looking for and where it was, it didn't take me very long to check the 1850 Census, as well.

NAMES	AGE	SEX	COLOR	OCCUPATION, ETC.	VALUE OF REAL ESTATE	BIRTH-PLACE
Hollaway, Greenberry	45	M	W	Farmer	$250	Tenn
" Mae	32	F	"			"
" Zach^y	12	M	"			"

Those names…The eerie coincidence gave me a queer feeling. And Mabel should have been twenty-seven, not thirty-two. (Or else she should have been forty-two in 1860.) But then I remembered Sara's cautions. How easy it was for enumerators to get names and ages wrong; and how the same names were used generation after generation.

Just one more spool, I promised myself. Then I head home.

Uncle Sugar had been less nosy in 1840. The census listed only heads of households. Everyone else was tallied by age bracket.

NAMES OF HEADS OF FAMILIES	FREE WHITE PERSONS, INCLUDING HEADS OF FAMILIES																							
	MALES												FEMALES											
	To 5	5-10	10-15	15-20	20-30	30-40	40-50	50-60	60-70	70-80	80-90	90-100	To 5	5-10	10-15	15-20	20-30	30-40	40-50	50-60	60-70	70-80	80-90	90-100
Green^y Holloway	1				1												1							

The "white female" was surely Mabel, and she was in her twenties. So her age in 1860 had been wrong. She must have been forty-two, not thirty-seven. Twenty-two, thirty-two, forty-two. That made sense. I folded the sheet with the information and stuffed it in my briefcase. Sara had been right about cross checking the documentation. The census takers had not always gotten the straight skinny. Mabel had probably looked younger than her years in 1860 and a neighbor, asked for the data, had guessed low.

"She looks younger than her years." The phrase wriggled through my mind and I thought fleetingly of Dee-dee looking older than her years. For every yin there is a yang, and if the universe did balance…If for some reason Mabel herself never spoke to the enumerator and a neighbor in the next holler guessed her age instead, the guess would be low. So, twenty-seven, thirty-two, thirty-seven made a weird kind of sense, too. And it actually agreed better with the written documents!

And what if she kept it up? I laughed to myself. Now there was a crazy thought! Aging five years to the decade, by 1870 she would have seemed… mmm, forty-two. And today? Add another sixty-odd years, and Mabel would appear to be…A hundred and five or thereabouts. About as old as Mae seemed to be.

I paused with one arm in my jacket.

About as old as Mae seemed to be? I stared at the spool boxes stacked in the carrel, ready for pick-up.

Greenberry and Mabel. Green and Mae? No, it was absurd. A wild coincidence of names. *The census records are not that reliable. And it's only that Dee-dee is aging too fast that you even* thought *about someone aging too slow.* I took a few steps toward the door.

And the 1830 Census? I hadn't bothered checking it. What if it listed a Green Holloway aged 20-29 and a "white female" *still* aged 20-29?

I turned and looked back at the reading room and my heart began to pound in my ears, and all of a sudden I knew why Dr. Bench had figured Mae for eighty-five three decades ago, and why Mae had feared for her sanity all her life.

> *So early in the month of May,*
> *As the green buds were a-swelling.*
> *A young man on his death-bed lay,*
> *For the love of Barbry Ellen.*

It was pitch black out when I finally arrived home. There was a light on in the kitchen, none abovestairs. I parked in the driveway and got out and walked around the end of the garage through the gate into the back yard. The crickets were chirruping like a swing with a squeaky hinge. Lightning bugs drifted lazily through the air. I walked all the way to the back of the yard, to the edge of the woods and leaned against a bent gum tree. The ground around me was littered with last year's prickly balls. I listened to the night sounds.

I had checked 1830 and found…I didn't know what I had found. Nothing. Everything. A few tantalizing hints. Greenberry, Mabel and Zachary. Mister, Mae and…Zach? Not a younger brother, but a son? And another entry: *Wm. Biddle, Jr., a free man of color.* Mae had spoken of "Will Biddle who farmed two hollers over from us when I was a child…" But in 1830? In *1830*?

There was a logical part of my mind that rejected those hints. Each had an alternative explanation. Coincidence of names. Clerical errors. Senile memory.

Sometimes we remember things only because we have been told them so often. I remember that I stepped in a birthday cake when I was two years old. It had been placed on the floor in the back of the family car and I had climbed over the seat and…But do I *remember* it? Or do I remember my parents telling me the story—and showing me the snapshot—so many times over the years that it has become real to me. Mae could be remembering family tales she had heard, scrambled and made *hers* by a slowly short-circuiting brain.

But there was another part of me that embraced those hints; that wanted to believe that Mae had known Margaret Sanger, had voted for Teddy Roosevelt, had danced on the White House lawn in a Sanitary Commission uniform, because if they were true…

I stepped away from the tree and a rabbit shot suddenly left to right in front of me. I watched it bound away…And spied figures moving about in the Carters' back yard. Henry and Barbara. I watched them for a while, wondering idly what they were up to. Then I recalled Henry's nickname for his wife—and a song that Mae had known.

I took the same route the rabbit had taken. Last year's dead leaves crackled and dry twigs snapped beneath my feet. I saw one of the Carters—Henry, I thought—come suddenly erect and look my way. I hoped he wouldn't call the police. Then I thought, Christ, they're newlyweds. What sort of back yard shenanigans was I about to walk in on?

I stopped and waved a hand. "That you, Henry? Barbara? It's Paul Wilkes."

A second shadow stood erect by the first. "What's wrong?" It was Barbara's voice.

"I—I saw you moving around back there and thought it might be prowlers. Is everything all right?"

"Sure," said Henry. "Come on out. You'll get tick-bitten if you stay in there."

"Why don't you have your yard light on?" I asked as I stepped from the woods. Stupid question. I could think of a couple of reasons. Brenda and I had once gone skinny dipping in our pool at three in the morning. *Stifled laughter and urgent play, and the water glistening like pearls on her skin.* That had been years ago, of course; but sometimes it was good to remember that there had once been times like that.

"It would spoil the viewing," Henry said.

Now that I was close enough, I saw that they had a telescope set up on a tripod. It was a big one. "Oh. Are you an astronomer?"

Henry shook his head. "I'm a genetic engineer, or I will be when I finish my dissertation. Barbry's going to be a biochemist. Astronomy is our hobby."

"I see." I felt uncomfortable, an intruder; but I had come there with a purpose. I made as if to turn away and then turned back. "Say, as long as I'm here, there is a question you might be able to answer for me."

"Sure." They were an obliging couple. The moon was half-full, the air was spring evening cool, they did not really want me there interrupting whatever it was that the sky-gazing would have led to.

"I've heard Henry call you Barbry," I said to Barbara. "And…Do you know a song called *Barbry Ellen?*"

She laughed. "You mean *Barbara Allen*. Sure. That's where Henry came up with the nickname. He's into folk singing. *Barbry Ellen* is an older version."

"Well, someone told me it was the 'old president's favorite song,' and I wondered if you knew—"

"Which old president? That's easy. George Washington. You see, he had this secret crush on his best friend's wife, and…"

"George Washington? Are you sure?"

"Well, there might have been other presidents who liked it. But Washington's partiality is on the record, and the song has been out of vogue a long, long time."

"Was that all you wanted to know?" asked Henry. There was something in his voice that sounded a lot like "good bye." He wasn't happy, I could tell. I had spoiled the mood for him.

"Yes, certainly," I said. "I thought you might have been prowlers." I backed away into the woods, then turned and walked quickly home.

I learned me that 'un when I was knee-high to a grasshopper. Pa told me it was the President's favorite song. The old President, from when his Pappy fought in the War.

The old President, from when his Pappy fought in the War.

> *Lost my partner, what'll I do?*
> *Lost my partner, what'll I do?*
> *Lost my partner, what'll I do?*
> *Skip to my love, my darling.*

✦

Brenda drank tea. She always allowed the bag to steep for a precise five minutes (read the package) and always squeezed it dry with her tea spoon. She always disposed of the bag in the trash before drinking from the cup. When she drank, she held the saucer in her left hand and the cup in her right and hugged her elbows close to her body. She stood near the French doors in the family room, gazing out toward the back yard and the woods beyond. I had no idea if she had heard me.

"I said, I think I'll go over to Sunny Dale today and look in on Mrs. Holloway."

Brenda held herself so still she was nearly rigid. Not because she was reacting to what I had said. She always stood that way. She spent her life at attention.

"You didn't have any plans, did you?"

A small, precise shake of the head. "No. No plans. We never have any plans." A sip of tea that might have been measured in minims. "Maybe I'll go into the office, too. There are always cases to work on."

I hesitated a moment longer before leaving. When I reached the front door, I heard her call.

"Paul?"

"Yes?" Down the length of the hall I could see her framed by the glass doors at the far end. She had turned around and was facing me. "What?"

"Why do you have to go in today? It's Saturday."

"It's…nothing I can talk about yet. A wild notion. It might be nothing more than a senile woman's ravings, but it might be the most important discovery of the century. Brenda, if I'm right, it could change our lives."

Even from where I stood I could see the faint smile that trembled on her lips. "Yes, it could, at that." She turned around and faced the glass again. "You do what you have to do, Paul. So will I."

It was odd, but I suddenly remembered how much we had once done together. Silly things, simple things. Football games, Scrabble, Broadway shows. Moments public and private. The party had asked Brenda to run for the state legislature one time, and I had urged her to accept, but the baby had been due and…Somehow, now we stood at opposite ends of the house. I thought for a moment of asking her to come with me to the Home, but thought better of it. Brenda would find those old, grey creatures more distressing than I did. "Look," I said, "this should only take a couple hours. I'll call you and we'll do something together this afternoon. Take in a movie, maybe."

She nodded in her distracted way. I saw that she had spilled tea into her saucer.

✦

Once at the Home, I sought out Mae in her garden retreat, hoping that she was in a better mood than yesterday. I had a thousand questions to ask her. A dozen puzzles and one hope. But when she saw me coming, her face retreated into a set of tight lines: Eyes, narrowed; mouth and lips, thin and disapproving.

"Go away," said Mae Holloway.

"I only wanted to ask a few—"

"I said, go away! Why are you always pestering me?"

"Don't mind her," said a voice by my elbow. "She's been that way since yesterday." I turned and saw Jimmy Kovacs, the retired printer. "Headache. Maybe you should give her something."

"You don't need a doctor to take aspirin."

He shook his head. "Aspirin didn't work. She needs something stronger. Might be a migraine. I had an allergy once. To hot dog meat. Every time I had a frank, my head felt like fireworks going off inside. So, my doc, he tells me—"

"I'll see what I can do," I said. Old folks chatter about little else than their ailments. They compare them the way young boys compare…Well, you know what I mean. "Mine is bigger than yours." They have contests, oldsters do, to see who has the biggest illness. The winner gets to die.

I sat on the stone bench beside Mae. "Jimmy tells me you have a headache," I said.

"Jimmy should mind his own affairs."

"Where does it hurt?"

"In my haid, jackass. That's what makes it a headache."

"No, I mean is it all over or in one spot? Is it a dull ache or sharp points. Is it continual, or does it come in bursts? Do you see or hear anything along with the headache?"

She gave me a look. "How do you make a headache into such a contraption?"

I shrugged. "There are many things that can cause a headache. When did it start?" If I could relieve her pain, she might be willing to answer the questions I had about her family history.

She squinted at the ground, her face tight as a drum. I heard her suck in her breath. Bees danced among the flowers to our right; the fragrances hung in the air. "Yesterday afternoon," she said. "Yesterday afternoon, after you left. It was like the sun come up inside my head. I was lying down for a nap when everything turned blind white for a few seconds and I heard a chorus a-singing hymns. I thought I'd surely died and gone to heaven." She took a deep breath and massaged her left temple with her fingers.

"Somedays I'ud as lief I were dead. All these here aches and pains…And I cain't do the things I used to. I used to dance. I used to love to dance, but I can't do that no more. And everybody who ever mattered to me is a longtime gone."

Her parents. Little Zach. Green Holloway. Gone a very long time, if I was right. Joe Paxton. Ben Wickham. There must have been plenty of others, besides. Folks in Cincinnati, in California, in Wyoming. She left a trail of alienation behind her every place she had ever been. It was a cold trail, in more ways than one.

"When the white light faded out, I saw it weren't an angel choir, after all. It were Christy's Minstrels that time when they come to Knoxville, and Mister and me and…" She frowned and shook her head. "Mister and me, we tarryhooted over to hear 'em. Doc, it was the clearest spell I ever had. I was a-settin' in the audience right down in front. I clean forgot I was a-bedded down here in Sunny Dale."

Sometimes migraines triggered visions. Some of the saints had suffered migraines and seen the Kingdom of God. "Yes?" I prompted.

"Well, Mister was a-settin' on my left holding my hand; and someone's man-child, maybe fifteen year, was press't up agin me on my right—oh, we was packed in almighty tight, I tell you—but, whilst I could see and hear as clear as I can see and hear you, I couldn't feel any of them touching me. When I thunk on it, I could feel that I was lying a-bed with the sheets over me."

I nodded. "You weren't getting any tactile memories, then. I think your—"

She didn't hear me. "The troupe was setting on benches, with each row higher than the one in front—Tiers, that be what they call 'em. They all stood to sing the medley, 'cept 'Mr. Interlocutor,' who sat in a chair front and center. Heh. That was the out-doin'est chair I ever did see. Like a king's throne, it was. They sang *Jim Along Josie* and *Ring, Ring the Banjo*. I h'ain't heared them tunes since who flung the chuck. The interlocutor was sided by the soloists on his right and the glee singers—what they later called barbershop singers—on the left." She gestured, moving both hands out from the center. "Then the banjo player and the dancer. Then there was four end-men, two t' either side. Those days, only the end-men were in the Ethiopian business."

"The Ethiopian business?"

"You know. Done up in black-face."

Images of Cantor singing "Mammy." Exaggerated lips; big, white, buggy eyes. An obscene caricature. "Black face!"

My disapproval must have shown in my voice, for Mae grew defensive. "Well, that was the only way us reg'lar folks ever got to hear nigra music back then," she said, rubbing her temple. "The swells could hear 'em any time; but the onlyest nigras I ever saw 'fore I left the hills was Will Biddle and his kin, and they didn't do a whole lot of singing and dancing."

"Nigras?" That was worse than black-face. I tried to remind myself that Mae had grown up in a very different world.

Mae seemed to refocus. Her eyes lost the dreamy look. "What did I say? Nigra? Tarnation, that isn't right, anymore, is it? They say 'coloreds' now."

"African-American. Or black."

She shook her head, then winced and rubbed her temple again. "They weren't mocking the col— the black folks. The minstrels weren't. Not then. It was fine music. Toe-tapping. And the banjo…Why, white folks took that up from the coloreds. But we'uns couldn't go to dark-town shows, and they couldn't come to us—not in them days. So, sometimes white folks dressed up to play black music. Daddy Rice, he was supposed to be the best, though I never did see him strut *Jim Crow*; but James Bland that wrote a lot of the tunes was a black man his own self. I heared he went off to France later 'cause of the way the white folks was always greenin' him."

"I see. Has your headache subsided since then?" *Minstrel shows*, I thought.

"It's all so mixed up. These memories I keep getting. It's like a kalideyscope I had as a young'un. All those pretty beads and mirrors…"

"Your headache, Mrs. Holloway. I asked if it was still the same." Try to keep old folks on the track. Go ahead, try it.

She grimaced. "Why, it comes and goes, like ocean waves. I seen the ocean oncet. Out in Californey. Now, that was a trek, let me tell you. Folks was poor on account of the depression, so I took shank's mare a long part of the way, just like Sweet Betsy." She sighed. "That was always a favorite of mine. Every time I heared it, it was like I could see it all in my mind. The singing around the campfire; the cold nights on the prairie. The Injuns a-whooping and a-charging…" She began to sing.

"The Injuns come down in a great yelling horde.
And Betsy got skeered they would scalp her adored.
So behind the front wagon wheel Betsy did crawl.
And she fought off the Injuns with powder and ball.

Mae tried to smile, but it was a weak and pained one. "I went back to

Californey years later. I taken the *Denver Zephyr*, oh, my, in the 1920s I think it was. Packed into one of them old coach cars, cheek by jowl, the air so thick with cigar smoke. And when you opened the window, why you got coal ash in your face from the locomotive."

"Look, why don't you come to the clinic with me and I'll see if I have anything for that headache of yours."

She nodded and rose from her bench, leaning on her stick. She took one step and looked puzzled. Then she staggered a little. "Dizzy," she muttered. Then she toppled forward over her stick and fell to the ground. I leapt to my feet and grabbed her by the shoulders, breaking her fall.

"Hey!" I said. "Careful! You'll break something."

Her eyes rolled back up into her head and her limbs began to jerk uncontrollably. I looked over my shoulder and saw Jimmy Kovacs hurrying up the garden path. "Quick," I said. "Call an ambulance! Call Dr. Khan! Tell her to meet us at the hospital."

Jimmy hesitated. He looked at Mae, then at me. "What's wrong?" he said.

"Hurry! I think she's having another stroke."

Jimmy rushed off and I turned back to Mae. Checkout time, I thought. But why now? Why now?

I have always loved hospitals. They are factories of health, mass producers of treatments. The broken and defective bodies come in, skilled craftsmen go to work—specialists from many departments, gathered together in one location—and healthy and restored bodies emerge. Usually. No process is one hundred percent efficient. Some breakdowns cannot be repaired. But it is more efficient to have the patients come to the doctor than to have the doctor waste time traveling from house to house. Only when health is mass produced can it be afforded by the masses.

Yet, I can see how some people would dislike them. The line is a thin one between the efficient and the impersonal.

Khan and I found Mae installed in the critical care unit. The ward was shaped like a cul-de-sac, with the rooms arranged in a circle around the nurses' station. White sheets, antiseptic smell. Tubes inserted wherever they might prove useful. Professionally compassionate nurses. Bill Wing was waiting for us there. With clipboard in hand and stethoscope dangling from his neck, he looked like an archetype for The Doctor. We shook hands and I introduced him to Khan. Wing led us out into the corridor, away from the patient. Mae was in a coma, but it was bad form to discuss her case in front of her, as if she were not there.

"It was not a stroke," he told us, "but a tumor. An astrocytoma encroaching on the left temporal lobe. It is malignant and deeply invasive." Wing spoke with an odd Chinese-British accent. He was from Guandong by way of Hong Kong.

I heard Khan suck in her breath. "Can it be removed?" she asked.

Wing shook his head. "On a young and healthy patient, maybe; though I would hesitate to perform the operation even then. On a woman this old and weak…" He shook his head again. "I have performed a decompression to relieve some of the pressure, but the tumor itself is not removable."

Khan sighed. "So sad. But she has had a long life."

"How much longer does she have?" I asked.

Wing pursed his lips and looked inscrutable. "That is hard to say. Aside from the tumor, she is in good health…for a woman her age, of course. It could be tomorrow; it could be six months. She has a time bomb in her head, and no one knows how long the fuse is. We only know that the fuse…"

"Has been lit," finished Khan. Wing looked unhappy, but nodded.

"As the tumor progresses," he continued, "her seizures will become more frequent. I suspect there will be pain as the swelling increases." He paused and lowered his head slightly, an Oriental gesture.

"There must be something you can do," I said. Khan looked at me.

"Sometimes," she said, "there is nothing that can be done."

I shook my head. "I can't accept that." Holloway could not die. Not yet. Not now. I thought of all those secrets now sealed in her head. They might be fantasies, wild conclusions that I had read into partial data; but I had to know. I had to know.

"There is an end to everything." Noor Khan gazed toward the double doors that led to the medical CCU. "Though it is always hard to see the lights go out.

I drew my coat on. "I'm going to go to the University Library for a while."

Khan gave me a peculiar look. "The Library?" She shrugged. "I will stay by her side. You know how she feels about hospitals. She will be frightened when she recovers consciousness. Best if someone she knows is with her."

I nodded. "She may not regain consciousness for some time," I reminded her. "What about your patients?"

"Dr. Mendelson will handle my appointments tomorrow. I called him before I came over."

All right, let her play the martyr! I tugged my cap onto my head. Khan didn't expect thanks, did she? I could just picture the old crone's ravings.

The hysteria. She would blame Khan, not thank her, for bringing her here.

As I reached the door, I heard Khan gasp. "She's singing!"

I turned. "What?"

Khan was hovering over the bed. She flapped an arm. "Come. Listen to this."

As if I had not listened to enough of her ditties. I walked to the bedside and leaned over. The words came soft and slurred, with pauses in between as she sucked in breath: "There was an old woman…at the foot of the hill…If she ain't moved away…she's living there still…Hey-diddle…day-diddle…de-dum…" Her voice died away into silence. Khan looked at me.

"What was that all about?"

I shook my head. "Another random memory," I said. "The tumor is busy, even if she is not."

It was not until mid-afternoon, buried deep in the stacks at the University Library, that I remembered my promise to call Brenda. But when I phoned from the lobby, Consuela told me that she had gone out and that I was not to wait up for her.

> *But the summer faded, and a chilly blast*
> *O'er that happy cottage swept at last;*
> *When the autumn song birds woke the dewy morn,*
> *Our little "Prairie Flow'r" was gone.*

In the year before Deirdre was born, Brenda and I took a vacation trip to Boston and Brenda laid out an hour-by-hour itinerary, listing each and every site we planned to visit. Along the way, she kept detailed logs of gas, mileage, arrival and departure times at each attraction, expenses, even tips to bellboys. It did not stop her from enjoying Boston. She did not insist that we march in lockstep to the schedule. "It's a guide, not a straitjacket," she had said. Yet, she spent an hour before bed each night updating and revising the next day's itinerary. Like an itch demanding a scratch, like a sweet tooth longing for chocolate, satisfying the urge to organize gave her some deep, almost sensual pleasure.

Now, of course, everything was planned and scheduled, even small trips. Sometimes the plan meant more than the journey.

Brenda frowned as I pulled into the secluded lot and parked in front of an old, yellow, wood-frame building. A thick row of fir trees screened the office building from the busy street and reduced the sound of rushing traffic to a whisper.

"Paul, why are we stopping? What is this place?"

"A lab," I told her. "That phone call just before we left the house…Some work I gave them is ready."

"Can't you pick it up tomorrow when you're on duty?" she said. "We'll be late."

"We won't be late. The Sawyers never start on time, and there'll be three other couples to keep them busy."

"I hope that boy of theirs isn't there. He gives me the creeps, the way he stares at people…"

"Maybe they changed his medication," I said. "Do you want to come in, or will you wait out here?"

"Is there a waiting area?"

"I don't know. I've never been here before."

Brenda gave a small sound, halfway between a cough and a sigh. Then she made a great show of unbuckling her seat belt.

"You don't have to come in if you don't want to," I said.

"Can you just get this over with?"

Inside the front door was a small lobby floored with dark brown tiles. The directory on the wall listed three tenants in white, plastic, push-pin letters: a management consulting firm, a marriage counselor, and the genetics lab.

When Brenda learned that S/P Microbiology was situated on the third floor, she rolled her eyes and decided to wait in the lobby. "Don't be long," she said, her voice halfway between an order, a warning and a plaintive plea to keep the schedule.

The receptionist at S/P was a young redhead wearing a headset and throat mike. He showed me to a chair in a small waiting room, gave me a not-too-old magazine to read, and spoke a few words into his mouthpiece. When the telephone rang, he touched his earpiece once and answered the phone while on his way back to his station. Clever, I thought, to have a receptionist not tied to a desk.

I was alone only for a moment before Charles Randolph Singer himself came out. He was a short, slightly rumpled-looking man a great deal younger than his reputation had led me to expect. His white lab coat hung open, revealing a pocket jammed full of pens and other instruments. "Charlie Singer," he said. "You're Doctor Wilkes?"

"Yes."

He shook my hand. "You sure did hand us one larruping good problem." Then he cocked his head sideways and looked at me. "Where'd you get the samples?"

"I'd…rather not say yet."

"Hunh. Doctor-patient crap, right? Well, you're paying my rent with this job, so I won't push it. Come on in back. I'll let Jessie explain things."

I followed Singer into a larger room lined with lab benches and machines. A dessicator and a centrifuge, a mass spec, a lot of other equipment I didn't recognize. A large aquarium filled with brackish water, fish and trash occupied one corner. The plastic beverage can rings and soda bottles were dissolving into a floating, liquid scum, which the fish calmly ignored.

"Jessie!" Singer said. "Wilkes is here."

A round-faced woman peered around the side of the mass spectrometer. "Oh," she said. "You." She was wearing a headset similar to the receptionist's.

"Jessica Burton-Peeler," said Singer introducing us, "is the second-best geneticist on the face of the planet."

Peeler smiled sweetly. "That was last year, Charlie." She spoke with a slight British accent.

Singer laughed and pulled a stick of gum from the pocket of his lab coat. He unwrapped it and rolled it into a ball between his fingers. "Tell Doctor Wilkes here what we found." He popped the wad of gum into his mouth.

"Would you like some tea or coffee, Doctor? I can have Eamonn bring you a cup."

"No, thanks. My wife is waiting downstairs. We were on our way to a dinner party, but I couldn't wait until tomorrow to find out."

Singer gave me a speculative look. "Find out what?"

"What you found out."

After a moment, Singer grunted and shrugged. "All right. We cultured all three cell samples," he said. "The 'B' sample was normal in all respects. The cells went through fifty-three divisions."

"Which is about average," Peeler added. "As for the other two…One of them divided only a dozen times—"

"The 'A' sample," I interjected.

"Yes," she said after a momentary pause. "The 'A' sample. But the 'C' sample…That one divided one hundred and twenty-three times."

I swallowed. "And that is…abnormal?"

"Abnormal?" Singer laughed. "Doc, that measurement is so far above the Gaussian curve that you can't even see abnormal from there."

"The 'A' sample wasn't normal, either," said Peeler quietly.

I looked at her and she looked at me calmly and without expression. "Well," I said and coughed. "Well."

"So, what's next?" Singer demanded. "You didn't send us those tissue samples just to find out they were different. You already knew that—or you suspected it—when you sent them in. We've confirmed it. Now what?"

"I'd like you to compare them and find out how their DNA differs."

Singer nodded after a thoughtful pause. "Sure. If the reason is genetic. We can look for factors common to several 'normal' samples but different for your 'A' and 'C' samples. Run polymerase chain reactions. Tedious, but elementary."

"And then…" I clenched and unclenched my fists. "I've heard you work on molecular modifiers."

"Nanomachines," said Singer. "I have a hunch it'll be a big field someday, and I'm planning to get in on the ground floor." He jerked a thumb over his shoulder at the aquarium. "Right now I'm working on a bacterium that eats plastic waste."

"Dear Lord," said Burton-Peeler in sudden wonder. "You want us to modify the DNA, don't you?"

Singer looked from me to his wife. "Modify the DNA?"

"Yes," I started to say.

Burton-Peeler pursed her lips. "Modify the 'A' sample, of course. Whatever factor we find in the 'C' sample that sustains the cell division…You want us to splice that into the short-lived sample."

I nodded, unable to speak. "I thought it might be possible to bring it up to normal."

Singer rubbed his jaw. "I don't know. Splicing bacterial DNA is one thing. Human DNA is another. A universe more of complexity. Of course, there is that business with the multiple sclerosis aerosol. They used a modified rhinovirus to carry the mucus-producing genes into the lungs. If the factor is gene specific, we could do something similar. Infect the cells with a retrovirus and…"

"Then you can do it?"

"Now hold on. I said no such thing. I said *maybe* it was possible, *if* the chips fall right. But there'll be some basic research needed. It will cost. A lot."

"I'll…find the money. Somehow."

Singer shook his head slowly. "I don't think you can find that much. You're talking about maybe three to five years research here."

"Three to—" I felt the pit of my stomach drop away. "I don't have three to five years." Dee-dee would be dead by then. And Mae, too, taking the secret in her genes with her.

"We'll do it at cost," said Burton-Peeler. Singer turned and looked at his wife.

"What?"

"We'll do it at cost, Charlie. I'll tell you why later." She looked back to me. "Understand, we still cannot promise fast results. When you set off into the unknown, you cannot predict your arrival time."

Go for broke. Damn the torpedoes. "Just try is all I ask."

Burton-Peeler saw me out. On the landing to the stairwell she stopped. "You're the father of the young girl with progeria," she said. "I saw it in the paper a few years ago. The 'A' sample was hers, wasn't it?"

I nodded. "Yes, and the second sample was my own. For comparison." I turned to go.

Peeler stopped me with an arm on my sleeve. She looked into my eyes. "Whose was the third sample?" she asked.

I smiled briefly and sadly. "My faith, that the universe balances."

In the lobby, Brenda was just handing a tea cup and saucer back to Singer's red-haired receptionist when she saw me coming. With a few brisk motions she collected her things and was already breezing out the door as I caught up with her.

"I'll drive," she said. "We're way behind schedule now, thanks to you."

I said nothing and she continued in what was supposed to be an idly curious tone. "Who was that woman with you? The one on the landing."

"Woman? Oh, that was Jessica Burton-Peeler. Singer's wife."

Brenda arched an eyebrow and made a little moue with her lips. "She's a little on the plump side," she said. "Do you find plump women attractive?"

I didn't have the time to deal with Brenda's insecurities. "Start the car," I told her. "We'll be late for dinner."

> *They say we are aged and gray, Maggie*
> *As spray by the white breakers flung;*
> *But to me you're as fair as you were, Maggie,*
> *When you and I were young.*

Mae Holloway lay between white sheets, coupled to tubes and wires. She lay with her eyes closed, and her arms limp by her sides atop the sheets. Her mouth hung half-open. She seemed grey and shrunken; drawn, like a wire through a die. Her meager white hair was nearly translucent.

She looked like a woman half her age.

Noor Khan was sitting near the wall reading a magazine. She looked up as I entered the room. "They told you?"

"That Mae has recovered consciousness? Yes. I'm surprised to see you still here."

Khan looked at the bed. "I have made arrangements. She has no family to keep watch."

"No," I agreed. "They are long gone." Longer than Khan could suppose. "Is she sleeping?"

She hesitated a moment, then spoke in a whisper. "Not really. I think that as long as she keeps her eyes closed she can pretend she is not in hospital. Those memories of hers…The consciousness-doubling, you called it. I think they play continually, now. The pressure from the tumor on the temporal lobe."

I nodded. Suppress all external stimuli and Mae could—in a biological kind of virtual reality—live again in the past. If we spoke too loudly, it would bring her back to a time and place she did not want. "Why don't you take a break," I said. "I'll sit with her for a while."

Khan cocked her head to the side and looked at me. "You will."

"Yes. Is that so surprising?"

She started to say something and then changed her mind. "I will be in the cafeteria." And then she fluttered out.

When she was gone, I pulled the chair up to the bedside and sat in it. "Mae? It's Doctor Wilkes." I touched her gently on the arm, and she seemed to flinch from the contact. "Mae?"

"I hear yuh," she said. Her voice was low and weak and lacked her usual snap. I had to lean close to hear her. "It'ud pleasure me if you'd company for a mite. It's been mighty lonely up hyar."

"Has it? But Doctor Khan—"

"I kilt the b'ar," she whispered, "but it stove up Pa something awful. He cain't hardly git around no more, so I got to be doin' for him." She paused as if listening. "I'm not so little as that, mister; I jest got me a puny bone-box. I ain't no yokum. I been over the creek. And I got me a Tennessee toothpick, too, in case you have thoughts about a little girl with a crippled-up Pa. What's yore handle, mister?"

"Mrs. Holloway," I said gently. "Don't you know me?"

Mae giggled. "Right pleased to meet you, Mister Holloway. Greenberry's a funny name, so I'll just call you Mister. If you'll set a spell, I'll whup you up a bait to eat. H'ain't much, only squirrel; but I aim to go hunting tomorry and find a deer that'll meat us for a spell."

I pulled back and sat up straight in my chair. She was reliving her first meeting with Green Holloway. Was she too far gone into the quicksand of nostalgia to respond to me? "Mae," I said more loudly, shaking her shoulder. "It's Doctor Wilkes. Can you hear me?"

Mae gasped and her eyes flew open. "Whut...? Where...?" The eyes lighted on me and went narrow. "You."

"Me," I agreed. "How are you feeling, Mrs. Holloway?"

"I'm a-gonna die. How do you want me to feel?"

Relieved? Wasn't there a poem about weary rivers winding safe to the sea? But, no matter how long and weary the journey, can anyone face the sea at the end of it? "Mrs. Holloway, do you remember the time you were on the White House lawn and the president came out?"

Her face immediately became wary and she looked away from me. "What of it?"

"That president. It was Lincoln, wasn't it?"

She shook her head, a leaf shivering in the breeze.

I took a deep breath. "The Sanitary Commission was the Union Army's civilian medical corps. If you were wearing that uniform, you were remembering the 1860s. That business on the lawn. It happened. I looked it up. The dancing. *Listen to the Mockinbird.* Lincoln coming outside to join the celebration. The whole thing. You know it, but you won't admit it because it sounds impossible."

"Sounds impossible?" She turned her head and looked at me at last. "How could I remember Lincoln? I'm not *that* old!"

"Yes, you are, Mae. You are that old. It's just that those early memories have gone all blurry. It's become hard for you to tell the decades apart. Your oldest memories had faded entirely, until your stroke revived them."

"You're talking crazy."

"I think it must be a defense mechanism," I went on as if she had not spoken. "The blurring and forgetting. It keeps the mental desktop cleared of clutter by shoving the old stuff aside."

"Doc..."

"But, every now and then, one of those old, faded memories would pop up, wouldn't it? Some impossible recollection. And you would think..."

"That I was going crazy." In a whisper, half to herself, she said, "I was always afraid of that, as long back as I can remember."

No wonder. Sporadic recollections of events generations past...Could a sane mind remember meeting Lincoln? "Mae. I found your name in the 1850 Census."

She shook her head again. Disbelief. But behind it...Hope? Relief that those impossible memories might be real? "Doc, how can it be possible?"

I spread my hands. "I don't know. Something in your genes. I have some people working on it, but...I think you have been aging slow. I don't know how that is possible. Maybe it has never happened before. Maybe you're the only one. Or maybe there were others and no one ever noticed. Maybe they were killed in accidents; or they really did go mad; or they thought they were recalling past lives. It doesn't matter. Mae, I've spent the last week in libraries and archives. You were born around 1800."

"No!"

"Yes. Your father was a member of Captain James Scott's settlement company. The Murrays, the Hammontrees, the Holloways, the Blacks and others. The overmountain men, they were called. They bought land near Six Mile Creek from the Overhill Cherokees."

I paused. Mae said nothing but she continued to look at me, slowly shaking her head. "Believe me," I said. "Your father's name was Josh, wasn't it?"

"Josiah. Folks called him Josh. I...I had forgotten my folks for such a long time; and now that I can remember, it pains me awful."

"Yes. I overheard. A bear mauled him."

"Doc, he was such a fine figure of a man. Right portly—I mean, handsome. He cut a swath wherever he walked. To see him laid up like that... Well, it sorrowed me something fierce. And him always saying I shouldn't wool over him."

"He died sometime between 1830 and 1840, after you married Green Holloway."

She looked into the distance. "Mister, he was a long hunter. He come on our homestead one day and saw how things stood and stayed to help out. Said it wasn't fittin' for a young gal to live alone like that with no man to side her. 'Specially a button like I was. There was outlaws and renegades all up and down the Trace who wouldn't think twice about bothering a young girl. When Pa finally said 't was fittin', we jumped the broom 'til the preacher-man come through." She stopped. "Doc?"

"Yes?"

"Doc, you must have it right. Because...Because, how long has it been since folks lived in log cabins, and long hunters dressed up in buckskins?"

"A long time," I said. "A very long time."

"Seems like just a little while ago to me, but I know it can't be. The Natchez Trace? I just never gave it much thought."

Have you ever seen a neglected field overgrown with weeds? That was Mae's memory. Acres of thistle and briar. All perspective lost, all sense of elapsed time. "Your memories were telescoped," I said. "Remember when you sang *Sweet Betsy from Pike* for me, and you said how real it all seemed to you? Well, after the Civil War, sometime during the Great Depression of the 1870s, you went out west, probably on one of the last wagon trains, after they finished the railroad. After that, I lost track."

She stayed quiet for a long time and I began to think she had dozed off. Then she spoke again.

"Sometimes I remember the Tennessee hills," she said in a faraway voice, "all blue and purple and cozy with family." She sighed. "I loved them mountains," she said. "We had us a hardscrabble, side-hill farm. The hills was tilted so steep we could plow both sides of an acre. And the cows had their legs longer on the one side than the other so's they could stand straight-up." She chuckled at the hillbilly humor. "Oh, it was a hard life. You kids today don't know. But in the springtime, when the piney roses and star-flowers and golden bells was in bloom, and the laurel hells was all purpled up; why, doc, you couldn't ask God for a purtier sight." She sighed. "And other times...Other times, I remember a ranch in high-up, snow-capped mountains with long-horned cattle and vistas where God goes when He wants to feel small. There was a speakeasy in Chicago, where the jazz was hot; and a bawdy house in Frisco, where I was." She let her breath out slowly and closed her eyes again. "I remember wearing bustles and bloomers, and linen and lace, and homespun and broadcloth. I've been so many people, I don't know who I am."

She opened her eyes and looked at me. "But I was always alone, except in them early years. With Mister. And with Daddy and my brother Zach." A tear dripped down the side of her face. I pulled a tissue from the box and blotted it up for her. "There weren't nobody left for me. Nobody."

I hesitated for a moment. Then I said, "Mae, you never had a brother."

"Now what are you talking about? I remember him clear as day."

"I've checked the records. Your mother died and your father never re-married."

Mae started to speak, then frowned. "Pa did tell me oncet that he'd never hitch ag'in, because he loved the dust of Ma's feet and the sweat of her body more than he loved any other woman. But Zach—"

"Was your own child."

She sucked in her breath between clenched teeth. "No, he weren't! He was near my own age."

"You remember Zach from 1861 when he followed your husband into the army. He was twenty-two then, and you...Well, you seemed to be thirty-seven to those around you. So, in your memory he seems like a brother. By the time you rejoined him on his ranch in Wyoming, he was even a bit older than your apparent age. Remembered how you thought he resembled Mister? Well, that was because he was Mister's son. I think...I think that was when you started forgetting how the years passed for you. Mae, no one ever ran out on you. You just outlived them. They grew old and they died and you didn't. And after a while you just wouldn't dare get close to anyone."

Tears squeezed from behind her eyes. "Stop it! Every time you say something, you make me remember."

"In all this time, Mae, you've never mentioned your child. You did have one; the clinical evidence is there. If Zach wasn't your boy, who was? Who was the boy sitting next to you at the minstrel show in Knoxville?"

She looked suddenly confused, and there was more to her confusion than the distance of time. "I don't know." Her eyes glazed and she looked to her right. I knew she was re-seeing the event. "Zach?" she said. "Is that you, boy? Zach? Oh, it is. It is." She refocused on me. "He cain't hear me," she said plaintively. "He hugged me, but I couldn't feel his arms."

"I know. It's only a memory."

"I want to feel his arms around me. They grow up so fast, you know. The young 'uns. One day, they're a baby, cute as a button; the next, all growed up and gone for a soldier. All growed up. I could see it happening. All of 'em, getting older and older. I thought there was something wrong with me. That I'd been a bad girl, because I kilt my Ma; and the Good Man was punishing me by holding me back from the pearly gates. If'n I never grew old, I'd never die. And if I never died, I'd never see any of my kin-folk again. Doc, you can't know what it's like, knowing your child will grow old and wither like October corn and die right before your eyes."

For a moment, I could not breathe. "Oh, I know," I whispered. "I know."

"Zach...I lived to see him turn to dust in the ground. He died in my own arms, a feeble, old man, and he asked me to sing *Home, Sweet Home*, like I used to when he was a young 'un. Oh, little Zach!" And she began to cry in earnest. She couldn't move her arms to wipe the tears away, so I pulled another tissue from the box on the tray and dabbed at her cheeks.

She reached out a scrawny hand and clutched my arm. "Thank you, doc. Thank you. You helped me find my child again. You helped me find my boy."

And then I did an odd thing. I stood and bent low over the bed and I kissed Mae Holloway on her withered cheek.

I'm going there to see my mother.
She said she'd meet me when I come.
I'm only going over Jordan,
I'm only going over home.

My days at the Home passed by in an anonymous sameness, dispensing medicines, treating aches and pains. Only a handful of people came to see me; and those with only trivial complaints. Otherwise, I sat unmolested in my office, the visitor's chair empty. I found it difficult even to concentrate on my journals. Finally, almost in desperation, I began making rounds, dropping in on Rosie and Jimmy and the others, chatting with them, enduring their pointless, rambling stories; sometimes suggesting dietary or exercise regimens that might improve their well-being. Anything to feel useful. I changed a prescription on Old Man Morton, now the Home's Oldest Resident, and was gratified to see him grow more alert. Sometimes you have to try different medications to find a treatment that works best for a particular individual.

Yet, somehow those days seemed empty. The astonishing thing to me was how little missed Mae Holloway was by the other residents. Oh, some of them asked after her politely. Jimmy did. But otherwise it was as if the woman had evaporated, leaving not even a void behind. Partly, I suspect, it was because they were unwilling to face up to this reminder of their own mortality. But partly, too, it must have been a sense of relief that her aloof and abrasive presence was gone. If she never had any friends, Mae had told me, she wouldn't miss them when they were gone. But neither did they miss her.

I usually stopped at the hospital on my way home, sometimes to obtain a further tissue sample for Singer's experiments, sometimes just to sit with her. Often, she was sedated to relieve the pain of the tumor. More usually, she was dreaming; adrift on the river of years, connected to our world and time by only the slenderest of threads.

When she was conscious, she would spin her reminiscences for me and sing. *Rosalie, the Prairie Flower. Cape Ann. Woodsman, Spare that Tree. Ching a Ring Chaw. The Hunters of Kentucky. Wait for the Wagon.* We agreed, Mae and I, that a wagon was just as suitable as a Chevrolet for courting pretty girls, and Phyllis and her wagon was the ancestor of Daisy and her bicycle, Lucille and her Oldsmobile, and Josephine and her flying machine. And someday, I suppose, Susie and her space shuttle.

It was odd to see Mae so at peace with her memories. She no longer feared them; no longer suppressed them. She no longer fled from them.

Rather, she embraced them and passed them on to me. When she sang, *Roisin the Beau*, she remarked casually how James Polk had used its melody for a campaign song. She recollected without flinching that she had voted for Zachary Taylor. "Old Rough and Ready," she said. "There was a man for you. 'Minds me some'at of that T.R. Too bad they pizened him, but he was out to break the slave power." It gave her no pause to recall how at New Orleans, "*There stood John Bull in martial pomp / And there stood Old Kentucky.*" It must have been an awful relief to acknowledge those memories, to relax in their embrace.

There were fond memories of her "bean," Green the Long Hunter. Of days spent farming or hunting or spinning woolen or cooking 'shine. Of nights spent 'setting' by the fire, smoking their pipes, reading to each other from the Bible. Quiet hours from a time before an insatiable demand for novelty—for something always to be *happening*—had consumed us. Green had even taken her down to Knoxville to see the touring company of *The Gladiator*, a stage play about Spartacus. Tales of slave revolts did not play well elsewhere in the South, but the mountaineers had no love for the wealthy flatland aristocrats.

She recalled meeting Walt Whitman, a fellow nurse in the Sanitary Commission. "A rugged fellow and all full of himself," she recalled, "but as kind and gentle with the men as any of the women-folk."

She still confused her son sometimes with a brother, with her father, with Green. He was younger, he was older, he was of her own age. But there were childhood memories, too, of the sort most parents have. How he had "spunked up with his gal," "spooned with his chicken," or "lollygagged with his peach," depending on the slang of the decade. How they had "crossed the wide prairie" together after the War and set up a ranch in Wyoming Territory. How he met and wed Sweet Annie, a real "piece of calico."

Not all the memories were pleasant—Sweet Annie had died screaming—but Mae relished them just the same. It was her life she was reclaiming, and a life consists of different parts, good and bad. The parts make up a whole. I continued to record her tales and tunes, as much because I did not know what else to do as because of any book plans, and I noticed that, while her doubling episodes often hopscotched through her life—triggered by associations and chance remarks—the music that played in her mind continued its slow and inexorable backward progression, spanning the 1840s and creeping gradually into the mid-thirties.

Slowly, a weird conviction settled on me. When the dates of her rememb-heard tunes finally reached 1800, she would die.

✦

Time was running short. Most brain tumor patients did not survive a year from the time of first diagnosis; and Mae was so fragile to begin with that I doubted a whole year would be hers. Reports from Singer alternated between encouragement and frustration. Apparent progress would evaporate with a routine, follow-up test. Happenstance observation would open up a whole new line of inquiry. Singer submitted requests for additional cell samples almost daily. Blood, skin, liver. It seemed almost as if Mae might be used up entirely before Singer could pry loose the secret of her genes and splice that secret into my Deirdre.

I began to feel as if I were in a race with time. A weird sort of race in which time was speeding off in both directions. A young girl dying too old. An old woman dying too young.

One day, Wing was waiting for me when I entered the hospital. Seeing the flat look of concern on his face, my heart faltered. *Not yet*, I thought; *not yet!* My heart screeched, but I kept my own face composed. He took me aside into a small consultation room. Plaster walls with macro designs painted in happy, soothing colors. Comfortable chairs; green plants. An appallingly cheerful venue in which to receive bad news.

But it was not bad news. It was good news, of an odd and unexpected sort.

"Herpes?" I said when he had told me. "Herpes is a cure for brain tumors?" I couldn't help it. I giggled.

Wing frowned. "Not precisely. Culver-Blaese is a new treatment and outside my field of specialty, but let me explain it as Maurice explained it to me." Maurice LeFevre was the resident in genetic engineering, one of the first such residencies in the United States. "Several years ago," said Wing, "Culver and Blaese successfully extracted the gene for the growth enzyme, thymidine kinase, from the herpes virus, and installed it into brain tumor cells using a harmless retrovirus."

"I would think," I said dryly, "that an enzyme that facilitates reproduction is the last thing a brain tumor needs spliced into its code."

Wing blinked rapidly several times. "Oh, I'm sorry. You see it's the ganciclovir. I didn't make that clear?"

"Ganciclovir is—?"

"The chemical used to fight herpes. It reacts with thymidine kinase, and the reaction products interfere with cell reproduction. So if tumor cells start producing thymidine, injecting ganciclovir a few days later will gum up the tumor's reproduction and kill it. There have been promising results on mice and in an initial trial with twenty human patients."

"What is 'promising'?"

"Complete remission in seventy-five percent of the cases, and appreciable shrinkage in all of them."

I sucked in my breath. I could hardly credit what Wing was telling me. Here was a treatment, a *deus ex machina*. Give Singer another year of live tissue experiments and he would surely find the breakthrough we sought. "What's the catch?" I asked. There had to be a catch. There was always a catch.

There were two.

"First," said Wing, "the treatment is experimental, so the insurance will not cover it. Second…Well, Mrs. Holloway has refused."

"Eh? Refused? Why is that?"

Wing shook his head. "I don't know. She wouldn't tell me. I thought if I caught you before you went to see her…"

"That I could talk her into it?"

"Yes. The two of you are very close. I can see that."

Close? Mae and I? If Wing could see that, those thick eyeglasses of his were more powerful than the Hubble telescope. Mae had not been close to anyone since her son died. *Since her child died in her arms, an old, old man.* Inwardly, I shuddered. No wonder she had never gotten close to anyone since. No wonder she had lost an entire era of her life.

"I'll give it a try," I said.

When I entered her room, Mae was lying quietly in her bed, humming softly. Awake, I knew, but not quite present. Her face was curled into a smile, the creases all twisted around in unwonted directions. There was an air about her, something halfway between sleep and joy, a *calm* that had inverted all those years of sourness, stood everything on its head, and changed all her minus signs to plus.

Setting on her cabin porch, I imagined, gazing down the hillside at the laurel hells, and at a distant, pristine stream meandering through the holler below. At peace. At last.

I pulled the visitor's chair close by the bedside and laid a hand lightly on her arm. She didn't stir. "Mae, it's me. I've come to set a spell with you."

"Howdy there, doc," she whispered. "Oh, it's such a lovely sunset. All heshed. I been telling Li'l Zach about the time his grandpap and Ol' Hickory went off t' fi't the Creeks. I was already fourteen when Pa went off, so I minded the cabin while he was away."

I leaned closer to her. "Mae, has Dr. Wing spoken to you about the new treatment?"

She took in a long, slow breath; and let it out as slowly. "Yes."

"He told me you refused."

"I surely did that."

"Why?"

"Why?" She opened her eyes and looked at me; looked sadly around the room. "I been hanging on too long. It's time to go home."

"But—"

"And what would it git me, anyways. Another year? Six months? Doc, even if I am nigh on to two hunnert year, like you say, and my bone-box only thinks it's a hunnert, *that's still older'n most folks git*. Even if that Doctor LeFevre can do what he says and rid me of this hyar tumor, there'll be a stroke afore long or my ticker'll give out, or something. Doc, *there ain't no point to it*. When I was young, when I was watching everyone I knew grow old and die, I wanted to go with them. I wanted to be with them. Why should I want to tarry now? If the Lord'll have me, I'm ready." She closed her eyes again and turned a little to the side.

"But, Mae…"

"And who'll miss me, beside," she muttered.

"I will."

She rolled out flat again and looked at me. "You?"

"Yes. A little, I guess."

She snorted. "You mean you'll miss whatever you want that you're wooling me over. Always jabbing me with needles, like I was a pincushion. There's something gnawing away at you, Doc. I kin see it in your eyes when you think no one is looking. Kind of sad and angry and awful far away. I don't know what it is, but I know I got something to do with it."

I drew back under her speech. Her words were like slaps.

"And suppose'n they do it and they do git that thang outen my brain. Doc, what'll happen to my music? What'll happen to my memories?"

"I—"

"You done told me they come from that tumor a-pressing against the brain. What happens if it's not pressin any longer?"

"The memories might stay, now that they've been started, even with the original stimulus removed. It might have been a 'little stroke' that started it, just like we thought originally."

"But you can't guarantee it, can you?" She fixed me with a stare until I looked away.

"No. No guarantees."

"Then I don't want it." I turned back in time to see her face tighten momentarily into a wince.

"It will relieve the pain," I assured her.

"Nothing will relieve the pain. Nothing. Because it ain't that sort of pain. There's my Pa, my Ma, Green, Little Zach and his Sweet Annie. Ben and Joe and all the others I would never let cozy up to me. They're all waiting for me over in Gloryland. I don't know why the Good Man has kept me here so long. H'isn't punishment for killing Ma. I know that now. There must be a reason for it; but I'm a-weary of the waiting. If'n I have this operation like you want, what difference will it make? A few months? Doc, I won't live those months in silence."

> *My Chloe has dimples and smiles, I must own;*
> *But, though she could smile, yet in truth she could frown.*
> *But tell me, ye lovers of liquor divine,*
> *Did you e'er see a frown in a bumper of wine?*

There is something about the ice cold shock of a perfect martini. The pine tree scent of the gin. The smooth liquid sliding down the throat. Then, a half second later, wham! It hits you. And in that half second, there is an hour of insight; though, sometimes, that hour comes very late at night. You can see with the same icy clarity of the drink. You can see the trail of choices behind you. Paths that led up rocky pitches; paths beside still waters. You can see where the paths forked, where, had you turned that way instead of this, you'd not be here today. You can even, sometimes, see where, when the paths forked, people took different trails.

"Paul!"

And you can wonder whether you can ever find that fork again.

I turned to see Brenda drop her briefcase on the sofa. "Paul! I *never* see you drinking."

Subtext: Do you drink a lot in secret when I can't see you? Sub-subtext: Are you an alcoholic? Holding a conversation with Brenda was a challenge. Her words were multi-layered; and you never knew on which layer to answer.

I placed my martini glass, still half-full, carefully down upon the sideboard, beside the others. It spilled a little as I did, defying the laws of gravity. I faced her squarely. "I'm running out of time," I said.

She looked at me for a moment. Then she said, "That's right. I'd wondered if you knew."

"I'm running out of time," I repeated. "She'll die before I know."

"*She...*" Brenda pulled her elbows in tight against her sides. "I don't want to hear this."

"That old woman. To live so long, only to die just now."

"The old woman from the home? *She* has you upset? For God's sake, Paul." And she turned away from me.

"You don't understand. She could save Dee-dee."

Brenda's head jerked a little to the left. Then she retrieved her briefcase and shook herself all over, as if preparing to leave. "How can a dying old woman save a dying old girl?"

"She's yin to Dee-dee's yang. The universe is neutral. There's a plus sign for every minus. But she wants to go over Jordan and I...can't stop her. And I don't understand why I can't."

"You're not making any sense, Paul. How many of those have you had?"

"She's two centuries old, Brenda. Two centuries old. She was a swinger and a sheba and a daisy and a pippin. She hears songs, in her head; but sometimes they're wrong, except they're right. The words are different. Older. *Old Zip Coon*, instead of *Turkey in the Straw*. *Lovely Fan'*, instead of *Buffalo Gals*. *Bright Mohawk Valley*, instead of *Red River Valley*. She read *Moral Physiology*, when it first came out. Mae did. Do you know the book? *Moral Physiology*, by Robert Dale Owen? No, of course not. It was all about birth control and it sold twenty-five thousand copies even though newspapers and magazines refused to carry the ads *and it was published in 18-god-damned-30.* She voted for Zachary Taylor, and her Pa fought in the Creek War, and her husband died at Resaca, and she saw Abraham-fucking-Lincoln—"

"Paul, can you hear yourself? You're talking crazy."

"Did you know *The Gladiator* debuted in New York in 1831? 'Ho! slaves, arise! Freedom...Freedom and revenge!'" I struck a pose, one fist raised.

"I can't stand to watch you like this, Paul. You're sopping drunk."

"And you're out late every night." Which was totally irrelevant to our discussion, but the tongue has a life of its own.

Through teeth clenched tight, she answered: "I have a job to keep."

I took a step away from the sideboard, and there must have been something wrong with the floorboards. Perhaps the support beams had begun to sag, because the floor suddenly tilted. I grabbed for the back of the armchair. The lamp beside it wobbled and I grabbed it with my other hand to keep it still.

Awkwardly twisted, half bent over, I looked at Brenda and spoke distinctly. "Mae Holloway is two centuries old. There is something in her genes. We think. Singer and Peeler and I. We think that with enough time. With enough time. Singer and Peeler can crack the secret. They can tailor a...Tailor a..." I hunted for the right word, found it scuttling

89

about on the floor and snatched it. "Nanomachine." Triumph. "Tailor a nanomachine that can repair Dee-dee's cells. But Mae is dying. She has a brain tumor, and it's killing her. There's a treatment. An experimental treatment. It looks very good. But Mae won't take it. She doesn't want it. She wants to sleep."

I don't know what I expected. I expected hope, or disbelief. I expected a demand for proof, or for more details. I expected her to say, "do anything to save my daughter!" I expected anything but indifference.

Brenda brushed imaginary dust from her briefcase and turned away. "Do what you always do, Paul. Just ignore what she wants."

I was in the clinic at the Home the next day when I received the call from the hospital. My head felt as if nails had been driven into it. I was queasy from the hangover. When the phone rang and I picked it up, a tinny voice on the other end spoke crisply and urgently and asked that I come over right away. I don't remember what I said, or even that I said anything; and I don't suppose my caller expected a coherent answer. My numb fingers fumbled the phone several times before it sat right in its cradle. *Heart attack*, I thought. And as quickly as that, the time runs out.

But they hadn't said she was dead. They hadn't said she was dead.

I hope that there was no traffic on the road when I raced to the hospital, for I remember nothing of the journey. Three times along the way I picked up the car phone to call the hospital for more information; and three times I replaced it. It was better not to know. Half an hour, with the lights right and the speed law ignored. That was thirty minutes in which hope was thinkable.

Smythe, the cardio-vascular man, met me in the corridor outside her room. He grabbed me by both my arms and steadied me. I could not understand why he was grinning. What possible reason could there be?

"She'll live, mon," he said. "It was a near thing, but she'll live."

I stared at Smythe without comprehension. He shook me by the arm, hard. My head felt like shattered glass.

"She'll live," he said again. His teeth were impossibly white.

I brushed him off and stepped into the room. *She'll live?* Then there was still time. Everything else was detail. My body felt suddenly weak, as if a stopcock had been pulled and all my sand had drained away. I staggered as far as the bedside, where I sank into a steel and vinyl chair. Smythe waited by the door, in the corridor, giving me the time alone.

Dee-dee lay asleep upon the bed, breathing slowly and softly through a tube set up her nose. An intravenous tube entered her left arm. Re-mote sensor implants on her skull and chest broadcast her heartbeat and breathing and brain waves to stations throughout the hospital. Smythe was never more than a terminal away from knowing her condition. I reached out and took her right hand in mine and gently stroked the back of it. "Hello, Dee-dee, I came as fast as I could. Why didn't…" I swallowed hard. "Why didn't you wait for me to tuck you in."

Dee-dee was still unconscious from the anesthetic. She couldn't hear me; but a quiet sob, quickly stifled, drew my attention to the accordion-pleated expandable wall, drawn halfway out on the opposite side of the bed. When I walked around it, I saw Consuela sitting in a chair on the other side. Her features were tightly leashed, but the tracks of tears had darkened both her cheeks. Her hands were pale where they gripped the arms of the chair.

"Connie!"

"Oh, Paul, we almost lost her. We almost lost her."

It slammed against my chest with the force of a hammer, a harder stroke for having missed. *Someday we will.* I took Connie's hand and brushed the backside of it as I had brushed Dee-dee's. "It's all right now," I said.

"She is such a sweet child. She never complains."

Prognosis: The life span is shortened by relentless arterial atheromatosis. Death usually occurs at puberty.

"She's all right now."

"For a little while. But it will become worse, and worse; until…" She leaned her head against me and I cradled her; I rubbed her neck and shoulders, smoothed her hair. With my left hand, I caressed her cheek. *It is not the end; but it is the beginning of the end.*

"We knew it would happen." The emotions are a very odd thing. When all was dark, when I believed myself helpless, I could endure that knowl-edge. It was my comfort. But now that there was a ray of light, I found it overwhelming me, crushing me so that I could hardly breathe. A sliver of sunshine makes a darkened room seem blacker still. I could live with Fate, but not with Hope. I found that there was a new factor in the equation now. I found that I could fail.

"Where is Brenda?" I asked.

Connie pulled herself from my arms, turned and pulled aside the cur-tain that separated her from Deirdre. "She didn't come."

"What?"

"She didn't come."

Something went out of me then, like a light switch turned off. I didn't say anything for the longest time. I drifted away from Connie over toward the window. A thick stand of trees filled the block across the street from the hospital. Leaves fresh and green with spring. Forsythia bursting yellow. A flock of birds banked in unison over the treetops and shied off from the high tension lines behind. I thought of the time when Brenda and I first met on campus, both of us young and full of the future. I remembered how we had talked about making a difference in the world.

I found Brenda at home. I found her in the family room, late at night after I had finally left the hospital. She was still clad in her business suit, as if she had just come from the office. She was standing rigidly by the bookcase, with her eyes dry and red and puffy, with Dee-dee's book, *The Boxcar Children*, in her hands. I had the impression that she had stood that way for hours.

"I tried to come, Paul," she said before I could get any words out. "I tried to come, but I couldn't. I was paralyzed; I couldn't move."

"It doesn't matter," I said. "Connie was there. She'll stay until I get changed and return." I rubbed a hand across my face. "God, I'm tired."

"She's taken my place, hasn't she? She feeds Deirdre, she nurses her, she tutors her. Tell me, Paul, has she taken over *all* my duties?"

"I don't know what you mean."

"I didn't think there was room in your life for anyone beside your daughter. You've shut everyone else out."

"I never pushed you away. You ran."

"It needs more than that. It needs more than not pushing. You could have caught me, if you'd reached. There was an awful row at the office today. Crowe and FitzPatrick argued. They're dissolving the partnership. I was taking too long to say yes to the partnership offer; so Sèan became curious and…He found out Walther had wanted a 'yes' on a lot more, so we filed for harrass…Oh, hell. It doesn't matter anymore; none of it."

She was talking about events on another planet. I stepped to her side and took hold of the book. It was frozen to her fingers. I tugged, and pried it from her grasp. Slowly, her hands clenched into balls, but she did not lower her arms. I turned to place the book on the shelf and Brenda said in a small voice, "It doesn't go there, Paul."

"Damn it, Brenda!"

"I'm afraid," she said. "Oh, God, I'm afraid. Someday I will open up the tableware drawer and find her baby spoon; or I'll look under the sofa and find a ball that had rolled there forgotten. Or I'll find one of her dresses bundled up in the wash. And I won't be able to take it. Do you understand? Do you know what it's like? Do you have any feelings at all? How can you look at that shelf and remember that *her* book had once lain there? Look at that kitchen table and remember her high chair and how we played airplane with her food? Look into a room full of toys, with no child anymore to play with them? Everywhere I look I see an aching void."

With a sudden rush of tenderness, I pulled her to me, but she remained stiff and unyielding in my arms. Yet, we all mourn in our own ways. "She did not die, Brenda. She'll be okay."

"This time. But, Paul, I can't look forward to a lifetime looking back. At the little girl who grew up and grew old and went away before I ever got to know her. Paul, it isn't right. It isn't right, Paul. It isn't right for a child to die before the parent."

"So, you'll close her out of your mind? Is that the answer? Create the void now? You'll push all those memories into one room and then close the door? You can't do that. If we forget her, it will be as if she had never lived."

She softened at last and her arms went around me. "What can I do? I've lost her, and I've lost you, and I've lost…everything."

We stood there locked together. I could feel her small, tightly controlled sobs trembling against me. Sometimes the reins have been held so close for so long that you can never drop them, never even know if they have been dropped. The damp of her tears seeped through my shirt. Past her, I could see the shelf with *The Boxcar Children* lying flat upon it and I tried to imagine how, in future years, I could ever look on that shelf again without grief.

> *"Tell me the tales that to me were so dear*
> *Long, long ago; long, long ago.*
> *Sing me the songs I delighted to hear*
> *Long, long ago, long ago."*

Dee-dee was wired. There was a tube up her nose and another in her arm. A bag of glucose hung on a pole rack by her bed, steadily dripping into an accumulator and thence through the tube. A catheter took her wastes away. A pad on her finger and a cuff around her arm were plugged into a CRT monitor. I smiled when I saw she was awake.

"Hi, daddy…" Her voice was weak and hoarse, a byproduct of the anaesthesia.

"Hi, Dee-dee. How do you feel?"

"Yucky…"

"Me, too. You're a TV star." I pointed to the monitor, where red and yellow and white lines hopped and skipped across the screen. Heart rate, blood pressure. Every time she breathed, the white line crested and dropped. She didn't say anything and I listened for a moment to the sucking sound that the nose tube made. A kid trying for the last bit of soda in the can. The liquid it carried off was brown, which meant that there was still a little blood. "Connie is here." I nodded to the other side of the bed.

Dee-dee turned her eyes, but not her head. "Hello, Connie. I can't see you."

Consuela moved a little into her field of vision. "Good morning, Little One. You have a splendid view from your window."

"Nurse Jeannie told me that…Wish I could see…"

"Then, I will tell you what it looks like. You can see the north end of town—all those lovely, old houses—and far off past them, on the edge of the world, the blue-ridge mountain wall and, in the very center of it, the Gap; and through the Gap, you can see the mountains beyond."

"It sounds beautiful…"

"Oh, it is. I wish I could be here instead of you, just so I could have the view."

I looked up at Connie when she said that and, for a moment, we locked gazes with one another. I could see the truth of her words in her eyes.

And then I saw surprise. Surprise and something else beside. I looked over my shoulder—and Brenda was standing there in the doorway, smartly dressed, on wobbly legs, with her purse clutched tightly in her hands before her.

"The nurses," she said. "The nurses said she could only have two visitors at a time." Visiting was allowed every three hours, but only for an hour and only two visitors at a time. I was a doctor and Connie was a nurse and the staff cut us a little slack, but the rules were there for a reason. Consuela stood.

"I will leave."

Brenda looked at her and caught her lower lip between her teeth. She laid her purse with military precision on a small table beside the bed. "I would like to spend some time with Deirdre, Paul. If you don't mind."

I nodded. As I stood up I gave Dee-dee a smile and a little squeeze on her arm. "Mommy's here," I told her.

Connie and I left them alone together (a curious expression, that—"alone together") and waited in the outer nursing area. I didn't eavesdrop, though I did overhear Brenda whisper at one point, "No, darling, it was never anything that *you* did wrong." Maybe it wasn't much, not when weighted against those years of inattention. It wasn't much; but it wasn't nothing. I knew—maybe for the first time—how much it cost Brenda to take on these memories, to take on the risks of remembering; because she was right. If in later years you remembered nothing, you would feel no pain.

And yet, I had seen two centuries of pain come washing back, bringing with it joy.

Children recover remarkably well. Drop them, and they bounce. Maybe not so high as before, but they do rebound. Dee-dee bore a solemn air about her for a day or two, sensing, without being told, that she had almost "gone away." But to a child, a day is a lifetime, and a week is forever; and she was soon in the recovery ward, playing with the other children. Rheumatic children with heart murmurs; shaven-headed children staring leukemia in the face; broken children with scars and cigarette burns... They played with an impossible cheerfulness, living, as most children did, in the moment. But then, the Now was all most of them would ever have.

There came a day when Dee-dee was not in her room when I arrived. Connie sat framed in a bright square of sunlight, reading a book. She looked up when I walked in. "Deirdre has gone to visit a new friend," she said.

"Oh." A strange clash of emotions: Happy she was up and about again, even if confined to a wheelchair; disappointed that she was not there to greet me.

"She will return soon, I think."

"Well," I said, "we had wanted her to become more active."

Consuela closed her book and laid it on the small table beside her. "I suppose you will no longer need my services," she said. She did not look at me when she said it, but out the window at the new-born summer.

"Not need you? Don't be foolish."

"She has her mother back, now."

Every morning before work; every evening after. Pressing lost years into a few hours. "She still needs you."

"The hospital staff cares for her now."

I shook my head. "It's not that she *needs* you, but that she needs *you.* You are not only her nurse."

"If I take on new clients," she went on as if I had not spoken, "I can do things properly. I can visit at the appointed times, perform my duties, and leave; and not allow them such a place in my heart when they are gone."

"If people don't leave a hole in your life when they are gone, Consuela, they were never in your life at all."

She turned away from the window and looked at me. "Or two holes."

I dropped my gaze, looked instead at the rumpled bed.

"In many ways," I heard her say, "you are a cold man, Doctor. Uncaring and thoughtless. But it was the fruit of bitterness and despair. I thought you deserved better than you had. And you love her as deeply as I. If death could be forestalled by clinging tight, Deirdre would never leave us."

I had no answer for her, but I allowed my eyes to seek out hers.

"I thought," she said, "sometimes, at night, when I played my flute, that because we shared that love...That we could share another."

"It must be lonely for you here, in a strange country, with a strange language and customs. No family and fewer friends. I must be a wretched man for never having asked."

She shook her head. "You had your own worry. A large one that consumed you."

"Consuela Montejo, if you leave, you would leave as great a hole in my life as in Dee-dee's."

"And in Mrs. Wilkes'." She smiled a little bit. "It is a very odd thing, but I believe that if I stayed I might even grow to like her."

"She was frightened. She thought she could cauterize the wound before she received it. It was only when she nearly lost Dee-dee that she suddenly realized that she had never had her."

Consuela stood and walked to the bed. She touched the sheet and smoothed it out, pulling the wrinkles flat. She shook her head. "It will hurt if I go; it will hurt if I stay. But Mrs. Wilkes deserves this one chance."

I reached out and took her hand and she reached out and took mine. Had Brenda walked in then, I do not know what she would have made of our embrace. I do not know what I made of it. I think I would have pulled Brenda in with us, the three of us arm in arm in arm.

The really strange thing was how inevitable it all was in hindsight.

When I left Consuela, I went to visit Mae. It had been nearly two weeks since I had last seen her and it occurred to me that the old bat might be lonely, too. And what the hell, she could put up with me and I could put up with her.

I found my Dee-dee in Mae Holloway's room. The two of them had their heads bent close together, giggling over something. Deirdre was strapped to her electric wheelchair and Mae lay flat upon her bed; but I was struck by how alike they looked. Two gnarled and bent figures with pale, spotted skin stretched tight over their bones, lit from within by a pure, childlike joy. Two old women; two young girls. Deirdre looked up and saw me.

"Daddy! Granny Mae has been teaching me the most wonderful songs."

Mae Holloway lifted her head a little. "Yours?" she said in a hoarse whisper. "This woman-child is yours?"

"Yes," I said, bending to kiss Dee-dee's cheek. "All mine." No. Not *all* mine. There were others who shared her.

"Listen to the song Granny Mae taught me! It goes like this."

I looked over Dee-dee's head at the old woman. "She didn't tell you?"

"Noor brought her in, but didn't say aye, yea or no. Just that she thought we should meet."

Dee-dee began singing in her high, piping voice.

> *"The days go slowly by, Lorena.*
> *The snow is on the grass again.*
> *The years go slowly by Lorena…"*

"Her days are going by too fast, ain't they?" Mae said. I nodded and saw how her eyes lingered on my little girl. "Growing old in the blink of an eye," she said softly. "Oh, I know how that feels."

"Granny Mae tells such interesting stories," Dee-dee insisted. "Did you know she saw Abraham Lincoln one time?" I rubbed her thinning hair. Too young to know how impossible that was. Too young to doubt.

Mae's hand sought out Dee-dee's and clenched hold of it. "Doc, I'll have me that operation."

"What?"

"I'll have me that operation. The one that's supposed to make this tumor of mine go away. I'll have it, even if my music and my memories go with it."

"You will. Why?"

"Because I know why you been poking me and taking my blood. And I know why the Good Lord has kept me here for all this long time."

Noor Khan was waiting in the hallway when I stepped out of the room.

"Ah, doctor," I said. "How are things at Sunny Dale."

"Quiet," she said. "Though the residents are all asking when you will be back."

I shrugged. "Old people dislike upsets to their routine. They grew used to having me around."

Khan said, "I never knew about your little girl. I heard it from Smythe. Why did you never tell me?"

I shrugged again. "I never thought it was anyone's business."

Khan accepted the statement. "After you told Wing and me of Mae's remarkable longevity…I knew you were taking blood samples to that genetic engineering firm—"

"Singer and Peeler."

"Yes. I thought you had…other reasons."

"What, that I would find the secret of the Tree of Life?" I shook my head. "I never thought to ask for so much. Mae has lived most her life as an old woman. I would not count that a blessing. But to live a normal life? To set right what had come out wrong? Yes, and I won't apologize. Neither would you, if it were your daughter."

"Is Singer close? To a solution?"

"I don't know. Neither do they. We won't know how close we are until we stumble right into it. But we've bought a little time now, thanks to you. Is that why you did it? Because you knew that meeting my daughter would convince Mae to accept the Culver-Blaese gene therapy?"

Khan shook her head. "No. I never even thought of that."

"Then, why?"

"Sometimes," said Khan, looking back into the room where the young girl and the old girl taught each other songs. "Sometimes, there are other medicines, for other kinds of hurts."

> *I seek no more the fine and gay,*
> *For each does but remind me*
> *How swift the hours did pass away*
> *With the girl I left behind me.*

They are all gone now. All gone. Mae, Dee-dee, all of them. Consuela was first. Brenda's partnership arrangement with FitzPatrick—telecommuting, they called it—left no place for her at the house. She came to visit Dee-dee, and she and Brenda often met for coffee—what they talked about I do not know—but she stopped coming after Dee-dee passed on and I have not seen her in years.

Brenda, too. She lives in LA, now. I visit her when I'm on the Coast and we go out together, and catch dinner or a show. But she can't look at me without thinking of *her*; and neither can I, and sometimes, that becomes too much.

There was no bitterness in the divorce. There was no bitterness left in either of us. But Dee-dee's illness had been a fault line splitting the earth. A chasm had run through our lives, and we jumped out of its way, but

Brenda to one side and I, to the other. When Dee-dee was gone, there was no bridge across it and we found that we shared nothing between us but a void.

The operation bought Mae six months. Six months of silence in her mind before the stroke took her. She complained a little, now and then, about her quickly evaporating memories; but sometimes I read to her from my notes, or played the tape recorder, and that made her feel a little better. When she heard about seeing Lincoln on the White House lawn, she just shook her head and said, "Isn't that a wonder?" The last time I saw Mae Holloway, she was fumbling after some elusive memory of her Mister that kept slipping like water through the fingers of her mind, when she suddenly brightened, looked at me, and smiled. "They're all a-waiting," she whispered, and then all the lights went out.

And Dee-dee.

Dee-dee.

Still, after all these years, I cannot talk about my little girl.

They call it the Deirdre-Holloway treatment. I insisted on that. It came too late for her, but maybe there are a few thousand fewer children who die now each year because of it. Sometimes I think it was worth it. Sometimes I wonder selfishly why it could not have come earlier. I wonder if there wasn't something I could have done differently that would have brought us home sooner.

Singer found the key; or Peeler did, or they found it together. Three years later, thank God. Had the breakthrough followed too soon on Deirdre's death, I could not have borne it. The income from the book funded it and it took every penny, but I feel no poorer for it.

It's a mutation, Peeler told me, located on the supposedly inactive Barr body. It codes for an enzyme that retards catabolism. There's a sudden acceleration of fetal development in the last months of pregnancy that almost always kills the mother, and often the child, as well. Sweet Annie's dear, dead child would have been programmed for the same future had she lived. After birth, aging slows quickly until it nearly stops at puberty. It only resumes after menopause. In males, the gene's expression is suppressed by testosterone. Generations of gene-spliced lab mice lived and died to establish that.

Is the line extinct now? Or does the gene linger out there, carried safely by males waiting unwittingly to kill their mates with daughters?

I don't know. I never found another like Mae, despite my years of practice in geriatrics.

When I retired from the Home, the residents gave me a party, though none of them were of that original group. Jimmy, Rosie, Leo, Old Man Morton…By then I had seen them all through their final passage. When the residents began approaching my own age, I knew it was time to take down my shingle.

I find myself thinking more and more about the past these days. About Mae and the Home; and Khan—I heard from my neighbor's boy that she is still in practice, in pediatrics now. Sometimes, I think of my own parents and the old river town where I grew up. The old cliffside stairs. Hiking down along the creek. Hasbrouk's grocery down on the corner.

The memories are dim and faded, brittle with time.

And I don't remember the music, at all. My memories are silent, like an old Chaplin film. I've had my house wired, and tapes play continually, but it isn't the same. The melodies do not come from within; they do not come from the heart.

They tell me I have a tumor in my left temporal lobe, and it's growing. It may be operable. It may not be. Wing wants to try Culver-Blaese, but I won't let him. I keep hoping.

I want to remember. I want to remember Mae. Yes, and Consuela and Brenda, too. And Dee-dee most of all. I want to remember them all. I want to hear them singing.

AFTERWORD TO "MELODIES OF THE HEART"

I had begun writing "Melodies of the Heart" in late 1990 and got stuck. I wasn't certain whether to write the story omnisciently, from multiple third person, or from the singular first person of Dr. Wilkes. Each had its attractions. I composed different openings.

In March of 1991, I was invited to attend Balticon 25 to accept the Compton Crook Award for *In the Country of the Blind.* The Guest of Honor was Nancy Kress, who gave an intriguing speech over the scarcity of children and families in SF. Since "Melodies…" involved precisely a child and her family, I shyly introduced myself and asked her opinion. Her comments helped considerably to make up my narrative mind, and marked the beginning of a long friendship.

I've discussed the innards of the story before, so I won't repeat that here. The story is set around the time of "Soul of the City," in *The Nanotech Chronicles.* Singer and Peeler have not yet founded SingerLabs; and Henry and Barbara Carter from "Remember'd Kisses" are young newlyweds. The young boy from "Captive Dreams" is mentioned briefly toward the end, when Dr. Wilkes has become an old man.

The immediate inspiration came from an essay by Oliver Sacks in *The Man Who Mistook His Wife for a Hat,* in which he described patients haunted by re-heard melodies and re-seen visions of their youth. These were not memories. In normal memory, we remember the past precisely *as past.* These are more like retrieving files from computer "memory," by which the file becomes physically present in the now.

The speculative science involves "mundane immortality," that is, remarkably long life. Life spans follow a statistical distribution (actually three overlapping distributions) whose hazard rate in reliability engineering is called "the bathtub curve." We know of people who have lived to 120 years old; and if you go out into the tail of the distribution, there is a minute-but-nonzero probability of people even longer-lived.

So. The re-heard memories of an exceptionally old woman. I shudder to think how very nearly the story became a mere puzzle, as Dr. Wilkes pieced the memories together. The third (and key) element was to ask: "Who does this—re-heard memories evidencing a very prolonged life—hurt most?"

Some final advice came from Stan Schmidt, the editor of *Analog Science Fiction and Fact*, who helped with the progeria angle and who stiffened my spine as regards the ending. On a technological note, while it was not the first story I ever wrote on a computer, it was the first story I ever wrote on my very own computer, a Mac Performa 400. Don't laugh. It was finished in October 1992 and appeared in the January 1994 issue of *Analog*.

The advice from Nancy and Stan helped immeasurably. "Melodies…" placed first for novellas in AnLab, *Analog*'s annual reader poll. It was a Hugo nominee for best novella at Intersection (Glasgow, 1995) and was shortlisted for the Theodore Sturgeon Memorial Award for best short science fiction of the year. Gardner Dozois reprinted it in his 12th annual *Year's Best Science Fiction* and David Hartwell selected it for my own collection *The Forest of Time and Other Stories*. Altogether, it has been one of my most successful stories.

But the best recognition it received was from readers who wrote me or have commented on message boards that they wept uncontrollably when they finished it.

Thank you.

CAPTIVE DREAMS

*S*oft and warm. Looking here, there. Duckies, Lambie-pie, pretty red Ball. *I love Lambie-pie. Reaching for it. White fluffy-looking Lambie-pie soft smooth and round and Ball slipslides between the always-bars. Ethan-voice calling, "Lambie-pie." Falling bouncing, slowly, slowly, slowly. Catch Ball, he runs away. Ow! Bang the fingers on the always-bars.*

Closing the eyes and waiting for the dark. See Ball resting against lamp. Hear bouncy sounds: Boing-boing-boing. Blackness! Catch the hard rod always-bars. Up, up, and swing around; and down. On the floor; hard against the feet! Quiet, quiet. Hear crib springs squeaking; duckies rattle. Open eyes and wait for light.

Brightlighthurtheyes. Clumpthud. Hello, lamp. Hello, Ball. Reach for it. Reach for it. Too fast! Too fast! Leg caught; snakey tangle. Spinning tumble up down. Ow! Lamp totters. Catch it, catch it, catch it. Frozen falling lamp standing still. Noise. Clump. Clumpclump. Brightyellowflash.

Shat[CRASH]ter.

She turned at the sound of the crash and, shoving her fist to her mouth, ran for his bedroom. Heart thudding. Fearing what she might find. "Ethan!" He was out of his crib, smiling blankly, windmilling his arms as he staggered around the room. His left ankle was tangled in the cord for the floor lamp, which had toppled, smashing the shade and shattering the bulb. Tiny, sparkling shards of glass glistened in the carpet.

"Ethan!" She swept him up in her arms, untwisting the cord with a practiced movement. Anger fighting relief, she held him tight. "Oh, Ethan. Naughty boy. You could have been hurt."

"Baaall," said Ethan in his typically slurred voice. He held onto her neck and planted a wet smack of a kiss on her cheek. "Lamm. Me. Pie." She squeezed her arms and eyelids tight. Her cheek was cool where wetness lingered. He didn't even know her. He was off into his own personal universe where she couldn't follow.

"Is there anything I can do, Alma?" The gruff baritone voice behind her reminded her that she had left the front door open when she had run for the bedroom. She turned and faced him, cradling Ethan against her hip. Soon the boy would be too big to pick up; too big to handle. What then? What then? She would find a way. Something. She would cope.

"I'm sorry, Mick. You see how it is. I can't leave him alone for a second."

Mick reached out and tousled the lad's hair. "Hi, there, boy. Do you remember Uncle Mick?" Alma stiffened at the familiarity of the gesture.

"He has his good spells," she told him. "Some days he can follow simple directions. He can even speak a complete sentence. But most of the time…" She hesitated and caught her lip to keep it from trembling. "Most of the time he doesn't make sense at all."

"Mamma," said Ethan, smiling into Mick's face.

Mick gave the boy a shadowed look and an uncertain smile played across his mouth. *He doesn't understand, either*, she thought. None of them did. None of that procession of men that had passed through her life since Nate had run out on her. They all stumbled over Ethan, sooner or later. They all yearned for her undivided attention, and they couldn't have it. Not while Ethan needed her. Someday soon Mick would utter those hateful, selfish words. *Why don't you put him in a home?*

Mick could see the entire evening laid out before him as he rubbed the hand vacuum back and forth across the rug. The tiny shards of glass tinkled as they were sucked into its maw. From the kitchen he could hear Alma's voice canceling the baby sitter. Silly. She'd have to pay anyway. The agency supplied RNs to baby-sit special children. You couldn't book them and then cancel at the last minute. He shook his head and rubbed his hand through the carpet nap searching for uncollected fragments. He'd tried telling her that just one time; and, Jesus, you'd've thought he'd suggested dumping the kid on a country road.

He glanced up at the crib, where Ethan lay strapped on his back, staring at the mobile dancing inches before his face. Little wooden ducks with wings that beat mechanically as they circled. Up, down, around and around. Forever flying south for winter. The kid was too big to be in a crib anyway. And—a quick, almost furtive glance at the larger bed—too big to sleep in his mommy's bedroom.

Oh, yes. Alma and he would spend a Quiet Evening at Home. She would cook for him; and they would watch something halfway decent on the tube. The movie they'd planned on would be out on video eventually. And as for the restaurant…Well, Alma was a decent cook. Later, they would philander on the sofa; but always, always with one ear on the bedroom. And then she would take him by the hand and lead him in here softly tip-toeing. And half the time they would find Ethan still wide-eyed awake staring at them; and half the time Alma would stop half-aching-way and ask what if he did wake up; and half the time he couldn't do it himself because what kind of a pervert did it in front of a kid? And that made three-halves, which pretty much summed it up.

When he turned off the hand vacuum he could hear Alma's muffled sobs from the kitchen. He squatted on his heels, listening. Yeah. She wanted the freedom as much as he did; but the kid was an anchor around her neck dragging her down, down, down. She was killing herself and the kid didn't even know it. So far, once—exactly once—they had made it out of the house. And it was the grace of God that the restaurant and the movie theater had had public phones so she could check with the nurse-sitter every half hour.

"Kid," he muttered, "sometimes you're a real pain in the butt."

"Ethan bad. Ba'boy."

Mick jerked his head up. The kid had abandoned his mobile and was staring at him between the bars of his prison. He began to jerk his body, so that the crib shook rhythmically back and forth. "Mick!" Ethan beamed. "Uncamick!"

Ah, hell, you had to love the kid, didn't you?

She raced back to the bedroom with the tissue crumpled in her hand. "What is it?" she asked. "What was that noise?" Mick was squatting by the crib with his face half-stuffed between the bars. "What's wrong?"

He turned a silly smile on her. "Relax, Alma. Ethan and I were just making faces at each other, that's all."

"Did you get all the glass vacuumed up?" She dropped to her hands and knees and rubbed the carpet. "No. Here's a piece you missed. Christ, Mick, can't you finish a job? Those tiny reflections. He *notices* things like that. Things you and I would pass right over. What if he picked it up and swallowed it? Here, give me that vacuum." She snatched it from his hands. Mick stood up and stepped back. The motor hummed and she rubbed it back and forth through the nap of the rug.

His shoes moved at the edge of her vision, shifting his weight from side to side. "Make yourself useful," she said. "Start the meal. You can boil a pot of water, can't you? Start the spaghetti. Do *something*."

"Alma—"

"Leave me alone!"

She saw the feet shuffle and move away. A few moments later, she heard the front door close. She rocked back on her heels and turned off the vacuum, and hugged herself tight. *I won't cry. I won't* cry. *I won't cry. He would have dropped me anyway.* You could see it coming. Men liked divorcées: They were experienced, saddle-broken. But men didn't like them with children in tow; and they doubly didn't like them with retarded children in tow.

"Uncamick," said Ethan.

"Shut up!"

The boy's face crumpled and his mouth twisted into a knot. Alma sprang up, unstrapped him, and hugged him to her. "Oh, Mommy's sorry." She rocked him back and forth in her aching arms. "I didn't mean to yell at you."

Knifesharpsmell tickles nose. See white dress nurse close door. Soft-comfy-springy touch on heiney. Hum-hum. Hear door close. Sit on sofa next to Momma. Flash. Gentle breezes tickle arms and face. GreatBIGface! Babblebabble-bleEthanbabble. Deep voice not-Mick. Flicker! Bright spinning colors. Ghost hands reach for it; reach for it Hum-hum-hum. Nothing. Hands held tight and soft. Spinning colors move and turn and reach and. Got it!

It was a neat office; tidy, but not sterile. The walls were hung with comforting diplomas; and, amidst the clutter on the desk, sat a nameplate carved in oak: *Doctor Dave.* The man himself—thin and sporting a great big bird beak of a nose, beaming face encircled by a sunburst of hair—sat at ease behind the desk and smiled.

It was all supposed to relax her, she knew. A doctor's office, yes; but homey. Chocked with familiar features. Crayon drawings in childish hands thumb-tacked to the wall beside the stern diplomas. A somber row of medical texts...but festooned with colorful page markers. A stand-up, Lucite photograph on the desk featuring the doctor embedded in familial bliss. She shifted slightly to a more comfortable position on the sofa and straightened her skirt. She didn't know what she was doing here. Doctor Khan had referred her, but...She couldn't afford a specialist; certainly not a...She squinted at the diploma again. Certainly not a pediatric neurologist.

She glanced at Ethan, who was staring off at some infinite wonder, and put her arm around his shoulder. "Don't worry, Ethan," she whispered to him. "There's nothing to be frightened of." She did not expect a response; was not disappointed when she received none. What sort of vision was he staring at? What sort of dreams did he have?

The doctor folded his hands into a ball on his desk. "I'm glad you could come and see me today, Mrs. Seakirt. From what your pediatrician told me when she referred your case, I believe we may be able to do something to help little Ethan."

She had heard those words before. They had never meant anything except high hopes and disappointment. She shook her head. She would not allow herself to be disappointed again, even if it meant foregoing hope. "I won't see him institutionalized, Doctor Silverman. He's *my* obligation. I won't turn my back on him the way my husband did." *Ex-husband.*

Ethan pulled away from her. "Frightened?" he said.

"You're scaring the boy," she told the doctor, pulling Ethan to her. She stroked his hair gently and he snuggled against her. After a moment, he began to make small, contented noises. Alma looked back at the doctor. "He's happy with me."

"No one says otherwise, Mrs. Seakirt. We do not plan to institutionalize him."

"Then what? He's been in and out of every therapy there is. Play therapy; clown therapy." Even, God help her, aversion conditioning therapy. "None of it has helped and the insurance has long run out. Ethan is severely retarded. That's something I have learned to live with, that's all."

"I love you, mamma," said Ethan suddenly; and Alma tightened her hug on him.

"And I love you, too."

Silverman seemed about to say something, then changed his mind. Instead, he reached into a drawer and came from behind his desk with a brightly colored mechanical pinwheel. He squatted in front of Ethan. "Hi, Ethan," he said. "My name's Doctor Dave. I'd like to be your friend." He held the pinwheel in front of Ethan's face and caused it to spin by pumping the trigger with his thumb. The petals whirled and the colors seemed to dance.

Ethan did not react. He simply grinned into space.

"I told you, doctor. Ethan is retarded."

Silverman nodded. "Yes. I think that is exactly right." He paused. "Mrs. Seakirt," he said, "do you know much about computers?" He continued to pump the pinwheel while he studied Ethan's face.

Computers? Why on earth did he want to talk about computers? Well, let him explain things in his own way. The consultation was not costing her anything. She had been quite firm about that when Doctor Khan had suggested it. "I have a workstation at home. My office lets me telecommute because of Ethan. They are really very understanding. They know that…" She was babbling. She had met Mick because of her telecommuting. His company had the maintenance contract on the PCs, and one day he had come by personally to see how…Alma took a breath and smoothed her skirt once more. "I can operate a desktop and modem," she said, "but I don't know any of the theory."

Silverman's grin split his beard. "Neither do I. I leave that to Tom. But I do know that there is something called an I/O buffer." He transferred the pinwheel to his left hand and, holding it off to the side, he caused it to spin again. Ethan did not turn his head to follow the movement.

"Input/Output buffer," she started to say; except that Ethan began to bounce up and down on the sofa, waving his hands in the vacant air in front of his face. Alma caught her lip between her teeth. She knew the pattern. Soon he would start flailing about and crying. She reached an arm out to stop his agitation, but Silverman stopped her. "Excuse me," she said in a voice that tolerated no excuses.

"Pretty," said Ethan. "Pretty-pretty-pretty-pretty-pretty-pretty-pretty-pretty."

"Just bear with me a moment, Mrs. Seakirt. Tell me, does your I/O buffer ever become backed up?"

She spared an anxious glance at Ethan. "Yes, sometimes." She struggled against Ethan's jouncing. He was becoming unruly. He would embarrass her in front of the doctor.

Suddenly, Ethan twisted to the right and his flailing hands grasped hold of the pinwheel that Silverman had been patiently spinning all the while. Silverman closed his own hand over Ethan's so he would not drop the toy. A few seconds later, Ethan grinned.

Alma fell silent and stared at him; while Silverman waited, watching her. The silence lengthened a beat or two, until Ethan slurred, "Pretty-pretty," again. Alma's heart was suspended over a deep chasm. Silverman had held the pinwheel *here*, then *there*. And Ethan had reached for it *here*, then *there*. But late, seconds late. "Doctor…?"

Silverman pursed his lips and nodded. "I told you. He is simply retarded."

"Retarded," Silverman repeated a few minutes later, after she had composed herself. He had asked the receptionist to bring them both cups of tea, and he sat now returned to his throne behind the desk, dunking his bag up and down, up and down.

The hot, bitter liquid had helped calm her, but her heart still hung dizzyingly over the abyss. She watched Ethan playing with the pinwheel beside her on the sofa. The boy had discovered that the trigger made the blades spin. He would push the trigger (and the blades would spin, and slow, and stop.) And a moment later, his eyes would light up. And then he would laugh at the unmoving pinwheel. That behavior had never made sense before. Now…

She sat the trembling tea cup on the lamp table. "Ethan's I/O buffer is backed up," she recalled his earlier words.

"That's right," said Silverman, squeezing his teabag against a spoon. "Ethan's mind may be as sharp as yours or mine, but the sensations—the sights and sounds and such—arrive moments late, perhaps even out of synch; and the responses are delayed, as well. High viscosity sensation, I call it. Tell me, Mrs. Seakirt, does he cry often?"

A lifetime of reaching for things that were no longer there. Oh, God, the disappointment! "Yes," she said. And then, more firmly, "Yes, he does." She looked back to Ethan, sitting beside her, playing with the fascinating toy. When he dropped it, as he eventually would, he would not realize it for several seconds, because according to Doctor Silverman, he would still be seeing an "afterimage" in his hand. That was why he had trouble picking things up: he reached for an *image* of a fallen toy and, unless he had held—or had been held—completely still in the meantime, his groping fingers would close on nothing—or on the wrong thing.

It was strange, thinking that way. In a way, her son was blind. Blind to *now*; seeing only *then*.

"And his speech," continued the doctor. He took a sip of his tea. Alma had already downed hers in ragged gulps. She clenched and unclenched her fists in her lap. She wanted him to *get on with it. Explain my child to me!* "Since he doesn't hear his own voice when he speaks, he lacks the feedback we all use to control our timbre and intonation. He keeps hearing echoes of what he has already said. That—"

"I called a radio talk show one time," Alma said, "but I forgot to turn my radio down. You know how they use tape delay? I started hearing my voice saying what I had said three seconds before. It was impossible to think straight."

Silverman nodded. "Exactly. Ethan talks in short bursts most of the time so he can finish before the echoes start. I imagine that his longer vocalizations are very rhythmic, and full of repetitions."

Prettypretty. Once he had sat for nearly a quarter of an hour saying *mamma mamma mamma* over and over, until his tongue had finally tired and lost the rhythm. "Why, yes, they..."

"You know why, don't you? He is synchronizing his voice to the echoes. Ethan lives in a world of afterimages and echoes. It's amazing to me that he functions as well as he does."

"Doctor," she said suddenly. "Sometimes he hunches up with his eyes closed tight and his hands over his ears..."

"Waiting for the buffer to clear."

It annoyed her the way he sometimes finished her sentences. "What about his other senses?" she asked. "Smelling and touch and taste."

"His tactile and proprioception senses are probably unaffected. And likely his smelling, too. Odors go straight to the old reptile brain. If he dropped the pinwheel, he might notice something odd because while he could still see it, he could no longer feel it. He may have learned to use such moments as cues to enable him to cope somewhat. We'll run the usual tests to be sure; but that is how it has been with the other children."

"There are others like Ethan?" That surprised her: That there should be others like Ethan.

"Some. Not many. Autism and dyslexia are much more common I/O disorders. But I have described several cases in the *New England Journal*."

Ethan dropped the pinwheel. It fell to the floor while he continued to gaze happily at his empty hands. Alma quickly scooped the toy up and placed it back into Ethan's hands, as she had done with countless toys countless times before. Always in vain, because Ethan would drop them again. She had always thought that it had been from loss of interest. But she knew how to handle it now. *She knew how to handle it!* Ethan cried, "Oh!" and made his belated grab toward the afterimage of the fallen toy; but Alma held his hands tight around the pinwheel's handle and waited for his vision to catch up with his reality. When she released him at last, he again had a firm grip on the toy.

Three seconds later, he said, "Thankyoumamma."

She turned back to Silverman. "It's so simple. All those years, and I never noticed."

"Not so simple, really," Silverman assured her. "It just seems so with hindsight. It's not something we're conditioned to notice. We're so used to living in the Now that it's hard to imagine that others might be... living on tape delay. Only after a period of relatively constant inputs—say after napping or engaging in an absorbing, repetitive task—does the buffer clear. My colleague believes it is the variability of the inputs that somehow overloads the brain's buffer. Provide a low-sigma data stream and—" He stopped abruptly and laughed. "I'm sorry. I'm starting to talk like he does."

"Doctor Silverman, who is this colleague you keep referring to?"

"Oh. I didn't say? Doctor Zachariah. Tom Zachariah."

"He's not a pediatric neurologist, is he?"

A slow shake of the head. "No, he's a Ph.D., not an M.D."

Not a real *doctor, in other words.* "And his degree is in…?"

"Computer science."

"I see." She had known he would say that. All that talk of computers and buffers and they were sitting in a doctor's office, after all. "And what is it you propose to do to my Ethan?"

Silverman stared at her for a moment and rubbed the side of his ample nose. "Bypass the buffer," he said.

Food smells. Sweet and delicious. BabblebabbleEthanbabblebabbleMick. Hug Momma! Hug hard cold smooth Momma. Kiss her warm. Cold metallic taste. Flicker. *And…Momma gone. Silvermetal table leg reflecting long thin mirror-shaped Ethan. Warm tears flow. "Momma!" Babblebabble. Fly! [Vertigo.] Grab soft warm table leg. Sweet Momma smell. Smoothsoftouch. Hairs tickle. See Momma reaching down!*

"Yes, mother," Alma spoke patiently into the phone. "Yes, mother." It was hard balancing Ethan on her hip and the phone on her shoulder. "Nothing. He tried to kiss the dinette table leg, that's all. No, I've told you that before. This *is* his home." Ethan squealed in fright—of what? What had happened a few seconds ago?—and grabbed her choking tight around the neck. His breath was sweet and hot in her ear. He whimpered and Alma hitched him around so she could support him more easily. "I thought I would let Dr. Silverman test him. No, it won't cost me anything." *Not that that would affect you anyway, you tight-fisted bitch.* "Dr. Silverman said that part of the costs are being covered by a donation and the rest by a federal research grant. Research grant, mother. Yes, I know that means it's an experimental treatment. No, Ethan is not a lab rat. Mother, Ethan is my son and I will decide what's best for him. Certainly, mother, I always treasure your advice." *Whether I take it or not.* "Good-bye, mother. Yes, yes, I know you only want what's best for me."

She fumbled with the phone and it slipped from between her chin and shoulder and swung at the end of its cord, banging against the wall like a suicidal bungee diver. She set Ethan down—[and he danced in circles arms outstretched crying, "Mommymommymommy" and laughing]—and she hauled in the receiver like a fisherman hauling in a net. She checked quickly to see if Beatrice were still on the line. Beatrice would assume that the banging sound had been her daughter slamming the phone on the hook and they would go around and around about it.

But she heard the happy dial tone and, with a sigh of relief, cradled the wall phone. Mother's problem was a compulsion for micromanagement. Strategic advice was not enough for her; she was a master tactician, as well. She could not simply tell Alma what to do—half her friends were plagued with parents who still did that—but she had to tell her how to do it and when to do it, and she offered critiques afterward. It had never been simply: *Do the dishes, Alma, dear*, but *Why did you do the plates* before *the glasses?* Never just: *Get dressed for school, Alma, dear*, but *Why don't you wear the new plaid skirt with the pullover sweater?* And always, always, the orders were framed as questions. She had spent a lifetime trying to guess what Beatrice had wanted of her; and a lifetime guessing wrong.

It's not right to experiment with children. Oh, isn't it, mother? What was that medicine you made me take? Better than the Pill; better than a diaphragm. An implant inserted under the skin at the clinic, so you never had to worry about being careless, or forgetting, or the damn thing *leaking*, for cripes sake. So all you had to worry about was—

Chromosome damage.

And Ethan.

Thank you so very much, mother; but I will take it from here.

She took the phone off the hook again and scanned the bulletin board where she had pinned the doctor's card. She hurt her finger when she stabbed the buttons.

Tom Zachariah, to Alma's surprise, was an Indian. Not a wild west, whoop-em-up, paint and feathers Indian; but the short, tan kind from South Asia. He had an office of unbelievable clutter. Books, magazines, reams of machine paper—one accordion pile snaking onto the floor like a stationery slinky, a pulpish creature creeping off the desktop. Odd corners of desk, table and shelf were occupied by the eviscerated remains of computer equipment: slain, half-eaten and left for electronic jackals; circuit boards and the short ends of wires exposed like rib cages in their gaping carcasses.

Zachariah folded his hands as if praying. He smiled at her. Everyone smiled at her; pity or sympathy or even friendliness, she didn't know. His face was a muted coffee, thin and with a narrow nose, the cheeks pocked with the craters of ancient acne, as if he had been the victim of a very tiny shotgun blast.

"So, Mrs. Seakirt," he said, with his odd, melodious accent rising and falling in unexpected turns. "You are Ethan's mother."

She had the sudden disorienting notion that he was appointing her to that post. It hadn't sounded like a question. "Why, yes. Yes, I am. They are testing him now." She wondered if he could fail the tests. *What if he's not suitable for their "procedure"?* She picked at imaginary lint on the arm of the leather-clad captain's chair. *He's never been apart from me this long.* What if he panics? I should have remained with him. I should have insisted.

Zachariah nodded. "Dan will take several hours at it, but the preliminary results last week looked very promising. Tactation and proprioception are in real time, as we had thought. Otherwise, Ethan could hardly stand upright. Olfaction is only slightly delayed. Meanwhile, I—Yes?"

"Excuse me, Professor Zachariah, but I hope I'm not being personal…"

"Yes?" He waited smiling.

"You are Indian, aren't you?"

His smile broadened. "Oh, yes indeed. From Kerala State on the Malabar Coast."

"But, your name. Thomas Zachariah?"

"Ah, Mrs. Seakirt, India is no more homogeneous a sub-continent than Europe. There are twelve million Christians in India, a community that dates back to St. Thomas the Apostle. His missionary travels were not so well documented as St. Paul's, I fear."

"I see. I didn't mean to pry. I…"

He waved a hand. "No, no, no. It is perfectly all right. It is the fallacy of lumping. When I was a child in Kerala State, I thought all Americans were either cowboys or gangsters." He laughed at his childhood foolishness.

She laughed with him. "All right, Professor Zachariah—"

"Call me Tom." He leaned back in his desk chair and the springs and leather creaked. "Computer nerds are not formal."

She was suddenly fascinated by the coordination of her own senses. What must it be like, Alma wondered, if the creak of the chair and the sight of Zachariah leaning back entered the brain at different times? How could you ever learn to associate a sight with a sound with a touch with a smell with a taste? "All right, er, Tom. Dr. Silverman said that you would explain the computer side of the procedure to me."

"Yes. You understand it is still experimental. We have had excellent responses with chimpanzees, and a few preliminary studies with other children that look good. But, we cannot promise results."

"It won't hurt him, will it?"

"No." He seemed startled. "No, of course not. That much we can promise."

"Good. I won't let him be hurt."

He blinked. "None of us want to hurt him, Mrs. Seakirt. We will simply drill a hole through the skull—"

Drill a hole in my child's head.

"—to a certain area of the hypothalamus that Dan has identified. I am sure that he has already explained that all sensory inputs, indeed all neural impulses—"

"Are identical. Yes, he did. And the brain decides whether you are holding sandpaper or smelling roses based on the locations of the sensors and the destination area of the brain."

Zachariah seemed pleased. "Exactly. In some cases, the signals go to the wrong areas of the brain, so that the individual smells 'purple' or hears 'sour.' Very complex problem. Very complex. That, of course, is not your son's condition. Here we have a much simpler case—or we believe we have a much simpler case—in which the associative neurons of the hypothalamus are retarded. Am I, er, 'snowing' you, Mrs. Seakirt?"

"No. Dr. Silverman already explained about affectors and effectors—the input and output neurons—and the associative neurons that connect them." *I wonder what they are doing to Ethan right now? While I sit and chat nonsense with this smiling man with the funny name.*

She rubbed her hands forward and backward along the chair arms. Ethan would be frantic by now at his separation from her. Zachariah's words dipped into and out of her consciousness like a stone skipping on the water. "—an electronic device of my own devising—" *What if this procedure of theirs fails?* "—plug-in skull module—" *It is experimental, after all.* "—portable computer with neural net logics—" *I work with computers; I know how they can bomb off.*

"So in essence, Mrs. Seakirt, the sensory inputs will be routed through the computer directly into the receptor areas of the brain. You may think of it simply as a new sort of bypass surgery. Do you have any questions?"

What if it doesn't work?

✦

Fresh, bright laundry smell. Sharp odors. Smell of medicine.	*Gummy sour taste in mouth. Sticky sweet.*	*Soft, cool sheets covering gently. Head hurts [ow!].*	*White sheets cover body. Bed rails up like crib.*	*Soft rustle sounds.*
		Room spin slowly, slowly.	*White dress nurse walks by with tray. Smiles.*	*"Ow!" Rattle of glasses on tray. "Why hello, Ethan, awake already?"*
Sweet momma-smell.				
		Turn head. Still hurts!	*Mommy! sitting by bed. Tiredsadlook.*	*"Good morning, baby."*

She tried not to look at the cable snaking from her son's head; but it was impossible not to look. It was a flat cable, the ribbon kind, and it was coupled to a 50-pin intelligent port implanted in Ethan's skull. Tom Zachariah's "little device." The other end of the cable was a minicomputer. State of the Art, Zachariah had assured her. The cutting edge. And, for the life of her, she could not decide if her son was hooked up to a computer or if a computer was hooked up to her son.

He opened his eyes suddenly and jerked his head back and forth. A nurse walked by with a clattering tray and Ethan followed her movement. "Why hello, Ethan," the nurse said, "awake already?" She did not wait for an answer but continued on her mission. Ethan turned again and looked Alma in the eyes. Bright, aware, "real-time" eyes. "Mama," he croaked with a throat sore from the anaesthesia tube.

"Good morning, baby," she said. Mornings and after long naps were always the best times. They were the times when she felt Ethan was really there; when there was a human being behind the eyes and not a—God help her!—not an animated biological machine. But it never lasted. It never lasted. If Doctor Silverman were right, Ethan's sensory input channels quickly backed up.

Except that today was supposed to be different.

She studied the cable once more. Different. Whatever was wrong with Ethan's brain, Silverman did not know and could not repair. The brain was still an unplumbed mystery. The best he could manage was this…computer bypass. This experimental computer bypass. Something that would synchronize what Ethan's brain could not. If Doctor Silverman were right, Ethan could make sense of his inputs now. He could learn things. He could go to school. He could be like any normal boy.

She ran a finger along the computer cable to the computer with the convenient wheels and handle. A normal boy.

Only different.

✦

Beatrice sat all hunched into herself on the sofa. The coffee cup clenched in the right hand hovered above a saucer held firmly in the left. [China, of course, one never served Mother on plastic!] "Why does he stare at me that way?" she asked.

Ethan stood before her, solemnly silent. His mouth half open; his left hand gripping the handle of his "wheely." The umbilical snaked from his skull socket to the processor. His thoughts traveling up and down the wire so the machine, like a patient secretary, could sort them out. No, not his thoughts. Simply neural impulses, translated to electricity and back again by Tom Zachariah's electro-neural transformer. They were not *thoughts* until the proper region of Ethan's brain made them so.

Alma saw how her mother's eyes kept tracking on that cable, following it back and forth from machine to skull and back, and not once lingering on Ethan's face. "He is trying to make sense out of you, Mother." And she enjoyed the double take that triggered. *Good luck, Ethan. I've been trying for twenty-five years without success.*

Beatrice sniffed. "I thought that connecting him to that…thing was supposed to cure him."

"It's not so simple, mother. Tom explained that we have years of garbled cognition to unlearn. That's why the classes are part of the treatment. Ethan learned certain compromises of behavior and coordination that enabled him to get on despite the viscosity of his senses—"That was a good phrase. Viscosity of the senses. Trying to push a message through thick mud. Much like holding a conversation with Mother.

"So, it's Tom, now? What ever happened to Doctor Zachariah?"

"Mother, we're friends. He and Doctor Dave and—"

"At least your Silverman is just a Jew and not a jump-up, dark-skinned Hindu who—"

"Mother, he's a Christian." *Which you are not!* "He cares about Ethan."

"Oh, and I suppose I don't. I am only the boy's grandmother, after all. I only want what's best for the both of you."

Ethan jumped up and down. The cable snaked in sinusoid curves. "Gammah!" he announced, pointing at Beatrice. "Gammah!" His voice was still slurred a little, but at least he was hearing how his own voice sounded and the feedback was helping him correct it.

Beatrice looked at the boy. "I still say it isn't natural."

Mama was always warm and soft. Always the same. Never hard or cold or fuzzy or anything else. And Lambie-pie was always soft and fuzzy and always there when he reached for him and the music made the duckies fly and the flying duckies made the music whenever mama twisted the thing on its side and the bedroom was always over there and the living room over here and the voices only happened when people moved their mouths except for the box voices on the teebee though even there the box people moved their mouths and he could put his pretty ball down and go away and come back and it would still be there and he could reach out and pick it up and it was all so wonderful!

Mick pushed the doorbell once more and stepped back so he would be clearly visible through the peephole. Modern life had evolved its own code of etiquette. He glanced up and down the narrow road, lined with trees and bushes and plots of flowers. *The 'burbs.* Not the Mean Streets, but the Bland Streets. They twisted around each other in such a way that this group of houses formed a circle around a patch of woodland in the rear of the properties. The woods were inaccessible from the street and, hence, undevelopable. They formed a refuge for 'coons, muskrats, squirrels and other suburbanites. It was all supposed to make you forget that you were in the most densely populated state of the Union.

He wondered what Alma's neighbors thought of Ethan's prosthetic. Did they approve? Did they care? He would probably never know. Alma would probably never know. A man jogged along the blacktop past Alma's house. Mick watched him. The man looked neither left nor right. He wore a headset and his eyes were narrowed in concentration. *Sunk into his own private world*, thought Mick. *Does he even know he has neighbors?* How could people live so close together and yet be virtual strangers to one another?

The door opened just as he was about to ring again and Alma stood framed in the doorway. "Mick," she said, her voice laced with surprise. Not pleasure. Nor unwelcome. Just a neutral surprise.

"Hello, Alma." He kept his hands hidden behind his body. "Surprised to see me?"

"I—Yes. Yes, I am. After you ran out, I never expected to see you again."

Mick kept the smile on his face. *I didn't run out. You drove me out. You were stressed and I couldn't deal with it.* "Are you going to invite me in?"

Alma hesitated a fraction of a second, then stepped aside. Mick crossed the threshold and brought his right hand out. He held a copper bowl with a spray of daffodils and greens. Alma's face unfolded with delight and Mick sighed in quiet relief.

"Oh, Mick, they're lovely. And they're live, not cut. Thank you." She turned away from him and set them on the sideboard in the entry hall. The yellow of the flowers contrasted nicely with the dark wood; the mirror on the wall behind multiplied the flowers into a garden. Mick could see Alma's reflection smile down at the flower bowl. "And what's in your left hand, Mick?"

"Oh, this?" He held out a brightly wrapped rectangle. "It's for Ethan."

"Ethan." Alma's lips parted and her head bobbed once, slowly. "Of course, Ethan. What is it?"

"Let me give it to him." Mick stepped into the living room with Alma half a pace behind. "Ethan? Where are you?"

He heard a squeak-squeak-squeak, and the boy stepped from behind the breakfast bar that fronted the kitchen. His face brightened. "Unnca Mmick!" And he hastened toward him, with his computer appendage in tow. "Unca Miiick!"

Mick turned to Alma. "He recognizes me," he said with pleasure.

"Yes, he's become...What is that in his hand? A sandwich? Oh, my God." Alma ran to cut Ethan off.

Mick stood open-mouthed. A sandwich? And she freaks out?

"Oh, Ethan! Ethan. You know you shouldn't do that. You could have cut yourself."

Ethan held his other hand up. "Knife," he said. Alma grabbed it from him in a convulsive gesture.

"For God's sake, Alma. It's only a butter knife."

"He can hurt himself with it! He can."

Ethan's eyes went big and round. "Hurt?"

Mick hunkered down on his knees. "Hey. Hey, guy. Look what I brought you. Look here." He held up the brightly wrapped present and waved it.

Ethan forgot his fears instantly and turned to Mick. "Pretty," he said. Mick handed the gift to him and watched as he laughed and tore off the wrappings.

It was a Dr. Seuss book. The boy goggled at it; then looked at Mick. His mouth was a silent O. Then he turned and held it up to his mother.

She took the book from him and opened it. "Oh, Mick, he can't read."

"Not yet; but he will soon."

"It will take time. Doctor Silverman said it would take time. He still needs me."

"Of course, he does; but as time goes on, he'll be able to do all sorts of things on his own. Won't you, Ethan?"

"Only up to a point, Mick. After all, an artificial leg doesn't let you do everything that a two-legged person can."

"I suppose not." Ethan would always be slow, Dave had confided in him. Years of retarded sensation had inhibited his learning. He could learn now, but he would probably never function at age level.

Mick refused to feel sorry for the boy. Maybe Ethan would always be a few rungs down, but at least he was on the ladder. "Think positive, Alma. You won't have to worry so much."

"What do you mean?"

"When you go out. About his getting into trouble. You know."

"He can still get into trouble. Even normal boys get into trouble."

"Sure, but—"

"You don't care about him at all, do you?" She waved the Dr. Seuss book in his face. "You thought that just because he has his prosthetic I can abandon him, like other single mothers. Go out, have a good time, and never mind the kid."

"Now, wait a minute, Alma. That's not fair. You have a life, too."

"You're just thinking of yourself. All you've ever wanted to do was get inside my pants. Get between me and my responsibilities. Don't you know how much Ethan needs me? Who do you think you are? You come in here trying to run my child's life—" Mick ducked as she threw the book at him. Ethan jumped and tried to grab it as it arced over his head. "Go on. Get out of here!"

Outside, Mick shoved his hands in his pants pockets and kicked a stone down the driveway. What in the world had brought on that tirade? Did she resent him that much for walking out on her before? Running her child's life…Did she know? He looked back over his shoulder at the silent door. The federal grant would not have covered the surgery, let alone the remedial therapy. There just wasn't enough money in the public coffers. But Dave had promised that he wouldn't tell Alma where the rest of the money had come from. He had promised. And that ungrateful Alma—

He walked down the driveway toward his car. Silverman hadn't revealed anything. He cast a last look back at the door. Alma would have thrown it in his face if she had known. And so his savings were gone with last winter's snows and he didn't even have a thank you to show for it.

He remembered Ethan jumping for the book as it sailed past him. Living in real time, like any normal boy. He remembered Ethan's delight when he had torn the wrappings away.

He unlocked the car door. And caught himself whistling. *Funny. Alma was right. I did have selfish motives. I thought that if Dave and Tom could fix Ethan up, she could make room in her life for another person. For me. Alma and*

119

I could have a normal relationship. But the weight of the chains lingered long after they had been cut away, just as Ethan's vision had lingered after he closed his eyes. It hadn't hit Alma yet that the chains were gone. And when it did, it would be too late for him to step back into her life. Someone else would reap where he had sown. And yet, he was whistling.

Because he did have a thank you. A child's smile. Calculate the ROI on *that*.

The supermarket was never crowded this early on a Saturday, which was a good thing because Dave had told her that large crowds might still be stressful. Too much input all at once. Neural nets, Tom had explained, also need to learn. It wasn't as simple as "plug him in and turn him on."

She could feel, and sometimes saw from the corner of her eye, the way the other shoppers turned their heads to stare at Ethan. It did not seem to bother him. He strolled along the aisle by her side staring at the rows of brightly labeled cans. He pulled his "wheely" along in his left hand. One of the wheels on the computer had lost a bearing or something because it squeaked as he rolled it along.

Another mother, with a ten-year-old boy in tow, passed her in the aisle going the other way. Again, Alma saw how the eyes tracked the computer and then flicked ever so briefly to Alma. The other boy was overweight, his cheeks so full that they pinched his eyes into slits behind his glasses. He was eating from a torn-open bag of candy corn. He gawked openly at Ethan; then he pointed and laughed. "Get a Walkman," he said.

Alma ignored them and they disappeared down the aisle and turned into Baked Goods. Ethan tugged at her sleeve. "Mamma," he said. "Maamaa. Wassa Wawkmaan?"

"Never mind for now, Ethan. I'll tell you later." She checked her shopping list. "Let's see. We need cereal. And what else? Peas, carrots, green beans. And milk. No." She pulled the pencil from behind her ear and crossed that off. "We already have the milk, don't we Ethan?"

She looked down by her side and he was gone.

Her heart flipped over. Ethan? Where was he? Why hadn't she heard the squeaky wheel?

Before she could move, she did hear the wheel and Ethan turned the corner from the next aisle over. He had a colorful box of cereal balanced on his computer, which he pushed before him like a shopping cart. "Fouund it, maamaa!" he said. "Found it." He grabbed it off the computer and held it up to her.

"Oh, Ethan, you don't like that kind of cereal. You want the one with the jogger on the front. Don't worry. Give it to me; I'll exchange it. Stay right there and don't move."

She hurried to the dry cereal aisle and set the cereal box on a shelf at random. She ran her finger along the ranks of boxes, looking for...

A cry! Ethan!

She scurried back to the canned vegetable aisle to find the fat boy pulling on Ethan's umbilical cable. "Let *me* listen," the fat boy was saying. "It's *my* turn." Ethan was crying and waving his arms, trying to grab the cable. Every time the fat boy tugged, Ethan's head jerked.

"You let go of him, you awful boy! You let go!" Alma strode toward them.

The fat boy saw her coming and dropped the cable and ran, calling, "Mommy."

Alma dropped to her knees next to her sobbing son. He was rubbing the shaved spot on his head where the cable was attached. "It hu-hurts," he said. "It hu-hu-hu-hurts." He talked in gulps between the sobs.

"Don't worry, Ethan. He's gone. I won't let him hurt you again." She hugged him and stroked his head gently.

"What did you do to my son!" It was a loud, angry voice and Alma turned to see the fat boy clinging to the jeans of his mother. He was pointing. "She called me a name, mommy."

"What did you do?"

"What did *I* do?" Alma rose and faced the woman. "I found your boy assaulting my son and I chased him away. That's what I did!"

"Impossible," the woman replied. "His father and I believe in non-violence. We won't even let him watch those awful cartoon shows."

"I wouldn't know about that." Alma was aware of the other shoppers gathering at the two ends of the aisle. "All I know is that I found him yanking on my son's—" Sudden panic: *What do I call* it? "—my son's prosthetic."

"Prosthetic?" The other woman looked openly at what she had been eyeing surreptitiously. "What is it, some kind of boom box?"

"No. It's a sensory collator."

"You're Seakirt, aren't you?" It was another woman shopper, who had come up the aisle to eavesdrop. "I read about you in the *Enquirer*." She turned to the first woman. "Her son is retarded, so she hooked him up to a computer." Turning back to Alma. "It won't work, you know. Computers aren't really 'thinking machines.' All they do is crunch numbers."

"I know that. I—"

But the first woman drew herself up. "You allowed a retarded child to roam loose in the supermarket? What if he had hurt someone! What if he threw some sort of fit!"

Alma wanted to tell the woman that retardation was not like that. That being slow to process inputs and outputs was not the same thing as homicidal mania. But the woman was in no mood to listen. "It's only a prosthetic," Alma said, pointing to the computer. "Like your son's glasses."

"How dare you compare my son to…that!"

"Just remember, it was your son who threw the fit." She grabbed the shopping cart in one hand and Ethan in the other and pressed past them. Behind her she could hear the whispers. "It's just awful what she's done to him." "It isn't natural." "Computers are taking over everything."

When she checked out of the market, she told the manager to be sure to charge the other woman for the bag of candy her child had eaten.

There were pickets in front of the Janifer Institute for Electroneural Medicine: several clumps of them wielding placards and eyeing each other as warily as they eyed the tall metal-and-glass doors. Alma hesitated as she stepped from the parking garage down the block and she put her hand down by her side to stop Ethan.

"Whass wrong, mommy?"

"Hush." She backed up a hasty step and peered around one of the concrete support pillars. The protesters weren't actually marching. Some were leaning on their signs, drinking coffee. The four police officers standing between the protesters and the Institute chatted with each other or rocked back and forth on their heels as they watched the sign-wavers. They weren't expecting trouble, just nuisance; one more dull duty. The local Eyewitless Action News Team were already set up, but their cameras weren't running. The technical crew were having coffee and donuts while the on-camera personality put the finishing touches on his hair. Curious passers-by, seeing the cameras and the protesters, had stopped and were waiting.

For her.

They were all waiting for her to show up, Alma realized. The protesters were going to stage something dramatic and visual for the evening news. If they got themselves on TV they would be real; their ideas would be worthy of attention.

At least, those ideas that could be compressed to slogans and symbols and sound bytes. *End the Cruelty*, declared one sign, and what did that have to do with her? Another sign bore a red slashed-circle superimposed over a picture of a computer. And, yes, she had been getting a lot of *that* lately. Not from her friends and co-workers—they worked with computers themselves—but from strangers who felt duty-bound to tell her what was good for her. On a third sign she could make out the word "blasphemy" but nothing else.

Alma hated them. Why couldn't they leave her alone? Why did everyone have to tell her what to do? She backed away from the pillar. "Come on, Ethan. Let's get back in the van. We're going home. We'll see Doctor Silverman some other day."

"Let me see," he said, and stepped forward with his wheely. Alma seized him roughly by the shoulders and yanked him back.

"Don't let them spot you," she told him. "They'll come and scream at us so they can get on TV."

"Can I be on teebee?"

"No. Stay with momma." She turned toward the minivan, but Ethan shook loose from her grip and broke toward the sidewalk, pushing his wheely ahead of him. "Ethan!" She tried to shout and not shout at the same time, so Ethan would hear her and the protesters would not. But there must have been something wrong with the wheely's audio circuits because Ethan did not pause. By the time he "heard" her it would be three seconds too late.

Before he could turn the pillar, Ethan ran headlong into a man coming the other way. The man grunted and reached out and grabbed the boy's arm. "Steady, there, fella," he said. Then he stooped and rubbed his shin where the wheely had struck him. "You should watch where you're going. You could hurt someone." He looked up. "You must be Alma Seakirt. I thought I saw someone peek out from the parking garage."

He was a short, dark man, about 90% normal size. His features—nose, ears, hands, feet—were small, but of mature proportions; as if he were the product of a pantograph, a scaled-down version of a full-sized man. Somehow, that seemed to concentrate his energies, so that he projected an intensity that normal-sized men could not.

Alma stepped toward him and yanked Ethan's arm from his grasp. "Touch my boy again and I'll call for the police."

He blinked and pulled his hand away, as if Ethan had suddenly become white hot. "Hey, don't get me wrong. I'm not a child mol—I'm not differently-motivated sexually. I just wanted to talk to you for a moment."

"Your timing is off. The cameras aren't here yet."

"No one followed me. They think I left something in my car."

Alma had taken away two steps away, leading Ethan toward their minivan. She paused and turned back. "Why?" she asked.

He flushed, an attractive coloring against the dark, curly locks of his hair. "Not all of us are publicity hounds. I don't turn my convictions on and off for the cameras. I'll leave the posing to Gerald and Inga and the others at National. My impression is that you don't like confrontation, especially with a large group of activists."

"Is it."

"You had a judge issue an injunction to stop us from picketing at your home—"

"My God, you don't have to be a privacy freak for that! Everyone in the neighborhood was involved." And she had taken some heat from the neighbors herself, as if it were her fault that protesters threatened to disrupt their quiet little corner of the universe. Only Doc Wilkes, a retired G.P. who lived six houses around the block, had been sympathetic, calling her from time to time with words of encouragement. "So what?"

"So, I wanted you to *listen* to what we have to say."

She hesitated, resenting the trap of reasonableness. How could a fair-minded person reject anything without first studying it? Like those people who condemned movies they had never seen, or books they had never read. The ACLU had said that freedom of speech meant nothing if no one heard. And so by subtle steps the right to speak becomes the obligation to listen.

But she noticed that the other hadn't said that *he* wanted to listen to what *she* had to say. *Be reasonable* was always a one-way request. She had never heard of anyone pleading, *Please let* me *be reasonable.*

"Is something funny?"

She shook her head. How could she explain? She had no desire to plead her position to him and was not even sure what her position was. But he was good-looking in a miniature sort of way and under other circumstances she would not have minded getting to know him better. "Sorry, I'd love to hear what you have to say, but I don't want to hang around. One of your friends out there could show up looking for you."

"Where, then?" he asked, fast as a panther.

"Where?"

"If not here, where do you want to meet me?"

Over drinks in a small, intimate bistro…? Lord, what was she thinking? And what would she do with Ethan in the meantime? "One on one?" she said sharply. "No chanting crowds? No cameras?"

He nodded. "Just you and me."

Someplace where she could take Ethan along, like the public library? But if they met anywhere public, the vultures would gather. Someone

124

would notice the boy, and the silent, whispering crowds would stare. And the picketers, cheated of their prey at the Institute, might well hear of it and be waiting, cameras and all, when she stepped outside. Mick had thought that the neural bypass would free her from Ethan. That was how much he knew! She wished he were here so he could see how wrong he had been.

Her house? Oh, God, no. She didn't even know this man. She was not about to put herself alone with him.

So, they couldn't meet public and they couldn't meet private. Which let her off the hook.

"I have a neighbor," she heard herself say. "He might let us use his house." She was as astonished as if a stranger had spoken, and could do no more than give him a time and an address.

She watched him get into his own car, a small, gas-efficient foreign make. No surprise there. In a large car, a Caddy or a Lincoln, he would have looked like a child. She started her van and put it into gear. *Why did I agree to this?* she wondered. She took the back street exit from the garage so the people in front of the Institute would not see her or recognize her van. A glance in the rear-view mirror showed her that the little man was following. *I don't even know his name.* This wasn't right. Her life needed no more complications than it already had.

Doc Wilkes was a comfortable old gentleman who seemed as much a part of his house as the vines and flowerbeds. The wrinkles on his face were concentrated around the corners of the eyes and mouth, and his eyes took in everything with lively interest. Alma did not know him well; he was mostly a voice on the telephone, or a friendly wave when he jogged by her house with his Walkman. Yet, when she went to his door and made her strange request, he did not hesitate to agree.

Alma stepped inside to find herself surrounded by soft music: a quiet, bluesy tune she did not recognize. The sounds seemed to be coming from a room at the end of the hallway, but when she looked up she saw twin speakers in the wall. Doc Wilkes grinned. "It's a trick you can play with digital recordings. Musical ventriloquism. I have speakers in every room. I can even make different instruments sound from different directions, or seem to spin around you. Hello, there, little Ethan."

Ethan peeked out from behind Alma's skirts. "Hello?" he said uncertainly.

"He's a little shy around strangers sometimes."

125

Wilkes beamed and knelt in front of the boy. "I'll bet you don't remember me at all," he said. Ethan shook his head, but remained silent. "Never mind. You can call me Doc." He looked at Alma. "Who's your G.P.?"

"Doctor Khan."

He seemed startled. "Noor Khan? Is that a fact? I thought she had retired." He shook his head. "Well, some of us last longer than others." A strange, haunted look flickered briefly in his eyes. "Some of us last longer." Alma wondered what ancient hurt had been resurrected. "Well," he continued brusquely, "it's not how much time, but how well we use it. Noor Khan is a good physician; better than I ever was. Has she put any meat on those bones of hers, or is she still as scrawny as a crane?"

Ethan tugged at the old man's sleeve. "Doc?" He pointed. "Who's makin' th' music?"

Wilkes turned his attention back to the boy. "It's called *Careless Love*. Can you beat the time, Ethan? Like this?" And he tapped a slow, syncopated 4/4 rhythm on the top of Ethan's wheely. Alma fidgeted.

"Can I tell this fellow he can come in, then? I want to get this over with."

"What? You mean he's cooling his heels out on the porch? Of course, he can come in." Wilkes arose in a creaking of knees. "That was very good, Ethan. He's much improved, Mrs. Seakirt. Much improved."

Alma paused by the door and looked back at him. "In most ways."

She could see that he wanted to ask her what she meant, but he did not press the point. "You can use the living room, off to the left there. I'll make myself scarce. If I stick around, your friend is liable to ask me what I think, and if he does, I'm liable to tell him." He chuckled. "I'll take Ethan out to the kitchen, if you like."

"No, thank you. He'd be too much a bother for you."

"No bother at all." Doc took Ethan by the hand. "Come with me, Ethan. We'll play some more games with the music. Hum along with me. Dáaa da dá da dáa d-dáaaa…"

Alma watched them go. Ethan would be all right. Doc was a doctor, after all; even if he was retired. And she would be right down the hall if Ethan needed her. Her feelings, as she opened the door, were a curious blend of anxiety and anticipation.

His name was Vinnie Patterson and he thought she had done the wrong thing.

"No one has the right," he explained earnestly, leaning forward over the coffee table that separated them, "to profit from cruelty to others."

She shrank back from his intensity into the high-backed, upholstered wing chair. "What cruelty?" she asked, remembering the placard she had seen waving in front of the Janifer Institute. On the table before her, her barely sipped coffee slowly cooled. Doc Wilkes had offered them both a cup but, when he turned to Vinnie, the man had responded with a short dissertation on the rape of the Brazilian rain forest. What must it be like, Alma wondered, to live a life in which every act was a political act, even the drinking of a simple cup of coffee. For all Vinnie knew, the coffee had been grown in Colombia, not Brazil.

But there was probably something objectionable about Colombia, too.

"What cruelty?" Vinnie unzipped a black, vinyl carrying pouch and rummaged inside. "The surgery that you put your boy through was tested on animals, wasn't it?"

"Chimpanzees." Alma remembered Silverman telling her that.

"Yes." He handed her an 8x10 glossy photograph. It was black and white, not quite in focus. A chimpanzee, lips pulled back from its teeth, mouth open in what had to be a cry, stretched its arms through the bars of a cage. The pleading eyes stared out at Alma. She looked back at Vinnie.

"Torture," he said. "Innocent animals tortured so that a few white males could become rich and famous."

"So that my son could function like a normal boy."

"The mentally challenged have the right to their own lifestyle. Would your child have a right to use this technology if it had been tested first on Jews? Or on blacks?"

"What? Of course not. That would be horrible."

Vinnie leaned forward again, as if he were prepared to leap across the table. "Then why do you think you have the right to use technology tested on other living creatures?"

"But…They were only animals."

"Only animals." Vinnie shook his head. "Alma, a rat is a dog is a pig is a boy."

She reared back. "What does that mean? How dare you compare my Ethan to a rat!" Her mother had done that, she remembered. Beatrice had called Ethan a lab rat.

"No, no," he said. "I don't mean that Ethan is no better than a lab rat. I meant that rats—any living thing—has rights. That we humans are not entitled to use them as *things*. 'Anything that has eyes has a soul.'"

"Potatoes?" She couldn't resist teasing him, he was so earnest. "Laced shoes?"

For a moment, she thought she had offended him. His lips tightened and pulled back at the corners. But then, abruptly, he laughed. "Yes," he

said, "as a matter of fact, shoes do have soles. Potatoes, I'm not sure about."
She laughed with him.

"Sometimes," he continued, "we can take ourselves too seriously and
forget how to laugh. But—" And the laughter bubbled away like flattened
soda. "—would you have cracked a joke if we had been discussing women's
rights instead of animal rights?"

I might have, at that, she thought. "No," she said.

"It's always wrong to impose human ideas on nature. And it's especially
wrong to use them in research in some sort of mad quest for immortality.
There are more benign ways of doing the research. Epidemiological studies. Computer models."

"That sounds pretty good, young fellow." Doc Wilkes stood in the
doorway with a steaming coffee pot. "Animal rights. I never knew anyone
in the medical profession who wanted to mistreat animals. Hell's bells. If
the animals were mistreated, the test results wouldn't be valid. If ethics fail
to show the way, self-interest will do." He walked to the table and glanced
at Alma's still full cup. "Gone cold," he said. She looked away. For some
reason, Doc made her feel uneasy.

"Rights are a human notion," she heard him tell Vinnie. "There are no
'rights' in nature. Does the lion honor the lamb's rights? Or vice versa? No,
sir, she does not. So what entitles us to impose our human ideas of rights
onto animals?"

Vinnie stared at him. He opened his mouth and closed it. Then he said,
"That's a trick argument. Inga has shown that it is immoral to—"

Doc waved an irritated hand. "Save your moral judgments for church.
Don't try to force your beliefs on the rest of us."

Alma suddenly realized why Doc's presence made her feel uneasy.
"Ethan!" she said, suddenly rising from the chair. "You left him alone in
the kitchen!" She turned to push past him and her knee banged the coffee table, knocking the china cup over and sending a flood of cold coffee
across the glassed top. Behind her she heard Vinnie's voice.

"I don't blame her for being alarmed, doctor. Don't you realize how
unreliable computers are? What if it bombed off while the boy was un-
supervised? Suppose he was climbing off a chair when all of a sudden his
senses...?"

Alma didn't hear any more. She was halfway down the hall and saw
Ethan at the other end staring at a photograph hanging on the wall: two
old women, one of them a dwarf.

Yes, she thought suddenly. What if it *did* bomb off when she was not
around? She had never really thought of that before.

The colors were bright and clear. And he could make them appear on the paper by rubbing the "crayon" back and forth. Rub-rub. But stay inside the circle. The crayons had a pleasant, waxy smell. Rub-rub. He had smelled that smell before. Rub-rub. But he had never connected the smell with the colorful little cylinders. It was wonderful. Did the different colors have different smells? He put down the brown one and picked up the green one and held it to his nose. He took a deep breath. Maybe. It was hard to be sure.

Alma watched Ethan from the corner of her eye as she washed the dishes. He sat at the kitchen table with a box of crayons and a sheet of butcher paper. He clutched the green crayon in his fist, and the tip of his tongue peeked from the corner of his mouth. The fist moved over the paper.

"Don't put the crayon in your mouth dear."

Ethan blinked and looked at her, looked back at the crayon. He continued doodling. "No, momma."

Alma rinsed a plastic cup and set it in the drainer. "What are you doing, Ethan, dear?"

"Drawn a picher," he said without breaking his frown.

"Of what?"

"Jus' pichers."

"Pic-tures," she said, enunciating clearly. "Pictures have to be pictures of something, don't they?"

He shrugged and hunched over the paper. "Doggie," he said.

"Do you want a doggie?" She hoped not. She couldn't take care of an animal besides.

"No. Jus' drawn doggie pik-churs."

"But a green doggie? Why are you making the doggie green?"

He stopped drawing. "I dunno."

"You can make the grass green. And the trees." She finished the last of the dishes and opened the drain in the sink. She dried her hands on a tea towel.

"Can I dry the dishsh—dishes, momma?"

"You might drop them on the floor, dear. You know how you still drop things sometimes."

"Plastick don't break. I can pickup." Pride in the voice. *I can pick up.*

"I know you can, Ethan, dear. And it's wonderful. But I would have to wash the dish over again after it was on the dirty floor. Don't you like drawing pictures?"

Silence. She looked over at the table. Had the computer bombed? She hung the towel on its rack. Honestly. She had had such hopes for Zachariah's implant; but Ethan still dropped things, and he was still slow to answer sometimes. It was a bother having to run the diagnostic program every morning and drag the computer with them everywhere—and the stares they received! Not that she minded. It was for her Ethan. Still, it *was* extra work.

Ethan slid off the kitchen chair and put the crayon box atop his wheely. He reached for the butcher paper.

"Where are you going, dear?"

"Bedroom."

"There's no table in there to draw on. I don't want crayons all over my bedroom. Isn't it much easier to draw at the kitchen table? You can show the picture to Uncle Vinnie when he comes here tonight."

"Sto'room?"

"You know the storeroom is full—"

"Make sto'room *my* bedroom?"

"Then where would I put all the things that are in there?" Sewing machine. Ironing board. Winter clothes in the closet. And never mind the bright, happy wallpaper that Nate had hung himself. The smiling birds and happy squirrels. That had been when they had planned to use the room for something else. When they had thought they could have plans. Before they had known how impossible that would be.

"You'll be able to do much better work out here. You have the table and the sunlight coming through the window."

Ethan threw the crayon box onto the table. The lid came open and the little wax cylinders rolled across the formica surface. The red one reached the other side and fell to the floor.

"Ethan," she said. But the boy was already rolling his cart toward the bedroom. She shook her head. Most of the time his coordination was good, but every now and then something would screw up and Ethan would miss what he aimed at—as with the crayons just now—or he would fail to hear what she said to him. She should keep track of these glitches. Tell Zachariah. Maybe there was a bug in the software.

She bent behind the table and retrieved the fallen crayon. Then she sorted the crayons out into proper order and placed them back in their box. Ethan's drawing lay on the table. She picked it up and studied it. It was crudely drawn. Head and body were simple ovals. The legs were sticks. Both ears were atop the head; one of the eyes was outside the oval of the skull. Well, he was new to hand-eye coordination; and Picasso had become famous for work like this. Standing on a patch of green, the dog was brown after all.

She awoke that night from inchoate dreams into the darkness of her bedroom. What was it? What had woken her? A sound? Voices! Was it Vinnie? No, he had left early. She fumbled with the lamp on the night stand. Six o'clock? Something was wrong.

And Ethan's crib was empty.

He's roaming the house! She threw the covers aside and, clutching her nightgown tight around her throat, left the bedroom. They really should move to an apartment. Someplace smaller. There were only the two of them. There would only ever be the two of them. Rattling around in a half dozen rooms, it was too easy to lose track of him. She should have let Nate keep the house in the settlement.

She found him sitting on the living room floor with a bowl of cereal. The television was on and the roadrunner was giving it to the coyote again.

"Ethan!"

He jerked as if punched and a brief scowl crossed his face. "Yes, momma?"

"What are you doing up alone?"

"Watchin teebee."

"You know I don't want you playing with the TV. It's dangerous. You could electrocute yourself."

"You play it." He cast his eyes down as he said it. Alma thought there was a hint of fear in his voice. Was he afraid that his mother would electrocute herself?

"Don't worry, Ethan. Grown-ups know how to work the TV without being electrocuted." She stooped and took his bowl and spoon. "Here. I'll take care of that. I don't want you spilling on the rug."

"No, I throw't out. Lem*me*. Can do't myself." He tugged on the bowl and it tipped and the milk splashed on him and on the rug. He froze and stared at the stain. Then he cried and hugged her. "M'sorry, momma. M'sorry. Din't mean to do't."

After a moment, she hugged him back. Was it going to be like this from now on? Waiting for the next random computer glitch? What if the next time he fumbled something, it was not a bowl of milk and cereal but something dangerous? What if the next time he failed to hear her advice in time, it was a warning? She knew suddenly and clearly what she had to do.

Alma stepped into Doctor Silverman's office and was immediately struck by the number of people present. Silverman and Zachariah, of course. Zachariah looked especially distressed and his big, brown cow-eyes regarded her with puzzlement. And the thin, dusky woman standing by the bookcase must be the Institute's lawyer.

But Mick? What was he doing here?

Ethan wrested free of her grasp. "Uncle Mick!" he said, rolling across the room. Alma caught up with him just as Mick hoisted him up. "I missed you, Uncle Mick."

"And I missed you."

Alma seized Ethan under the arms and lifted him away. "Be careful," she told Mick. "You've got to remember how long the umbilical is."

She heard his voice over her shoulder as she turned her back on him. "Six feet, Alma. Six feet with a spring-loaded take-up reel. Plenty of slack for picking kids up and hugging them."

She turned and stared at him.

"Whose company did you think supplied the components?"

So, that was why he was here. An investment to be protected. Profits. "I should have known," she said.

She set Ethan with his legs dangling over the edge of the sofa and *(flash on the day she had sat there listening to Doctor Silverman explain what it was she had to deal with)* she turned and introduced the man still standing in the doorway. "This is Sèan FitzPatrick, my lawyer."

"Not Vinnie Patterson?" said Mick.

There was an odd twist to his voice. She looked at him. "What, do you follow me around, Mick? That's sad. Get a life. I have. Vinnie…makes me feel good about myself."

"Right."

"What do you mean by that crack?"

"For God's sake, Alma. He looks like a kid."

"Who, Vinnie? What of it?"

"So. I suppose you've always wanted one."

She took two long steps across the room and slapped him. A long, roundhouse slap that started nearly from her knees. It rocked his head to the side. "How dare you!"

Silverman stood up from behind his desk. "Please!"

FitzPatrick laid a restraining hand on her arm. She looked at him and nodded and let herself be led to the sofa to sit beside a bewildered Ethan. "Mommy, why? What? Uncamick?" She hugged him hard around the shoulders, feeling the way the umbilical draped across her forearm. There, let them see for themselves that the wheely did not always help Ethan process his sensory inputs. Sometimes they were still garbled. "This is business," she announced to the room at large. "Let's keep my social life out of it." She turned to the lawyer. "Sèan?"

FitzPatrick had dark brown hair threaded with white. His three-piece pinstripe suit fit him like a glove, and the trouser creases could slice cheese. Silverman favored the lawyer with a hard stare.

"We've spoken. On the phone."

FitzPatrick responded to Silverman's irony with a pleasant smile. "And had we settled the matter then, we would not have to have this meeting."

Silverman introduced the Institute lawyer as Antoinette daSouza. FitzPatrick gave her a three-fingered scout salute. "Hello, Nettie. It's been a while since we crossed swords, hasn't it? I haven't seen you down at Hogan's since D.A. Copperfield's retirement party."

"I've been back home to see my parents," she said, returning his handshake. She had an odd accent. Not quite Spanish. Brazilian, probably.

Hired guns, thought Alma. They didn't care about her Ethan *or* about the Institute. Tomorrow, paid by someone else, they would just as cheerfully argue the other side. Shake hands and come out fighting. It was the fighting that mattered, not the fight.

Silverman's first words were directed to her. "I don't understand, Alma. I don't understand, at all." Turning to face him, she seized her resolution and held it tightly to her. "What don't you understand, doctor? I want Ethan disconnected. Is that too hard to comprehend?"

Tom Zachariah was seated in a padded armchair beside Silverman's desk. He had his elbows resting on the arms of the chair and his hands were clasped into a ball under his chin. His eyes were troubled. "Why?" he asked.

Before she could respond, FitzPatrick laid a hand on her arm. "Mrs. Seakirt does not have to answer any questions. It is her decision not to continue the extraordinary medical treatment that her son has been receiving."

"But that is foolish," said Zachariah. He looked at Alma, but she would not meet his eyes.

"Irrelevant," said FitzPatrick. "*In re Maida Yetter*, citing *Roe v. Wade*, the constitutional right to privacy includes the right to refuse medical treatment even if the refusal is 'unwise, foolish or ridiculous.'"

"Alma can decide for herself if she wants medical treatment," Mick interrupted. "But is that what Ethan wants?" The mark of her palm stood out dull red against the pale skin of his cheek. *I shouldn't have slapped him,* she thought. *I shouldn't have given in like that.* It made her look foolish and hysterical.

FitzPatrick looked at Mick. "Being retarded, Ethan is incompetent under the law. A court would hear his preferences, but they would not be controlling. Alma Seakirt, as Ethan's parent, is entitled to make his decisions in his name."

"But the electro-neural transformer has reduced Ethan's retardation," Silverman pointed out.

"True," FitzPatrick riposted, "but it does not make him any older. He is still under eighteen and still legally incompetent." He smiled at the doctor.

A lawyer's trick, thought Alma. A rhetorical ambush. FitzPatrick used words the way a fencer used a foil. What was it he had said to her when Vinnie had introduced them? *Among the Irish, conversation is regarded as one of the martial arts.* But he didn't have to look as if he were enjoying himself.

DaSouza spoke up. "The state also has *parens patriae* interests, Sèan, to look out for those who cannot look out for themselves. That's the basis for child labor laws and mandatory school attendance. *In re Mildred Terwilliger,* the court must consider only the interests of the incompetent person, and *not* merely the interests or convenience of the parent."

"*My* convenience?" said Alma. "*My* convenience? Do you know how difficult it is to—" FitzPatrick raised his hand palm out and she stopped herself. Yes, he was right. Why hire someone to argue your point and then argue it yourself? FitzPatrick knew what he was doing; and, at Vinnie's request, he was even doing it *pro bono.* Otherwise, the Institute might have been able to bully or trick her into backing down.

"The U.S. Supreme Court," FitzPatrick reminded daSouza, "held in *Parham v. J.R.* that simply because a parent's decision is disagreeable to the child or because it involves risks, the power to make the decision does not automatically transfer to the state. And a parent is *presumed* to be acting in the best interests of her child."

"*Parham* is federal law," said daSouza. "This will be tried in Orphan's Court."

FitzPatrick shrugged. "If it is tried, at all. State courts take cognizance of federal precedent on constitutional questions. Chief Justice Scalia—"

"Courts *have* appointed guardians to make the decisions in many cases," daSouza pointed out. "Parents may not refuse blood transfusions for their child's operation, for example—even where their religious beliefs are at stake. Nor may they refuse medical treatment for fetuses that remain viable after abortion. Besides, you're forgetting *Cruzan.* The State is not *required* to accept a family member's substituted judgment for an incompetent loved one!"

"Yes," FitzPatrick admitted, "but the examples you cite involve risk of death. *In re Green*, the court ruled that the state does not have *parens patriae* interest of sufficient magnitude to interfere with a parent's decision when the child's life is *not* immediately imperiled by his physical condition. So here the individual's liberty interest to refuse unwanted medical treatment—either for themselves or for their incompetent wards—is unaffected."

"Dammit!" Mick brought his hand down hard on the bookcase he had been leaning against. "What is the point to all this jawboning? Alma, it's *wrong* to take Ethan off that transformer. Ethan? Ethan." He stepped forward and stooped down to face the boy on the sofa. "Ethan, what do *you* want?"

Ethan took his finger out of his mouth. "I dunno."

"Do you *want* to be disconnected from your wheely?"

Ethan scowled and looked down.

"Do you?"

Alma put a hand on his shoulder. "You don't have to answer him."

He looked up at her and smiled. "I wanna do what momma wants."

Mick's head jerked up and he looked from Ethan to her and back. "He doesn't know what he's saying."

"Which is why," FitzPatrick reminded them, "children are legally incompetent to make this sort of decision for themselves."

Mick looked at her and she stared back without flinching. "You've brainwashed him," he said. "You and that Vinnie Patterson."

She set her jaw. "Why, because he pointed out the dangers of relying on the transformer? Because I don't feel right about torturing animals?"

"No animals were 'tortured,'" said Silverman. "That photograph you sent us was not of one of *our* chimpanzees. It was a sick monkey in Gabon being taken to a veterinarian, and was restrained only to prevent it from harming itself. That photograph," he added darkly, "reappears from time to time, always out of context."

"And none of the diagnostic records show any evidence of computer malfunctions," said Zachariah. "Why not give as much weight to what did happen as to what might have happened?"

"No," said Mick, still looking her in the eyes. "I don't think those are your real reasons."

She gave him an indignant look and held it between them. "And what are my real reasons?"

Mick shook his head and stood up. He dusted off the knees of his trousers. "The jailer envies the captive's dreams," he said, looking at no one in particular.

She wanted to know what he meant by that, but did not want to give him the satisfaction of explaining. "No one questioned me," she said, and they all looked at her. Silverman, Zachariah, Mick, the lawyers. "No one questioned me when I agreed to hook Ethan up to that thing. Why do you question me now that I've decided not to continue? Do I only have the right to choose when you approve of my choice?"

"It's not that," said Silverman. "It's—"

"Bad publicity for the Institute," she said, ignoring FitzPatrick's attempts to silence her. "After all the big announcements, how would it look when your star patient wants to be taken off? That's the only reason you're fighting me."

Silverman shook his head. "Not the only reason. And a trial would be just as bad."

"Worse," said FitzPatrick. "That's why it won't come to trial." He cocked an eyebrow in daSouza's direction.

"No, they'll fight it, Sèan," Alma told him. "If I take Ethan off, there'll be a big stink. How will they ever get anyone else to sign up their child?"

Zachariah spread his hands. "Mrs. Seakirt, I admit that no one *wants* to fail—"

"Or at least not many of us," said Mick.

"But the success of this research project is not why I urge you to reconsider."

"The Institute operates for a profit," she reminded them. Vinnie had told her that. Greed for profits blinded people.

"Alma, we care about Ethan," said Mick. "All of us do. You're not alone. He's not a burden you have to shoulder by yourself."

"What do you know about it?" she snapped. "You ran out like all the others. You're not concerned about my Ethan at all. It's the profit you'll make from building these prosthetics for the Institute."

"Alma." He straightened; shoved his hands in his pants pockets. Looked down; looked back up. "Alma, if it will convince you otherwise, I will donate every cent of profit on those machines to any charity you name."

Taking Ethan by the hand, she stood up. FitzPatrick stood with her. "No, I'm sorry. My mind is made up." She walked to the door, the lawyer trailing behind her. "I coped with Ethan for years before the operation. I can cope with him again."

"We'll fight you on this," said Mick. "We'll have the court name a guardian."

FitzPatrick nodded. "See you in court."

As she stood in the half-open door, Silverman spoke up. "One thing, Alma." She looked back at him. "The decisions are not easy, and you never, ever know if you are right. But if you go ahead, it won't be like it was before."

"Why not?"

"Because he'll remember."

Her skin tingled, and for the oddest moment she felt as if she were encased in glass and everyone in the room beside herself and Ethan were far, far away. Then the moment passed and Ethan tugged at her skirt and she looked down. "A' we goin now, momma?"

She knelt and hugged him, untwisting the cord with a practiced movement. "Yes, we're going now. And momma will take care of you forever and ever.

"Will ev'ythin be awright?"

She brushed at his clothes and hair, straightening any sign of disarray.

AFTERWORD TO "CAPTIVE DREAMS"

I wrote "Captive Dreams" whenever I was stuck on "Melodies of the Heart." Consequently, although it was started later, it was finished a year earlier. It appeared in *Analog* (Aug 1992) and placed second in its category in the AnLab voting. The time setting of the story coincides with the epilog of "Melodies of the Heart," and consequently old Dr. Wilkes makes an appearance.

The immediate inspiration for the story was a then-neighbor's daughter, who was developmentally disabled and to whom the divorced father was greatly devoted.

I noticed that sometimes when I greeted her, the young girl would not answer for a few moments, then would wave as if she had just heard me. There are likely any number of explanations for the behavior, but one that struck me at the time was literally retardation. The sensory signals were slower reaching the brain. In the story, I extended the notion to suppose that different sensory channels were reaching Ethan's brain at different times, and consequently he was seeing, hearing, touching different "moments." This would be an impairment of what Aristotle called the unifying or "common" sense. Such a perceived world would be inherently unintelligible. This led to the imaginary device for coordinating the sensory signals; but of course that was only the beginning of the story.

Recently, I read that one of the flaws in experiments that purportedly show decisions being made before the subject is aware of making them is that visual signals, auditory signals, and tactile signals really do arrive in the brain moments apart, but that some function in the brain combines them into a common sensation. Score one for the old Stagirite.

A reviewer once wrote of this story that it was "about" the ethics of animal experimentation. It wasn't, but you must be the judge. The title comes from Gérard de Nerval, *Fragments de Faust*: "The jailer is another kind of captive—is the jailer envious of his prisoner's dreams?" Alma Seakirt is another kind of captive.

The letters I received from the caregivers of children like Ethan showed that some people understood and were profoundly moved. That's all any writer can ask for.

HOPEFUL MONSTERS

It was a brilliant spring day when Karen Brusco brought home her perfect baby. It was of a piece with the day, which was likewise perfect. Flowers sported red and yellow among roadside bushes, burst from front gardens, and draped precipitous hillsides with bridal veils. Laurel and forsythia and daffodils sweetened the air, and Karen responded with her own glow. She was a mother. Like spring, she had burst forth.

It was cause for celebration, and so shortly after returning from the Choice Center, she and Bill invited family, friends, and neighbors over. All of them agreed that Rachel was perfect, perhaps the most perfect baby ever born. In part, this must have been no less than politeness, but much of it was no more than truth. Not only had Rachel scored a perfect 10 on her APGAR but going beyond appearance and activity, she exhibited a delicacy and symmetry of feature, an alertness and focus in her gaze, a genuine benevolence in her grimace that was given to few other newborns. Except, of course, for those others whose parents had used the Child Design Department.

"We didn't design for intelligence," Bill explained, though not because he discounted intelligence to beauty in baby girls. "We just haven't identified the gene for intelligence yet." The "we" was broadly construed, as when a sports fan says "we" won a game. Though down with architecture, piping, wiring, and HVAC, he could not have identified a gene if it had walked up to him on the street and shaken his hand.

"There *is* no gene for intelligence," grumbled Jessica Burton-Peeler, a matronly woman who lived around the corner—if a ring road can be said to have corners. Her husband, Charlie Singer, liked to call her "the second-best geneticist in North America" and, if she objected, amended that to "the second-best geneticist in our house." Charlie was in the kitchen chatting up Sarah and Andrew, who were Karen's parents, and a neighbor, Jamie Shaw, who had dropped in for the cake and ice cream.

"Well, yes," said Bill. "I meant 'gene' in a metaphorical sense." He was acutely aware that SingerLabs was a major player in genetics and nano-technology and that consequently he was talking to a pro.

Jessie leaned over the crib, set in a place of honor in the living room, and tickled Rachel under the chin. The baby responded by making a gro-tesque face. "Genes aren't metaphors," she told the proud father. "They're molecules. But the reason there's no gene for intelligence is because there's no one thing to call 'intelligence.'"

"The state of the art isn't there yet," said Bill, a bit defensively. "Beauty is an abstraction, too. But the complex of features that make it up—eye color, nose length, cheekbones—those are things we can get a handle on. We worked through composite sketches during the design phase of the project and…"

"And Rachel is not a 'project,'" said Karen, who had stopped by with a tray of hors d'oeuvres from the kitchen. She let several guests pick from the tray before setting it down on the coffee table and joining her husband at the crib side. "Just like an engineer, to talk about 'projects' and 'design phases' all the time."

Bill tucked up. "It's an analogy. They told us how genes aren't one thing in one place. So they have this MAGIC machine—a Multiplex Auto-mated Genome Integrator and Calibrator—that locates and replicates the DNA from multiple sites at accelerated speeds. It's like an acrostic. The letters that spell 'blue eyes' aren't in a contiguous string but hopscotch around the genome like…"

Charlie had come up behind them. "…like a little girl skipping through *Himmel und Hölle*," he said. "The interesting question is…who's the little girl? Besides this one," he added with an avuncular nod toward the crib. He looked down at the baby, but made no move to touch her. "What sur-prises have you in store for us, hopeful monster?" he said softly.

Karen bridled. "Monster? Rachel's no monster! How can you say a thing like that?" Charlie was a neighbor, a friend. They often had dinner together. She could not believe he had said that.

Singer ignored Jessie's kick to his ankle and unwrapped a stick of gum, which he popped into his mouth. "A 'monster' is just a large-scale muta-tion," he said. "Goldschmidt coined the term 'hopeful monster' because he thought evolution proceeded in big leaps and 'hoped for the best.'"

Bill nodded his head as if understanding. Karen was mollified, but still suspicious. "The genes are like lines of code," Bill said, "and the genome is the program."

"Well, only if each line of code were broken up and scattered throughout the program, and an instruction could mean something different depending on when it was read and what other instructions were read at the same time. Oh, and bits of the syntax could be roped into other instructions, like the letters in a crossword puzzle. But other than that, yeah, 'just like.'"

Sometimes Charlie could irritate Bill. "There was some scientist," Bill insisted, "who reformulated genetics in terms of information theory. I read an article about it once."

"Shapiro at Chicago," Charlie said. "Sure. It was his paradigm that led to Rachel. He showed how genetic change could be massive *and* non-random. When you look inside genes, you find biochemical activities that can rearrange DNA molecules. They 'recognize' particular sequence motifs, which means genetic change can be specific; and the same activity can operate at multiple sites in the genome, which means change is not limited to one genetic locus. That's what turned MAGE into MAGIC. Why, there are some critters that completely reorganize their genetic apparatus within a single cell-generation. They fragment their chromosomes into thousands of pieces—and reassemble a specific subset into something else." He leaned over the crib again. "So Goldschmidt wasn't exactly right; but he wasn't entirely wrong, either. And what Nature accomplishes by accident, our clever engineers hope to accomplish by intelligent design." He shook his head. "Next to genes, my nanomachines are simple Tinkertoys."

Bill said, "Oh, come on, Charlie. The nanos you build are…"

"Just machines. But an organism's not a machine, Bill; and a baby's not a mousetrap. You don't take a bunch of parts and assemble 'em from the outside. An organism *diversifies* into its own parts from the inside."

Karen tickled Rachel, a process the child did not seem to care for, since she squirmed and fussed. "She's a little miracle," she said.

"Charlie," said Jessica finally, "we're here to coo over their baby, not lecture them on genetics."

"It doesn't matter," Karen said with conviction, "she's under warranty." She bent over the baby and rubbed her gently. "Aren't you, you little cutie!" Rachel emitted a great belch and smiled at no one in particular.

Jessie frowned and looked at Charlie, but neither of them said anything.

"Of course there's no gene for intelligence," Bill explained patiently to his fellow engineers when he had returned to work from paternity leave.

Rachel and her beauty had become naturally the topic *du jour*. One could not examine the hologram without making some comment. It was expected. "That's because there's no one thing we can call intelligence."

Hugo, who had the desk next to Bill, laughed. "Maybe not, but there's a lot of things we can't! Hey, Winnie! You see Bill's new baby?"

Winnie had been passing through the bull pen with a flatscreen tucked under her arm and a hard-hat pushed back on her head. She was evidently just off a site visit. She hesitated, then came over and accepted the hologram, studying it for a moment from different angles before handing it back. "She's very pretty." But as she turned to go, Hugo stopped her.

"Is that all you have to say? Aren't you going to say something about the, you know, *process*?"

"Hugo," said Bill. "Leave her alone."

But Winnie gave Hugo a level gaze. "You know I didn't approve; and you know why. So why don't we leave it at that?"

Bill watched her go into her office and insert her flatscreen into the wall pocket. The wall came alive with circuit diagrams. Bill felt guilty about goofing off and made to return to his own project; but Talequah said, "I don't think she likes that you selected for beauty rather than brains."

Hugo guffawed. "You mean she wishes they'd been able to select for beauty when she was conceived!"

"I wanted to select for intelligence," Bill said, almost apologetically, "but it's not simple, like repairing genetic diseases. Those are usually specific defects in specific loci, and fixing what's broke is always easier than optimizing something that isn't. Besides, intelligence involves two brain hemispheres, the nervous and glandular systems, and who knows what else? So it's not even clear yet which genes to tweak in which direction."

Talequah glanced at Winnie's office and said, "Maybe it's because she doesn't have kids of her own."

"No," said Bill. "You weren't here last year. Winnie felt it was immoral."

"Immoral!" Talequah raised her brows. "That gorgeous little baby? Why?"

"Well," said Bill, feeling a twinge of discomfort, "there is trial and error involved."

Hugo snorted. "How else can they identify which genes control which features in the first place? They *have* to experiment."

"Well, they also analyzed my DNA and Karen's," Bill said. "And Karen's parents', too. They even exhumed my mom and dad and as many of our grandparents as we could locate. My sister, too. It wasn't all...experimenting. Even so, there's still a risk."

Hugo shook his head. "Sure, but there are risks to staying in bed with the covers pulled up over you. We needed a lot of basic research over a lot of years to get us where we are today." He glanced once more toward Winnie's office. "People shouldn't let religious beliefs get in the way of progress."

Karen took Rachel to her parents' house, which was only a half-hour's drive away. A new baby was a hassle, as Sarah and Andrew would no doubt remind her. *The Grandparents' Revenge*, Andrew had called the baby, and had promised to mark as a red-letter day the first time she said to Rachel things Sarah had once said to her. It was a cheerful sort of vengeance, withal, and today Karen wanted only some time off for the hair salon. A freelance technical writer could work from home—an important consideration when she and Bill had been planning to have a child—but sometimes she just needed to get out of the house. Bill was on the road this week—a site in upstate New York—and she needed someone to watch Rachel for a couple of hours.

"You were a rambunctious child," Sarah told Karen when she had taken little Rachel in her arms. "You once swung on the refrigerator door playing Tarzan and tipped it over. I ran out the front door and up the street to *my* mother because you were driving me crazy."

Karen had heard the story innumerable times before, the catastrophe growing with each telling. "Well," she said, making light. "Don't let the little wiggle-worm swing on any doors."

"Oh, she's a quiet little darling."

Rachel had been looking from voice to voice, face to face. The doctors all said that this was an important stage in her cognitive development, learning to recognize important people in her life. Karen smiled and Rachel looked at her with such round-eyed earnestness that she had to laugh. Rachel was supposed to return the smile, but her grave stare was just too comical.

Sarah said to Andrew, "What is Rachel staring at?" And Andrew—he had never been Andy, not even to his own parents—pressed the hold button on the newspaper and said, "What?"

The poor wriggler was trapped inside a playpen, and Andrew reflected for a moment on her unjust imprisonment. It was a small fold-out that they kept on hand for just such occasions—soft netting festooned with toys—but since the kid could not even crawl yet, it seemed to Andrew a bit of overkill. He crossed the room to where his granddaughter lay on her back, kicking her arms and legs like an old-time break dancer. A gaily colored mobile hung just above her—an ominous Toy of Damocles, Andrew thought—but the baby was staring intently at the hinge on the corner of the playpen instead, juking the base so that the hinge would flex slightly.

"I think she's going to become a mechanical engineer, just like her grandpa. Aren't you, sweetie?"

If Rachel had an opinion in the matter, she did not share it. Andrew jiggled the mobile to attract her attention, but to no avail. He decided to turn her over.

"I think she's done on this side," he told Sarah, and his wife looked away from the television long enough to approve. "Let her exercise her neck muscles," she agreed. "She doesn't hold her head up well yet."

Rachel fussed a little when she was turned, but then discovered her left hand and spent the next fifteen minutes in its contemplation.

Karen was afraid something was wrong with Rachel. She had propped the baby up on the floor with pillows to cushion any fall and, to encourage crawling, had placed brightly colored toys just beyond her reach, like the pediatrician had said; but so far she had had no joy of it. Rachel would simply fix her gaze on one of the toys and stare at it and stare at it. When Karen leaned in front of her, she stared right past her.

"Each baby progresses at a different rate," Bill reminded her at dinner when she had mentioned this. The pediatrician had told her the same thing.

"And her fingers twitch."

"Babies are always twitching. It's a sort of isometric exercise hard-wired into our instincts."

"No, she twitches her fingers always in the same order; first one hand, then the other. Then she laughs."

"No telling what amuses a rug rat."

"Bill, she's not crawling yet. It worries me. Yesterday I set a ball in front of her and all she did was look at it. Then she looked at the clock—or I think she looked at the clock. She stared in that direction, anyhow. Then she looked at the picture of your grandparents."

"The round one on the wall?"

"That's the one. I don't know what she found so fascinating. She can't see anything but the shape at this age."

Bill had been reading specifications on his flat screen, which he liked to prop up at the table when he ate, and so he had only half his mind on the conversation. "I'm sure she's all right."

But then later, after they had done the dishes, he stepped quietly into

Rachel's room. The baby lay wide awake in her crib, and she was reaching for the mobile, then for the netting on the bedside, then for the mobile again. Bill thought she might be gauging distances. "Planning your escape, are you?" he said.

Rachel glanced at him, then just as quickly glanced away. He wondered why she now seemed to avoid eye contact.

"Aaa," said Rachel. "A aa a aaa."

Bill nodded. According to the PERT diagram he had made of infant development, babies began breaking their sounds into "syllable-like" intervals in imitation of the voices they heard around them. But she had already been doing so at five months, and ought to have started adding consonants by now. If the truth be told, he was waiting for her first "da-da."

Her leg was definitely twitching.

Bill returned to the living room and began absently to gather up the papers he had spread out on the coffee table.

"I'm sorry, dear," Karen said. "I thought you were done with the drawings and I folded them up."

Bill was still thinking about Rachel's actions. He stuffed the hard copies into a drawing folder and zipped it up. "Don't worry," he said. "I've looked at them often enough I don't need to look at them anymore."

Karen found Rachel sitting up in her crib and instead of napping she was dropping toys over the safety rail. One of the things babies do, their pediatrician told them, was to throw toys. Early on, something in the brain completes itself, and the baby connects the rattling sound she hears with the rattle she sees in her hand. After that they try to learn what kind of sounds everything makes. They also try to put them in their mouths, not only to learn the taste, but to learn the texture. The lips are the most sensitive organ of touch.

Most of the toys were already on the floor, and Karen sighed and bent to pick them up. "You shouldn't throw your toys on the floor," she told Rachel, even though she knew the baby ought to do precisely that. "You make Mommy pick them up."

Rachel shot her a glance that almost seemed to say, *well that's what mommies are for!* Then she took Lambie Pie, a plush animal nearly as big as she was and pushed it to the rail. In her other hand she had a lightweight rubber ducky squeeze toy. She pushed both of them over at the same time and watched them fall. Her left hand twitched, thumb, forefinger, middle finger. When the toys hit the floor, she laughed and bounced, beating both arms in tempo.

Karen sighed. "You did that on purpose, didn't you? To give Mommy more work."

Rachel said, "Fah seh!" She followed this with a raspberry sound. At least she was finally using consonants.

Rachel had discovered how to splash the water in her bath. Karen had placed her in her Baby's Own Tub and Rachel stared as if hypnotized at the water line as it rose. When Karen raised the washcloth, Rachel fussed and shook her head. Since she was usually cooperative in her bathing, Karen hesitated, wondering if something were wrong. Rachel placed her hand on the surface and kept it there in perfect stillness, as if entranced by the winking water. Then she pushed her hand slowly underwater. She repeated this several times with a look of such intensity that Karen almost laughed. The last time, Rachel smacked the water hard with her palm, splashing herself and Karen.

This was evidently very funny. But then her left arm and leg began to spasm uncontrollably and the baby began to cry.

"The tremors have been getting worse," Karen told Jessica one day when they had been invited to dinner with the Singers. SingerLabs was flourishing, and so the Singer house was one of the better homes in the neighborhood. The computer guru around the other side of the ring road might have a better one, but he never had guests in, so the matter was indeterminate.

It was one of those long, balmy summer days when the sun lingered and the clouds were golden brush-strokes high in a deep blue sky. After the meal, the four of them retired to the deck with drinks and contemplated the sunset over the small woodland behind the house. During the high summer, when the trees were fully clothed, it was hard to make out the backs of the houses on the other side and one could pretend that the woods ran primeval to the river.

Jessica Burton-Peeler frowned and asked about the tremors, and Karen told them of the toy-tossing, the water splashing, the leg jerks, and all the rest. Charlie smiled at the account of Rachel's concern with the rising water in her tub and said, "Did she cry 'Eureka!'?" But the Bruscos didn't get it and a sharp glance from Jessie forestalled any explanation.

"Mom came over to watch her," Karen said, "and she said she's noticed it, too. I think it's something neurological."

Bill shook his head and paused with his drink raised. "I think someone at the Design Center screwed up."

147

Charlie Singer pursed his lips. "Maybe not," he said, then he left the deck and went into the house to fetch a notebook from his office. When he returned, he asked Bill, "Did your doctor…"

"Dr. deNangle."

"Did Dr. deNangle explain the complexity of the gene-to-trait relationship?"

"Everyone knows it's complicated stuff."

"Hm. Well, there's different sorts of complication. Disorganized complexity is marked by large numbers of variables whose effects can't be understood analytically, only statistically. Organized *simplicity*, on the other hand, has few variables tied together in deterministic relationships. In between, we have organized complexity. In the early stages of design, the relationships can be understood analytically, although there may be strong variables and weak variables; but in later phases unanticipated factors—environmental factors, for example—come into play, what we call noise factors, and again we're faced with random fluctuations and stochastic processes. With me so far?"

Bill nodded with more certainty than he felt.

"Now genetics, like quantum mechanics, is a case of organized complexity. There are analytical equations—but with stochastic outcomes. Take a look at this…" He opened the notebook.

	X_1	X_2	X_3	X_4	X_5	X_6	X_7	X_8
Y_1	b_{11}	0	b_{13}	b_{14}	0	0	b_{17}	b_{18}
Y_2	0	b_{22}	b_{23}	0	0	b_{26}	b_{27}	b_{28}
Y_3	0	0	b_{33}	b_{34}	b_{35}	b_{36}	b_{37}	b_{38}
Y_4	0	0	b_{43}	0	0	0	b_{47}	b_{48}

"…This here puppy is a second-level indenture for a nanomachine we're building at the plant. It's supposed to be a transmission pump for metering…Well, that doesn't matter. It's got itself four functional requirements—the Ys—and each is affected by one or more of eight design parameters—the Xs. The b coefficients indicate the amount by which *this* X affects *that* Y."

Bill nodded. "Yes, I can see that, but what has it got to do with Rachel?"

"Most traits are affected by many genes," Charlie said, "and most genes affect many traits. That's why the genome is like a mobile. Jiggle one part, and other parts wiggle; sometimes in ways you don't expect." He pointed to the matrix. "Think of the Ys as traits and the Xs as genes. Now suppose you wanted to optimize Y_1. Maybe that's nose length. Then you would have to work on the genes X_1, X_3, X_4, X_7, and X_8. Now, I can jigger X_1 wherever I want, and it only affects nose length. But when I target X_4, it'll also affect Y_3. And targeting X_3, X_7, and X_8 will impact *all* the other Ys. You see? This design is what we call 'coupled.' Like a faucet where you have a hot and a cold knob to control both the volume *and* the temperature of the water. Now, this is a simple nanomachine, and only the second indenture of the design. A human will have thousands of Ys and thousands of Xs and Lord-knows-how-many indentures. You had the design center optimize a set of Ys—let's say Y_1, Y_2, and Y_3—that added up to physical beauty. To do that, they had to target this set of Xs. But evidently, one or more of those Xs had an effect on Y_4, on Rachel's nervous system; and as those genes have realized during her somatic development, they've given her the twitchies."

Bill sighed and said, "I wish *you* had explained this to me, and not Dr. deNangle." But Karen began to weep quietly, and Jessie kicked Charlie's ankle under the patio table and gave him the Look.

Charlie understood and clapped his mouth shut. He always leapt to factual explanations when emotional comfort was needed. So he did not add that the matter became even more uncertain when you realized that in a complex organism like a human being most of the matrix entries contained question marks.

It took three tries for Karen to see the specialist. First, their primary caregiver made an error entering the neurologist's federal registration number; then they had to go back to the Choice Center to get the certified genetic profile; and only then were they properly scheduled. By that time, Rachel was using recognizable words like dada and mama and wawa in proper context, and the periodic spasms on her left side were an almost daily occurrence.

In some indefinable sense, Rachel seemed aware of this; for she scowled mightily whenever her leg or arm began to jerk; and once Karen saw her hit herself in the leg, saying "nono," as if the leg were a disobedient toy.

The pediatric neurologist looked tired. The appointment was late in the day and the waiting room had been crowded. Dr. Powell—please call me Harriet—had studied carefully the lab results from Dr. Khan, the pediatrician, and the genetic tables from Dr. deNangle, and had made a very thorough examination of Rachel herself.

"Who was Stephen Hawking?" asked Karen when Dr. Powell had tried to explain.

"He was a famous scientist who had a condition similar to Rachel's."

Something in the smug announcement irritated Karen. "Why should I care if someone else had the same problem?"

"Not 'problem,' but 'condition.' A problem is what you make it. Hawking was a brilliant man and accomplished great things in physics."

"Why do you think that would comfort me?" Bill, sitting silently beside her, placed a hand on her arm, but she shrugged it off.

"Because," said the doctor—and only a touch of her weariness seeped through her words, "because it is a manageable condition. So is the autism."

"Autism? What do you mean 'manageable'? Autism, too?" There was glass in Karen's voice. She had not broken yet, but she might.

"The two are not unrelated," the doctor told her in that evasive, backward-turning way that scientists had. "Mild autism is often associated with genius. The ability to *focus*, to dwell unreservedly in that interior world has led to great insight in mathematics, science, the arts..."

"You mean 'idiot savants'..."

The doctor frowned and pursed her lips. "We don't like that term."

"I don't like what the term means."

Bill, that useless lump, finally spoke. He said only, "Karen..." But at least he had said something.

"There are programs," the doctor assured them. "You may even be eligible for state funding, since cases like this have been increasing in the past few years. With the help of therapists, there is better than a fifty percent probability that Rachel could be almost like other children, with only the odd quirk and a bit of absentmindedness."

"Manageable...," Karen said through numbed lips.

"What doctor Powell means...," said Bill.

"Is that she can't be *cured! I know what* manageable *means, Bill!* I don't think you do. And neither does she."

The doctor did not react to the verbal slap, and it occurred to Karen that Dr. Powell had heard such things unnumbered times before. She handed Karen a sheaf of documents that had to be completed to qualify for the government money, but when Karen rose without taking them she handed them to Bill instead.

"Thank you, doctor," he said.

"Call me Harriet."

Karen had to think things over, to come to terms, and she could not do that surrounded by noise. Rachel was tired and cranky from the drive to see the specialist; and all Bill could do was yammer foolishly about the support program, the federal money, and the ten-hours-a-day therapy. Karen left the baby with him and took a long walk around the neighborhood.

Two roads fishhooked into one another, forming a rough oval and enfolding in their handshake a woodland surrounded by private property. Technically, the woods were public land, part of the Green Acres program, and there was actually an easement along the creek where it ventured out of its culvert to wind through the north quarter of the woods. But as a practical matter it was almost like a private reserve. Karen caught glimpses of the trees and bushes between the houses she passed. The leaves were just turning russet and orange.

When she was three-quarters around the oval and approaching the culvert, the door flew open on one of the houses and a woman came out with a small boy in tow. Karen did not know her neighbors on this side of the woods, so she delivered an anonymous hello. For answer she received a suspicious glance. A pedestrian? Here? And the woman stepped between Karen and the boy. "Hello," she allowed. Then, to the boy: "Get in the car, Ethan. Vincent! Are you coming?"

A dark-haired, scaled-down model of a man emerged from the house. He was half a head shorter than the woman, as if his last adolescent growth spurt had never taken place. A walking optical illusion, he seemed a little farther away than he actually was. He noticed Karen and nodded in a cool, but friendly fashion.

"I'm from around the other side, on Edward Road," Karen explained. "I've been taking a walk." She had not wanted to explain anything; she had wanted only to be alone with her thoughts. "Have a nice day."

She started to move on, but at that moment little Ethan, who had been standing stock still, stepped for the car door and bumped into it, whereupon he froze once more. That was when Karen remembered. "Oh! This is the house where those demonstrators were making all the noise a few years ago. That was just before we moved in, but the realtor was worried about what it would do to property prices."

"What it would do to his commission, you mean," said the little man. He wasn't small enough to be a midget, but Karen found it hard not to stare at him.

"Your boy," Karen said, but then stopped unsure of how to continue. The boy in question had closed his eyes and reached out to grasp the handle of the door, which he did with no trouble. He opened it and it bumped him a little so that he staggered. The woman quickly gathered him up and lifted him into the back seat to buckle him securely in place.

The woman rose from her task and favored Karen with a hostile look. "What about him?"

"Well, my daughter…" Now it was Karen's turn to hesitate. But then a moment later she was pouring out all her frustrations on two perfect strangers. They listened, first with surprise, then with close attention, finally with sympathy.

"My Ethan's problem is different," said the woman, who finally introduced herself as Alma. "He's retarded. Did you know that what you see and what you hear and what you touch reaches the brain at different times? It's true. But something in our brain coordinates all our senses and knits them together. Ethan's time lags are too long and he can't coordinate them properly. So he is always seeing and hearing something a few moments in the past; and what he hears and what he sees are not always the same thing. I've been trying to teach him to close his eyes before he tries to do anything. That 'clears the buffer' for a short while. Until his senses get all out of synch again."

Karen made sympathetic sounds. "Does it ever get to you? Are there ever times when you think you can't do it anymore?"

But Alma shook her head. "Ethan is my life." Ethan, in the back seat, cried out something blurred and uncertain, like a deaf boy. Karen shuddered and knew that Alma was lying, perhaps most of all to herself.

"It's the pollution," Vincent said firmly. "Electric power lines, fracking, you name it. That's why we see more and more birth defects."

Karen made a wan smile. "Not in my case. It seems to be a design problem, what the genetic engineers call 'functional coupling.'"

Alma's smile froze and Vincent pursed his lips. "It's a designer baby?" Karen nodded and Vincent said, "Then you brought it on yourself."

When Karen went to see Dr. deNangle she was surprised to learn that he already knew about the baby's neurological problems. But all practitioners and specialists were required by law in the case of designed babies to inform the originating Design Center of any quality control issues. A few years earlier, Dr. deNangle reminded her, there had been a big recall.

"And that's the good news," he told her. "Rachel is still under warranty. You can still bring her in for non-conforming material control." He smiled as the babies in the holograms on his wall smiled: beautiful and broad. He even resembled them somewhat, with his chubby cheeks and soft features.

"I don't know about that," Karen said. "I mean, the defect has nothing to do with the design. We asked for a beautiful child, and that's what we got. The neurological problems…"

"…are probably a side-effect of the genetic adjustments we made, so they'd be covered. Don't worry, the warranty replacement costs are backed with the full faith and credit of the United States Government. In a way, it's even good news. We can take samples from Rachel and study them and learn what went wrong. That way, the next rev level will be an improvement."

Karen recalled the explanation that Charlie Singer had given Bill: how one gene might affect multiple functions, depending on a complex interplay of timing, environmental cues, and neighboring genes. She hadn't understood everything Charlie and Bill had talked about, but as a technical writer she could grasp the essentials of any topic.

"I don't know," she told the baby designer. "I don't think I can go through this a second time."

"I understand how you feel just now; but in another year or two, you may be ready for another try. We keep learning, not only from Rachel, but from others like her. They teach us so much."

Karen rose, gathered her purse. "I'll talk to Bill about it."

That evening she watched Rachel play by herself in her perfectly sealed-off world. She might as well have been on another planet for all the attention she paid to others, and Karen remembered that, even while nursing, the baby had seemed abstracted.

When she put Rachel down for the night and turned off the light, Rachel began to cry and fuss. But when Karen returned and flipped the light on, she quieted immediately. Then she stuck her hand out—her right hand—and pointed to the light switch. Karen sighed and flipped it off again. In the darkness, Rachel laughed.

The next day, Rachel sat up in the living room and stared at the light switch by the kitchen door. She fussed and pointed and fussed some more, until Karen relented and flipped it, turning on the pole lamp. That kept Rachel amused while Karen cut the vegetables for dinner. Her head swiveled back and forth from the lamp to the switch, from the switch to the lamp. Then something about the lamp caught her eye and she scrootched her face in ferocious concentration.

That used to amuse Karen because she looked so terribly serious when she did it. But now she saw that it was only another symptom of that merciless focus that some autistics often had.

Rachel's attention came to rest on the lamp cord. She looked back at the switch, scanned the wall to the socket, then the cord to the lamp.

She did this several times—repetitiveness being another symptom of autism—and then, unexpectedly and unexpectedly fast, she crawled across the carpet toward the lamp cord.

Karen dropped the celery and the chopping knife and ran across the room and scooped up Rachel before she could grab the cord. "No, no, no!" she cried. "You could hurt yourself!"

But Rachel paid her not the least attention. She strained in Karen's arms, still trying to get to the lamp cord. It was as if her mother were nothing more than an inanimate obstacle keeping her from reaching her goal. "No, Rachel!" she cried, although the child showed no reaction to her name. "You could get electrocuted and die."

And the hateful thought arose unbidden that that might really be best for everyone.

Bill laid his fork down on the plate so carefully that no sound could be heard. He stared across the table at Karen. "What do you mean 'we should send her back'?"

Karen would not look at him but fiddled with the spaghetti with her fork, twisting it around and around. "She's still under warranty. Two years, they said. We can send her back for any reason related to the design…"

"Kill her."

Karen shook her head violently. "No, no, no. We just sign some papers saying that this is the best thing for her. Then the hospital takes her and… She just goes to sleep. Really, Bill, it's the merciful thing to do. She would never have had an adequate quality of life. She would never have been normal. And how could I have gotten my work done if I were supervising therapy ten hours a day, like they said. For at least five years."

"I would help…"

"Bill, you're on the road half the time. How much help would you be?" Most of her spaghetti was wound up on her fork by then. She lifted the fork and it slid off onto the plate. Karen blinked in surprise, then began winding the spaghetti up again. "Promise me you'll think about it, at least."

Doctor deNangle was all assurance. He met them in a different office, in the other wing of the hospital. It was an altogether more spartan room. The walls sported diplomas, but no smiling babies. There was an antiseptic smell to the air. Dr. deNangle sat across the desk from them with his hands clasped into a ball atop it.

"Ethical progress always meets with resistance," he explained. "Alarmists like to go on about a so-called 'slippery slope,' but, people are resilient

154

and once the step is taken, they get used to it. Now it is the law of the land. The world didn't come to an end."

Bill opened his mouth to say that at least one world would come to an end, but before he could speak, the doctor explained how the body parts could be used to save the lives of other children, children who would have a more fulfilling life than Rachel could ever have had. "It would maximize total human happiness, and give her life meaning," he insisted. "She would have lived for a purpose."

Bill saw the pain in Karen's eyes, and knew that pain would only worsen. Trying to care for an autistic child would suck the life out of her, leaving only a husk of the vivacious woman he had married. He thought the baby was smarter than she seemed, but he could not deny that she had withdrawn into a self-contained world of her own.

Karen was right. His job did take him out of town, out of state, sometimes even out of country for days or weeks at a time. There was a pending project in Turkey that might last six months, continuous residence there. All the labor would fall on Karen, and that was not really fair. He really could not ask that of her.

Leaving the doctor's office, Bill had still not said anything. Ultimately, on the forms the doctor had given them to fill out, his signature was not strictly required. But it would delay matters—there would be a review board—and it would drive a wedge between Karen and him that might not be removed. Silently, he reached out and took her hand, and their fingers intertwined.

At the door, after a tense, uncomfortable visit, as Karen and Bill were leaving, Sarah's stone-tight face crumbled and she told Karen that she would never speak to her again. "It's horrible what you are doing. Horrible!"

Karen broke into tears. "You can't think I *want* to do it! But it's the best thing for all of us." Bill gave his mother-in-law a disapproving glare. It really wasn't any of her business. There was no place on the Warranty Return forms for a grandmother's signature.

Andrew was not happy, either. He put his arm around his wife and guided her back inside the house; then he returned to the door. "It was a shock to her," he told Karen and Bill. "She'll get over it. You just have to give her time."

Karen was crying too hard to answer, but Bill gave his father-in-law a nod. Sarah and Karen were mother and daughter, after all. Sarah would not cut her off completely.

Later, Andrew went to his wife, who sat in the bedroom with a photograph of Rachel. Like Karen, she was crying unreservedly, and Andrew thought it was for much the same reason. It was a hard decision to make, but he knew Karen had not made the decision lightly. It had to have been hard for her, as well. It had to have been hard to let go.

He told Sarah what he had told their daughter. "Honey, you'll get over it," he said as he sat down beside her. "We have other grandchildren. Johnny's two boys, and Betty's girl. And Karen and Bill can have another baby, one who doesn't have all those neurological disorders."

"It's just so awful…"

"They're not doing anything criminal. It's legal. And more and more people are doing it. People won't accept inferior work anymore. Remember Joanna and Harry Douthet? Their boy was almost two years old, and that's the limit under the law."

Sarah raised to him red-hot eyes. "Don't tell me you agree with them! Please don't tell me that!"

Andrew shook his head. "No. No, I don't. But it's their baby. We can't impose our opinions on them. And you know, you know that, that Rachel would never have had a full life. Maybe Karen was right when she said this was the best decision for their daughter."

But Sarah would not be consoled and after a while Andrew gave up and left her to cry alone.

Jessie was horrified when they told her. They had been having drinks on the Singers' patio deck, enjoying the brisk autumn air. A sense of peace and contentment had settled over Karen since she had made her decision, and she had been certain that Jessie would share her happiness—or at least her relief.

But Charlie Singer settled back into his great stone face, and stared at her and Bill as if they had become parents manqué, and Jessica Burton-Peeler seemed genuinely angry. "You can't do that," she said. "Rachel is your baby. She's been part of your family for, what, eight months. Part of your life."

But Karen was thinking that Rachel would have become not only a part of her life, but the whole of it. A parasite eating up every hope and dream she had ever had. "She wasn't really a part of the family," she told their friends. "She didn't connect to anyone. She didn't relate. Her autism would probably have gotten worse. It would have been cruel to force her to live like that. It wasn't a life worth living."

"*Lebensunwertes Leben*," said Charlie, breaking silence and the great stone face.

Bill scowled at him. "What does that mean?"

Charlie shook his head as if to clear it. "Just a term they once used, the last time they looked for the superman. Quality of life...And God help you if you fall below the lower tolerance limit."

"You're geneticists, both of you," Karen said. "I thought you'd understand."

Jessie's mouth flattened into a line; but she managed to say, "Maybe that's the point. We do. Karen, you can't just up and kill her!"

And who was this *outsider* telling her what she could and couldn't do. "We won't be killing her," Karen explained. "It's all done in a hospital. And, and Dr. deNangle agrees with us."

"Well," said Charlie, "good for him."

It was a short walk home, but it seemed longer. Evening fell earlier this time of year, but the streetlamps lighted their way. "That Charlie is such a prig," Bill ventured when they had rounded the bend onto the Edward Road section of the circle and were out of earshot of the Singer home. "I never thought he would be one of them."

"Isn't the Center named for him? That's why I thought he would..."

Bill shook his head, took Karen by the elbow so they could walk more closely together. "Different Singers. No relation."

"And Jessie...The way she looked at me."

"She can't stop us. That's against the law. It's our choice."

Karen wasn't really listening. "I don't think I could go over there again. For dinner, I mean, or drinks."

Bill glanced behind toward the curve in the road. "I don't think they'll be asking."

It was a wind-whipped autumn day when Karen Brusco took back her perfect baby. Red and yellow lurked among the bushes, stained the sumac and hazel, and spotted the maples with rust. Cyclones of fallen leaves tumbled and swirled in the air, and Karen responded with her own sigh of regret.

It wasn't as bad as she had feared. The protesters had been kept by law across the street, and the Center had cleverly made the entrance common to the rest of the hospital so that they would not know why any particular person was entering. There had been a celebrated incident several years ago when the protesters had shouted at a woman taking her baby in for a leukemia treatment, thinking that she was exercising her rights under the Quality of Life law. That had been enough for the courts to enjoin silence on all protesters.

Dr. deNangle was waiting for them in the lobby, and led them not to the right, to the Baby Design Center, but to the left, down a long hallway to a cheerful and colorfully appointed waiting room. "You'll see," he told them as he held the door for them. "We learn a lot from these cases, and next time things will work out better. Every year we learn more about which genes to alter to get the results we want. Don't let this discourage you. Sometimes things just don't work out; but you can try again. This," he said, waving about, "is the Departure Lounge. You can say goodbye to Rachel here. A nurse will be with you shortly."

He cautioned them that the next couple were scheduled at the quarter hour and it was hospital policy not to have multiple clients in the room at the same time. Then he left through a set of swinging doors and they heard him very briefly call out to someone with a number before the doors swung shut and enclosed them in silence.

Karen did not understand how she was supposed to say goodbye to something that paid no attention, that would not even look at her. And indeed, no sooner had she set Rachel on the carpet than the child crawled off to a pile of toys that were kept in the room. Patiently, she began sorting them, placing them in rows, aligning them carefully, but in no discernable order. A ball, some blocks, a plastic car, a plush cat,…

Bill said, "Well, good-bye, Rachel," with a sort of awkward self-consciousness.

Rachel waved an arm. "Ba-ba," she said, and Karen almost believed she had said "bye-bye," except she continued to jerk the arm and repeat "ba-ba-ba-ba" until Bill reached down and picked her up. Then she stretched her arms out toward the toys that she had been setting in rows, crying "na da! na da!" over and over.

It was a relief when the nurse came out through the same set of swinging doors. She had a flatscreen in her hands and looked up from it. "Karen Brusco?"

Karen jerked her head up and down in small motions, but did not speak up.

"I'm sorry, Ms. Brusco, but you'll have to speak aloud for the record. And I'll need to see some identification to make sure you have the rights to return this baby."

"Yes," said Karen. "Yes, I'm Karen Brusco," and she pulled out a Federal Identity Card from her purse.

The nurse turned to Bill, and he seemed about to affirm his own identity, but the nurse instead indicated the baby in his arms.

"And is this Rachel Brusco?"

"Yes," said Karen; and Bill, in order to register his presence, also said, "Yes."

"Could you remove her shoes, please? I need to compare her footprints with those made at birth." She looked up. "It's procedure. We wouldn't want to process the wrong baby."

They did so, and the nurse placed the bare feet against the scanner on her flat screen. While she was doing so, she said to Karen, "I know how hard this is for you. Believe me, I know. This is the worst day of your life, isn't it? It was for me. No, go ahead, dear. It's okay to cry. Lots of mothers do. It's part of the grieving process. Sometimes things just don't work out the way we hoped."

But what Karen felt then was not sorrow, so much as a vast relief. The nurse was right. She had done the right thing for everyone—for herself, for Bill, and even for poor Rachel, who would never have been truly happy.

The nurse took the baby from her arms and Karen watched her as she passed through the doors to the part of the hospital where babies were put to sleep.

It was a long time afterward, but eventually Sarah began to speak to her daughter again. But it wasn't the same; and it was never the same ever again. Sarah remained unconvinced. She remembered how little Rachel had stared solemnly and intently at things, almost as if she were studying them. She had never laughed much, but surely gravity was not a capital offense.

There had been a picture of Rachel on her dresser, the one that had been taken shortly after Bill and Karen had brought her home, and before the neurological problems had surfaced. The baby had such a smile on her face.

At Andrew's urging, Sarah put the photo away in a drawer. But every now and then, when no one else was around, she opened the drawer, and looked at the picture, and remembered Rachel.

AFTERWORD TO "HOPEFUL MONSTERS"

This is one of the new stories; and the title admits of multiple readings, not all of them comfortable. The search for the superman, now called "transhumanism," is fraught with peril, not least in that to proceed from the present state A to the future state C, we often must pass through the intermediate state B. And B can be very messy.

The skeleton of the story was suggested to me by a scenario in "A Curious Encounter with a Philosopher from Nowhere" by Fr. Richard John Neuhaus (*First Things* v.120, February 2002) in which he reflected upon his debate with Peter Singer. Singer was then an advocate of post-birth euthanasia for lives unworthy of life, and Fr. Neuhaus mused on what things might be like if it became normal. The scenario is used with the earlier permission of the late Fr. Neuhaus and the later concurrence of George Weigel, executor of his estate.

The other element—and what makes it a *science* fiction story—was suggested by a chapter in Mary Midgley's book *Evolution as a Religion* (Routledge Classics, 2002), in which she discusses the problems inherent in genetic engineering and the search for the superman; viz., on which children will we experiment? And what sort of people conduct such experiments?

The difficulties of achieving design intent with multiply-coupled design parameters came up while developing course materials for teaching a seminar in *Design for Six Sigma*. For those brave enough, reference *Design for Six Sigma*, by Kai Yang and Basem El-Haik, specifically their Chapter 8 on "Axiomatic Design."

The time setting for the story is later than both the preceding stories, as Singer and Peeler have become SingerLabs and are already major players in the biotech/nanotech fields. A minor touch: Rachel's pediatrician, Dr. Khan, was Ethan's pediatrician in "Captive Dreams" and the on-call doctor for the nursing home in "Melodies of the Heart." There is also an

160

incidental mention of "the computer guru around the other side of the ring road…"

These three stories all involve children and families, so Nancy Kress' GoH speech at that long-ago Balticon must have made an impression.

PLACES WHERE THE ROADS DON'T GO

Jared Holtzmann and Kyle Buskirk met in college and became from the start fast friends. In part, this was quite literal, for they were both track stars who had set State records in their respective high schools—Kyle in the 100-meter dash and Jared in the 5000-meter run. Kyle used to joke that he could win fifty races to every one of Jared's, and Jared would counter that Kyle was always rushing into things.

But even off the track they found a lot in common. They both liked to hoist a cold one at the Avalanche after school. They both enjoyed the threedies, crude as they were in those days. They both had the same taste in women, which led to their one serious quarrel in college.

Jared was short and dark, and Kyle was tall and fair. They differed on any number of topics, and many were the debates that made short the night—first in the dorm; later in the commune, which is where I met them and became their referee. In three of four pro sports, they rooted for different teams.

But they did not insist on mutual agreement in all matters. If a friendship cannot withstand a difference of opinion, it is not a friendship at all.

Kyle majored in computer science, which is the 100-meter dash of contemporary technology, while Jared majored in philosophy, surely a marathon among human endeavors. Kyle used to twig Jared about entering a field of no practical use, but Jared told him that while good computer science might stop our machines from making mistakes, good philosophy might stop people from making them.

Then came graduation, and they went their separate ways—Jared to graduate school and Kyle to his parents' garage, where he set up a software company in the usual fashion. They promised to stay in touch, and for the most part they did.

Later, one of them decided to live forever.

TURISTS

The European Philosophical Association held its meeting in Vienna one summer, ten years after graduation, and Jared was a featured speaker. Even at that point in his career, it was inconceivable to hold such a conference and not invite the *enfant terrible* of metaphysics. And it so happened that there was enough overlap between analytical philosophy and mathematical logic that I had been invited to speak. A few texts and tweets discovered that Kyle was in Leipzig that week on business, and a few more arranged a get-together for the three of us. Kyle took the Bullet to Vienna and then a cab to the University and was waiting for us in the *Stadtpark* outside the campus when the conference broke up.

Jared had made reservations at the Palmenhaus, and it was such a brilliant afternoon that we walked to the Burggarten from the University. That section of the Ring features brightly flowered parks, outsized statues of half-forgotten heroes, and immense buildings in the ponderous Hapsburg style. Amidst these great stone giants, the Butterfly House was a glittering confection of iron and glass. We strolled down the barrel-vaulted greenhouse, through a rain forest, under waterfalls, past hollow trees, surrounded all the while by a kaleidoscope of tropical butterflies. The Palmenhaus itself had been at one time the Imperial-and-Royal orangery, and the long summer day flowed through the glass walls and ceiling and coated everything in the afternoon light.

Talk ran high. We hashed over Old College Days and brought one another up to speed on life since then. That was mostly for my benefit. Kyle and Jared had stayed in touch, and I was the third man in a duet.

Kyle told me about his latest app; Jared tried to explain something or other metaphysical; and I learned that his wife, Gladdys, was even then roaming the Kärtner Strasse, credit card in hand, and would join us in time for after-dinner drinks.

"Which reminds me," Kyle said to me. "How's your sister?"

I should explain that my sister Maddy had been the source of that one true quarrel the two friends had shared in college; and Kyle's question was a none-too-subtle reminder to Jared that Gladdys had been his second choice.

Jared ignored the jibe and asked about my paper at the conference, so I explained as much about paired adjoint functors as dinner conversation could handle. One map runs from problem to solution and the other from solution to problem. The solving function finds the best solution to a given problem, and the posing function finds the biggest problem that a given solution solves. So if a set of things can be described by a collection of properties, then by Stone-Čech compactification, a finite collection will suffice, and that meant you could test for properties in a finite time.

Kyle sat with his hands pressed together as if in prayer, tapping his teeth with them. Then he pulled a card from his wallet and handed it to me. "Get in touch with me later, Mac. I'd like you to go over that with some of my people, both barrels. I don't know that it can solve my problem, but I trust my intuitions."

Dessert had arrived by then. "What problem is that?" Jared asked over a forkful of Malakoff dumpling.

Kyle grimaced. "Oh, reason I was in Leipzig. I tried to hold a meeting with a client over the Net using a simulacrum, but he twigged to the gig and I had to fly over personally to smooth feathers."

"I can see where he might be ruffled," said Jared. "You disrespected him, sending a sim to do a man's job."

Kyle flipped a hand. "Yeah, so I'm telling him now it was a marketing gimmick for our next-gen simulations. It did take him fifteen minutes before he figured it out."

I cut a slice of Alsatian munster off the cheese board and ate it with a soda cracker. "You mean the Turing test? Fifteen minutes to realize he's talking to a machine? Not bad."

"Yeah, but he shouldn't have realized it at all. *My* problem—aside from selling him a new simulator app for his auto assembly design team—is to figure out how he figured it out. I mean, the in-house alpha tests were almost perfect. So why the fail on the first beta?"

Jared smiled briefly over his dessert. "I can tell you why."

Kyle was drinking tawny port and savored it before setting the snifter down. "Okay. This ought to be good. I've had people going over the architecture, the output screens, the response matrices…And you know *philosophically* why the alphas worked and the beta failed."

"Well, yes," said Jared. "Your staff thought the sim was acting human because…that's the way *they* act."

I couldn't help the laugh, and Kyle gave me an unhappy glance. "You never did have a great sense of humor, Mac."

Jared was very pleased with his jest, and wiped his lips with his napkin.

But as he lifted his port he grew more serious. "It's human nature, Kyle. No utterance is self-explaining. The listener always hears things through the filter of his own preconceptions. You and your internal testers *expected* the simulation to work, so you 'heard' the simulated responses as human-like. Your customer in Leipzig had no such expectations, and something struck him as false."

"Yeah, but what?" Kyle leaned forward and put both hands on the table. He said, pronouncing each word carefully, "The cat sat on the mat."

Jared blinked. "What?"

"You said the listener always brings his own expectations to the—what'd you say?—the utterance. So what do you get out of *that* utterance. 'The cat sat on the mat.' Go ahead." He sat back and crossed his arms.

Jared frowned for a moment, then looked to the glass ceiling of the restaurant and mused: "Perhaps it was for counterfeiting…"

Now it was Kyle's turn. "*What?*"

"The mat," said Jared. "Mats are plates used in flexographic printing. But why would the dude hide them and not give them up…?"

"The dude?"

"Yes, the 'cat.' Don't hear that slang much since the 70s, except among jazzmen, so maybe he was a musician in a jazz band, or an old hippie. But what sort of flexible printing plates would you 'sit on' for someone?"

"Counterfeit plates," said Kyle slowly.

"Well, that was just a guess. But you see my point? The meaning of a text depends on the *con*-text, and that includes the listener's expectations. Among hippies, 'cat' meant one thing; among boatmen, it would mean the tackle used to hoist an anchor to the cathead."

Kyle picked up his glass and swirled the port around. Then he sighed and drank. "Jared, I hate to say this, but…You may be onto something." He set the snifter down and fell silent as his gaze lit on a small white butterfly that had escaped the Butterfly House. Then, he leaned across the table, taking us into his confidence.

"I'm going to do it, guys. I'm going to create the first artificial intelligence."

Jared grinned. "I'm still looking for the natural kind."

But Kyle was in earnest. "Don't laugh, Jared. Children will study about me in their schoolbooks."

"A helluva thing to do to the poor kids," I suggested.

Jared pursed his lips and looked distant. "I don't know. The airlines use flight simulators and you can get inside one and it's just like piloting a 787 from New York to LA; but with one crucial difference."

"What's that?" Kyle asked.

"When you get out of the simulator, you won't actually be in LA."

Kyle thought for a while, finished his port, then leaned forward again. "Tell you what. Why don't you come out and see me in St. Louis. You too, Mac. We'll do a Turing Test on my best sim, and you can tell me what strikes you as false."

That was how it all started. It seemed innocent enough at the time.

We had just agreed on a date when Gladdys found our table. "Hello, boys," she said and laid a stack of packages beside the fourth chair. "You can run, but you can't hide." She gave Jared a peck on the cheek and turned to me with that look of vague recognition that announced that she knew she knew me but could not recall my name.

"Mac," I said. "John MacKenzie. The math whiz," I added.

"Oh! Yes." She pointed a finger at me. "Maddy's brother. How are you?" But she did not wait for an answer before turning to Kyle, who had risen from his chair. "Kyle!" Then, in a stage whisper: "We've got to stop meeting like this. I think Jared is beginning to suspect!" Kyle grabbed her around the waist and swung her horizontal in a parody of an old romance movie.

"Don't worry about Jared," Kyle said. "I'll distract him. Jared, look, a butterfly!"

He returned Gladdys to vertical and, laughing, she took the fourth seat. The waiter swooped in and she ordered a glass of sherry. "So, where's Denise?" she asked when all was settled. "She couldn't come?"

Kyle shrugged and tossed his head. "She and I aren't together anymore."

While Gladdys expressed sympathy, Jared leaned toward me and whispered. "He was always good at the hundred-meter dash."

ORIGINAL SIM

Two weeks later we visited Kyle in St. Louis. He was still *Vaporetti* back then—vapors, cloud computing, get it?—and still pushing the eccentricity of "Silicon Prairie." I gave the seminar on adjoint functors to his staff. I think two of them understood it and one of them may have eventually made something of it.

Kyle wanted to apply the theorem to the frame problem. After each action, the AI has to update its "inventory" of what the world is like. But how does it know which items to update? The "common sense law of inertia," also known as the "let sleeping dogs lie" strategy, is for the system to ignore all states unaffected by the action. The problem is: How many *non*-effects does an action have? Using the Harris-MacKenzie Theorem, that infinite set might be compactified in practice to a finite set, thus reducing response times.

The day after the seminar, Jared showed up and Kyle steered us into a conference room where two wide-screens perched on a boardroom table surrounded by comfortable black leather high-backed chairs. Each monitor displayed a human figure against an office cubicle backdrop. Both seemed very busy at something, but glanced out of the screen from time to time as if waiting for the session to begin.

"Behold, Adam and Bob!" Kyle announced with a sweep of his arm. "Those are code names," he added as an aside, and Jared said with mock incredulity, "No, really?"

"Why two?" I asked.

Kyle perched himself on the edge of the board table. "Simple. Since you guys already know you're here to do a Turing test, you might bring— what'd you call 'em, Jared?—'filters of your own preconceptions' to the way you perceive them. So, I decided to present you with one sim and one real dude. 'Your mission, if you decide to accept it,' is to tell me which is which."

That seemed fair enough. Jared said I could go first and Kyle asked him to go next door to the break room so he would not be influenced by my session. Jared clapped me on the shoulder as he left and said, "Go get 'em, tiger."

Kyle would not think he had a foolproof sim if the image itself was an obvious animation; and indeed both Adam and Bob seemed realistic. Adam's office had no obviously personal décor—no children's drawings, no award certificates, no vacation threedies pinned to the wall—but that proved nothing. If Adam were on staff at Vaporetti, he might not have a life.

I said Hi to Adam and he asked how I was doing, and I said fine, and things went on from there. Because the sim was a prototype designed to discuss software design needs with clients, Kyle had asked us to confine our discussions to that area and the normal chit-chat such a call might entail. That seemed fair enough. So I asked Adam about his family, and he responded that his mother was under the weather. Any kids? No, he said, and I thought that might explain the absence of cubicle art. I asked him what project he was working on and he told me and I asked him how far along he was and he said eighty-five percent by the PERT, and so it went. After ten minutes of this, I thanked him, and he said I was welcome, and I turned to Bob.

Bob's office did contain personal items: a certificate hanging on the wall behind him, a child's crayon drawing, a trophy on the bookshelf. We went through the same pleasantries and I learned that his daughter Carolyn wanted to be a dancer. Then I asked him the same project questions I had asked Adam.

When I had finished, I decided that Bob was the human because his background seemed more fleshed out and because I thought I had detected a slippage between lip movement and voice on Adam. I wrote my choice on a piece of paper and folded it.

Then it was Jared's turn. Kyle fetched him from the break room and he took the seat in front of Adam's monitor and looked into the screen camera.

And said nothing.

The silence stretched on, and I began to wonder if Jared were at a loss for the right questions to ask. But after a few minutes, he said, "Hey, how about those Cards?"

Adam frowned and said, "What do you mean?"

Jared nodded and, without saying good-bye, rolled his chair over to face Bob. He repeated the same procedure: a long silence, and a question about the local baseball team.

"They're *both* sims," Jared announced when he had finished and spun his chair around. Kyle's sour look was sufficient confirmation. I quietly slipped my own choice into my jacket pocket, hoping no one would ask to see it.

Jared said, "You thought that once I had decided one of them was a sim, I would automatically accept the other as human, and you would have your Aha! moment."

"You suspected right off."

Jared shrugged. "I suspected before I came here. I knew you would try to stack the deck. I didn't know just how."

Kyle flushed and looked away for a moment. "All right, you got me. *Mea culpa.* But what was that business sitting there like a bump?"

Jared just looked at him. After a while, Kyle said, "Well?" in a very impatient tone.

"I was waiting to see if your sim would do what you just did. Humans grow impatient. Computers simply idle."

Kyle closed his eyes and let his breath out. "Okay. You're right, as usual. We can work up some subroutines for that. Throw in some random number generators…" He did not make notes, but I thought an audio pick-up might be recording him. "I notice you didn't say 'the cat sat on the mat.' I

168

was ready for that one. But…"

"How about those Cards?" Jared chuckled. "I wondered if your sims might not be able to deal with equivocation—where a word like 'card' might have more than one sense…"

"I know what equivocation is," Kyle said with a flash of irritation.

"Based on syntax, it might have been a question about baseball or a question about poker; so your sims were cued to say they 'didn't understand the question' to resolve the ambiguity. But syntax isn't semantics, and no one living near St. Louis could be confused about which Cards I meant. Even if they didn't follow baseball, they would say something like, 'I don't follow baseball' or 'I didn't catch the game.'"

"Okay. I need better context filters for ambiguities. More fuzz in the fuzzy logic…"

Jared hesitated, then shrugged. "You can't program intellect, Kyle. As Feser explained, intellect is the ability to grasp abstract concepts—like 'man' or 'being mortal,' to put them together into complete thoughts—like 'all men are mortal,' and to reason from one thought to another—like when we infer from 'All men are mortal' and 'Socrates is a man' to 'Socrates is mortal.'"

"Computers eat logic for breakfast," Kyle responded. He looked to me as for support, but I kept out of it.

"Green is an electromagnetic wave," said Jared. "Grass is green. So grass is an electromagnetic wave. The syntax is the same, but no human would make the mistake. We would recognize that 'is' has more than one meaning. Socrates *is* a man in a different way than grass *is* green. But to a computer, it looks the same." He spread his arms, "Kyle, how is it even possible for holistic, open-ended, context-sensitive *relevance* to be captured by a set of propositional, language-like representations of the sort used in classical AI?"

But teeth showed in the patented Kyle Buskirk grin. "Look. You can do long division in your head, right? Well, so do computers. So, obviously human mental processes can be described by algorithms."

"*Some* human mental processes," Jared allowed.

Kyle ignored him. "And for each algorithm there's a Turing machine that can implement it."

"A credo of faith. The Church-Turing thesis can't be formally proven."

"Yet we've developed Boltzmann machines," Kyle said, "that can categorize, perceive visible objects, understand language…"

"Scanning and pronouncing text is not the same thing as 'understanding language.'"

"It's only a matter of time," Kyle insisted. Simulate enough brain processes and you have a brain, hence a human-like mind."

"Isn't there an upper limit on Boltzmann machines?" I asked. "The Heisenberg-Boltzmann limit. Outside my specialty, but I understand it's like the Carnot limit on heat engines."

Kyle glanced my way. "That's a technical obstacle, Mac. Something beyond Boltzmann machines wouldn't have the same limits."

Jared shrugged. "The real problem is that your system is too Platonic."

Kyle did a double-take. "Platonic…Okay. I gotta admit that is one critique I never thought to hear about an AI. What do you mean?"

"I mean your systems accept inputs passively, like wax accepting a signet ring. Your text-reading machines…You have to input the text it is supposed to pronounce."

"So what's the cure?"

Jared smiled faintly. "Aristotle. Your system needs to gather inputs actively, not receive them passively. Look. Do you see this chair?" Jared pointed to the padded boardroom chair beside him.

Kyle looked, scoffed. "Duh?"

"Right. But how? Photons are cascading into your eyeballs not only from the chair, but from the table, me, the computers, the other chairs, the wall behind me, and on and on. Yet, somehow you are privileging *these* photons and not *those* photons. You are *looking at* the chair. Everything we know comes from unintelligible energy fragments—not just photons, but sound waves, molecules—impacting against our senses like a wave on a beach. And from these fragments of meaningless sensory inputs we *construct* an understanding of the world. Humans—most animals, really—have *intention*. We seek out sensory stimulations and select among them to guide our decisions. We don't just *see*, we *look*."

"You make it sound like a baleen whale," I interjected, "seining the sensory ocean for the krill of information."

Jared laughed and slapped the table. "That's good, Mac! I'm going to steal that for my lectures."

"Well," said Kyle. "You do have a talent for putting your finger on the key points. It's the frame problem again, isn't it? How does my AI know which inputs are relevant and which it can ignore?" He stood and began pacing. "This is frustrating," he admitted. "And the Turing test is just the first step. To get the electronic computer to mimic the performance of the human computer…"

Jared shook his head. "It's not that simple."

A multitude of responses chased themselves across Kyle's face—impatience, irritation, dismissal. But then he folded his hands under his chin as he often did when he turned thoughtful. "I hadn't thought I was describing something simple."

Jared smiled. "Visit me in Princeton, and I'll show you."

THE GREAT ROOM OF CHINA

Jared and Gladdys lived in an old apartment building that had been refurbished into suites back around the turn of the century and leased to faculty members. The rooms were comfortable, with flowered wallpaper and upholstered wooden furniture. "It looks positively retro," said Kyle, after he had hung his coat in the hallway and looked around.

Jared thanked him, but I had seen Kyle's home in St. Louis, and I don't think he had meant "retro" as a compliment.

Kyle made a showy bow and kissed the back of Gladdys' hand. "Madame!" he said, and patted the kiss firmly in place. Gladdys laughed and told Kyle he could never be serious.

"I've made dinner reservations at Prospect House," Jared told us. "I'm afraid I've co-opted our own dining table for the structured experience."

"Structured experience..." I suggested.

"Yes, I'll set up a scenario, give you your instructions, and turn you loose."

The table was dark wood with lion's-paw legs and an extender in the center. It had been set up with two chairs placed across the narrow direction from each other. On the table between them was a stiff, foldable plastic screen with two horizontal slots on either side labeled IN and OUT. Jared seated Kyle on one side of the screen, and me on the other. Gladdys disappeared into the kitchen, where she busied herself making hors d'oeuvres and drinks. "I've watched him do this with his grad students," she explained.

Once we were settled, Jared said, "Now the first rule of this structured experience is..."

Kyle cried out, "First rule of Structured Experience is you *do not* talk about Structured Experience!"

Jared did not get the reference to *Fight Club*. "Well...," he said uncertainly, "yes. No talking until the debriefing. But here's the scenario. Mac, you will select cards from this white deck..." He handed me a thick pack of laminated cards, printed in red Chinese symbols. The one on top read 喂 or *wai³*. I looked at Jared curiously.

"But I only know a little..."

"I know." He hushed me, and handed me a cheat sheet along with a set of instructions. The cards had index numbers in their corners and the cheat sheet listed the translations. A second sheet was indexed by context: In the Café, On the Bus, and so forth. My only instruction was "Respond to the output as seems best to you. Record on the log sheet the card number inserted and the card number received in response.

Then he handed Kyle a tabbed tray of red cards bearing white symbols. I learned later that these were indexed in strict numerical order with no translations provided. Kyle pulled the first card from the tray to inspect it and muttered, "Searle...?" before Jared shushed him, too.

"Are we ready?" Jared asked. Kyle asked for another minute or two to arrange his cards and instructions. When he finally admitted readiness, I inserted card 001 in the slot. *Hello.*

A moment later a red card emerged from Kyle's side. *Hello.*

I was startled but Jared squeezed my shoulder and put a finger to his lips. So I shrugged and consulted the conceptual index, where I saw a group titled Lost Luggage; and since I had once misplaced a bag in Shenzhen Bao'an Airport, I decided to lead with that. I found card 250 in the pack and inserted it. *Excuse me! I think I left my suitcase here. Have you seen it?*

I could hear some fumbling around on the other side and was just about to make some comment when a red card emerged. I recognized the symbol for *I'm sorry*, and when I checked the rest of the translation it read *There is no suitcase here.*

I hunted through my deck and found four responses appropriate to Kyle's statement. I selected one: *Then my suitcase is lost! All my clothes and personal things were in it.*

Our silent conversation continued in like manner. When Jared called a halt, I had my imaginary suitcase back and Kyle had received an imaginary tip for his imaginary initiative in helping me. All's well that ends well.

"Okay," Jared said. "Time for the debrief."

I started to say, "Kyle, I didn't know you could read Chinese!" But Kyle was saying, "Searle's Chinese Room..." Then, to me, he added, "I can't."

"I only had that cram course when I went to the Shenzhen Conference, but..."

"Look, Mac, all I had was a matrix that said if I got a card with *this* number, I was supposed to give you a card with *that* number. I had no idea what was going on...Oh, shit!"

Gladdys had returned with a tray of cheese, meat slices, and crackers and some wine glasses. "About half his students have the same reaction, dear."

I was a beat and a half behind, but I got it, too. "The Turing Test is meaningless," I said. "Even if you mimic human output, you haven't necessarily captured the same algorithm the mind uses."

"Kyle," said Jared, "you carried on an intelligible, if stilted, conversation in Chinese. Did you understand what was on the cards? Did you even *know* that you were conducting a conversation? Did you have the same mental experience you have when you speak English?"

Kyle pursed his lips. "No," he admitted. "You know, it's one thing to read about Searle's Chinese Room, quite another to experience it…" He fell to introspection. "The usual rebuttal," he said after a moment, "is that the room *as a whole* is intelligent…"

But Jared only smiled. "Kyle, if *you* didn't know what the conversation was about, what makes you think the *card deck* knew?"

"Could be the analogy just doesn't hold. To fully simulate a Chinese speaker you would need millions of filing cabinets and response matrices, and responses would take so long that…"

"The principle is the same. Kyle, you were acting just like a digital computer: processing syntax according to an algorithm. But even if you capture all the syntactical rules in a super matrix you can't capture the semantic meanings."

"If the system were complex enough…," I suggested.

Jared nodded. "Complexity is necessary, but…'Methinks it is like a weasel' is just a string of marks, and *making the marks does not generate the meaning*. It's necessary but not sufficient."

Kyle began to nod. "I see what you're getting at."

By then Gladdys had led us into the parlor where she had laid out the appetizers. I followed along. "So," I said as we settled into the chairs and sofa, "mimicking human performance—the Turing Test—is the easy part. But establishing that the human and machine outputs are produced by the same process is the hard part. All this 'Chinese Room' stuff…I hate to puncture Jared's balloon; but I think there *was* a Chinese-speaking intelligence involved. *Whoever wrote the cards* and put together the response matrices had to know Chinese."

Now it was Jared's turn to appear troubled, and Gladdys laughed as she handed us our wine glasses. "Jared has a problem extending the analogy." She tapped the side of her head with her index finger. "That intelligence has to be outside the box." Then she smiled and lifted a drink in toast.

ONE FLU OVER

It was five years later, during the big epidemic, when everyone went about wearing those face-masks and getting their shots, when we all met again. Jared had contracted the flu and had fallen deathly ill. And while he was not as close to me as he was to Kyle, still he had dated my sister and we knew each other better than most.

The worst of it was over by then and the airports were open once more, so I caught a regional to Newark, rented a car, and drove down to Princeton Hospital. Traffic was light and people still tended to avoid one another. Like soldiers in the waning days of a war, those lucky enough to have escaped so far had no desire to become the last fatality. It was, sadly, the smoothest trip that anyone had ever taken down the Jersey Turnpike.

The University Medical Center stood on a side street, past an old cemetery, which struck me as bad *feng shui* for a hospital. I drove through to the parking lot and walked back to the main building. It was a chilly, blustery spring quite in keeping with the mood of the country. The information desk was enclosed within a Plexiglas shell under positive air pressure so germs would not waft into the booth. I presented my certificate of inoculation and passed through the sanitizing airlock into the main hospital. The UV lamps, air jets, and gas spray were supposed to sterilize visitors, but I thought they might be only to reassure them. It certainly cut down on the number of visitors.

I found Jared in a third-floor room originally designed for two but now holding six beds. Two were empty, which I took to be a good sign. Jared was closest to the window, with an enlightening view of the cemetery on Witherspoon Street. He seemed to be asleep, and I turned to tip-toe out; but he opened his eyes and said, "Gladdys…? Oh! Mac! You came all the way from Chicago? You didn't have to do that."

"Chicago's not exactly the far side of the moon," I told him. "You look… good."

"I look awful. But at least I don't look dead, and that's good enough. You seem fit, though. You never caught it, did you?"

I felt as if I should apologize. "The incidence rate in Chicago was way below national average. No one knows why. Random chance. Gladdys emailed me. She said you were recovering."

"She didn't catch it, either. Lucky."

"Where is she?"

"Down in the cafeteria with Kyle."

"Kyle's here, too?"

"Sure. He moved to New Jersey a year ago; lives an hour or so up north. And no, not so much as a sniffle for him, either. It's a conspiracy, I tell you." He paused and coughed into his arm. It was a dry, hacking cough and by conditioned reflex I pulled back a little from the bed. "And Maddy?" he said.

There was a small commotion by the door, where the duty nurse blocked a middle aged couple from entering. "But we're her parents," I heard the man say. The nurse told them only one visitor at a time was allowed per patient and the man deferred to the woman.

I turned back to Jared. "So, when do they let you out?"

"When the government subsidies run dry. No, that's too cynical. They're all scared that they'll release someone too soon and the epidemic will start up again, and they'll be blamed. So, they'll hang onto me a while yet."

"There was more than one epidemic, you know. Atlanta identified three different strains. That's why the preventive program didn't seem to help."

"'Screw the Flu!'—and it broke out anyway."

I shrugged. "If they hadn't done it, there would have been four."

"I suppose. I heard you developed the mathematical model for the epidemic."

"Me and a bunch of others, for all the good it did. When we identified areas where the new vaccines would do the most good—the Firebreak, we called it—we ran smack dab into a wall of congressmen horrified that we didn't regard every district as *equally* entitled to the shots. Look, they told me not to get you all agitated."

Jared chuckled. "It's you getting all agitated." We chatted for a few minutes longer. He pretended to be interested in my new paper, but was too fatigued to pull it off. Finally, he lay back and said, "Could you go down to the cafeteria and send Gladdys up here?"

"We'll talk again later."

"Sure. I'm not going anywhere."

Same old Jared. I took the elevator back down and found the cafeteria just off the lobby. Gladdys sat at a table in the corner. Kyle was holding her hand, saying something in a soothing tone. He looked over when I entered, leapt up, and pumped my hand. "Mac! Great of you to come!" Gladdys, too, rose and hugged me briefly.

"Have you seen him?" Gladdys said. "Is he awake again?"

"Yes, he asked for you."

Gladdys hesitated and Kyle put a hand on her wrist. "It's all right," he said. "The contagious phase is over or they wouldn't allow visitors at all."

"Then why all the safeguards? Will you come with me?"

Kyle shook his head. "One at a time. You know the rules."

When Gladdys had gone, Kyle sighed. He looked at me sidelong. "The razor's edge, Mac. Once you've been on it, nothing is ever quite safe again.

She and Jared live in an apartment suite here in Princeton. You've been there. Breathing the same air half the day; breathing each other's exhalations. He caught it; she didn't. The bullet missed her by this much." His thumb and forefinger calibrated the miss. "Do you blame her for being scared? Ten percent mortality for those who caught it."

"Which means ninety percent survival," I told him. "And not everyone caught it. The odds were in her favor."

Kyle gave me a look of pity. "Mac, there's more to risk than mathematics."

"Now you're sounding like Jared."

He made the vampire cross with his forefingers. "Avert the evil," he said. Then, turning serious, he picked up his disposable coffee cup. "Jared can make light as much as he wants; but he was scared, scared clean through. Ten percent may be small next to ninety; but it looks big enough when it's in your face." He drank, put the cup back down, and looked around the nearly empty cafeteria. He did not look at me when he continued. "I was scared, too."

"Jared told me you didn't even get the sniffles."

"No. For him. I was scared for him. He and I have been…" He searched for a word.

"Korpsbrüder?" I suggested.

"Whatever the hell that is."

"Jared described you that way once. It's some Heidelberg thing where students fight with sabers and give each other scars and then are bound together for life."

Kyle barked a short, sharp laugh. "Did he say that? Then I guess that's what we are. Korpsbrüder…" He tried the word out. "Friendly fights. Friendly scars. We have given each other a few…"

"Are you still with Angela?" I asked before he too could bring up Maddy. My sister and the kids had come through the epidemic, but her husband Paul had not.

"Angela…" Kyle faced me once more. "It's hard to keep a relationship going when people won't touch each other even with ten-foot poles. Maybe I'll find someone new, now that it's over." He stood and carried his cup to the mulcher and shoved it in. When he sat back down, he said, "You know what's the problem with life? Death. That's the problem with life."

I allowed as how it might well be. I decided I needed a soda and went to the vending machine. Kyle shadowed me.

"I couldn't bear to lose him…," he said. "I know. It makes me sound like he and I were…But you know we weren't. It's just…There's got to be a way around it. If we were to download our entire mind into a computer…"

I turned, puzzled by the non sequitur. "Around what?"

"Death. Around death. If we can load our minds into computers, we would never get the flu. Never die."

"Computers get viruses, too," I pointed out. "Systems crash."

"Yeah. But you can always back-up and restore. It was Jared who finally convinced me that I had the wrong approach to the sims."

We sat down again at the table and I popped my soda can. "How?"

"We were trying to simulate a human being. When was the last time you ever met a human being?"

"Is that a trick question?"

Kyle's lips broadened. "He tricked *me* with it. We were trying to program a generic human; but people are all particular. Each one of us has certain capacities, learnings, interests, hobbies, experiences that make us who we are. There is a *wholeness* to a person. That's what people were picking up on with our sim. It lacked depth."

"So you've decided to simulate a specific human being, complete with backstory…" He nodded and I said, "It sounds like science fiction."

"Everything does," Kyle said, "until it gets done."

THIS GÖDEL IS KILLING ME

Years later, historians would say that it had been the "Flash Flu" that really gave the impetus to telepresence. People grew reluctant to gather in confined spaces—like offices, airplanes, and the like. Flashmobs, even after the ban was lifted, became smaller and fewer. A great many theaters and concert halls closed. Easier—and safer—to work solo in the Cloud—which by then was being called the Grid. Other historians pointed out that the magnitude of the epidemic had been greatly exaggerated by the blogosphere, and did not justify the degree of anxiety that gripped the country. Yet, what happens in history is to a great extent inseparable from what people *think* has happened.

And so when Kyle indicated a need to consult with me, I struck a blow for personal contact and flew out from Chicago for a colloquium with his math people. Only two came in person; the rest "fibered," as we used to say. We discussed some new theory I had developed from Savage that treated decisions as mappings from the system state Y into the space of consequences Z, and used a proximity on the consequences to determine which decisions were "close" to one another.

Kyle called Jared to let him know, and our philosophical friend drove up from Princeton to spend what was supposed to be a fun weekend.

Kyle's home was also *Flapjack*, which was the name of his company *du jour*. Since graduation, he had made four fortunes and lost three. "Companies don't matter," he had explained once. "They've become commodities. I've invented the virtual company, the flash-corp. When I need the talent, I bring them together. We incorporate, finish the job, then disband, each to our own affairs."

The house sat on a half-acre lot in a township along the Northeast Corridor. Two roads entered the area and curved around and into each other so that between them they formed an irregular oval with two stems. The houses lined the inside of the oval, enclosing a woodland in the center. "The woods are sealed off from the township," Kyle told us as he showed us about the property, "so it can never be developed."

It was not very large as wildernesses went—in fact, you could make out the backs of the houses on the far side of the oval—but Jared thought this an endearing and unexpected feature and I was inclined to agree with him.

Kyle was then living with a network architect named Ling-ling, though he had not made the arrangement formal. Companies were not the only things in his life that came and went. She was pleasant to Jared, but just a little reserved, as if sensing that the short, intense philosopher occupied a niche in her lover's life that she could never fill.

We spent the night in two guest rooms and in the morning Kyle and Jared went out on a run. The irregular oval formed by the two roads provided a track, and both of them had kept up the practice since their championship track days. I left running and jogging to those better suited to it, and sat on the patio in Kyle's back yard and thought long thoughts. Or else I napped. Later, Kyle and Jared joined me there to await dinner, which Ling-ling was preparing. The sun was setting behind us, so the treetops glowed in an unseen, faerie light and the shadow of the house advanced across the lawn toward the woods like the army of darkness.

We talked a bit about Kyle's line of "InterFaces," simulations that people used as avatars. Why answer your vidphone in your own persona when you could answer as Napoleon or the latest gaming hero? Since they were supposed to be masks, neither autonomy nor deep realism mattered.

Kyle drank "treated" coffee, infused with low-lactose whey protein and a blend of compounds from acai, pomegranate, blueberry, grape seed and green tea. "Full of anti-oxidants," he declared as he lifted the cup in toast. "Never grow old."

Jared returned the salute with a cup of Earl Grey. "Too bad. I've been looking forward to becoming an *éminence grise*. But, Kyle, *all* plants contain antioxidants."

"And Rust-Oleum is an antioxidant, too," I added. "Drink it, and I guarantee you'll never grow old."

Kyle laughed, then frowned a little into his cup, perhaps wondering at its cost/benefit ratio.

I handed him my beer. "Here, try this. No organism harmful to man can live in beer."

We japed some more, but inevitably the talk turned to Kyle's project. He had given up on directly modeling human behavior and was focusing now on emergent properties, using methods a neighbor of his was developing at SingerLabs.

"Emergent properties," mused Jared. "That's what we used to call formal causes in the old days."

"I thought it meant 'then a miracle happens,'" I grinned.

"Isn't SingerLabs a biotech firm?" said Jared.

"Bio- and nano-," Kyle told us. "You know how complex behavior, like flocking in birds, can emerge from a set of simple rules…?"

"Mmm." Jared put his tea down. "Right. What is it, three rules?"

Kyle nodded. "Yeah. So…How do you derive a complex organism from a simple genome."

"Genomes are simple?" I asked.

"They aren't big enough to contain a full set of blueprints and step-by-step construction drawings," Kyle insisted. "So there must be some way to 'unfold' them from a generating set. Now, that's not my problem; it's Henry's. My problem is to simulate a complete personality. The trick is to discover the smaller set of recursive instructions that it emerges from, then use subsumption architecture to build it up in layers. That's where Ling-ling comes in. Reflex behaviors—that's the generating set—go on the lowest layers; like 'avoid crowding your neighbors' or 'steer towards the average heading of your neighbors.' The more abstract behaviors are layered incrementally atop the simpler ones, and they control the direction to be taken to achieve an overall task."

"In other words," Jared responded, "your higher layers deal with final causation. That makes sense to me. But I thought your customers weren't looking for well-rounded sims for their InterFaces."

"They aren't. I am."

"Oh, that's right. You want to download a mind into the computer."

"You've been talking to Mac." Kyle shook his head. "Who needs the Grid when we have Mac? Did he tell you his sister is a widow? Her husband died in the Flu."

"I think Mac was trying not to tell either one of us. Tell me you're not heading for Elmira to make a play for the grieving widow. She has two kids, you know; and you don't seem the paternal type."

"Me? No. I've got Lorraine."

"Ling-ling."

"Right. Ling-ling. No, I just thought you'd want to know."

"College was years ago, Kyle. I'm happily married."

"Sure, *you* are; but is *Gladdys?*"

An uncomfortable silence enveloped us. Either Kyle was making a bad joke—like the man who says of his seven-year marriage that it was the happiest two years of his life—or he was making a serious observation. Gladdys was outgoing, a musician, and Jared was not exactly your party animal. I remembered how Kyle and Gladdys had been tête-à-tête in the hospital cafeteria. In her anxiety, had she whispered some confidence to him, some discontentment? Kyle began to redden slowly under Jared's flint-faced scrutiny.

I didn't like the way they sometimes ignored me when I was with them. After all, it was my sister they were talking about, and in the end, Maddy had rejected both of them. Jared was dating Gladdys within the week, while Kyle had flitted to Denise, then Lorraine, Audrey, Katya, and now Ling-ling. I had thought Maddy long forgotten.

So, as I had done so often in the past, I put myself verbally between them.

"Will subsumption architecture help you download minds into computers?"

Kyle shot me a grateful glance. He could be offensive, but usually not by intention, and he was always surprised when others took his jokes to heart.

"There are several promising avenues," Kyle assured us. "We figure on success in maybe fifteen years." Then he turned to Jared with the peace offering. "What do you think, Jared?"

What Kyle wanted was that Jared should give him some encouragement, or at least wish him good luck. But Jared's one great character flaw was his remorseless honesty. Perhaps he was nettled by Kyle's jape and decided to give him both barrels of the philosophical shotgun.

"Not in fifteen years," he said. "Not in fifteen hundred years. It's flat-out impossible."

That was when Ling-ling came to the patio door and told us that dinner was on the table. There was a certain hardness to her features, and I wondered if she had earlier overheard Kyle garbling her name. It was not unlikely, as she maintained a stony silence during much of the meal that followed.

The table was long red maple, with ceramic tiles inlaid down the center on which hot dishes might be placed. Jared's seat faced the French doors and the wooded lot that was the kernel in the residential shell. Kyle sat across from him, while Ling-ling sat at the head, near the kitchen door, a little apart physically as well as symbolically. I was relegated to the foot.

"So," Kyle said, "tell Ling-ling what you meant when you said it's impossible to download a mind into a computer." As if it was Ling-ling who cared.

Jared already regretted his acerbic dismissal. He should have said something vague and non-committal. He did in fact think that AI was impossible and it would be a waste of Kyle's time and talent; but Kyle would not be the first to hare off after El Dorado. What he should have said, as he admitted to me later, was "If anyone can do it, you can."

Instead, he sighed. "How much do you know about Gödel?"

Kyle was feeling snappish by then. "Never heard of it." Of course, being in AI, he had heard of Gödel's theorem and the Lucas-Penrose thesis; but being in AI, he had also long ago dismissed it. One marker distinguishing the scientist and engineer from the logician and mathematician is the use of the term "impossible." To Jared—and to me—it meant just that, like "a married bachelor." But to Kyle, it meant "we don't know how to do it yet."

But Jared took him at his word. "Gödel showed that any consistent computational system complex enough to support simple arithmetic will produce true sentences that cannot be proved *within-the-system.*

Kyle scoffed. "If a proposition can't be proved, how do you know it's true?"

"I said the proposition cannot be proven-*within*-the-system. Say you specify a computational system W_i. It consists of a finite set of axioms and a finite set of rules for developing propositions from those axioms. Those proof-sequences are like roads leading from the axioms to the propositions. The propositions at the end of the roads are 'provable.' What Gödel proved was that *there are places where the roads don't go.* Some propositions are undecidable; and the statement of their undecidability must lie outside the system."

Kyle threw his hands up at that point. "*That's* the catch. Expand the system. Why not a chain of machines, W_i, W_j, W_k,..., each proving the consistency of the preceding one. At some point they reach 'critical mass' and consciousness emerges."

Ling-ling spoke for the first time. "Even I see why that not work." Yes, she had heard his earlier remark. I could hear it in her voice and deliberately exaggerated accent.

Kyle shot her a look, but he could not have achieved his successes had he been unable to reason clearly. He sighed, and dropped his fork to the plate. "Right. Then the bigger system will also be incomplete and have true, but unprovable sentences."

"And that leads to an infinite regress," said Jared, "and to an infinitely large machine."

"But why does that mean downloading is impossible? It's just a matter of running the mind-program on a different substrate."

Jared had gone too far to back off now, and sometimes the quickest way out of a bad situation is to push on through to the other side. "Because a computer is a physical embodiment of a formal system. So Gödel's theorem applies, and it follows that the computer will be incapable of generating a proof of consistency without external help. But the human mind *is* so capable, and from that it follows that no machine can be a complete model of the human mind."

"But your reasoning applies to any statement-maker. What about 'Jared can't assert the truth of this statement'? It's true, but you can't assert it. So, you're subject to the same limitation. The whole Lucas-Penrose argument is vacuous."

But Jared was already shaking his head. "Assertion is not the same as proof. Provable statements are a subset of true statements; but a mere assertion need not be true at all. A computer can't even *see* an unprovable statement."

Kyle laid down his knife and fork. "It can if we insert the unprovable propositions into the system as axioms."

Jared cocked his head. "Which one, the proposition or its negation? They'd both be undecidable, you know."

Kyle made a gesture. "Both!" Ling-ling sighed in an exaggerated fashion.

Jared said, "Then the system would be inconsistent."

"So what? Humans are inconsistent, too."

"So nice," said Ling-ling. "Inconsistent AI."

"Humans are rational," Jared said. "Human reasoning is not just a set of formal steps but includes the ability to reflect on the correctness of those steps. And this is precisely what a purely formal system cannot do."

Kyle sighed and turned to me. "What do you think, Mac?"

Long ago, in college, I had fallen into the role of referee, and so expecting the question, I had been mulling over what my answer ought to be. I did not know any mathematical logician who failed to find the Gödelian argument at least "interesting," which is a term mathematicians use that means "I want to believe it's wrong, but I don't yet see how." As Polyani once said, *a formalized deductive system is an* instrument *which requires for its logical completion a mind* using *the instrument in a manner not fully determined* by *the instrument*. And Jared had said something about subsets, so…

"There ought to be a proximity on the set of all coherent propositions within the system," I hazarded, thinking out loud. "Suppose Jared is right, and your AI can only yield *provable* propositions. But if these sentences are topologically dense in the space of all propositions, then every true proposition would be arbitrarily close to a provable one. So you could both be right. You can't make an AI 'just like' Jared—though God knows, one of him is enough—but it might be possible to construct an AI indistinguishable for all practical purposes from a human intelligence."

The secret to getting on with Kyle was to tell him not the unvarnished truth, but the varnished truth. It helped if you slapped a coat of paint on it, too. Jared had told him that what he wanted most in the world was impossible. I had told him he might be able do something indistinguishable from it; and that was good enough. I'm not going to get into Harris proximities, closure operators, or the function space 2^Y, or for that matter how I extended the concept of Dedekind cuts. That sort of thing is an acquired taste. Suffice it to say that I received the Fields Medal for the work a few years later. The interesting thing is that if Jared had not taken the liberty of friendship to slap him in the face with the intellectual equivalent of a dead fish, Kyle would not have turned to me, and I would never have achieved my brief moment of fame. Such are the vagaries of fate.

But that came later. At dinner that evening, the silence was finally broken by the sound of Ling-ling's silverware as she finished her meal. "All word-play," she said when she looked up.

Kyle took heart. "That's right," he said, gathering confidence. "Word-play, like all of philosophy. You're asking me to drop my lifelong dream *because of a damned metaphor?*"

"I'm not asking," Jared said quietly, "that you do anything. Look. Even if it is impossible, so what? You can still dream the impossible dream."

"Well thanks a whole freaking lot."

Afterward, as he was gathering the empty dishes together, Kyle smiled, though it was a rueful smile. "You had me going, Jared. You really had me going. But what about the brain? When you get right down to it, the brain is a computational engine, too. That means there's a flaw in your argument somewhere."

"No," said Jared. "It means minds are not brains."

Kyle stared at him for a moment, then threw his head back and laughed. "You really had me going," he said again.

SLEEPING DOGS LIE

A few years later, Kyle used his fourth fortune to fund the independent NM Foundation. By that time, he was simply *Kyle Buskirk and Associates,* having nothing more to prove. Sims had become in that decade what operating systems had been in the previous century, and Kyle's underlying protocols had become by popular demand so much the standard for the industry that the government had contemplated intervention in the name of his less popular competitors. Kyle, who had never before contributed to a political cause, got the message and began to do so. Replacing his fourth fortune with his fifth was not a problem.

NM stood for *Nou Mechanima,* which most took as a fanciful rendition of "New (or Now) Mechanisms." Humanists knew that it would have meant "Mind Machine" in Greek, had -*anema* not been coyly misspelled as -*anima,* which in Latin meant "life." Packing mind, machine, and life into the name seemed more subtle than Kyle's usual playful approach to nomenclature. I suspected Jared's hand in it.

Kyle did not broadcast the NM Foundation's goals, but neither did he try to hold them secret, and eventually the word spread. "Sim Guru to Build Brain in a Box" will give you a rough idea of the newsfeeds that followed. That set off the blogosphere. On the one hand were those accusing him of blasphemy for trying to create a human soul; and on the other hand were those who volunteered to cut off and freeze their own heads so that their minds could be downloaded when Kyle finally succeeded. Jared and Kyle had disagreed on more than a few things over the years, but that both these groups were nutty beyond all measure was something on which they found common ground. *They don't even know what a soul is,* Jared complained to me in an email. *They think it's a substance.* Since I didn't know what he meant either, I let it ride.

Blogs thrive on leaping to conclusions. They accept all inputs credulously, the excuse being that they can always correct the post later. Before long, anyone who had ever known Kyle—relatives, playmates, schoolmates, business associates, and former lovers—was sharing Kyle Buskirk stories. So it was not long before they discovered Jared.

But while Jared was quite willing to argue with Kyle into the small of the night, he was disinclined to do so for the entertainment of strangers. When a well-known blog host asked him what he thought of Kyle's project, Jared smiled and answered that "if anyone can do it, Kyle can." A lot of people took this as a vote of confidence, but I noticed the conditional clause, and of course so did Kyle.

Attention-deficit disorder is the disease of the age. Whether this is a Pavlovian consequence of weaning children on the flickering, transient imageries of *Sesame Street* or the general replacement of reading by surfing, people seem to have misplaced the ability to concentrate. Which is to say that the proverbial fifteen minutes of fame now barely lasts five. That Kyle Buskirk proposed to create intelligent computers, let alone that Jared Holtzmann thought them impossible, flashed across the public awareness like a white-hot meteorite. The afterimage lingered for a few eyeblinks, then people were onto the latest antics of Stephanie Bloom or the possibility of mandated regime change in Algeria.

I cannot say that Jared was not relieved. He disliked the spotlight in any case. But I think Kyle was equally thankful. He knew, if the public did not, that real achievement comes incrementally from painstaking attentions paid to fine details, regardless how sudden and unexpected the press releases might seem to an inattentive public. It was okay to paint goals in broad brush strokes, but getting there was another matter. He was less unwelcoming of attention than Jared, but he did find it distracting.

I did not see either man for a couple of years, though the occasional email showed up in my comm. box, and once Jared posted a comment on my math blog regarding a point on modal logic, and a vigorous debate ensued. We exchanged cards at appropriate times of year. Kyle hinted at some mysterious sort of breakthrough imminent at NM. Otherwise, matters remained quiet and polite. I supposed that, since they lived nearer each other, Jared and Kyle got together more often. Only later did I learn that I was mistaken.

Then one semester Jared came to the University of Chicago as a guest lecturer. He came without Gladdys, who was soloing with the Philadelphia Orchestra for a concert series, so he and I spent time together. After his final lecture, he came to see me in my office in the old Statistics and Mathematics building, a three-story brick residence across the street from Ryerson and covered with the traditional ivy. Most of the offices belonged to the Financial Mathematics group, but they put up with a few of us more exotic spillovers. Years ago, a fire had damaged the roof, but the only reminder of it now was a very faint smoky smell that emerged during heavy rainstorms.

My office was about what you might expect. Stacks of papers, shelves stuffed with textbooks, monographs, and the like. Two or three computers and ebooks even more stuffed than the shelves. I had seen Jared's office in Princeton, and it was an altogether more orderly place. Of course, I had a couple of flatscreens, with lots of file storage, too. Very portable. But when I'm thinking through a problem, I like to spread papers over a table, or tape things to the wall. There's a lot to be said for gestalt.

"Kyle texted me last week," I told him. "He asked me why you keep trying to block his AI project."

Jared had settled into a big soft chair with an old copy of Slattery balanced on the arm, and last semester's term papers stacked on the end table beside him. He had picked up the textbook with the intent of placing it somewhere, and had seen with a blink of despair that he dared place it nowhere without the likelihood of triggering an avalanche. I took it off his hands to take it off his mind.

"I'm not trying to block him," he said, as he settled back. "The Great Wall of China could not block him." In those days he liked to affect a tweedy "English" look, complete with elbow patches on his jackets. "He keeps asking for my opinion, and I keep giving it. A couple months ago, I kirked his system."

"Kirked?"

"You remember that TV character, Captain Kirk? He used to pose paradoxes to computers and they would get all tied up in logical knots and start smoking and sparking. That's because computers are innocent. They believe what you tell them. What Kyle wants to accomplish is not just difficult; it's impossible *in principle*. He doesn't contact me as much anymore. I asked him why, and he said he didn't need the negativity." Jared bit his lip and shoved his hands into his jacket pockets. "He was wrong."

"Wrong not to ask you?"

"Wrong about not needing the negativity. No one learns anything in an echo chamber." He sighed. "And you, you're his enabler."

"Me!" Jared could be awfully blunt. "I proved he could approximate human intelligence arbitrarily closely for all practical purposes."

"Maybe so; but not all human purposes are practical. An approximation is still an approximation, and the devil is in the details. If your Density Theorem is correct, Kyle may *believe* he has succeeded."

That "if" nettled me. Mathematics, it seemed to me, dealt in absolutes in a way philosophy and science never could. "What's the harm in that?"

"What's the harm in any illusion? If we grow accustomed to sims indistinguishable from humans…"

"We'll start treating sims as if they were real people. But how can that…?"

"No, Mac. The danger is that we'll start treating people as if they were sims."

I considered that for a moment. "Seems pretty far-fetched."

Jared seemed on the brink of responding. Then he shrugged and settled back in the chair. "Maybe I worry too much. Never mind. We should head up to the Quadrangle Club for lunch."

I checked my watch. "Wait a while. I called Beth Phillips—you remember her from the commune? She's teaching history up at Northwestern now and I asked her to come down and meet us there." *Anything else,* I had thought. Let's talk about old commune days, about history, Beth's new book, *Jared's* new book—anything but the interminable subject of Kyle and his damned AI project.

So of course my computer chimed, and it was Kyle calling. Whatever other divine attributes God may have, a sense of humor is among them.

Kyle was using his own product, appearing on-screen as a Bill Gates imago, with the features morphed enough to look like Kyle disguised as Gates.

"Hey, Mac!" the image said. "Jared there yet? He is? Good. Turn the cam so I can see him." I shifted the angle of the computer to take in the rest of the room, and Kyle/Gates waved. "Yo, Jared. Still thinking those long thoughts?"

Jared had leaned forward with his arms on his knees and peered intently at the screen. "Hi, Kyle," he said. "Sorry to hear about Michele."

Kyle made a brushing motion with his hand. "I don't want to talk about that right now. I called to ask you out to Detroit next week, for the holidays. My expense."

"Gladdys and I…"

"I'll fly her out, too. We can all get together, like in Vienna. God, how long ago was that?"

"What's such a big deal?" Jared asked, with a touch of suspicion in his voice.

The Kyle Buskirk grin split the Bill Gates face. "NM has made a breakthrough. We've created the artificial neuron, what we call a 'neuristor.' It's a nano-scale self-powered integrated circuit that can be spliced in place of faulty axons. It works just like a prosthesis…"

187

"That's wonderful," I said. "That's tremendous!"

Jared's congratulations were also heartfelt. He had always believed that in reaching for the unattainable Kyle would grab hold of something remarkable. "That could revolutionize treatment not just for brain surgery, but for epilepsy, ALS, Alzheimer's, even schizophrenia."

It could and did, and the research team at NM—Boland, Singh, et al.—would later receive the Nobel Prize in medicine. NM was Kyle's baby and he deserved part of the credit. But the medical possibilities took second place in his enthusiasms.

"I don't want to talk about that right now. I want to talk about AI. We can record the neural patterns that pass through the neuristors. Now tell me," he said earnestly, leaning toward the camera. "What's the difference between replacing one damaged axon with a neuristor and replacing all of them? Just quantity. It's the breakthrough we've always wanted. If we replace all the axons in the brain with neuristors, we can record the entire suite of neural patterns, and that means we can download the entire mind into a mainframe. The computer would have to be massive but there is no defeater blocking us. It's all engineering now. Come out to the NM Lab in Detroit and I'll show you something that'll knock your socks off. You're done with the lectures, right? How about you, Mac, when are you free?"

We agreed on a date and as Jared returned his data pad to his jacket pocket, he said casually. "How's the weather in Detroit?"

Kyle said, "I don't want to talk about that right now."

Jared smiled and pulled a phone from his pocket. "I didn't think you would."

He punched a number. "Hello," he said, "put me through to Kyle Buskirk. Yes, it's important, or I would not have called his private number." He waited a few moments, then said in a cheery voice, "Kyle! Jared. That's a *great* sim you have there."

I could hear Kyle's "damn!" from where I sat. The mask on the computer screen dissolved and an unaltered Kyle replaced it. He was sitting behind his desk in his office. "What tipped you off?"

Jared shrugged. "I don't want to talk about that right now."

Kyle drummed his fingers on his desk. "Damn. It was supposed to randomize those responses. We couldn't give our net knowledge for every possible topic of conversation, so we set boundary responses."

Jared said, "Your topic field was too constrained. There is always topic drift. And you need to work on your grammar engine. It sounded like you were reading a technical paper."

"It was only a demo," Kyle said. "Mac, what about you? Did it seem human to you?"

I was loath to appear more gullible than Jared, but I nodded. "I didn't think to question it; but in hindsight, it's obvious."

Jared nodded. "Kyle...How *is* the weather in Detroit?"

Kyle smiled. "I don't want to talk about that right now."

"Make me a promise," I told Jared as we bundled up for the walk to the Quadrangle Club. An early winter wind was blowing off the Lake, drilling the dry cold into the bone. Chicagoans have no idea what temperatures might be without the wind chill. "Promise me that we won't talk to Beth about Kyle and his project."

"That was a telling prank he pulled at the end there."

I paused before tightening my muffler. "Yeah, you should've seen your face. Promise."

"I promise. Mac, if Kyle wants to approximate an AI, there are two problems he has to overcome. The credulity problem..."

"I don't want to talk about that right now."

Jared gave me a sour look, and I could tell that that line would become a running gag among the three of us. "Look," I pleaded with him. "Beth has an important new book out on the Elamite Tablets and their relationship to Harappa and the Dravidian language family. We are *not* going to burden her with this business with Kyle."

Jared pulled the fur cap over his head. "She'll ask about him. You know she will."

"Besides," I muttered, "humans can be credulous, too."

Jared simply waited, and I finally succumbed. "Okay, okay. What's the second obstacle?"

"Intuition," he said. "Insight. Creativity. Whatever you want to call it. Look, Kyle is right about this much: a lot of human thought really is algorithmic. Habit, culture, genetics—eighty percent of life is on autopilot, and should be. But he hasn't considered that not *all* thought is computational. Thinking is fluid, dynamic, tentative, spontaneous, sometimes creative. It's not rule-bound, rigid, static, mechanical, and formalized. Computation and thinking are two distinct activities. Read Feser on Leibniz' Mill. There's no prospect of AI at all, as long as computers are machines."

"Well," I suggested, "isn't that exactly what Kyle is trying to change?"

We walked a little while in silence, bundled against the biting wind and bitter sleet. When we came to the corner, Jared turned abruptly and put his back to the wind, facing me. "Speaking of Beth and old commune days," he said, "you know that Kyle has been in contact with your sister."

I did not deny knowing.

"He'll have no joy of it." Jared spun about and continued toward the club.

COMPUTER MOUSE

Jared and I booked first-class tickets on the 80-90 Bullet the following week, connecting with the local at Toledo, and so north toward Detroit. A limo met us at the maglev station in Romulus and whisked us in comfort to the labs in River Rouge. Kyle had made a policy of locating his facilities in regions that had been in economic decline. Cynics said this was because land there was cheap. Kyle wondered how many communities the cynics had helped revitalize.

The driver took us directly to the labs—a complex of tall, streamlined buildings connected by walkways on their upper stories. Chrome-and-glass were by then very retro and Kyle hated retro, so the façades had been faced in a white-to-cream ceramic. There were plenty of windows on three faces, but much of the fourth façade was unbroken wall decorated in geometric patterns and bas-reliefs. From the highway, the complex resembled nothing so much as the white-washed castles of the middle ages, and how was that for retro?

The limo dropped us off with a promise to deliver our luggage to our hotel rooms, which were in the nearby Turing Towers and Suites. The Lead Investigator for the Network Topology group, a Young Turk named Neill, met us at the door and took us around the building. I was stroked and praised by the staff for the Density Theorem that had made all their work possible.

That might have been painting with too broad a brush, but Kyle had always known how to lay egoboo on with a trowel. I noted a general consensus that I was "on their side" and not among the "denialists" and the "religious nuts." I don't know if they meant Jared and did not ask. So far as I know, Jared had never made a *religious* argument against AI, and those arguments I had heard him make were sound ones well-deserving of serious rebuttal. If anything, some of the "transhumanists" who had blogged on "the Great Project" came across as more overtly religious. They were certainly more faith-based.

"*It's an old dream,*" Jared had said during the train ride. "*Put away the old corrupted body, and put on the new body, renewed in the spirit of your mind.*"

"*That sounds like a quote,*" I commented.

"*Paraphrase,*" said Jared. "*It's from the Bible.*"

✦

Kyle was perfectly capable of "duding up" in coat and tie. He often had to do so in Japan and China, and sometimes even in Europe. But here in his own environment, he was content in tan slacks and forest green polo shirt. He hopped to his feet when Jared and I entered the demonstration lab and pumped our hands, introducing us to others, most of whose names I have now long forgotten.

He allowed the Lead Investigator for Sims to explain the computer mouse. This was a holographic image of a mouse in a virtual environment. "Cheaper than building a robot," Kyle interjected. I made a private bet with myself that the staff called the thing "Mickey," and might have grown wealthy had not the odds against been so poor.

Then the Lead Investigator for Neural Recordings—her name I do remember as Danielle—introduced us to a real mouse, called "Algernon" for some reason. Algernon, it seemed, could learn mazes with astonishing rapidity. For this demonstration, they brought in a fairly simple maze-box, and Kyle invited Jared to assemble the walls into whatever configuration pleased him. Afterward, Algernon mastered it with the breezy competence of a professional.

"Now here," Danielle said, handing me a half-wall. "Snap this hurdle into the post holes anywhere along the main run."

I did so, with the comment that Algernon could easily leap over it and continue his quest.

"Of course," she replied. "We're counting on it."

Within a few trials, Algernon was hopping over the barrier with ease. Then Danielle removed the barrier and let Algernon run it once more.

When the mouse came to the place where the hurdle had once been, he leaped.

"Even though it's not there anymore?" I said with some wonderment. Jared blinked, startled, but said nothing.

"Even though it's not there anymore," the Lead Investigator agreed. "Mice are blind. Their eyes see only vague shapes and shadows. They navigate by smell, touch, and memory. Algernon remembers there was a barrier at this point in the run and leaps over it by habit."

Then it was time to record the mouse's brain. This involved, of all things, a little cap that fit over Algernon's head that would scan the neuristors installed earlier by nanomachines. Danielle adjusted the fit and settings and explained what the cap would do. That was the first time I heard the "flashbulb in the head" metaphor.

"We're going to record only the cognitive parts of the brain," Danielle explained. "We've modeled the somatic aspects with the computer. Those are pretty much the same from mouse to mouse."

I was still mulling over "the cognitive parts" of a mouse's brain, when Algernon began to flail about.

Kyle, who had been sitting in a chair in the corner, leaning forward with his hands clasped between his knees, spoke up. "Don't worry. The mouse doesn't feel anything, and we haven't killed it, since we've only flashed the cortex and the hippocampus. The somatic part will keep the body alive and kicking. It will be a zombie for a while, but…"

"But," said Danielle, "eventually the mouse will 'recruit' the remaining portions of its brain to other functions. There's a certain plasticity to the thing. Learning actually changes brain shape. Specific regions grow or shrink in response to changing environmental demands."

Kyle grinned at me. "What do you make of *that*, Jared?"

Jared smiled. "It demonstrates that learning is something that the mouse does to its brain, not something the brain does to the mouse."

"He's loaded," announced a young man at the computer console. Kyle nodded to the screen.

"Watch this."

The image showed a wire-frame mouse, which I assumed was the "somatic simulation" mentioned earlier. The operator spread his finger and thumb and the viewpoint panned back, so that the mouse appeared placed at the entrance to a maze. I glanced aside at the plastic and wood box on the table. The simulated maze replicated the physical one that Jared had assembled. I thought I knew what was coming.

"That's why you had us arrange the pattern in the maze," I said to Kyle, "so we wouldn't suspect you had preprogrammed anything."

He answered only with a smile, but Jared murmured, "Now where would we have gotten the idea that Kyle would stack the deck?"

"Cyber-Algernon is all set," the operator told us. "And…go."

The simulation scurried through the maze, making all the correct turns. When it came to a certain point on the straight-away, it leaped.

I sucked in my breath and jerked my head to look at Kyle.

"That's why you had me set that hurdle. So we'd know. No other mouse in the universe would have been trained to hop at that precise point in that particular maze."

Kyle had slouched in his chair, long legs protruding, hands balled together and tucked under his chin. He nodded toward the computer. "That's Algernon in there. That is freaking Algernon."

Afterward, we went to an upscale restaurant in River Rouge, just the three of us; not to celebrate the success of the experiment—Kyle had run the test many times before he dared invite us to witness it—but just because the three of us had not dined together for some time. On the way over in the limo, Kyle ran on about the experiment and the possibilities it opened up. I asked enthusiastic questions; but Jared remained monosyllabic, which I did not take for a good sign.

At *Courier du Bois*, we were shown to Kyle's "usual table" and left to study the menu, which was burned into elk hide, in keeping with the theme.

"The central human ability," Jared said finally, "is our ability to 'see what matters when.' And data, no matter how much there is, never adds up to context."

"Don't get all metaphysical on my ass," Kyle said. "You beat that drum too often. Theoretical objections don't matter now that we have empirical success." The sommelier brought a wine list to us and Kyle pointed. "Two bottles of the '12. Those should be old enough to drink, d'you think?" He handed the wine list back and picked up the menu. "Let's see here… Hmm. I don't see crow on the menu. Do you, Mac?"

I preferred to stay out of it, but saw no way to duck a direct question. There was something going on between my two friends that ran deeper than philosophy and computers. I turned to Jared. "He couldn't have preprogrammed that demo. I don't think it's a trick this time." It wouldn't hurt to remind Kyle that he had tried to trick us before, and we had empirical reasons to be skeptical.

"No, it wasn't a trick," Jared admitted. "But it might not mean what you think it means. Facts never explain themselves. We—you, me, people—we have to *apply* meaning to them. Everything we saw cyber-Algernon do was physical, it can be accounted for by sensation and imagination, and those are purely material powers. You can't extrapolate that to immaterial powers like conception and volition."

"Mice don't have such powers," Kyle objected.

Jared gave him a level stare. "No, *mice* don't."

"Look, guys," I pleaded with them. "Can't we just have a pleasant dinner together? Forget cyber-mice, forget metaphysics; but never forget friendship."

Jared and Kyle both looked away at the same time. Kyle muttered something under his breath. Jared said, "Just for you, Mac."

And it was a fine meal, a companionable refection full of humor and bonhomie. There was wine and talk and laughter, and by mutual and unspoken assent we avoided any mention of the AI project, or indeed of philosophy or computers of any sort. Sporting teams were mentioned and their prospects assessed. A new threedy, *Beggars in Spain*, was quietly building an audience by word of mouth. Chef Brian was called forth from his culinary domain to receive our approbation. There was a book that the critics all agreed simply *must* be read which we decided by a vote of two to one ought not. There was an election coming up and we agreed there was an outside chance one of the parties would nominate a candidate of substance. We had not shared such a meal since Vienna, now many years distant, and while we talked of many things, very few of them, thank God, were of any grave importance.

But toward the end, as we prepared to leave the restaurant, Jared said something odd to Kyle. Kyle had said he was sorry that Gladdys couldn't make it and Jared said, oddly, "Remember Gödel's theorem. There are things that are true that can't be proven."

Kyle's face closed up after that and the handshakes that followed were perfunctory. After Kyle was gone, I asked Jared what he had meant, but he would not say.

Kyle took the red-eye flight to Budapest that night; and when I awoke in the morning at the hotel, Jared was already on the New Twenty-first Century Limited sliding toward the City to connect with the Metrocela. Not too long afterward I was heading back to Chicago on the 80-90 Bullet.

It was the last time all three of us would be together in the flesh.

A FLASH IN THE BRAINPAN

Some wag in NM called the neural transcription process a "flashbulb in the brain." They soon discovered from their experiments on mice that they could not proceed piecemeal. Each transcription fried the neuron it copied; and when a sufficient number of nodes had been broken the neurological network fell into disjoint segments. Neurologists grew excited because the surviving mice would behave in various peculiar ways. There was some evidence of multiple personality disorder, although it was difficult enough to tell if a mouse had a personality, let alone more than one. Other mice became obsessive-compulsive or developed even shorter attention spans than usual. It all depended on which parts of the brain's neural net were disconnected from which other parts. As usual, in his pursuit of eternal downloaded life, Kyle's researchers had stumbled on half a dozen useful spin-offs.

So there was no help for it but to record the entire neural net at once. This, of course, fried all the neurons, so there were not even disjoint segments left. Kyle proffered me a contract to analyze the topological connectivity of the brain's neural structure. It was a handsome fee, but I hesitated too long and shortly received a message from the Dean informing me that if I did not accept the contract the University would lose a substantial bequest. Nothing more needed saying. It was long, difficult research and while useful, the results were hardly spectacular.

A few years after we had watched Algernon do his thing, Kyle spun off *Com-Pet-itive Solutions* to market a line of virtual pets. These were simulated dogs and cats imprinted with the neural patterns of actual pets flashed in the process of euthanasia. Anyone who has owned one knows that dogs and cats have distinct personalities, and those who opted to flash their dying pets rather than put them down in the usual way swore up and down that their virtual reconstructions had all the quirks of their corporeal predecessors. Either it was wishful thinking on the part of grieving pet owners or Kyle had actually captured their pets' essences by copying their brain patterns.

Jared pointed out that since modern science did not believe in "essences," this raised grave philosophical problems about what *Com-Pet-itive Solutions* thought they were actually copying. *You would think the Old Jogger would be grateful*, Kyle texted me shortly after Jared had raised that point. *Haven't I proved the existence of souls?* Me, I took Kyle at his word. He cared less about the logical coherence of his basic assumptions than he did about the results.

Naturally, parents began to request the same for their dying children, but the FDA withheld approval. There was also a degree of pushback from the general public, those who objected to human euthanasia. It was a tragedy for a child to die; it was murder to kill him.

"That someone faces inevitable death," Jared told me on a pix-call, "does not justify pushing him into the abyss."

"Why not?" I had asked him.

"Because *all* of us face inevitable death, Mac. So that puts all of us at risk. Remember what I told you once about the danger of one day treating real people as if they were sims? The real danger of gadget worship is what it does to our conception of ourselves."

The public debate boiled over when the right-to-die people joined in. They issued a press release stating that while they opposed flashing children because children could not give consent, the same objection did not apply to terminally ill adults.

The FDA still balked and even NM weighed in saying that the necessary primate studies had not been performed to ensure the process would even work at the human level. A dog or cat was one thing; apes, dolphins, or humans were orders of magnitude more complex. A chimpanzee has twice the encephalization of a dog or cat, a dolphin twice that of a chimp, and a human twice that of a dolphin.

It's not simply a matter of scaling up, Kyle said in a podcast during the height of the controversy. *Vertebrate brains are the most complex structures known to science. Do you want to know what a* billion *synapses looks like? It looks like one cubic* millimeter *of human cerebral cortex. The human cortex contains something on the order of twenty billion neurons, each with 10,000 synaptic connections. That makes two hundred* trillion *synapses. Friends, that's bigger than the national debt. Now...We can cut this down by eliminating most of the purely somatic circuits, but there's still a lot more complexity remaining than you'd find in a dog or cat. So before we can flash a human mind, we must cut down the number of synapses we need to record, and increase the capacity of our qubes. Only after we achieve a meeting between the size of the mind and the capacity of the q-bit computer, will human virtual immortality be within our reach.*

"No, it won't," Jared texted me afterward. "A man might achieve immortality in an analogous sense by writing his autobiography; but that biography, no matter how detailed and extensive, will not be *him.* Neither would a biography written in an alphabet of synapses, let alone a photocopy of it."

I asked him if he had told that to Kyle and he answered, "Why bother?"

And so NM itself took the matter off the public table and a shroud of silence descended on their public relations releases. We heard no more on human flashing. As far as the newsfeeds were concerned, all work on it seemed to cease. There were two possible reasons that I could see. Either Kyle had run into an insuperable obstacle, or he was continuing the work in secrecy.

"Do you really think Kyle would ever give up?" Jared texted me when I broached the possibility. "He probably finds the work goes a lot faster without a lot of noise." And then he added something that puzzled me at the time. "I never thought it would go this far." It was only later that I realized that it was not an admission of defeat, but a fear of success.

THE GUEST IN THE MACHINATIONS

Among the three of us, communications slowed. Kyle threw himself into his work; Jared, into classes and closely-written papers that no one read. Living on the far side of the moon in Chicago, I found myself more and more out of the loop. Besides, I had my own interests.

One of those interests was Beth Phillips. I had been a bachelor for so long that I barely recognized what had come upon me when it did. After that winter when we had dined with Jared, she and I began to find excuses to text, to meet, attend shows and showings, and generally provide pretenses to be in one another's company. I am glad to say that we were friends before we were anything else. Jared evinced no surprise at the news. *I knew it at that first dinner*, he texted me when I announced our engagement. Kyle responded by assuring me that I would thoroughly enjoy living with Beth. I'm not sure which response irritated me more.

In any event, our association proved fruitful for both her archeology and my mathematics, as we found a confluence of interests in building upon old work by Rashevsky, Renfrew and others on mathematical history. So I was able to make certain probabilistic statements regarding the size and distribution of Elamite pueblos along the Iranian coast and Beth was able to discover the sites of six of them and establish the connection between Elam and Harappa beyond reasonable doubt.

This might not excite anyone who has never heard of Harappa or Elam, which on the evidence would constitute the vast majority of the population, but the tablets she unearthed established sufficient overlap in inscriptions to permit Khan and Gazdar a few years later to finally crack the Harappan cuneiform. Best of all, none of it had any connection to Kyle's AI project.

It did, however, result in my invitation to the AMS convention when it was held in Valley Forge, Pennsylvania, to sit on a panel on the mathematical study of history. Daniel Hotchkiss, the pure historian on the panel, declared that history could not be captured by numbers, and I surprised him by agreeing. The world had metrical properties and non-metrical properties, and only the former could be netted by mathematics. The remainder required a different kind of understanding. Maybe that concession was due to Jared's influence.

It was funny that I thought of Jared, for that very evening in the Blue Grotto, after my dining companions had gone, Gladdys Kenrick-Holtzmann slipped into the chair across the table from me.

"Mac!" she said. "How delightful to see you! It's been years, hasn't it?"

My gap-mouthed silence expressed my surprise. "Gladdys," I said when I had found my voice. I started to rise; but as she was already seated, aborted the motion. "What are you doing in Valley Forge?"

"Major shopping expedition," she confided. "King of Prussia Mall."

By that I knew Jared was not with her. Princeton was only forty or fifty miles up the highway, but still it seemed a ways to travel just for shopping. She said it was a coincidence running into me, but I could run the probabilities. I very much doubted that a department store clerk had mentioned the mathematics conference to her, as she claimed. It wasn't the sort of chatter that department store clerks passed on to their customers.

"Is Beth with you? I'm so sorry we weren't able to come to the wedding."

"No. I'm traveling back home tomorrow." The wedding had been a small family affair. Invitations had been sent, but I hadn't really expected Kyle to interrupt his Chinese negotiations or Jared to leave the symposium in Oxford. I waited for Gladdys to get to her point, which she did with commendable dispatch after a few perfunctory questions about my own well-being.

"Have you heard from Kyle lately?"

"Not really," I said. "We exchange emails now and then, especially after NM came up with that neural prosthetic. I expect he and Jared communicate far more often than he and I."

Gladdys unfolded one of the napkins on the table, refolded it, smoothed it out. "He and Jared aren't as close as they once were."

"Oh. Did they quarrel?" And I could not help but recall their quarrel in college.

"No. No, it's not like that. They just…grew distant."

The opposite of love, Jared had once told me, was not hate, but indifference. And of the two, indifference might be the worse. Hate has a sort of vitality; but indifference was like one of Beth's Elamite pueblos, forgotten and enveloped by drifting time.

"He's only twenty miles away," Gladdys said with a strangle-grip on the poor napkin. "And he never comes by or even calls."

Yet I was certain that Kyle had moved to New Jersey to be closer to Jared. Did she want me to make excuses for him? Did she think I could make him call?

"I remember how you used to referee their debates, back in the day. Maybe you could…"

"I hardly ever hear from him, myself," I reminded her.

"But…He's so much fun to be around. I…Jared needs that in his life. He needs someone carefree and frivolous. He needs…"

"A sprinter?"

"What? Oh. Yes, I suppose so. Jared is so…steady, dependable…"

"That's pretty terrible," I agreed. "Dull?"

"Oh, *he* doesn't think so; and I guess among his like-minded friends he can be a real live wire. But he's like a monotone—la, la, la—and that's fine.

That's a ground, a tenor; but there ought to be a bit of, of *duplum*, don't you think? There ought to be improvisation, jazz. Kyle is attentive. He knows how to turn a, a compliment. Jared…gathers dust."

"He doesn't attend your concerts?"

"Oh, of course he does. But it's like it's his duty, and…" She suddenly fell silent and looked away from the table. "I suppose I ought to be heading home."

"Yes," I said. "I suppose you ought."

She looked at me with a curious glance, as if I had said more than I had. Then she reached across the table to take my wrist. "Poor Mac! Always caught in the middle. I'm sorry I unloaded on you. But tell me this. Your sister. Why *her*?"

The question brought sudden fear. Maddy doesn't tell me everything. "Jared hasn't been…"

"What? Jared? No, but Kyle has!"

"Ah." I pondered that for a moment. "Maybe because she's like his AI: forever just out of reach. She told him not to call anymore, you know. She has her own world, and Kyle doesn't fit. Gladdys, Kyle has trouble sometimes remembering the name of the woman he's with. Maddy doesn't want to be just another notch on his gun. She's the only woman he ever set his sights on and never bagged."

Gladdys shivered a little. "Maybe. But he ruined it for Jared. He broke them up."

"Oh, Jared was never that serious about Maddy. He was dating you within a week of the break-up."

"Mac, do you know what 'on the rebound' means? He *settled* for me. How do you think I've felt all these years, knowing that I was second choice?"

"Isn't that better than being Kyle's n^{th} choice?"

"Don't you think I've noticed how similar 'Maddy' and 'Gladdys' are?"

"Fifty percent correlation," I muttered. The names had half their phonemes in common. But I don't think she was listening to anything I said.

"I almost wish he would moon after her. I almost wish he would make secret, late-night phone calls. At least he'd be honest with himself."

"Gladdys, I don't think you're being fair to Jared; and I don't think you should be telling me this."

She finally relinquished the napkin, dropped it on the table. "That's right. You're Mac. You never get off the fence. When you're not agreeing with Jared, you're agreeing with Kyle."

"You can't pick a fight with me, Gladdys. And you shouldn't pick a fight with him, either."

She rose from the table, and I rose with her. "I'm sorry I came," she said. "This was a mistake. Forget everything I've said."

"If you can't vent to a friend, Gladdys…"

"Is that what you are?" Then, she crumpled in on herself. "No, I'm sorry. You really have been. It's just…Did you ever wonder whether everything might have turned out different?"

"We all reach a point," I assured her, "where we start to wonder about our lives."

"But…I heard a 'but' in there."

"But we only have one, and it is what it is. You can only go forward with what you have. Sometimes I wonder what it might have been like if Beth and I had connected years ago. Looking back, I can see how lonely I was all those years. But I never realized that when I was living through them. Yet…What if she and I *had* gotten together back in the commune, or straight out of college? Who can say but that might not have been a catastrophe? She wasn't then who she is now, and neither was I."

"So it all works out for the best?"

"Maybe, maybe not. But it does all work out for what *is*."

She smiled briefly, and I noted that when she smiled it was hard to notice the plainness of her features. "Thank you, Mac," she said, and took my hand briefly before turning and walking from the restaurant.

A LEAP OF FAITH

Both Jared and I were elected chairmen of our respective departments and spent the next few years in the Great Dismal Swamp of administration and bureaucracy, which proves that if you stick around long enough you eventually get handed the short end of the stick. I would rather have been doing mathematics than dealing with departmental kabuki, but what can you say when you are the last person to duck? I think Jared felt the same way. We both received polite congratulatory cards from Kyle; but I think he knew that while it was an honor just to be nominated, it was a pain in the butt to be elected.

In any case, new duties kept both of us busy. Seasonal greetings circulated as usual, and Kyle would occasionally drop us a personal message just before some new breakthrough hit the science newsblogs. But he no longer asked either Jared or me for our opinions.

I contacted him one time on some pretext and asked him in passing how Jared was doing. He looked away from the computer camera. "We haven't spoken much lately."

"Really? You two were always so close."

"Yeah, well, maybe I outgrew him." It was characteristic of Kyle that the other possibility did not occur to him. But it was also characteristic of him that he could hear what he said, and he added, "I still love the guy. I send e-cards. But…Our interests don't intersect that much anymore. Even track meets. I mean, it's not even track anymore. It's who has the best exoskeleton. Aah, nothing stays the same anymore."

"It never did," I assured him. "But why don't you give him a call, maybe drop in and see him? I'm sure he'd like that."

Kyle grimaced. "I'm sure he would. He hasn't told me I'm full of crap for some time now. Must hurt to hold that in for so long."

We chatted for a while longer. We had both heard that Jared had swum the Tiber a couple years before, and Kyle was certain that Holtzmann ancestors must be spinning in their Lutheran graves. He surprised me by revealing some awareness of my recent work in the new field we were calling cliology, mathematical history, and even wondered if some sort of app could be developed that would project possible path bundles for historical development. He asked about Beth, who was doing field work in Gujarat.

But the conversation soon dried up and we eventually logged off with promises to stay in touch. I wondered if it might have been different if we had met in the flesh for drinks or dinner. There is something distancing about the Intergrids.

When I contacted Jared, he was entirely different, all full of Mac-it's-great-to-hear-from-you and It's-been-too-long. I didn't point out that the grids worked both ways. After all, I was always a marginal figure in his world and Kyle's. Then too, he had always been the quieter one and it was quite possible for him to go weeks or months without communicating with anyone at all. If Kyle needed Jared to damp his oscillations, Jared needed Kyle to excite his quantum state.

Since his work tended not to make headlines, I was less aware of what Jared was up to than I had been of Kyle. He had drifted out of metaphysics into moral philosophy, and when I asked him what he thought of Kyle's neuristors, he was non-committal. "I don't know if they can do what he wants them to do. But I think I've said all I needed to say about AI."

An arm reached into view handing Jared a cup and saucer. Then Gladdys leaned in front of him and waved at the camera. "Hi, Mac. Long time, no see." She disappeared, and I took her cue and let it go at that.

"You haven't heard from Kyle lately?" I tried to make it sound like a guess. A puzzled and vaguely hurt look passed across his face. "No," he said.

"No, I haven't. I'm afraid I must have offended him in some way."

Maybe by calling his life's work a fool's errand? But I did not voice that thought. "Have you contacted him?"

"If he doesn't want to talk, I won't force myself on him. I think he must be pretty busy, judging by the newspapers. Dashing from one thing to another, as usual."

It seemed to me that Kyle had remained remarkably focused over the years on creating machine intelligence and downloading minds into computers. Living forever as software. If that was not a marathon, what was? I suggested as much to Jared.

"No, he's still rushing into things. He's making a terrible mistake. He seems to conceive of the mind—the soul, life—as a distinct substance. But there is no Cartesian theater; there is no ghost in the machine."

"I thought you, of all people…"

"Look, Mac. When you see a basketball, do you see rubber *and* a sphere? No. Even if Kyle can record and copy his brain patterns into a computer, they won't be *him*, any more than copying the sphere into granite or into algebraic equations will be the *basketball*."

"Oh, I don't think you need to worry about that."

"You think not? It's what he has been yearning for his whole life."

"But the technology is…"

"Immature? Of course it is. But do you think he will wait until it is mature? No, it's a, it's a religious desire with him. It always has been. Immortality. A new body. But humans are rational *animals*, Mac. *Animals*. Form *and* matter. And formal systems cannot capture the material side. Whatever he obtains—if he ever does 'download' a mind into a computer—it won't be human, and it won't be Kyle Buskirk."

I was holding a graduate seminar on Thron's theory of grills, addressing Flynn's "pitted filters," which were the duals of grills satisfying the Π-closed property, when Patsy, one of the departmental secretaries, slipped into the conference room with a note. She leaned close over my shoulder as she handed it to me and whispered, "He says it's extremely urgent." I glanced at the note: *Private. Urgent. Call now.* And it gave Jared's private pix number. An unfocused dread whelmed up within me. Jared used words precisely, and would not have told Patsy *extremely urgent* unless in fact it was.

Turning the seminar over to my post-doc, I excused myself and hurried to the department offices. I told Geetha to hold all other calls and closed the door to the private office behind me. Within moments, I was connected to Jared over the pix.

He seemed drawn and his eyes were dark-rimmed. He was at home and in the background I saw Gladdys at the dining table weeping into her hands. "Jared!" I said. "What's happened?"

Jared had been standing when the pix went through, turned away from the camera and looking at Gladdys. Now he faced me and slid into the desk chair. "Mac," he said. "It's Kyle. Ling-ling called and…"

"Ling-ling?"

"Mac, listen. Ling-ling works for NM at River Rouge. She called me and told me that Kyle has been diagnosed with multiple myeloma…"

I called up a summary window on the disease before Jared had finished the sentence. "What stage?" I asked.

"Stage one; but Mac…"

"Good. The median prognosis is five years with chemo and hematopoietic stem-cell transplantation. With luck…"

"Mac, listen to me!" Jared had to pause and visibly control himself. "Mac. Ling-ling said that Kyle has come to River Rouge. He's come to the NM lab. Do you understand?"

For a moment I could not speak. "My God. He's going to flash himself." Almost unbidden, my hands called up the mag-rail schedule, then the air schedule. "Maybe we can head him off, stop him."

"Stop him? Then you don't believe it will work, either."

"I…That's…Beside the point. Even if it does work, he'll be throwing away five goddamn years of his…his somatic life. Maybe more. How soon can you reach Detroit?"

"I can catch a commuter train to Thirtieth Street Station in time to make the Long Rifle and change to the Michigander at Toledo."

"Jared, that's four hours by mag-lev. Break down and fly. Flight time's only an hour."

"Plus travel time to the airport, two hours for security screen, and boarding and flight delays. Even if there is no delay getting out of Detroit Metro, trust me, it's just as fast by rail. Besides, Mac, *he's already there*. He was there when Ling-ling called. I think he told her to call us. Do you really think he would have summoned us if there were any chance we could have stopped him?"

THE GHOST IN THE MACHINE

When I added ground time to a nominal half-hour flight time, I found the Midwest Rambler put me in Detroit faster than air travel as well; so

I made arrangements, went home to pack a few things, and called Beth and told her what was happening. She remembered Kyle less fondly than some, but she promised to follow the next day. "I'm not exactly sure," she told me. "Is this supposed to be a wake or a rebirthing?" Then I took the Green to the Loop and a cab across town to Union Station. The Rambler was not as fast as the Twenty-first Century, but it made the circuit several times a day and I found myself on the train platform in Romulus half an hour before Jared was scheduled to arrive. I occupied myself by renting a car and getting ground directions to the Labs.

When Jared showed up, Gladdys was with him; and to all appearances had cried herself out on the four-hour trip. She was dry-eyed, but stood limply by his side as he scanned the station for me.

We shook hands silently and said nothing about the reason that had brought us together once more. I told them I had a car and had confirmed both our reservations at the Turing Towers. "You have a beard," Jared said irrelevantly. "And it's white."

I glanced at his hair, but said nothing. "This way. Beth is coming out tomorrow. Does Ling-ling know we're here?"

Jared patted the jacket pocket where he carried his pix. "She will meet us at the main entrance. Do you know the way? Of course, you do."

Tall and thin and garbed in an immaculate white lab coat, Ling-ling greeted us at the main door, along with some of the researchers involved in the project. I remembered a few faces from my earlier visit. Some appeared grave or troubled; others were grinning or bearing a look of satisfaction. They greeted me with handshakes, Jared with wariness.

Jared took Ling-ling's hand. "It seems you and Kyle parted on friendly terms," he said.

Ling-ling endured his attention. "We enjoyed each other, and when our time was up, the time was up. Why nurse hard feelings? Follow me, and maybe now you'll believe." I noticed that her years in the States had wiped away her accent.

We followed her down a long hallway, escorted by a cloud of witnesses. I heard some of them talking among themselves. Some saying "we've done it," others murmuring "maybe." Jared, his eyes turned inward, head tilted slightly downward, hands again thrust in jacket pockets, must have heard the same sotto voce commentary, but he showed no reaction. Gladdys walked on my other side. She seized my hand and squeezed it.

The room to which Ling-ling escorted us was broad and dimly lit by translucent display screens that tiled the walls. At the far end, two high-backed chairs of blond wood and padded black leather faced an empty holostage. I heard Gladdys catch her breath, and her hand tightened.

Ling-ling said, "We'll get an extra chair for the woman."

"No." The voice issued from hidden speakers, but seemed to come from the space over the holostage. "I'll speak with Jared and Mac alone."

It was Kyle's voice. The overtones were different—the acoustics of speakers versus those of larynx and mouth—but it was his voice.

"Everyone leave now," the voice said. "And, while I can't physically stop you, I ask that you not record this session for study."

"Kyle?" said Gladdys.

"Is that you, Gladdys? Just a moment." There was a faint whirr. Cameras pivoting somewhere. "Ah, yes. You shouldn't have come. I told Ling-ling to call Jared and Mac. Hello, Jared. Hello, Mac. What do you think now?"

"Kyle!" Gladdys wept, her cheeks gleaming with tears. "How could you do this?"

"It's just a radical make-over, is all. How we accomplished it is not something you would understand."

That was Kyle's wit, too. But Gladdys sobbed uncontrollably. Jared gathered her in his arms, but she shook him off. Ling-ling took her by the shoulder and she seemed to deflate and followed her meekly. "There's no cause for tears, Mrs. Holtzmann," Ling-ling told her. "You see. Our friend is transformed, but not gone."

Jared and I stood dumbly while the research staff filed out. One of them paused by a control panel, but the voice said, "No recordings, Bob. I said I couldn't stop you, not that I couldn't feel it." The researcher grimaced and gave us a sheepish look before following the others.

When the door clicked shut, Jared and I remained motionless in the center of the room, Jared staring at the door; I, at the holostage. Uneasily, I lowered myself into the left-hand chair. Kyle's voice said, "Jared, have a seat." Flashing lights caught the corner of my eye and for a moment I watched one of the panels flickering. Perhaps it monitored the voice synthesizer. I don't know.

Jared took the right-hand chair and slumped forward in it. He and I faced each other at an angle, and I could see now that Jared too had been crying, in that tight, stoic way of his. I have only known him to let loose a handful of times in our acquaintanceship, and sometimes I wished he would do so more often, save I am afraid of pressure contained so long.

"Well," said the voice. "I've done it."

"Yes," Jared told the floor in front of him. "But the question is what have you done?"

I swallowed. "You're looking well, Kyle," I said. Jared turned a red-rimmed, accusing gaze on me.

"Let me show you," Kyle said. The holostage took on a pearly glow. Ruby lasers rastered the volume. A wire-frame human took shape, then garbed itself in flesh and clothing. Furniture appeared around him: a chair, a lamp, a side-table. The figure sat as Kyle so often sat—long legs thrust out before him, crossed at the ankle; hands steepled under his chin. The Kyle Buskirk grin split his features. "Hi, guys."

Jared rose from his chair and slowly circumnavigated the holostage, examining the image from all sides. The Kyle-image turned and followed Jared with his head, causing an eerie tingle down my spine. Jared noticed the same thing, straightened, and looked around the room. "Cameras," he said. "They enable the computer to triangulate on any object in the room and adjust the image accordingly. Probably, the software gives first priority to moving objects."

The Kyle image spread its hands. "Duh?" he said. "You use binocular vision; I use cameras. Different bodies, different physiques."

Jared had finished his examination. "Different bodies," he said, "different persons."

Kyle cocked his head. "How so?"

"Because the person is a complete substance, composed of matter and form. The same form applied to different matters is different substances. Fido and Spot both have the form of 'dog,' but Fido is this matter and Spot is that matter."

"Trust a philosopher," said Kyle with an exaggerated sigh, "to take something hard and fast and make it all fuzzy and conceptual." Then he sat up in his chair. "You're right, of course, to some extent. I've lost almost all my somatic functions. I can see and hear; but I can't smell and taste."

"Then I guess we're not going out to dinner tonight," I said. Jared froze, then looked away from the holostage and from me.

"Mac," he said. "Please."

"I suppose I must feel different," Kyle went on. "Like phantom limb syndrome, only it's 'phantom body' syndrome. There are certain operations I perform that are analogous to reaching, for example. But I can't actually grip anything."

"You suppose," said Jared. "You don't *know* if you feel different?"

Another phantom shrug. "My somatic memories are gone. But Jared, I still remember being Kyle Buskirk."

"So does a digital recording."

"Jared, what will it take to convince you it's me? Ask me anything."

206

Jared had returned to his chair and lowered himself into it. His eyes were pinched. "I concede that the memory record is faithful and complete."

"Incomplete, actually. Anything I had forgotten in the flesh was lost before the flash. And I lost other memories when the files were compressed. A q-bit computer has enormous capacity; but not as enormous as the human brain. The losses were random."

Jared trembled, taking long deep breaths, the only sign of his inner turmoil. "It was cruel of you to do this to me," he said, "to bring me here and put me through this agony. This is my fault. I goaded you on, didn't I? But I never meant it to go this far."

"Emotions are a matter for the glands; and I don't have those anymore. I know what I did and why, but I don't feel them in my gut." The figure smiled. "I suppose I should say 'in my core.'"

"What *does* it feel like?" I asked. "I mean, to have a computer for a body."

"Would 'indescribable' do it for you? I get visual and auditory inputs. We recruited the optic and aural neurons for that. I know—somehow—when a channel is open or a monitor. It's like…Like an itch, I suppose. I'm a real whiz at math too; but there's an encyclopedia in an auxiliary server that I can't seem to access, so don't ask me the capital of Azerbaijan. The staff actually has to transfer the right files. As for the rest, how aware are *you* of your own spleen?"

Jared straightened. "What happened to Kyle?"

"I am Kyle."

"Okay. What happened to Kyle's body?"

"It's still animate, if that's what you mean. It can't see or hear, but the rest of its somatic functions were not touched. It breathes, eats, digests, craps. It can even make sounds, like barking or crying. Would you like to see it?"

Jared covered his face. "Like a blind, deaf animal…I loved that guy. I couldn't bear visiting the husk; and I know damn well Gladdys couldn't."

"Kyle." I said. "When did you decide to do this? Was it the cancer?"

"From the flesh to the flash! No. The cancer only places a time limit. The goal, I've had since the Flu, when Jared almost died. Jared's objections have nothing to do with it."

"Mac," Jared said in a voice strained for patience. "You're talking to a Chinese Room. It isn't Kyle—it can't be—and I wish you would stop talking to it as if it were. My best friend committed suicide just to make a digital recording of himself; *and you're talking to the video.*"

"Jared," the Kyle-image said, "how can I prove myself to you?"

I noticed he did not ask how he might prove himself to me.

207

Jared stood and buttoned his jacket, shoved his hands in the pockets as he often did, and shuffled a few steps. The hologram tracked his movements. "Tell me," he said. Then he fell silent.

Before the silence could drag on, the image spoke. "Tell you what?"

"Tell me when your affair with Gladdys started."

I do not know which chilled me more: the content of the accusation or the casual tones in which it was made. *But it was all burlesque,* I told myself. *Too obviously over the top, and right in front of Jared.* That was when I knew that the old quarrel over Maddy had never really ended.

"So you know?" said Kyle. "From the beginning?"

"That depends on when it started, doesn't it?"

"When you were in the hospital," Kyle said, also matter-of-factly. "She is a lonely woman, Jared. She needs company."

"So out of your generous spirit…"

"It is not physical, if that is what concerns you."

"Physical? That would be easy to forgive. But to seduce her affections… Friend, that cut far too close to the bone."

"It was not my initiative. And when she wanted to make it physical, I stopped coming to visit. I stopped texting."

"And so you added cruelty to betrayal. You were only toying with her affections, like you did with Maddy. You could not stand that I could love anyone but you, so you had to take them away from me. Then after you had her affections in your hand, you dropped them in the dirt and shut her out with not even a word of explanation. You cannot imagine that it is more pleasant to watch her moping after you than it was to see her going off on 'shopping trips.'"

"I'm celibate now, Jared. And I've shut myself up in a monastery. Jared, I stopped short. I would not cross that line. Do you understand? It wasn't just the cancer that tipped my decision."

Jared fell momentarily silent at this. "You killed yourself so you wouldn't take Gladdys from me? But you moron! You took Kyle from me! And why would that hurt me any less?"

"But I haven't gone away. I'm here."

"No, you're not. You are a…a damned scrapbook!" He turned away from the hologram. "Come on, Mac. We're done here."

"Jared," said the sim, "you would have lost me anyway. I received the death sentence two years ago. And then what would you have had? Scrapbooks and picture files and digital recordings. What sort of conversations could you have held with them?"

"Are you coming, Mac?"

I swallowed, nodded, and rose from my chair. The sim followed my movements. "Et tu, Mac?"

I went to Jared's side and threw an arm across his shoulder. "We'll all miss him."

He looked at me though moist eyes. "I thought you were convinced."

"I was. Until you asked about Gladdys. Kyle would never have answered like that. Everything was a recitation of facts. There were no feelings, no emotions."

The sim also rose from its virtual chair. "You can visit any time you like. I'll be on the Grid in another month or two, and you'll have a special password."

Jared grabbed the handle for the door, and the sim said, "Jared? Don't go." And for just a moment, Jared froze. Then he pulled the door wide and it swung shut behind us. "Call me," I heard the voice behind us. "Promise you'll call."

THE FLASH IN A PAN

Every year thereafter, Jared and I would receive cards on the holidays purporting to come from Kyle. Now and then, Jared's pix will ring with an incoming call from the Lab and later, off the Grid. He doesn't answer them. He has hung a picture in his office: he and Kyle from university days, garbed in their track uniforms, standing side by side on the cinders with their arms around each other's shoulders. When we get together with our wives, which we try to do twice a year, we always tell stories about Kyle, and they are always funny and full of good memories.

AFTERWORD TO "PLACES WHERE THE ROADS DON'T GO"

I wrote this one just before writing "Hopeful Monsters," but it received a substantive rewrite afterwards, so we could say it was written after "Hopeful Monsters," as well. This novella is another of the stories that appear here for the first time.

While the arguments for artificial intelligence and for "downloading minds" into computers are well known to science fiction readers—Ray Kurzweil's *The Singularity Is Near: When Humans Transcend Biology* (Penguin, 2006) is typical—the arguments against them are not. By this I do not mean arguments that we *should not* do these things, but that we *cannot* do them.

The idea for the story came from reading the Gödelian papers of the Oxford philosopher, John Lucas, specifically "Minds, Machines, and Gödel," *Philosophy*, XXXVI, 1961, pp. 112-127 copied along with subsequent replies and responses on his website: *http://users.ox.ac.uk/~jrlucas/* (scroll down to *I Gödelian Papers*). I later learned that the physicist Roger Penrose had taken up the argument, and that Gödel himself argued against the mechanistic concept of the mind.

Another argument against mind-as-mechanism came from philosopher John R. Searle's presidential address to the APA, "Is the Brain a Digital Computer?", which expands on his earlier Chinese Room thought experiment: *http://users.ecs.soton.ac.uk/harnad/Papers/Py104/searle.comp.html* Additional material came from Stanley L. Jaki, *Brain, Mind and Computers* (Herder & Herder, 1969) and Walter J. Freeman, "Nonlinear Brain Dynamics and Intention According to Aquinas," *Mind & Matter*, Vol. 6(2), pp. 207-234.

So the idea came to me of a philosopher and a computer scientist debating the issue. Nothing can be more boring than that; so they became two friends, Jared and Kyle, whose friendship is sorely tested by the disagreement—because the disagreement is a surrogate for something else.

The narrator shifted from omniscient to a third friend, Mac the topologist, who is both odd man out and the center of the argument. The various arguments—the Turing Test, the Chinese Room, the Gödelian argument, etc.—were made physical as much as possible. Dramatizing what is essentially a philosophical debate proved to be some of the most difficult writing I've attempted. Whether I succeeded you must judge.

Write what you know. I was a topologist in my storied youth, proving a couple of original theorems regarding function space topologies. A topology is a formalized concept of closeness or proximity, and makes a "set" into a "space." It struck me as I was reading Leonard Savage, *The Foundations of Statistics* (Dover, 1972), that his conceptualization of decisions as functions mapping state space into a consequence space would give rise to a topology on decisions based on the proximity of the consequences.

By some quirk of fate, I shortly after received an email from my former topology professor, J. Douglas Harris of Marquette University, asking about my old paper, as function space topology was becoming a hot topic once more. He had in the intervening years been working in computer architecture and writing a book on networking, but was thinking about some new theory in topology. Proximities have applications in programming, he wrote. Hmm.

Gödel's theorem showed that there are true statements that cannot be proven. I had the intuition that just as the rational numbers are dense in the reals perhaps the provable statements were dense in the true statements. So I asked Doug if he would be willing to vet Mac's role in the story. In particular, was there any reason why Mac's "Density Theorem" could not be true. He, in turn, brought in a colleague, Mike Slattery, an algebraist and computer scientist (and science fiction fan) to vet Kyle's role.

Well, then, someone ought to vet Jared. So I asked Edward Feser at Pasadena City College in California if he had any thoughts on the philosophical side of the argument. Ed is the author of a helpful book: *Philosophy of Mind: A Beginner's Guide* (Oneworld, 2007).

I also asked my friend Nancy Kress if she would look at the first draft, since I had a feeling that it was slow-paced and bloated. She graciously agreed, both to read the draft and that the draft was slow-paced and bloated. Consequently, the version you have read is shorter by nearly a third and altered in several other ways. I also received helpful comments from Doug Harris, Mike Slattery, and Ed Feser. All of them make cameos in the text. Whatever improvement resulted is due to their kindness.

REMEMBER'D KISSES

*C**lick.*

A mechanical sound. A relay, perhaps. A flip-flop switch or maybe a butterfly valve. Very soft. Almost muffled.

Sigh.

And that was hydraulics. Escape gas bleeding off. Pressure relief. Again, a muted sound, not particularly obtrusive.

Click.

It was a metronome. A syncopation. If you focused all your attention on it, it could become—

Sigh.

—quite relaxing. Hypnotic even. It would be easy to lose oneself in its rhythm.

Click!

The sudden hand on his shoulder made him start.

"Mr. Carter?"

Sigh.

He turned, unwilling; guided by the gentle but persistent pressure of the hand on his shoulder. His vision rotated, camera-like. Away from the equipment; along the tubing, hanging in catenary loops; past the blinking monitors; toward the sight that he had been avoiding ever since he had stepped into the room.

Click.

"Yes, Doctor?" His voice was listless, uninterested. He heard it as if he were a spectator at a very bad play.

"We did all we could, Mr. Carter. The medics stabilized her as soon as the police cut her out of the car. But I'm afraid there was little else they could do."

Sigh.

He looked at the doctor, turning his head quickly, so that the bed itself flicked across his vision without registering. But his subconscious saw the subliminal afterimage and began sending messages of pain and fear.

Click.

"I understand, Doctor..." He glanced at the name tag pinned to the white uniform, trying not to notice the little splashes of red on the sleeves and on the chest. "I understand, Doctor Lapointe. I'm sure you did everything possible."

"If we had gotten to her sooner, or if the trauma had been less severe, we might have been able to repair the damage. There have been incredible advances in tissue repair nanomachines in the last several years..."

Sigh.

Henry Norris Carter wondered if the doctor thought he was being comforting. Tell me more, he thought. Tell me all the different ways you might have saved her. If only. If only this advance had been made; if only that had been done sooner. If only. If only.

Well, take it as he meant it. "Yes, Doctor Lapointe; but I'm sure you understand that such speculations cannot make me feel any better about what's happened." [And a part of his mind curled up and gibbered, *Nothing's happened! Nothing's happened!*] "I'm quite aware of the advances in nanotechnology. My wife and I both work—" He suddenly realized he had used the present tense and stopped, confused. "—no, worked—" But that wasn't right, either. Not yet. "I mean we were both genetic engineers at SingerLabs over in New Jersey. We both donated DNA to the cell library there. As long as we're talking 'if only's,' if only I had had her cell samples with me—"

"No, Mr. Carter, you mustn't think that. As I said, the trauma was too severe. Even the most advanced nanomachines are still too slow to have saved your wife before irreversible brain damage set in."

So. Finally. He forced himself to look directly at the figure on the bed. The maze of tubing crawled snake-like around it. Encircling it; binding it; piercing it. Up nose. Down throat. Into vein and groin. Pushing the fluids and the gasses in and sucking them out, because the body itself had given up the task. The click/sigh of the respirator faded into the background.

The contours of the sheet were not quite right; as if parts of what was under it were missing. The doctors, he supposed, had cobbled the body back together as best they could, but their hearts hadn't been entirely in it. The whole left side of her face was an ugly purple bruise. And the symmetry of her nose and cheekbones and jaw was irretrievably lost. The right eye was closed, as if sleeping; and the left—The left eye was hidden under a mass of bandages. *If it's there at all.* Judging by the extent of the damage on that side, it was doubtful that the eye had remained in its socket.

He wanted to scream and his stomach gave a queer flip-flop and his knees felt suddenly weak. He trembled all over. Don't think about that. Think about anything else. Think about…

Quiet evenings at home. She, reading her favorite Tennyson in a circle of soft light cast by the goose-neck lamp; while he pretended to read, but watched her secretly over the lip of his book and she knew he was watching her and was waiting for just the right moment to—

Running through the rainstorm down 82nd Street from the Met, his trenchcoat an umbrella over both their heads. Laughing because it was so silly to get caught unprepared like that and they were soaked to the skin already and—

Hiking the Appalachian Trail where it lost itself in the granite mountains of New England and stopping to examine the wildflowers by the edge of the path and wondering why on earth the stems would always branch in just exactly that way and—

Four-wheeling over Red Cone that summer in Colorado and how he had frozen at the wheel because all he could see out either side of the Bronco was sky because the road ran up a ridge only a little wider than the car itself and how could anyone expect to drive over a knob of rock that steep? and how the sign on the other side, by Montezuma, had said dangerous road travel at your own risk and wasn't that a hell of a place to put it and—

Her eyes had been a most lovely shade of hazel.

"Pardon me?"

Henry looked at the doctor and blinked away the memories that had blurred his vision. "I said her eyes were hazel."

"Oh."

He turned and looked again at his wife. The doctor seemed at a loss for what to say and for a crazy instant Henry felt sorry for *him*. The doctor wanted to say something; anything to pierce Henry's shell of misery; but there was nothing that anyone could ever say or do that would make the slightest particle of difference in how he felt.

He felt…Nothing. He was numb. He refused to accept what he saw.

"Barbara."

"She can't hear you. She's far too deep in coma for that."

He ignored the doctor's comment. It was patently absurd. Voices made sound waves; and sound waves vibrated eardrums; and eardrums made nerve impulses; and somewhere, somewhere deep inside that dying body there had to be a tiny, glimmering spark, wondering why everything was growing so much dimmer and fainter and he would be *damned* before he let that spark flicker out all alone in silence.

He drifted toward the bed; and the doctor, sensing his intention, guided him toward her relatively uninjured right side. The doctor lifted the sheet, exposing her hand and Carter took it in both of his. He noticed the mole on her right side, just above the curve of the hip, and touched it briefly with his forefinger.

"The other driver," the doctor said, "the one who ran the red light, was killed instantly. An eighteen-year-old kid and dead drunk. Now he's just dead."

Henry shook his head. Did the doctor think that that thought would comfort him? He felt a brief regret that the drunk hadn't suffered; and a second regret that he would wish such a thing of anyone; and then he felt nothing once more.

"Barbry, I'm here. I came as soon as they called." He stroked her hand gently, fingertips on palm, and let his palm run under her limp fingertips; and was embarrassed to notice how his body, for a brief instant, responded to the remembered touch.

He began telling her about his day, because there wasn't much of anything else he could think of to talk about. [And why had she taken the day off to shop for his birthday? They should have been together in the lab, safe. Instead—]

Instead, he told her how he and Bill Canazetti had finally made some progress on the Barnsleyformer; because the trick wasn't in the morphogenesis after all, but in the fractal geometry of the genes. They had gotten a brief, tantalizing glimpse of a simple and elegant recursion formula and would have continued to work on it well after quitting time except the phone call had come from the hospital and—

And the traffic at the tunnel ramp had been terrible. Backed up all the way around halfway to the turnpike gate. Wasn't it always that way when you were in a hurry?

At any rate, he told her, 'Dolph Kavin was doing a slow burn because he'd been passed over for project leader on the cloning team. Old Lady Peeler had picked Amanda Jacobs and 'Dolph had complained bitterly to anyone who would listen [and there weren't that many] how women always stuck together; but you know how it is with office politics. And he said it was a lot different in the old days before Singer had died and the Lab was run on a more personal level.

And—

"She's gone, Mr. Carter."

He jerked for the second time at the unexpected touch; and looked from the hand tentatively laid on his wrist, up the arm to the doctor's sympathetic face.

"What?"

"She's gone. All brain activity has ceased. I—" He broke off, looked uncomfortable, mustered his resolve. "If you would sign a few forms, please. Many of her organs can still be saved, if we act quickly." The doctor looked at him in mute appeal. Your wife is dead, his eyes seemed to say; but we can still save others if you help.

Others.

Strangers.

And why should he care about strangers?

Donate organs. A nice way of saying, let's cut up your wife's body into little chunks and sew them into other people. Intellectually, he and Barbara had always supported the organ donor movement; but it was different when the actual time came. And what the hell did it matter? Barbry didn't live there anymore.

"Yes," he said; and his voice came out in a sort of croak. "Yes," he repeated. "Go ahead. It's what she would have wanted."

"You're doing the right thing," the doctor assured him. "Your wife may be dead, but part of her will go on living through others."

Click.

The most awful thing about the whole business, Henry decided as he rose shakily from the chair, was the way the respirator continued to pump air and the way in which the sheets continued to rise and fall. As if the person beneath them had only fallen into a deep slumber and would awaken when the morning came.

Sigh.

Of course, they insisted that he stay and rest. They gave him a mild sedative and they made him lie down for an hour or so. He closed his eyes, but his mind wouldn't shut down. It kept spinning and spinning, trying to find a way out of accepting what had happened. When he arose only a short while later, he was unrested and unrefreshed.

It was the early morning pre-dawn hours when he left Roosevelt Hospital and made his way down 9th Avenue toward the Lincoln Tunnel entrances. There was a mist off the Hudson that gave the West Side a ghostly and unreal appearance. Sounds echoed as if on a damp and abandoned stage set. His was the only car on 9th Ave., and in the distance a single pair of headlights drifted crosstown. If New York was The City That Never Slept, during these hours it at least dozed fitfully.

Some part of him had taken over from the gibbering, helpless personality crouching in the back of his head. It was a part of him that felt nothing and thought nothing. It was an automaton that made his body do all the right things, like some faithful robot dutifully carrying home its injured master.

The neighborhood north of the tunnel ramps had once been called Hell's Kitchen; but the new yuppy-fied City was a little ashamed of its rough-necked, blue-collar past, so they called it Chelsea North now. They could call it what they damn well pleased, but some things never change. It was still Hell's Kitchen and, if the police no longer walked the beat in squads of five as they once did, it was because they seldom left their patrol cars.

If Henry had been entirely himself, he would never have made the wrong turn. But automatons do make mistakes and the sign with the arrow pointing toward the tunnel was placed ambiguously. He meant to turn right at the *next* corner; but his eyes saw the sign and his hands spun the wheel, and there he was.

He realized his error almost immediately. He cursed for a moment or two and checked the street sign at the next intersection to get his bearings. He turned, and turned again, and then he saw her.

The streetlight was a stage spot highlighting a tableau. Brown, ratted hair hanging low around familiar eyes and nose; her body wrapped in a tattered pea jacket, and huddled over a heating grate; hugging a tattered shopping bag to her. Three men—two black, one white—loomed over her, laughing, giving her little shoves, while her eyes darted like mouse eyes back and forth, looking for escape.

"Barbry!"

Henry hit the brakes, twisted and grabbed the jack handle from the floor in the back. He burst from the car. "You! You, there! Leave that woman alone!"

The men laughed and turned on him and the laughter died. If Henry had been entirely himself, they would have pounced without a thought, like any wolfpack. But he was not entirely himself, and he had a jack handle in his hand, and there was something in his eyes. They used to call it the berserker look. It was the look that said that, whatever came, life or death, he would accept it gladly.

The three liked long odds in their favor. Three strong young males against a lone woman, that was acceptable. But against a crazy man with the berserker look? No. They might walk out of it; but maybe not all three; and certainly not all whole. So they sought the better part and walked away, throwing obscene words and gestures after them to show they hadn't been afraid after all, not really.

Henry walked to the woman on the grate and took her by the hands and raised her to her feet. She looked at him with fear in her eyes.

"Barbry?"

And she didn't really look like Barbara at all; and that broke the spell. Henry blinked and his surroundings came crashing down around him. Hell's Kitchen? How had he gotten here? He could remember nothing since lying down at the hospital. And who was this woman?

She looked like—. But, no. Her hair was brown, like Barbara's; but it was a shade darker. The face had the same shape; but the cheekbones sat lower. And there was a scar that ran from under the right eye, across the cheek toward the ear. She stank: of sweat and booze and excrement. Whoever it was, it wasn't Barbara. And why on earth would he ever have thought that?

"Who are you?" he asked.

She didn't answer and tried to pull her hands from his. Henry remembered leaping from the car and looked around with sudden alarm. Those three punks might come back any moment. He began to shake as he realized what he had done.

He turned back to his car, remembered the woman, and hesitated. He couldn't just drive off and leave her here. If those punks came back, she'd be worse off than if he had never stopped.

"Come on," he said. "Get in the car."

She looked at him doubtfully and backed away a step, holding her shopping bag like Hector's shield. Henry pulled open the passenger's door. "Get in," he repeated. "They might come back."

That seemed to get through to her. She glanced down the street in the direction her tormentors had gone, then looked back at Henry's Town Car. Her tongue swept out and around her lips. She looked at him again. Then she made up her mind and darted into the safety of the automobile.

Henry slammed the door, ran around to the driver's side, and slid behind the wheel. He hit the door lock and all four doors snapped at once. The sound startled the woman who jerked around anxiously. She tried the door and it wouldn't open; so she slid across the seat from him as far as she could go, putting her bag between them and clutching it to her.

✦

He took her with him back to Short Hills because he didn't know what else to do and it was easier to make no decisions than to decide anything. Once home, he hustled her inside his house, glancing over his shoulder while he did so, to see if—despite the hour—any of the neighbors were watching.

In the kitchen, she pulled away from him and ran to the farthest corner and crouched there, making small sounds in her throat. Henry wondered how much human being was left imprisoned within her skull. There but for the Grace of God…Barbry and this bag lady looked somewhat alike, enough to be taken for sisters if not for twins; yet, Barbry had lived here, in comfort if not in luxury, while this woman had lived on a heating vent in Hell's Kitchen. How easily it might have happened the other way. What trauma might have been enough?

"Now that I've got you," Henry told the woman, "what do I do with you?"

She seemed to shrink within herself and Henry held out what he meant to be placating hands. "Don't worry. I won't hurt you. If you want, you can have a shower and a meal. And a change of clothes." The thought of giving this woman one of Barbry's dresses was distressing. He wasn't ready to part with anything of hers, not yet. But there was a trunk in the attic, with some cast-offs that she had meant to donate to charity anyway.

He took the bag lady by the hand, noticing as he did so the track of needle marks up the inside of her arm, and showed her the shower in the bathroom. He gave her a washrag and towels and one of Barbara's old housecoats and told her to leave her dirty clothing for disposal. The woman glared at him suspiciously, so he shrugged and walked away.

In the kitchen, he opened a can of beef broth into a pot and turned on the heat. Something not too taxing for her system. As the odor filled the room he realized he was hungry, too, and he added a second can to the pot. After it had come to a boil, he reduced the heat to simmer and walked to the kitchen window.

The kitchen faced on a woods protected by "greenbelt" legislation from development. No danger of ticky-tacky working class homes depressing the property values. The canopy of the trees looked like a silhouette cut from black construction paper, the false dawn providing an eerie back-lighting.

He still didn't know her name. He had asked twice on the drive back, but she had remained silent, staring at him with ferret eyes, and he began to wonder if she even realized what was happening to her. Probably not much intelligence left. Etched away by years on the streets and a constant drip-drip-drip of heroin on the brain cells. Odd, how much—and how little—she looked like Bar— Like Barb—.

He squeezed his eyes shut and willed himself not to think of her. The sound of her voice. A wisp of perfume. Remembered kisses.

After a while, he realized that he couldn't hear the shower running upstairs. What was that bag lady doing?

When he checked the bathroom she wasn't there, so he searched from room to room until he found her. She was hiding in the closet in the guest bedroom. She had taken the few odd garments hanging there and made a sort of nest of them. The wire hangers swung and tinkled like Japanese wind chimes. She looked at him with those ferret eyes; expecting anything, surprised at nothing.

Somewhere, she had found an old bag of salted peanuts. A relic of some airline flight Henry had long forgotten. She had poured the nuts into her palm and was gnawing at them. When she saw Henry at the closet door, she clutched the foil bag to her, as if she expected him to try to take it away.

Eventually, she did eat. Not the peanut bag, but the soup Henry had prepared. She wolfed it in great greedy gulps, her left arm encircling the bowl, and her right wielding the soupspoon like a shovel. She kept her eye fixed warily on him the whole time, except when she darted quick looks around her, like an animal guarding its prey.

When she was done he took the bowl, which she released only reluctantly; and this time when he led her to the shower she seemed to understand. She grabbed the towels from his hands and stared at them. Then she stared at him.

"Go on," he said gruffly. "You shower now. I'll go up to the attic and see if I can find some old clothes for you."

When he returned from the attic with an armful of clothing, Henry found the woman in the library, sitting in Barbry's favorite reading chair. Showered and scrubbed, she seemed like a different person. Certainly, she smelled different: fresh and clean. From the rear, in the soft light and wearing Barbry's bathrobe, she looked enough like Barbara to make Henry's heart freeze for a moment. The dresses fell from his arms and he braced himself against the back of his own reading chair.

And the illusion vanished. All he saw was a bag lady holding the portrait photograph that Barbara and he had had taken only eight months before.

"That was my wife," he said, and she jumped a little and turned and looked at him. Her eyes were childlike. Green, he saw, and not hazel. They didn't look at all like the suspicious ferret eyes he had seen earlier. "My wife, Barbara," he explained, pointing to the photo. "She was, she was killed today in an automobile accident."

There. He had said it out loud. Now it was true. All of a sudden, he couldn't look at the photograph. The bag lady looked from the portrait to him and back to the portrait. Then she stroked Barbara's face gently. She nodded her head up and down in a slow cadence and made a low keening sound. Henry dropped into his chair, crushing the dresses he had laid there. He covered his face with his hands and a time went by.

When he looked up again, he saw that the woman had gone to the mirror by the bookshelves and was staring at her own face. She was holding the photograph in her right hand so she could see both herself and Barbara side-by-side. With her left, she held the front of the housecoat gathered together.

"Yes, you do look a little like her," Henry said. "Not much, but that's what made me stop there on the street. I—" He suddenly realized he had as much as said he wouldn't have stopped otherwise.

But the bag lady seemed not to have noticed, or, if noticed, not to have cared. "I'm Sadie," she said and Henry jerked his head in surprise at hearing her speak. "Sadie the Lady. That's me." She said it in a kind of sing-song voice. She returned her attention to the study of herself and the photograph.

Henry stood up and walked behind her so he could see the two faces from the same angle. "Yes. You know, if you did your hair up the same way, you would look even more like her." Barbry had always worn her hair piled up.

Sadie the Lady smiled, showing an incisor missing on the upper right. She put the photograph down and reached with both her hands to gather her hair into a rough approximation of Barbara's. She primped for the mirror, turning this way and that. Henry, watching her reflection, blushed. He should have known she would need new underwear, too.

The tableau in the cemetery seemed unreal. As if he were watching it from far away. Voices buzzed. Puppet figures stood about. He felt things only as if through layers of cotton. People he knew kept coming up to him and gripping his arm and telling him how sorry they were. He couldn't understand why they were so sorry, but he smiled and said everything was going to be all right.

Bill Canazetti, his lab partner, told him it was all right to cry. That he shouldn't hold it in. But Henry just shook his head. Later he would do that for Her. Just now, he couldn't.

There was a preacher. Barbara had been a church-goer, High Church, and Henry had sometimes gone with Her. He wished now he had gone more often. It was a portion of Her life that he could no longer share.

The preacher (Priest, he supposed. There was a difference). The priest spoke of comforting impossibilities. Eternal life. The immortal soul. Barbara had gone to a better world. She had left behind this vale of tears. Henry listened. He wanted to believe it. He tried to believe it. It was better to believe such things than to believe that there was no Barbara at all, anywhere. Death was the Great Proselytizer.

"Most of all," the man in the funny collar said to the assembled group, "Barbara lives on in the hearts and minds of those of us who knew and loved her. We carry some piece of her with us always…"

Now, that was certainly true. At least, since he had donated Her organs. There were no doubt several people already who carried a piece of Her with them. And there was the DNA sample at the lab. Under proper conditions it should last nearly forever. Immortality of a sort, though he doubted that that was what the priest had meant.

Henry decided that, if Barbry did live somehow in his memories, the first thing he should do when he got home was to record those memories on tape. Everything about Her. That way he could never forget.

He had kept Her clothes and other things. He couldn't bear to part with them just yet. They were memories, too, in a way; and he wasn't quite ready to cast them out. In fact [and it would shame him if it ever got out], he slept at night with one of Her slips tucked beneath his pillow.

And then there was Sadie the Lady.

Henry had talked her into staying. He didn't know why. He had put her up in the guest bedroom and let her wear Barbara's old things. Suspicious at first, she had gradually adjusted. She spoke now, at least once or twice a day; and had wandered off to her closet nest only once. She was still hoarding food, Henry discovered, in several caches around the house, which Henry left undisturbed. It seemed…right that she should be in the house.

The worst part had been the heroin withdrawal. Henry hadn't believed that such agony was possible. Sadie had moaned and sweated and begged him to find her connection. But her connection was in Manhattan and Henry had not allowed her out of the house, despite her pleading, her tears, and her threats. At times, he had to restrain her, physically; and found that, for her condition, she was surprisingly strong. Together, they had finally weathered the crisis; and when it was over they were both drained.

Afterwards she had begun to show more interest in herself. She bathed more regularly, and brushed and combed her hair. She became a kind of housekeeper, doing odd chores around the house. Cleaning. Cooking his meals. Sometimes mumbling to herself. Once or twice saying a few words out loud. Perhaps it was gratitude. Her way of repaying him for what he had done for her that night on the streets. Or perhaps she was trying to help him through his bereavement. Henry didn't know.

Sometimes when he saw Sadie in the hall or in the kitchen, Henry squinted his eyes and pretended to himself that she was actually Barbara. The mental Novocain was wearing off and Henry was starting to feel the pain of Barbara's loss. His little game with Sadie helped numb the pain, at least for a little while. It was a harmless bit of self-deception.

And it was only a game, of course. He knew when he did it that he was only pretending.

It was two weeks before he returned to work.

No one else was in the lab yet. Henry had come to work early on purpose. His cubicle was at the far end of the common room, farthest from the door, and he hadn't wanted to face the others, to run the gauntlet of their pity. Not right away. He had wanted some time alone, with Barbara, in the cell library.

She really was there, in a way. The culture dish contained all the information that was Barbara. Everything, that is, except the experiences and memories that had made Her a *person* rather than an organism. He told Her how much he missed Her, but mostly he was just silent, remembering things. Then he noticed the time and slipped hastily out of the cell library before anyone could see him there. People wouldn't understand and might think him a little odd.

He returned to his cubicle and looked around vaguely, as if he were in a strange country. He fiddled with the clutter on his desk and wondered how far Bill had gotten on their project. Bill hadn't been idle, he was sure. The guy was a certified workaholic. The two of them worked well together. The tortoise and the hare. Bill was a great one for leaping ahead in flashes of intuition; while Henry was the plodder who filled in the details and proved whether Bill's gut feeling was something more than what he had eaten for breakfast.

Well, he couldn't sit here all day looking like a zombie. Lord knows what the others would read into that. He activated the terminal screen and began studying the logbook. Minutes went by.

"Henry!"

He turned and saw Bill Canazetti shrugging out of his jacket. Was it 0800 already? Canazetti laid a hand on Henry's shoulders, a heavy hand that was supposed to be reassuring. "I'm so sorry about Barbara," he murmured. "We all are. She was the best."

Henry took a deep breath. He had been dreading this ritual all morning. Everyone would feel obligated to say something to him. Something to remind him of what he only wanted to forget. The fact that most of them had already done so at the funeral wouldn't stop them. Perhaps it satisfied some inner need; a need to participate in another's grief. For Henry, it did nothing except pick at the psychic scab. But he could face their awful sympathy now. He really could.

"Never mind that," he told Canazetti, more gruffly than he had intended. Bill looked hurt, so he added, "It's over with. And besides, Barbry's not really gone. She's still with me. Now it's time to get on with life."

"Yes, I suppose. Canazetti looked uncomfortable. "Is there—well, anything I can get you?" He was like all the others: eager to help where no help was possible.

"A cup of decaf would be nice," Henry told him. "I do need to catch up on our project. Let me just read the notes here and then you can fill me in on the details."

Canazetti nodded slowly. "All right." He left and Henry immersed himself in the notes on the Barnsleyformer.

He and Bill had been working to improve SingerLabs' line of cell repair nano-machines. To achieve the elusive goal of Whole-Body Repair.

C/R nannies had changed the face of medicine over the last ten years, ever since Singer had created the first one. Repairing damage to tissues was easy now. All the doctor had to do was inject a dose of microscopic machines into the affected tissue. The nannies would visit each cell; compare it to the blueprints stored in the nucleus; disassemble any proteins not to spec; and reassemble them properly.

The problem was that, if multiple trauma was involved, only one tissue at a time could be treated. Each nanny was designed specifically for a certain tissue; and, if two nannies were introduced into the body at the same time, each would perceive the other as a foreign body and engage in a war of mutual extermination.

The information load was the limiting factor. The nannies were controlled by microscopic processors, dubbed Big NIM, that compared DNA strands in triplicate and directed the myriads of C/R machines. But even a single tissue complex involved an incredible amount of data. There were hundreds of different proteins: enzymes and hormones. There were mitochondria, granules, and countless other cellular structures; each with a detailed set of "drawings" that described what it should look like. The limit seemed to be one tissue per nanny. Whole Body Repair seemed out of reach. There was just too much data to store and process. Big NIM always ran out of memory, no matter how much they stretched its capacity.

Bill and he had been ready to quit at one point. They had gone to see Old Lady Peeler to tell her it was impossible. There was a natural barrier, they had said, like the speed of light. Information bits must be carried on matter-energy "markers," and that set a lower limit on the scale for information processors. The machine could not be smaller than its information content. So, there was no way nano-scale processors could ever handle the data load for an entire organism, at least for an organism at the human level of complexity.

Dr. Peeler had listened to them in silence. Then she stared thoughtfully into the distance, working her lips. Finally, she had shaken her head and muttered, as if to herself, "I wonder how genes manage to do it."

And of course she was right.

Genes were natural nanomachines; yet they managed to build an entire complex organism from a single, undifferentiated cell. Morphogenesis, the biologists called it. The "unfolding" of structure from simplicity. Somehow, a zygote managed to contain all the information needed to grow a complete adult.

And that was a paradox.

Because the genes really weren't big enough to handle the information load. There just wasn't room for a complete set of elaborate blueprints in such a small space. Yet there had to be. Finally, in frustration, Henry had blurted out, "Maybe there aren't any blueprints at all!"

And that had reminded Bill of something. A dimly recalled oddity of the early 1980s. Michael Barnsley, a pioneer in complexity theory, had discovered that random inputs to certain recursion formulas always generated the same precise shape. Take a simple random process, like tossing a coin, and define a positioning rule for each outcome. If the coin lands "heads," move a specified distance and direction from the current position. If "tails," a different distance and direction. Then start somewhere—anywhere!—on a grid and flip a coin. After the first fifty moves or so, start marking the positions where your random process takes you. Eventually, the recorded points will accumulate into a definite shape—the "limit shape." Iterate the process thousands of times. The limit shape will always be the same, regardless of the particular series of coin tosses.

Somehow, the end result was encoded in the formula itself, irrespective of the input. It was like a magical machine that always produced the same product, no matter what raw material it was fed.

One set of Barnsley's recursion formulas generated a drawing of a fern leaf. The same leaf appeared every time he ran the simulation, regardless of the particular inputs. That led him to suggest that the genes contained information, not on how the leaf was shaped, but on how to run the recursion formulas. With that information in hand, random chance took care of all the rest.

Many biologists, and even some other chaos scientists, had objected. There is no room for randomness in biology, they had argued. In biology, randomness is death.

Which was true, but they had missed the point. Randomness was embedded in the universe. The physicists had shown long ago that randomness underlay all phenomena. It impinged constantly upon biological growth and evolution. Yet, individuals within a species always matured into the same basic shape. Sometimes, two people, unrelated to each other, even wore the same face. And species living in similar ecological niches evolved into similar forms. There had been sabre-tooth cats in Pleistocene North America. There had been sabre-tooth marsupial "cats" in Pleistocene South America. Everywhere the same shapes asserted themselves. The stems of a flower species always branched precisely so. Every flower.

Once again, science had shown that there were always simple answers to complex questions. Barnsley's algorithm was a transformer. Like an electrical transformer, it changed one thing into another. In this case, it transformed random causes into deterministic effects. Bill had dubbed the mechanism a Barnsleyformer, but Henry had his own private name.

He called it the Template of God.

Thus far, their work on that fatal Thursday, two weeks ago. Bill and he had learned how recursion formulas generated structure; but they had been stuck on the inverse process. Generating the structure from the formulas was one thing. Deducing the recursion formulas from the structure was more difficult. Now Henry saw that Canazetti had found a promising solution and he followed the reasoning closely in the log. Bill had decided that the recursion formulas worked the way they did because certain features of the generated structures were "fractal." That is, they were invariant under changes of magnitude. He had developed a technique he called "tyling," in which the structure was tyled with smaller and smaller replicates of itself. In this way he was able to create inductively the generating equations.

"The trick," he said in Henry's ear, "was getting the number of dimensions right."

Canazetti's unexpected voice made him jerk and he looked around over his shoulder.

"Sorry," said Canazetti, handing him his coffee.

Henry frowned and sipped the brew. He grimaced and looked at the cup. It was as bad as he remembered. He set it aside. "Dimensions," he prompted.

"Right." Canazetti pulled out his desk chair and rolled it under his backside. "A coin toss gives you a Barnsleyformer with up to two dimensions, a plane. But how many do we actually need?"

"Three," Henry replied. But he suspected he was wrong. Otherwise, why would Bill have asked him?

"Wrong." Canazetti shook his head emphatically. "And, once again, the physicists have been there ahead of us. Damned mechanics. Every time a bio-scientist rolls over a new rock, he finds a physicist underneath it. No, Henry, there are actually eleven dimensions." Henry looked skeptical, and Canazetti shrugged. "Take my word for it." He held up his fingers. "Three gross spatial dimensions," he said, counting them off. "Length, height, and breadth. Seven quantum hypo-dimensions rolled up in what they call subspace. And…" He had run out of fingers and he looked blankly at his hands for a moment before shrugging. "And time. I've logged the references in there." He pointed at the disc drive.

Henry decided he would review the literature later. It sounded bizarre to him, but then, most of modern physics did. "Then Barnsleyformers must generate biological structure in all eleven dimensions," he murmured. "Son of a bitch. The morphogenesis must be incredibly more complex than we thought. No wonder our three dimensional models—Hey, wait a minute!" His head shot up.

"What?"

"*All* the dimensions? Including time? That can't be."

"Oh? Why not?"

"Because the time dimension of an organism is its lifespan. How can the gene know ahead of time how long the organism will live?"

Canazetti shrugged again. "I don't know. It's a hunch. Ever read Heinlein's story *Lifeline*? But I suspect that the time dimension of the structure only specifies endogenous death. You know, from internal causes, like old age or birth defects. Exogenous death comes from outside the organism.

Accidents, like being hit with a virus or an automo—" He cut off abruptly and looked embarrassed. "Sorry."

Henry was more offended by Canazetti's circumspection than by any reference to Barbara's death; but he kept his silence. What did happen to the morphogenetic pattern when death came from the outside? Eleven dimensions. Might not some part of the pattern survive the truncation, at least for a while longer. At least until the original time span was reached? The Egyptians had believed something of the sort. The spirit lived on— but only for a while—somewhere beyond our normal senses. There were, after all, those seven other dimensions Canazetti had mentioned. Sub-space. Might the "soul" live there?

A thought began to form in the back of his head. Something nebulous and disturbing, that made his chest tremble inside. He ignored it. "Have you begun *in vivo* experimentation?" he asked.

"Just last week. I reprogrammed a scyphozoan cell-repair machine with recursion formulas tyled from its own DNA."

"A jellyfish?"

Canazetti waved his hand the way only an Italian could. "I wanted something simple enough for a first try, but complex enough to be interesting."

"And?"

Canazetti reached past Henry and pressed a few buttons on the computer terminal. A damaged molecular chain appeared on the screen. A phosphorus group was missing entirely and several carbon rings were broken. "These are the scans recorded through the digital microscope," he told him. "Watch."

Something crawled across the molecules. It looked to Henry like a slime mold; or like tarnish growing at high speed across a set of copper Tinkertoys. The colloidal agar for the cell repair nano-machines. After a few moments, it faded and the molecules underneath reappeared. Henry whistled.

"Like brand new," he said. "And fast."

Fast. What if it had been available two weeks ago? Would it have been fast enough? Henry refused to let himself think about that.

"Yeah." Canazetti's voice was less than ecstatic and Henry looked a question at him. Canazetti waved his hand in frustrated loops. "There're still a couple of stumbling blocks," he admitted. "For one thing, if you program the nanny with the DNA of one jellyfish, it doesn't work so well on other jellyfish."

"How so?"

"Well, every jellyfish carries the basic 'I-am-a-jellyfish' information; but it also carries information that individualizes it: 'I-am-Joe, the-jellyfish.' So, if you use it on a different individual, the nanny tries to restructure it as well as repair it."

Canazetti called up another visual on the terminal. "The jellyfish on the left," he said, "was repaired with nannies grown from the DNA of the one on the right."

Henry inspected the two cell diagrams. "How close is the match?"

"Eighty-seven percent."

"Nearly complete." Henry's own voice sounded far away. He could hear the rush of his blood in his ears. He felt light-headed. Nearly complete.

"Only if the donor and recipient are the same species," said Canazetti's voice. "Otherwise it doesn't work at all. Rejection sets in. Even within a species, I suppose the greater the initial similarity, the better it would work. That's just a hunch. But it doesn't help the doctors any. We want to repair cells, not rearrange them."

Henry tapped the screen with a fingernail. "Then why not clone the nannies from the patient's own cells; tailor them individually for each patient?"

"That would be fine, except for stumbling block number two. It takes time to tyle the material and to deduce the recursion equations. Remember, there are eleven dimensions to consider. And then it takes more time to grow the nannies. What's the patient doing in the meantime?"

Dying, obviously.

We could have saved her, if only—

If only—

If only—

Henry felt faint. He sagged in his chair and Canazetti's hairy Italian arms reached out and braced him.

"Easy there. Are you all right?"

"Yes," Henry told him after a moment. He rubbed his face with his hand. "Yes, I'm all right."

"Easy there. Are you all right?"

"Yes," Sadie told him after a moment. She rubbed her face with her hand. "Yes, I'm all right."

"You don't look all right."

It was Friday evening and he was seated at the kitchen table, eating the late supper that Sadie had prepared for him. Setting the pot back on the stove, she had staggered and slumped, almost spilling the pot. Henry wiped his lips with his napkin and pushed himself from the table. He went to Sadie and took her by the arm. He felt her forehead.

"You look flushed. Why don't you go upstairs and lie down. I'll bring you some medicine."

"No. 'M a burden, me. Too good to ol' Sadie. Time t' move on."

"Nonsense. You go upstairs. You've been working too hard these last two months. Maybe you've picked up a flu bug, or something."

He watched her leave and waited for her footsteps to die away. Then he went to his briefcase on the table in the hallway and opened it.

The zip-locked baggie lay on top of everything else. He picked it up and held it. There were three gelatin capsules inside. One was a specific against the flu that Sadie had. The other two—He began to open the bag but found that his hands were shaking too badly to break the seal. He set it down and leaned with both his hands on the table. He closed his eyes and breathed several long slow breaths.

"*...the nanny tries to restructure as well as repair.*"

She's only a bag lady, after all; and an addict. It's for her own good.

"*I suppose the greater the initial similarity, the better it would work...*"

She'll just find her way back to the streets again. I can't baby-sit her forever. She'll find her connection again. An addict's need never really dies.

"*...the time variable only specifies endogenous death...Exogenous death comes from outside the organism....there are eleven dimensions to consider.*"

And what kind of life was it, living from a shopping bag on a heating grate? She'll be much happier.

When he felt calmer, he opened the bag and poured the three capsules into his hand. He looked at them and rolled them back and forth in his palm. They felt cold and heavy, like stones; but he knew that was only his imagination.

Before he could think about it, he turned and climbed the stairs, two at a time. He stopped in the washroom and filled a glass of water and took it with him to the guestroom.

Sadie the Lady was lying in the bed. She hadn't bothered to take her clothes off. She seldom did. Henry still had to remind her to bathe about once a week. She was propped up on the pillows, but her eyes were closed and her breathing was shallow.

"Sadie?" he asked. She had to be conscious to swallow pills.

The bag lady opened her eyes and mumbled something incoherent.

"It's only an autumn cold," he told her. "Here. Take these." He thrust his hand out. The capsules seemed to have grown warmer. They were like small coals in his palm. "Take them," he said again. And his voice trembled.

Sadie reached out her arm and Henry saw the tracks of the needle marks lining the inside. Small red circles. Craters left from years of meteoric bombardment. "Here. Take these pills." And the words came more easily this time; and the capsules had ceased to burn his skin.

She plucked them from his outstretched hand and placed them one at a time in her mouth, following each one with a swallow of water. Her throat worked and they went down. She gave him back the glass. "T'anks."

The glass rattled when he set it on the end table. He waited. The minutes dragged out. Sadie's breath came more and more slowly, until finally a light snore told Henry that she was asleep.

For a few minutes he stood there, clenching and unclenching his hands. Finally, he nerved himself and reached down and lifted her in his arms. He was surprised to discover how light she was.

He carried her to the master bedroom and laid her down on Barbara's side of the bed. He pulled off her shoes, and adjusted the sheets around her. Then he went to the stereo in the wall unit and fumbled a cassette into the tape deck. He hit Play.

The voice that issued from the speakers was his own. He turned the volume down low, so the words were barely audible. The speakers whispered. Memories of Barbara. Her family; her history; how they had met; her life with him. Henry listened for a few minutes, but after a while he couldn't take any more, so he tip-toed out of the bedroom and eased the door shut. Behind him, memories played into sleeping ears.

The next morning, he began calling her "Barbry."

The first couple times earned him curious glances, but the bag lady seemed just to shrug it off. She seemed to accept everything he did with an odd mixture of blank fatalism and a pathetic eagerness to please. Henry dug out the old photo albums and spent all day Saturday showing the pictures to her. The techniques for planting false memories were well known. This is Barbry when She was six. This is the house She grew up in; and those are Her parents. Sadie nodded and grinned her gap-tooth grin. Once, passing a photograph back and forth, their hands touched and Henry was caught between a sudden desire to clasp her hand and an equally sudden desire to pull away.

She studied the pictures carefully, holding them close to her eyes, squinting, as if something had gone wrong with her vision. As if her eyes were not what they had been the previous night.

Henry peered at her face. Did it already look a little different? Were the cheekbones a little higher? The hair a little lighter? The scar a little fainter?

Or his imagination a little wilder?

A human body was more complex than that of jellyfish; and the process should take a good deal longer. But Bill Canazetti's tyling algorithm was wonderfully simple; and growing a Barnsleyformer from Barbara's DNA had taken more time than brilliance. For three weeks, Henry had remained at work, after the others had gone for the day. Bill had given him some quizzical stares over the extra hours but seemed to assume that Henry was using the work as a way of dealing with his grief.

And, in a way, of course, he was right.

Henry thought he had covered his tracks pretty thoroughly. The recorded weights of the specimens in the cell library would still tally. All the reagents and other supplies were properly accounted for. There was nothing out of place that they could trace to him. Not even the flu virus. Certainly not Barbara's cell samples.

"You must have loved her very much."

He emerged, startled, from his reverie. Sadie the Lady was holding out a snapshot. It was a picture of him and Barbara, taken during their vacation in the Rockies. There they stood, his arm around Her waist; both of them smiling foolishly, waving to the stranger who had held their camera. They were posing in front of their rented Bronco on the old railroad trestle on the Corona Pass Road. Behind them, the Devil's Slide fell a thousand feet into the forest below. Barbry was pointing back toward the Needle's Eye Tunnel that they had just negotiated. A frozen moment of happiness.

Henry remembered every detail of that day. The bite of the insects. The sawtooth sound of their chirping. How the sun had beat down on them, and how, despite that, it had been chillingly cold at the summit. Corona Pass was not a real road, but the remains of a narrow-gage railroad bed that switchbacked up the sheer side of a mountain. It was one lane wide, which made for interesting decisions when upslope and downslope traffic met. The Needle's Eye, a hole pierced through solid rock, had once been closed for several years by a rockslide, and the trestle over the Devil's Slide did not inspire great confidence, despite its solid timbers. The ruins of the old train depot lay astride the Continental Divide, and Barbry and he had found a secluded spot off the nature trail there, and had necked up a storm as if they had been teenagers.

"Yes. Very much," he said. "I miss her." More than anything else in the world, he wanted her back. "I love you very much, Barbry." And he looked Sadie straight in the eye when he said that.

Fear danced in her eyes, and then something else. "And I lo—"

The snapshot flicked from her fingers and floated like an autumn leaf to the carpet. Sadie's left cheek twitched and she stood and trembled like a fawn. "Don't feel good," she said.

Henry caught her before she fell and carried her back to the bedroom. "You're still sick, Barbry," he told her. [Yes, her hair was definitely lighter now.] He laid her down on the bed. "Rest up. Everything will be all right in a little while. A couple of days, at the most."

The cheek was twitching constantly now. It tugged at the nose and the corners of the mouth and eyes. Henry could swear he saw the cheekbone beneath it flow. He pulled a chair up next to the bed and sat there rubbing first one hand then the other.

Sadie began to pant, short gasps, bitten off. Her eyes bulged and sweat rolled off her forehead staining the pillowcase. She arched her back and her eyes rolled up in her head. Her hands clenched into fists that twisted and wrung the sheets. A scream trickled through her tightened throat.

Henry saw a tremendous spasm run through her right thigh muscle. It jerked once, twice, three times. Then Sadie collapsed, her mouth hanging slack and her fingers curling and uncurling. Her breathing grew long and shallow, as if she had just finished a long race.

Henry could not move. The nanny will try to restructure as well as repair. But he had never imagined that it would hurt. How long will this go on, he wondered? He bit into his knuckles and drew blood.

Her breathing began to quicken again, rasping like a saw through pine, and Henry saw the tension build in her muscles. It was like childbirth, almost. Worse than childbirth. She began moaning and the moaning increased in pitch and tempo and would have ended in a scream except her jaw was so tightly clamped that nothing but a whine escaped. Her whole body jerked this time and she rolled halfway onto her side.

I can't take this, Henry thought and he pushed himself from the chair to go.

But her eyes snapped open and pinned him there, like a butterfly to a board. She spoke; and the timbre of the voice was more than Sadie, but not quite Barbara, and there was pain and hurt in it. "What are you doing to me?" she cried. And she spoke again; and again there was pain and hurt, but of a different kind. "Why are you doing this to me?"

The scream, when it finally came, was Henry's.

For the next three days, Henry avoided the room except to bring meals, which she did not touch; and pain-killer, which she did; and to reset and play the tapes that he had made. Through the door, he would hear cries; cries that were now weeping as often as they were screaming. They were muffled and Henry knew that that was because she would thrust her face into the pillows to stifle the sound of it.

Barbara had been like that. She hated to cry and always tried to hide it.

He did not linger when he heard the crying, but fled instead to the quiet of the kitchen and, once, to the solitude of the greenbelt behind the house.

He got no sleep that weekend and when Monday came, he called in sick. Bill Canazetti took the call and Henry wanted to tell him that Barbry wasn't feeling well so he was staying home to take care of her. But he said nothing, because Bill might not have understood.

Or perhaps, he might have understood too well.

Late Monday afternoon a hammering sound brought him running up the stairs. He burst into the room and found Barbara/Sadie banging her head against the headboard of the bed. She would lean forward and then throw her head back hard against the carved wood. There were dark stains there.

His heart dropped like a stone. He bounded to her side and wrapped his arms around her to hold her back. "What are you doing?" he cried.

She grabbed her head in both her hands. "Make it stop!" she sobbed. "It hurts so much! Please make it stop!"

The brain, he thought. The nannies have reached the brain and are restructuring it to look more like Barbara's brain. Synapses and neurons were being rewired. Network configuration was changing. It shouldn't hurt, he told himself. It wasn't supposed to hurt. He held on to her more tightly and she buried her face in his shoulder, making small, animal sounds.

And what will happen now? Wasn't memory stored in the arrangement of synapses? In the network? No one really knew. No one understood how the brain worked. And there were always those seven "ghost" dimensions in Barbara's DNA.

He tried giving her headache medicine; but that didn't seem to work; so he tried a sedative and that at least stopped the whimpering, although in her sleep she continued to moan and toss.

And then, after a very long while, it was Tuesday.

He was in the kitchen, drinking breakfast. Bourbon, neat. An anesthetic to dull his own pain. He had not showered nor changed his clothes since Friday and they were stained at the collar, at the armpits, at the small of the back, in the crotch; and smelled of sweat and fear. Four days of stubble had made sandpaper of his face. His eyes were rimmed with red. He had not slept since Sunday.

And he heard a footstep in the hall.

He jerked his head up. She stood there, unsteady, leaning against the doorpost from the hallway, her jeans and blouse as filthy and disarrayed as his. More so, since she had been unable to visit the bathroom during her ordeal. Her hair, dirty from sweat and oil, was ratted and tangled. It was as if she had never left the heating grate in Hell's Kitchen.

He put his shot glass down so hard that the amber liquid splashed onto his hand. He half-rose from his chair. "Barbara?"

She stared at him vacantly. After a few moments, she shook her head. "No, I—Henry?"

He stood and walked around the table to her. "You've had a bad accident," he told her. "Amnesia."

As he got closer to her he began to see more clearly that she was not quite Barbara. The facial scar was gone; but a faint line remained. The missing incisor was still missing. There were other, more subtle differences that thirteen years of marriage had made plain.

He took her hands in his but stopped short of embracing her.

"How do you feel."

"Bad as you look," she replied. "I—" A pause. A grimace. "Twinges, time to time." Her face tightened and she looked at him hard. "Y'gimme somethin', dincha? Some kinda pill."

"It was medicine. You were sick."

"I never been sick."

Henry swallowed. "Yes, you were. Five years ago. We took you to St. Barnabas. Don't you remember?"

She pulled her hands away. "Don't! Yer crazy, you." She turned, took one step, and stopped. Three heartbeats went by; then she looked back over her right shoulder. "Bright pastels," she said. "The room was painted in bright pastels. The TV set was broken and you made them replace it."

"Yes."

"No!" She put her hands to her head. "Never happened. I'se in Rochester, me. Five years 'go I'se'n Rochester!" Her hands dropped slowly. "I think I was. I—" She began to cry. "'M confused. So confused. Henry? Help me."

He led her back upstairs to the shower and gave her Barbry's favorite baby doll pajamas. While she washed up, he stripped the bedsheets and replaced them with fresh linens. He took the soiled sheets to the laundry in the basement, but he remembered in time not to start the load while the shower was running.

While he waited for the water to stop he gradually became aware of his own condition. He rubbed a hand over the stubble on his jaw and caught a good whiff of his own odor. I need a shower, too, he thought. And a shave.

The shower felt good, and it relaxed him to the point where his lost sleep caught up with him. He decided to take a nap, so he wrapped himself in a towel and went to the master bedroom to find a pair of pajamas.

And Sadie was in the bed, asleep.

Henry stopped short and wondered why that should surprise him. After all, he had been putting her there himself. But, this was the first time she had gone there on her own. She had finished showering and then come to this bed, as if it were the most natural thing in the world.

His mouth twitched and he tiptoed to his dresser, where he reached around the bottom drawer for a pair of pajamas. Her breathing behind him was soft and regular. Relaxed, even; although a slight nasal blockage made a clicking sound whenever she breathed in.

He straightened and turned and looked at her. She was lying atop the sheets, her back to him. The rust-colored camisole top had ridden up to reveal her matching panties and a small, dark mole on the lower right side of her back.

He stared at the mole for a long time. He knew that mole. Even in the dark, he could have pointed to its exact location. It was not possible for two people to have that same mole.

He dropped the pajamas, and the towel, and crept gently into the bed. When he put his arms around her from the back, he felt her stiffen; but he stroked her gently, along the flank, and up and down the back—with a light touch, the way She always liked it—and, after a little while she relaxed and began making contented sounds in her throat.

Gradually, his hand widened its area of search. Up. Around. Here. There. Her breathing quickened and she twisted to face him. Her eyes were still closed, as if she were still asleep; but her mouth sought his and they embraced.

A quiet and desperate urgency followed, with quickly breathed assurances of love and pleasure. The baby dolls joined his towel.

"Barbry," he said. "Oh, Barbry."

And she stiffened again; but only for a moment. "Oh, Henry. I've missed you."

In the morning, he and Barbry lay contentedly side-by-side. The remnants of some bad dream nibbled at the edges of his mind; but he could not remember what it was. Something terrible. Something too distressing to be borne. He felt like a swimmer who had been sucked under by a sink-ing ship; who had kicked desperately toward the shining surface above until, lungs bursting, he had broken through into the cool, pure air.

Everything was going to be all right now.

Barbry was still asleep and Henry watched her silently for a while, admiring the smoothness of her body, the peacefulness of her face, the way her breasts rose and fell. He kept thinking that there was something he was supposed to do for her. Something important that he had forgotten. Well, it would come to him.

He eased out of bed and put his housecoat on. Then he slipped out of the room to the kitchen, where her made breakfast for the two of them. He felt like he was on his honeymoon; but that was ridiculous. Barbry and he had been married for donkey's years. He put the breakfasts on a tray and carried them back to the bedroom.

Barbry was awake when he entered, just beginning to get out of bed. She saw he was bringing her breakfast and laughed. "Breakfast in bed? Oh, Henry. No one ever done that for me." She put herself back under the covers, sitting up against the pillows.

Henry knew that the accident had given her partial amnesia, so he didn't make an issue of how often they had done this in the past. He opened the legs of the tray and set it across her, then he crawled in next to her.

She explored her breakfast with her fork. "What's this?" she asked.

"Poached eggs. Just the way you like them."

"Just the way…Course. Forgot."

While they ate, Henry noticed her giving him sidelong glances out of the corners of her eyes. She was watching him. Waiting for him, to do what? Henry took a bite of his toast and chewed. When he glanced back at her, he noticed a tear had worked its way down the side of her right cheek.

"Barbry! What's wrong? Why are you crying?"

"Nothing." She shook her head. "Nothing. Someone's died, is all."

"Died?" An unaccountable shiver ran through him. "Who?"

She looked at him and he saw there were tears in both her eyes. Tiny tears. She seemed more wistfully sad than bereaved. She shook her head again. "No one you ever knew," she said. "No one you ever knew."

She was in the library, sitting in her chair, but with her legs pulled up under her. She had a book open and she was reading it intently. A frown creased her brows and her lips moved silently as she followed the words across the page. He came up behind her and leaned on the back of the chair.

"What are you reading?" he asked.

"The poems of Tennyson," she replied. "Tennyson was h— Tennyson is my favorite poet; but I don't remember any of his poems."

He rubbed her shoulders with his hands. "It was a bad accident," he told her. "It will take a long time to remember everything. The doctors didn't have much hope for you, you know. But we showed them, didn't we?"

She twisted and looked at him. She patted his hand. "Yes, we showed them. You'll play the tapes for me again tonight, won't you, dear?"

"Of course."

"Good. Meanwhile…" She turned back and re-opened her book. She ran her finger down the page. "This poem. Could you explain what it means? It's called 'Tears, Idle Tears.' I'll read it to you."

She hefted the book and cleared her throat. Then she began to recite:

> 'Dear as remember'd kisses after death,
> And sweet as those by hopeless fancy feign'd
> On lips that are for others; deep as love,
> Deep as first love, and wild with all regret;
> O Death in Life, the days that are no more.'

He felt it rise in his throat. A feeling of intense longing and loneliness. There was no question about it. The old Brit knew how to string words together. But why should those words affect him so?

He felt the tears warm his cheeks. He tried to excuse himself to Barbry, but no words came out, only uncontrollable sobbing. It was embarrassing. He was crying like a baby. He had not cried like this since…Since…

There was something that was supposed to have made him cry like this, but he had forgotten what it was. Forgotten when it was. Forgotten everything, except that he was supposed to have cried; and that now the crying may have come too late.

Bill Canazetti fidgeted nervously by the front door, waiting for…her to get his coat. Dinner had been uncomfortable. A mostly silent affair, broken only by the tink of glasses and silverware. Afterwards, a few awkward sallies into conversation. Then he had made his excuses to leave.

She brought his coat to him and helped him into it. "Now, be sure to button up, Bill. It's chilly outside. The leaves are all off the trees. It's a lot colder here than where we used to live. It's too bad we don't get together more often."

"It's a long trip to Morristown," he agreed. He only wanted to leave. To get away from this place. To forget everything he had seen.

When he looked at his hostess, he saw Barbara Carter, smiling, waiting. He had always kissed her when leaving their house. A quick pass across the lips and a murmured quip about her husband finding out. It was a little game they had played between themselves; but there was no way this woman would know about it. Henry's theories about the seven hidden dimensions holding a person's soul and memories were just so much nonsense.

Weren't they?

He put his hand on the doorknob and twisted. The chill autumn air swirled in around him. He hesitated. He had to know.

"Barbara," he said, turning around. "Tell me one thing." He searched her eyes. "Are you Barbara?"

Changes chased themselves across her eyes. Surprise. Curiosity. Wonder. Perhaps, wistfulness. "Most of the time," she said. "More and more nowadays."

"But—"

"But am I really her?" She laughed and shook her head. "No. I'm just an old junkie bag lady, me. He gave me something. A nano…"

"Nanomachine."

"Yes, thank you. A nanomachine. It rebuilt my body. It rewired my brain. I remember Sadie; but it's faint, like an old dream. And I remember some other things. Things that happened to Barbry. They're faint, too. Did they come from the tapes? Or from somewhere else? I don't know. And there are other odd memories. Things that never happened at all, either to Barbry or Sadie."

Canazetti's throat felt tight. "Sadie's memories patched onto different circuits. They're hallucinatory, those memories."

"Maybe. Still. I know who I am. Most of the time, anyway."

"Then why do you do it? Why do you stay with him and pretend? I've done some experimental work. With frogs. The nerves. When they change. It—" He didn't know how to put it. "It must have been painful," he said, not looking at her.

"Yes. Yes, it was. Very painful. But Henry saw me through it."

He turned to her. "He might have killed you," he blurted out. "He didn't know enough to try it. We still don't know enough to try it. Dammit, he had no right to do what he did to you!"

"Bill, do you know what my life was like before he rescued me?"

He shook his head.

"How can I explain it? I can go to sleep and not be afraid that I'll freeze to death before morning, or that some kids will set me on fire just for the hell of it. And my new body, it's healthy. It don't need snow or crack like my old body did. And I can see and understand so much that I couldn't before, because my brain has been detoxed."

Canazetti looked past her shoulder, down the hallway, into the kitchen where he saw Henry carrying dinner dishes to the sink. He was humming to himself.

"Do you love him, then?"

"Yes. Both of us do."

His head jerked and he looked at her.

"When I'm Barbry," she explained, "I love him for Barbry's sake. But Sadie loved him, too. Because he saved her life. Because he took care of her. He's given her more than she ever dared to dream about. Except for one thing."

Canazetti's voice was choked. "What's that?"

"He never told Sadie that he loved her. He never saw her."

"Damn him!"

"No, don't say that."

"But, what he did to you. What he put you through. The selfishness."

"He couldn't love anyone else. He loved Her. He wasn't rational. What would you have done in his place?"

"I feel responsible, you know. It was my invention."

She put a hand on his arm. "Don't blame yourself for that, Bill. He would have tried something, even without your nano. I don't know. Brain-washing, maybe."

"I just can't help thinking that he did something wicked. A crime. And he should be punished."

She turned and watched Henry through the kitchen doorway while he rinsed the dishes and put them in the dishwasher. He noticed them watching him and grinned and waved.

"He is being punished," she said. "The worst punishment of all. He thinks he's happy."

AFTERWORD TO "REMEMBER'D KISSES"

This was the first-written of these "neighborhood" stories, having been finished in March 1988. The immediate inspiration was in James Gleick's book, *Chaos: Making a New Science* (Viking Penguin, 1987), where he discusses Michael Barnsley and his fern. This was a system of recursive equations that Barnsley devised that would create the form of a fern out of random initial inputs. It is discussed here: *http://en.wikipedia.org/wiki/Barnsley_fern*

Nothing in the equations says "this is how to draw a fern." Yet a fern emerges no matter what random inputs are used. If this represents what actually happens in morphogenesis, it tosses all arguments involving probabilities of this or that outcome into a cocked hat, and the unlikely may be no more than inevitable.

Years later, in 2010, the Craig Venter Institute succeeded in implanting a synthetic genome into a bacterium, causing it to act like the donating bacterium. That is pretty much what Henry was trying to do, in concept if not in complexity. But is it only the physical form that is built; or is the inner life of the organism built up also?

"Remember'd Kisses" appeared in *Analog* (Dec 1988) and placed 4th in the AnLab. In it, Henry Carter is older than in "Melodies of the Heart," and Singer has died. Peeler now runs SingerLabs. It was reprinted in *The Nanotech Chronicles* (Baen, 1991) and in the anthology *Nanotech* (Ace, 1998), edited by Jack Dann and Gardner Dozois. It's a story about letting go; or rather not letting go, and the terribly ambiguous consequences of doing so.

BURIED HOPES

The chair in the counselor's office was soft and cool to the touch. Leather, perhaps, but almost like buckskin. It was a bit large and high off the floor, so that Rann felt smaller than usual. The walls were adorned with comforting diplomas, and the windows muted the raucous sounds of the Manhattan traffic far below. The décor was composed in gentle earth tones. On the table between them, the counselor had set bone china cups filled with tea. All the little tricks of the trade, deployed to put the patient at ease. He squirmed a bit in the chair, seeking that elusive ease. He did not care for tea, but it was the least obnoxious of the alternatives she had offered.

Rann said, "I don't know why I've come here, doctor."

The counselor wore her hair in an authoritative bun and dressed in mannish, but mammalian fashion. Her large-framed glasses gave her a distancing, professional mien. She sat in a second chair facing him at an angle.

"You don't have to call me doctor," she said. "Call me Liz, or Ms. Abbot, if that is more comfortable for you."

Yes, she was trying to reduce the doctor-patient distance while maintaining a professional detachment. Friendly, yet not too friendly; at least, not until she could understand how close she might come without breaching the wrong psychological barriers.

Rann said, "Yes, 'Ms. Abbot.' Yes, that would be fine." He could see from the way she cocked her head that she had heard the residue of his accent. Once it had been thicker and had drawn quizzical glances, but diligent practice over the years had shaved nearly all the edges from it.

"Should I call you Mr. Velkran, or will Rann do?" she asked him.

Rann considered the alternatives. If she was "Ms." and he was "Rann," that would place him on the wrong end of a parent-child divide; but "Ms." and "Mr." created another and broader divide. Rann thought he would rather like being treated as a child, at least for the next hour, and told her to call him Rann.

"Is that short for 'Randolph'?" she asked him as she made a note.

He answered with a shrug into which she could read any answer she chose. "Don't call me Randolph."

She looked up and arranged her notes in a leather folder against her knees. "Something is bothering you."

Rann looked for the question mark at the end, but of course it was not there. He would not have come to her if nothing bothered him. Rann said, "Depression, I think."

Ms. Abbot glanced at the questionnaire he had filled out. "Don't you know?"

"I've always been given to melancholy and nostalgia. It's in my blood, and who can gage whether it is a little more or a little less. But it seems to me that it has deepened these past few weeks..."

"What is it that causes you to feel depressed?"

"I thought you might tell me. I mean, that's your job, isn't it?"

Ms. Abbot made a brief moue with her lips. "My job is to help you tell yourself. To help you search, as it were. But why don't we start with something else. Tell me a little about yourself. You live in New Jersey..." She tapped the forms he had filled out. "But you've come all the way into Manhattan to see me."

"You should feel flattered."

"I would if 'Abbot' were not the first listing in the index."

"Then I think you know why. I would rather not do this closer to home."

"There's no stigma to seeing a counselor."

Rann answered with another shrug and then, when the silence had dragged on, suddenly blurted, "Did you know that the international space station was de-orbited?"

Ms. Abbot seemed accustomed to conversational left turns. "I saw something about it on the news. It was worn out and abandoned, wasn't it?"

"It didn't have to be. It could have been maintained, upgraded, replaced."

"Is that why you've been feeling depressed? Because the old space station was decommissioned?"

"I..." *Was it?* he wondered. "I'm sentimental. I hate to see things end. The last moonwalker died...oh, years ago. No longer lives there anyone who has walked upon the moon."

"Ah, that was before my time, I'm afraid. And didn't it turn out to be a hoax?"

Rann leaped from the chair and began to pace the room, agitated beyond measure. "No, it was not! It was not!"

Ms. Abbot maintained her composure and said mildly, "But if the story is true, it would mean that people went to the moon *before* they built a space station in Earth orbit. Does that make sense? To go all that way, and then to backtrack?"

His pacing had brought him to the window and he looked down on the thumb-sized pedestrians teeming along the sidewalk. "It seemed a good idea at the time."

"Did the space program mean a lot to you? You don't appear old enough to remember it."

He turned from his contemplation. "It meant a lot to all of us," he told the counselor. "If only we had at the time realized it." He sought out the patient's chair and sank once more into it. "Who knows what might be out there? On the moon, on, on Mars there might be…" Rann fell silent. "There might be anything. Now, how few are left! Sometimes…" He paused and ground one hand in the other, like a mortar in a pestle. "Sometimes," he added more quietly, "I feel so lonely."

He saw the counselor nod, and he knew he had revealed something of himself. Automatically, the old guards went up. But then, why had he come here unless it was to reveal something of himself? "I miss the old country," Rann said, deliberately. "The music, the foods, the festivals—oh, how the young boys and girls dressed so fine on those days! Even the sound of the old tongues on the lips of friends. Sometimes sees my mind over the Oorlong Hills the sun set so great and red, painting in every color the clouds."

"Have you ever gone back to visit?"

Rann shook his head. "No. There are…difficulties."

Ms. Abbot said "ah" in such understanding tones. The world was full of people unwelcome in their own homelands. That was not precisely Rann's problem, but he decided not to complicate matters. "It helps to talk about it," he added.

"Do you have family back there? Is there anyone in particular you miss?"

For a moment Rann could see the Miss Kopál as if she stood directly before him, the dandi-flowers round her crown, the golden lace about her throat, the tattoos winding like vines along her arms. Then…the moment was lost and he realized that he no longer remembered what she

244

had looked like. He fumbled in his jacket pocket for a kerchief, but the counselor leaned across to hand him a tissue. "I'm sorry," he said. "Sorry. There were, once. But they have all by now forgotten me." He squared his shoulder, felt the unexpected crack of bone, and deliberately relaxed. "I suppose this seems silly to you. A bad case of homesickness."

"No, not silly at all. Have you been in this country long?"

Rann looked at the floor and clasped his hands. He waited for the inevitable question.

"If you are undocumented," Ms. Abbot said, "don't worry. My job is to help you deal with your depression, not to do the government's work for them." She reached out and touched Rann briefly on his wrist. Reflexively, Rann pulled back.

"A double-dozen of us came to the, to the New World together," Rann admitted, "but we've to the drogo scattered and seldom anymore do we see one another."

"The drogo?"

"Ah. Did I say that? I am falling into the rhythms of my suckling tongue. Drogo is in my country a seasonal wind—hot, dry, brisk—and as a way of speaking we say that we have blown off with it."

"Tell me, Rann, how long have you felt these pangs of loneliness?"

"Always. Ever since we landed here. It was not so bad when we all lived near one another; but…"

"But the old neighborhood has 'scattered to the drogo.' Tell me, is this feeling of loneliness persistent, or does it come and go? How did you feel, oh, last year? Two weeks ago?"

Rann closed his eyes and tried to imagine what he had been doing a fortnight since. His neighbors had invited him to a cookout. There had been burgers and franks and beer, discussion of the Giants and the new cable series on Teddy Roosevelt. The neighborhood dogs did not like him much and the beer had upset his digestion, but…"If you had asked me then, I would have said I was reasonably happy. Perhaps no less happy than most people believe they are."

"Do you think everyone unhappy?"

"Of course," he said. "It is only a matter of one's awareness. Have you no regrets, doctor? Is there nothing that in quiet moments might tinge with melancholy your thoughts? An old fiancé who slipped away? A brother or sister untimely gone? A childhood friend fallen out of touch? A…a calculation performed incorrectly?"

"A calculation? You're a mathematician, then?"

"I teach at a small college in New Jersey."

Ms. Abbot nodded and added notes to the folder. Rann admired the way she could write of one thing while talking of another and without even a glance at her paper.

"Then something happened," she said.

"What?"

"Something happened. You were ordinarily happy…Very well, you were not too unhappy. Now two weeks later you are deeply depressed. The BDI-4 you filled out prior to our meeting…There were some anomalies, but it did indicate sadness, guilt feelings, past failures, weeping. But no self-dislike, loss of pleasure, or change in appetite. As I said, a mixed…"

"Excuse me. BDI-four?"

"Beck Depression Inventory. It's a standard instrument for…"

Rann chuckled. "Oh. An inventory? An instrument? Do you keep depression on shelves in your stockroom? Do you at the QC bench measure it?" He knew he was deflecting, and he knew that Ms. Abbot knew. "No, doctor, I intend no mockery. It is only that such words fall on my ears oddly. Ish! I try so hard to speak standard American. Bear with me, please. It is my homesickness. It will hear the cadence of the suckling-tongue even through the mask of other words."

"Would you like to say something in your mother tongue? I should like to hear the sound of it."

"Will you mark it then on that sheet you have beside you? Ah, well. A poem, then." He thought for a moment, conjuring the syllables, feeling them sweetening his mouth before he ever spoke.

"Offen mere killanong
Kay-kaka doolenong
Waffen tok ishanong
Ish, doo kill-koffen.

Which I would translate not literally, but to give you some idea of the word-play involved:

'Long have I longed
To say aye for an aye,
To close while so close.
Oh, the time is too short!'"

Dr. Abbot waited while Rann wiped a tear from his cheek; then she said, "That was charming."

Rann said, "It is hard to say in American. The play is of 'long' and 'aye' against 'close' and 'short.' And the title we might translate as 'The Long and the Short of It.'" He paused and closed his eyes, the better to see the sunset tints now so long past and to hear a faint echo of that sweet voice.

He had composed the poem himself, just before his departure and recited it in the sunset to she whose face was now lost to him. "'It,' of course, is love."

The counselor smiled. "Isn't it always? Tell me, despite the separation from your homeland and relatives, is life worth living?"

Rann laughed. "Is that one of the questions on your little list? 'Rann Velkran shows moderately suicidal tendencies.' Sorry to disappoint you, doctor; but Rann does not give up on life simply because it has become unbearably sad these past two weeks…'The saddest life is happier than none at all.' That is a proverb among my people. Only the dead never weep…because they never laugh."

He paused because in his imagination he saw the international space station entering the atmosphere, warming, glowing, turning red from the friction, white hot as it began to come apart, raining into the embrace of the broad Pacific, incinerating all aboard…

"But there was no one left on board by then," he whispered.

"What was that?" Dr. Abbot said.

Rann said, "Never mind." He reached blindly for his tea cup and, misjudging, tipped the thing over so that green tea spilled across the glass table top, twisting into rivulets. Rann stared in horror and began to hyperventilate, then to sob. Alarmed, Ms. Abbot said, "What is it? What's wrong?"

"What's wrong?" Rann cried. "How could this happen! Look at it, running all over! So shapeless, so empty and meaningless! Never will we save it; the drink will now forever be untasted." Rann covered his face with his hands, but between his fingers he studied the eddying streams of tea and he imagined the acid tang of the hot liquid never now to be experienced.

Ms. Abbot had fetched paper towels from her desk drawer. Now, she stared at him in astonishment. "Don't worry," she said. "We'll just mop it up." And she laid the paper towels in the puddle to soak it up.

Rann considered the counselor with something not too short of horror before reminding himself that she was not like his own people. The sudden sorrow with which he had viewed the spilt tea itself dried up as if dabbed with a psychic towel, to be replaced with a gentle and nostalgic melancholy that he knew would never go away whenever he thought on this incident in the future.

When Ms. Abbot took the now-sodden towels to the wastebasket, Rann stood and tugged at his clothing. Strange how current events could stir long-dormant memories. It hadn't been the space station at all; or at least not alone. "I think our time is up anyway, Ms. Abbot, and you have patients with more pressing troubles than I. I believe I understand the cause. And perhaps a solution."

The counselor watched him solemnly. "There are coping mechanisms," she said, "but no solutions."

It took Rann a week to obtain the backhoe and secure the necessary permits, only a little longer to learn which palms at the township must be crossed with what quantity of silver. He assured the rental manager that he knew how to operate a backhoe, signed forms and releases to absolve the man of any responsibility for what might happen, and arranged to have it delivered to his home by a flatbed. From the DIY store he secured stakes, cord, chalklines, and other paraphernalia.

Then he climbed into the crawlspace below the roof and found his old positioning module. He spent the afternoon cleaning, polishing, and calibrating the unit and determining that it could shake hands with the GPS system.

The next morning Rann made himself an omelet with a side of ham and buttered toast. During the past week he had eaten listlessly, but today he felt nearly cheerful and regarded the empty pockets in the egg tray in which the three eggs had so lately nestled with only a modest amount of wistfulness for the eggs-that-had-been. He pretended that the eggs were like those at home and that the ham had been cured with the same smokes and spices as the meats to which he had once been accustomed. But a great many years had passed since then and he was no longer sure that he remembered their flavors aright. This, too, was a sadness.

Perhaps the old surgery had affected his taste as it had his features, giving him at least in his imagination a savoring for alien foods.

He entered his back yard with a certain lightness of step and drove a marker stake into the ground to step off his baseline. He set up his theodolite using the module, which had a built-in EDM to measure distance, and tuned the instrument to the global positioning system. It surprised him sometimes how similar were the tools of his trade from place to place; but he reflected that there were not too many different ways to take levels and distances and angles, and so there was nothing astonishing that the instruments might be similar. It was only a matter of transposing the numbers.

"Only" a matter of transposing the numbers.

His yard, like all those around the block, backed onto a small woodland in the center of the neighborhood. The two roads into the area curved into each other forming a rough oval that enclosed a modest copse of trees and brush, providing shelter for rabbits and birds and sundry creatures. Every day toward sunset some large, furry, flattish thing crawled slowly from the forsythia bush toward the creek that bisected the woods. A muskrat, he thought, or maybe a badger. A short walk in any direction touched on more urban landscapes, where such unruly things as lazy muskrats and meandering creeks were properly kept in their places. The woods, his neighbors had told him when he moved in, sat on township land; but because private property enclosed it on all sides, it could not be developed. He had not corrected them on the matter.

He had run a line to a stake at the far end of his property when his neighbor to the south appeared at the fence with two cans of beer. His name was Jamie Shaw and he was a legman for a private detective agency. Beyond that, and that he had a very large extended family, Rann knew little about him. "Looks like hot work," Shaw said, and waved the second can in Rann's general direction.

Rann did not want to take a break at the very beginning of his work—if there can be such a paradoxical thing as a break at a beginning—but neither did he wish to appear un-neighborly. He joined Shaw at the fence, thanked him, and sipped a little from the can. Shaw asked him what he thought of the Giants' chances come fall; and Rann, who had calculated from game theory a losing season, said that a new quarterback often breathed life into a tired offense. Shaw nodded, gestured with his can at the markers he had driven into the ground.

"Building something?"

"Yes, a swimming pool."

"Really? I never saw you as the athletic type. You're doing the work yourself?"

"Some of it. I expect to have help later."

"You've marked it pretty close to the woods."

Rann said, "The property lines actually run a little way into the woods. I checked."

Shaw took a swig of his beer. "Better check your deed. There are covenants. No digging, and no 'diminishing the woods.' I'd hate to see you get half into it and the association comes along and shuts you down. The lady down the corner..." He gestured vaguely north with his beer can. "... is mighty touchy about the trees and rabbits—or her boyfriend is. Heck, I'd rather not see them 'diminished,' either."

"Jamie, are you threatening me with a lawsuit?"

The ruddy man reared back. "Me? No. I don't confuse my personal preferences with the laws of the universe. I'm just giving you a heads-up.

I'm not the only one on the block, you know." He pointed to the houses on either side, and to the backs of those on the far side of the oval, partly visible through the summer foliage. "Now, you're not quite encroaching, but you might want to think about those trees dirtying up your pool come the fall. That one over there is a sycamore and sheds bark all year long. Why not put in an above-ground pool and place it farther away from the trees."

Rann said, "I'm sure everything will work out." He took the beer with him when he returned to his work, but his stomach churned and as soon as he was able he scurried inside, poured the beer down the drain, and removed his bolus. He stood for a while gagging over the toilet bowl and wondered at the price of neighborliness. Then he rinsed, swallowed the bolus once more, and returned to work.

The sun grew hot as the afternoon wore on, but that did not trouble him. The warmth was rather pleasant, especially after the interminable winter. He was swarthy and did not burn like Jamie Shaw, who sometimes emulated a well-done lobster. Someone had once told Rann that he looked like an Egyptian mummy: delicate and rugged at the same time, tough as old leather.

When he realized that his last stake would be off by several digits, he cursed himself. The hash marks on his sights were on the *chegk* scale and he had forgotten to transform the digits at one point. It was a mistake anyone could make. Some American scientists had once confused the metric scale with the traditional scale when programming a Mars probe and the probe had not known it had reached the surface until it had already gone several feet past it.

It was a mistake that he had made only once in his lifetime.

Rann wiped his tears and backtracked until he found the point where he had inadvertently used the old *puralon* scale and he made the necessary correction. After that, the blocking proceeded square and on the level, though his hands shook more than they might ordinarily have done.

A few days later, the backhoe was delivered and Rann spent the day fencing off the open space between his house and the garage with chain-link. The backhoe was officially an "attractive nuisance," and so he must put "appropriate safeguards" in place. The township inspector came around and checked everything, then recommended fencing off the woods behind as well. Someone determined enough could cross a neighbor's yard, pass through the woods, enter Rann's yard, and so hurt himself with the backhoe. Rann thought that anyone that determined could climb the fence as well, but he appreciated the inspector's position. There were rules and it was not within her authority to ignore them.

Afterward, he invited the inspector inside for a cup of coffee, which was gracefully accepted. A lot of home improvement enthusiasts, Rann gathered from her conversation, spent their time arguing with the code inspectors rather than improving their homes. Rann made sympathetic noises. She had already seen and approved the drawings and levels, and had ascertained Rann's competency to do the excavation work himself. He had earlier discovered that the inspector's cousin owned a concrete firm and had put the cousin's name on his subcontractor list. It was not bribery. She had never mentioned him, nor had Rann pointed it out.

Of course she noticed the picture over the mantel. It was meant to be noticed. "That's…rather startling," she said. "Abstract expressionism? A Pollock, maybe?"

"It's what they call a supernova. A giant star exploded eleven thousand years ago, about the time people were just beginning to farm. Eight hundred years later, they would have seen in the night sky a second sun. This…," Rann gestured at the picture, "is all that's left. The shock wave. The gas flying off from the explosion reacts with the interstellar medium, knocking electrons off their atoms. When the electrons recombine with the atoms, they produce light in many different energy bands—ah, colors—and give us this."

"It's very pretty," the inspector said. "It looks almost like a photograph."

Rann said, "It is."

"Oh, that's right. There was a big telescope out in space for a while, wasn't there? What's that down in the corner?"

"A part of a ship's hull. The equivalent of accidentally getting your thumb in front of the lens."

The inspector nodded at this, then started and laughed. "After all that money! And they didn't even get a clear shot."

Rann said, "Come here. I have another photograph that might interest you." This one hung in the entry hall facing the front door, so visitors who entered in the normal fashion saw it first of all. "This is a sinkhole on Mars, called 'Dena.' It's one of seven spotted around the volcano Arisa Mons."

"Deep," said the inspector as she studied the picture. "The shadows at the bottom are so dark that it almost looks like an opening into an underground cavern."

Rann said, "Yes, it does, doesn't it? And heat comes out of the hole. Makes you wonder what might be down there."

The inspector looked at him. "A volcano, you said?"

"A dead volcano. All seven vents give off heat," he added, "but Dena most of all. Closest to the source, maybe? But look into those shadows. Don't they draw you in? Don't they make you wonder what lies in the darkness beyond?"

"More rocks, I suppose. It's not safe to poke into shadows. Are those circular things near the sinkhole *bubbles*? Oh. No, they're craters. Weird optical illusion. For a moment, I thought…But the shadows are wrong."

"Lipless craters. Maybe they were domes that have now collapsed into their foundations," Rann suggested.

The inspector laughed. "You should write that sci-fi stuff. Well, thank you for the coffee, but I have two more sites to check out today. Don't forget to call me when you finish digging."

After she had departed, Rann remained for a while before the photograph, staring into the depths of the shadows. Nearly everyone he had shown his pictures to over the years had had the same reaction. An incuriosity bordering on the morbid. Had something gone out of the human race in this past generation or two? Had some spark been extinguished? It had not always been that way. He could remember the excitement of the first satellites, the first men in space, the first men on the moon, the first space station. It had all been 'first' in those days. He had never thought that he would see the last, as well.

He wiped a tear from his cheek for lost old days, and returned to this back-yard project.

Neighbors drifted by to watch from time to time. Alma Seakirt, the woman down at the corner, asked him how close he was digging to the woods, and the old retired doctor on her other side traipsed through the trees and brush as if engaged on a survey of his own. He leaned on the back fence and watched in silence for a time, but asked no questions and made no comment before leaving the way he had come.

"They just want to make sure you're not harming the preserve," Jamie Shaw told him afterward as Rann relaxed on his patio with a lemonade and studied on how little he had accomplished. He offered a drink to Shaw and to his cousin, Sandra Locke, who was visiting that day. They came across and took lawn chairs around the patio table. Lemonade did not bother Rann as much as beer did, so long as he took a small pill with the drink. Shaw had a packet of papers tucked under his arm and Rann waited to see what surprise the man intended.

"There is something peculiar about your property," Shaw announced as he set the packet on the patio table.

His cousin brushed a stand of hair out of her face. "Jamie has been wasting his time as usual instead of servicing our paying clients."

"Hey," said Shaw. "This is important. I had DETECT trace the property records in the Wessex County data base. Did you know that the covenant against diminishing the woods goes all the way back?" He took a swallow of his lemonade and set the glass on the table. "Yessir, that's a fact. Each conveyance passed the encumbrance on to the next buyer." He took another drink. "Do you know where I had to go to find these records?"

Rann said, "Perth Amboy," and both Shaw and Locke raised their eyebrows.

"You're almost right," Shaw said slowly. "Perth Amboy was the capital for the East Jersey General Board of Proprietors. But they officially dissolved themselves in 1998 and deposited all their records in Trenton."

Rann was sorry to hear that, since his people took oathing very seriously and sometimes a thing ought to go on simply because it had already gone on so long. Sentiment came easily to him.

"And since the oldest documents had never been scanned," Shaw continued, "I had to go down to Trenton to finish the job in person."

"Poor baby," said Sandra. "Can't do *all* your legwork by computer."

Shaw waved a hand. "Even on the computer, DETECT does most of the donkey work." To Rann, he added, "DETECT is a neural net *cum* knowledge base that Sandra and I put together."

"Sandra and *who?*"

"Okay, Sandra and Sandra. It not only searches out the records we need, it can also identify which other evidence to look for. Our township was within the original Elizabeth Town patent. Then Daniel Peirce and some other men bought the southern half for Wood Bridge, and Peirce sold the southern third of that to some settlers, who called it Piscataqua. But it turned out that there was already a small settlement in the township: a band of shipwrecked Dutch sailors who had made their way inland from Point Ambo. They took the oath of allegiance required by the proprietors and for a quit-rent of a half-penny the acre, each received in return..." Shaw flipped through the sheaf of printouts until he found the one he wanted. "...each received homelots of five *morgens*—that's ten acres—plus sixty acres of upland and six of meadow for haying. Then—here it is—in lieu of the standard proprietor's seventh, 'the wyld Woode south and east of ye east Kill of Runamuchy Creek shall be set aside as Commons for such Activityes as byrding and fyshing and trapping of smalle Animals.'" Shaw handed the page to Rann, who pretended to read it. He studied the signatories at the bottom of the page, blurred a bit by the scanning and reproduction and the age of the original document. There was Daniel Peirce's name 'for ye proprietors' and the seal of Governor Carteret. Below that the twenty four freeholders granted domain by right of prior settlement. "Benken van Kottespool, captain," he read. "Ronholf vander Alkrenn, navigator. Giszberth and Alengonda Hengenwaller…" He read the remainder silently. Shipwrecked sailors, far from home.

Sandra mentioned that the Dutch had colonized the area before the English had taken it in one of the Anglo-Dutch wars. "Afterward, New York claimed all of East Jersey as part of New Amsterdam, 'til the Duke of York himself smacked them upside the head."

Rann said, "That is all very interesting, but…"

"But," Shaw said, "the point is that the prohibition on disturbing the woods long predates the construction of these homes here." He swept his arm around. "The woods aren't undeveloped because our properties encircle it. Our properties encircle it because the woods can't be developed. There was a mention in an early conveyance—Vander Alkrenn to Jeremy Pike—that the land was a Lenape burial ground and that Lenapes who so desired would have easement along the creek to visit it, but the original charter makes no mention of that."

Rann said, "I suppose I ought to get back to my digging…"

"Well, now, that's the funny thing," said Shaw. "The digging. Normally, a quit-rent buys back freeholder rights, like the right to hunt or to explore for minerals and so forth. Most freeholders back then ignored the quit-rent because they never supposed that fox hunts would cross their croplands or that the proprietor would sell someone else the right to dig for gold. Why buy back a right that no one else is likely to exercise? But the Dutch sailors paid their quit-rents dutifully every year and when they eventually sold out and moved away, they put a no-digging encumbrance on the conveyances. All but this one."

Rann said, "This one."

"Yes, your deed is the only instrument that permits digging—and always has."

"How about that?" Rann murmured.

"You don't fool me, Rann," said Jamie Shaw. "You must have done your homework, and the township inspector, too. You knew none of your neighbors could legally stop you. But why did they exempt only this one property?"

"Just in case," Rann suggested, "we might want to exhume an Indian."

Shortly after, Rann made a show of giving up and bringing in a professional excavator with a bigger backhoe. The man was named Steve and he looked over the smaller rental unit that Rann had been using as a wolf might study a poodle. They went over the plans together and Steve checked the GPS markers. "Ya done the survey good," he admitted, "but maybe ya should stick to that, steada tryin' to shave some bucks on labor."

The inspector came by and the three of them reviewed certificates together. Afterwards, when Rann offered refreshments inside, Steve surprised him by studying the photograph of the Martian sinkhole and saying he wouldn't mind climbing down into the opening of the cavern, just to see what was there.

"If it *is* a cavern," Rann suggested, "and not just a play of shadows."

"Nah, it's a cavern, I tell ya. If this was the moon, I'd say ya might be right. No air makes the shadows real black. But Mars got air. Not much, maybe, but some. And, ya know, this sounds real whacko, but that sinkhole looks like it mighta been excavated."

"A swimming pool on Mars?" offered the inspector with a laugh.

"Nah. Too deep. Say, how big is this thing, anyway?"

Rann said, "About one hundred and thirty meters deep."

The inspector whistled. "A forty-three story building could sit in there."

Steve took up his gloves and pulled them onto his hands before sparing the photograph another look-over. "That would be some honking foundation to dig, I tell ya."

A few days later, Venkaaszbuul came to the house. Rann held the door open for him. "Come in, captain. I've been expecting you." They did not shake hands.

Venkaaszbuul ignored the sinkhole picture and, brushing past Rann, went directly to the living room, where he sat with his back to the photograph of the Vela supernova. "We have not been in contact for decades, navigator," he said, "and yet you were expecting me?"

Rann shrugged. "Call it Fate."

"I'll call it Death. Jizzvarth has died."

Rann felt a tear track his cheek. "Jizz?"

"Yes, of your Ypuralon comrades, the last. I thought you would desire the knowing of it." He spoke in *chegk*, the language of the lowlands.

Rann buried his face in his hands. "Oh, the hills! Oh, the hills! And only I alone to remember them the now!"

Venkaaszbuul managed to convey distaste on his expressionless face. It was in the eyes, and very subtle; but the Chegka were a subtle folk. Rann had to remind himself that they, too, felt grief, though they showed it in different ways than his own highland folk.

"It was a natural death," Venkaaszbuul assured him, "and no autopsy was called for."

A sob escaped Rann's throat, and he knew shame before his captain that he had allowed it. "Is that a comfort? Am I to forget that he was of our lives a part, of our crew a part? Or how he struggled in the lifeboats safely to debark us? You are a cold man, flatlander."

"And you a forgetful one, hillman. Or do you recall *why* your beloved countryman bore the shepherding of us into the boats?"

Curiously, the jab calmed Rann, proving that it was possible, on some topics at least, to weep oneself dry. "Sometimes," he said, "there are days when I do *not*." He hugged himself. "I am sorry for the error."

"Sorry, you are," the captain said. "Sorry."

"A small transposition error…"

"From flaws the smallest, great failures burst. Their philosopher Aristotle said this."

"It was too late to correct…"

"Of course it was. Hillmen may weep their sorrows on their sleeves; but the universe is cold and has no pity. 'There are in nature no second chances.'" The proverb was *chegk*, but he delivered it in a thick *puralon* accent, the sort of accent Chegka used for a laugh in their night clubs.

Rann said in a low and miserable voice, "How long must I answer for it?"

"For all your life," the captain said. "For every heartbeat of it since we were marooned in this miserable place. But…"—And here the captain's voice took on something close to pity—"it is Rann who has the demanding of the answers from you. The Americans have a proverb: Don't cry over spilt milk. So don't."

Rann attempted a smile, and failed. "What, then? Should we cry over milk held safely in containers upright? Not long past have I bespoken a counselor regarding my melancholy. These people must know some secret to assuage the pain when it grows too great. While there, I knocked a cup of tea over."

The captain sucked in his breath and said, "Ah," but did not otherwise change expression.

"And this counselor said that she would wipe it up, and that would be the end of it. Wipe it up! And try to pretend that we never saw anything."

Venkaaszbuul said, "It is their response to everything. They ignore the truths before their own eyes."

"Or they lock it in, like flatlanders."

"Were you of the School, you would learn to weep in your heart, not on your sleeve; but you would not learn not to weep. We can pass among them without much remark, while you and Jizz and the others, they looked on askance, more emotional than their women. A terrible lacking was it, that the Schoolmen failed the winning of the hills."

Tears coursed down Rann's cheeks. A million worlds had died a-borning in that failure. He wept for a moment for all the things that might have been; but he detested the bottled-up flatlanders, and so it was only for a moment that he wept at their failure. "She thought that by wiping it from the table, she could wipe it from our minds. It was only some spilled tea, and so a small sorrow; but her reaction was typical. They are heartless, these humans. No wonder they kill one another, fight endless wars, and never developed their technology. They are too *rational.* Not about anything do they *care!*"

The captain touched him briefly and made a flatlander's gesture that meant he accepted a portion of the hillman's sorrow as his own. A hillman would have wailed and embraced him, but Rann knew he ought treasure this momentary touch as the best one Schooled could do.

Venkaaszbuul said, "Offer it up. One of their native Schools advises that, and it is very close to what the true School teaches. We are given no burdens that we cannot carry."

Rann said, "As well, that, or we should have gone extinct long since. It is how the Winnower sculpts life."

Venkaaszbuul grunted and made no comment. Flatlanders did not believe in the Winnower. He stood and went to the patio doors, which were glass, and lifted the curtain to gaze at the backhoe chugging in the yard.

"I heard him as I stood on your threshold."

Rann came to his side but made no reply.

Venkaaszbuul said, "This land looked different when last I saw it."

"The houses weren't here then. New trees have grown, and old trees have fallen—or grown taller." Faintly, from somewhere across the woods, came the sound of children playing. Yet another of the many-worlds in which he would never live was the world in which he had young in his steading. But he mastered himself like a Schoolman. Venkaaszbuul and his people had been right about one thing: to remain unremarked, they had to adopt the stoicism of this world's people. "Did you hear that they de-orbited their space station?"

Venkaaszbuul bobbed his head in the human style. "It was why I bethought myself the visiting of you, my crew."

"How many…How many of us are left?"

"Eight. You were the last on my list." After a pause, he added, "It was

257

not much of a space station."

"It was the only one they had. Perhaps the only one they will ever have. The fall recalled to me the plunge of our own ship, and plunged me into a deep melancholy. Do you think…Do you think the other lifeboats made it to shore?"

Venkaaszbuul made a gesture of uncertainty. It so resembled a hillman's gesture of assurance that Rann knew a moment of hope before he realized the error.

"We were fortunate," Venkaaszbuul said, "that your piloting skills brought us down here, where there were few people, and those easily over-awed. It gave us time for the learning, for the surgery, for the mastery of their language."

"Dutch."

"Suppose we had burned up in shoals, our angle of attack too steep; or plunged into one of the boundless seas that swamp this world; or ground-ed in civilized lands, where they would have quite rationally stoned us or burned us. When you ponder the many-worlds that the quanta tell us might have been, remember that most would have been worse than this. Why not approach the past with gratitude rather than tears?"

"A School trick. Because this is of the many-worlds the best? That may be cause for the greatest melancholy of all."

"Ah, Rann, I'd not have the stealing from you of that melancholy which you so treasure; but why not suppose that the others landed safely and have been 'lying low,' just as we have."

Rann said, "Then perhaps we should stand up straight."

Venkaaszbuul stood a while longer at the glass doors before letting the curtain fall. "Why? So we can be spirited off for the studying in some secret laboratory?"

"They would be insane to so risk the wrath of a star-faring people of unknown powers."

"If I am to place myself in trust of their sanity, your objection answers itself. Whether they burn us at the stake or dissect us in the lab, I would just as soon not face them with the choice."

"But if they knew we had among them come, they might strive again to reach the stars."

"To what point, navigator? Once there was a hope that they might find our old base on Mars—or the observation post on the Moon—and we could scavenge the materials to build a messenger packet or a com-municator and so secure rescue. But only a double-handful of us now remain, and each of us nearing the end of days." He glanced at his hands, turned them over. "Less than a double-handful. Forgive my error. If you must weep, Rann—and I know you must—weep that the humans never reached Mars when we were young enough and numerous enough for it to matter."

The backhoe's engine revved and the claw dug into the earth. Steve, perched in the driver's seat, worked the levers back and forth. He did not notice the watchers. Venkaaszbuul grunted. "Is that where he is?"

Rann understood. "Somewhere in there. When the wreck hit, it threw dirt over everything."

"The boat still lies beneath the trees?"

Rann gestured yes. "The inertial sheath would have long ago shut down; so the earth has been working on it."

"Poshtli should have worn his life vest; but lakelanders are more feckless even than hillmen."

"Maybe he did wear an inertia bubble, and it failed him when we were forced to leap. One more sorrow. One more might-have-been." Rann imagined all the possible Poshtlis whose lives had not been lived, even here among the savages.

"You expect this hired man of yours to dig up Poshtli's corpse?"

"A corpse unmodified by the nanosurgery. Our insides may be passing strange, but outwardly you and I appear merely foreign."

"Which is why we permit no autopsy."

"But Poshtli's mummy will appear more than passing strange. The humans will realize that aliens have been among them; they will restart their space programs in an effort to find our world. It is too late for us; but not for them."

"You vastly underestimate their capacity for self-deception. They will call it a hoax, or an odd and crippling mutation."

Rann hugged himself with both arms. "Captain, of the crew and science staff how many were still aboard *Vital Being* when she hit shoals and burned?"

Venkaaszbuul looked at him for a long time. Then, he said, "I believe all made it to the boats; and perhaps the boats all made it to shore and they have been living out their days concealed as we are."

Rann laughed. "Now you are overestimating *my* capacity for self-deception."

"But Rann, you know the law of the quanta. When you don't *know*, anything is possible."

That night Rann and his captain ate dinner together, and Rann prepared a meal that would not irritate their digestive tracts. They raised a glass—of filtered wine—to their comrades who had perished and another to those who inevitably would soon perish. Rann proposed a toast to the earth—the real earth, not this one on which they had been shipwrecked for so long—and he sang a poem in *puralon* to honor them, even improvising a stanza in praise of the flatlands. Venkaaszbuul declaimed a heroic ballad in *chegk* concerning some bold explorer of ages past; and it was good to hear the old tongues and the old songs, even in *chegk*, and to praise a world whose star did not so much as shine in this planet's skies. They both wept—even the flatlander captain so forgot his Schooling that tears wet his face in abundance—and they embraced and promised never again to allow the years to intervene so thickly.

In the morning, Venkaaszbuul secured Rann's promise that, should the excavation by wild chance unearth the body of Poshtli the Lakelander, he would not disclose in any manner that there were others yet living who wore such unlikely bones beneath their skins. And then he departed.

Later that same day, a sheriff's deputy served Rann with a court order to cease and desist all digging. His neighbor Alma Seakirt had objected that since the encumbrance against digging appeared in all the other deeds surrounding the wood, and because the clear intent had always been to protect the woodland, it must have been omitted in error from the Vander Alkrenn deed. Rann Valkran disputed the order in township court and when he lost, appealed to the State, where he lost again.

By that time, the hole that he and Steve had excavated had been filled in and, per court order, planted in wildflowers. As a sign of hope in the future, Ms. Seakirt said.

Rann took it hard, his neighbor later observed, and could be seen on his patio sitting before the filled-in swimming pool weeping into his lemonade. He had always been a sensitive soul, Shaw commented, much given to tears and melancholy as well as sudden enthusiasms. Even in his happier moments, he had seemed haunted by some great and terrible sorrow in his past whose memory would not release him.

So it came as no surprise when Shaw saw him one morning lying dead with a shovel in his hand in a hole he had dug in his ground. Like everyone else, he assumed at first that it had been suicide. But suicide over a swimming pool never dug? In the end, there were enough anomalies—the position of the body, the placement of the wound, certain papers he had filed with his lawyer, Sèan FitzPatrick—for the coroner to rule 'suspicious circumstances,' and order an autopsy.

Afterward, amidst the sensation that followed the autopsy and the strange artifacts found in Rann's attic, when his death had been ruled a suicide after all, Elizabeth Abbot, a grief counselor whom he had briefly consulted, remembered that he had once said that he would not give up on life out of despair, and she wondered if he might have done so out of hope.

AFTERWORD TO "BURIED HOPES"

The germ of this story was planted many years ago, when I discussed with a counselor who worked in our office building the notion of an undercover alien who goes to see a counselor. The unformed idea was that the usual clichéd alien-observer-for-the-Galactic-Union would suffer pangs of loneliness and separation from his home culture and the counselor would eventually pick up on this.

It was not that this was not much of a story, as that it was not a story at all. So not much happened, and the notion lay dormant until recently when I read a news story of a man who had unearthed mammoth bones while excavating a swimming pool on his property. That suggested the title "Buried Hopes." I began to noodle over what else someone might dig up. Hidden chambers? A doorway to other dimensions?

Then I read an essay by the philosopher James Chastek entitled "A Theme for a Sci-Fi Story That I'll Never Write," in which he laments the cliché by which the aliens are always logical and the humans are emotional, and emotion always wins. Being a Thomist philosopher, he thought this a false dichotomy and inverted the scenario to one in which the aliens cry over spilt milk while the humans try to be logical about it. I asked him if I could use it, and he said sure. You can find his essay here: *http://thomism. wordpress.com/2010/04/11/a-theme-for-a-sci-fi-story-that-ill-never-write/*

At some point, these three threads—the emotional aliens, the need to see a counselor, and the notion of buried hopes—came together, with the results you have just read.

At this point in the "neighborhood stories," Singer is dead, Henry relocated, and Kyle uploaded (or not). However, Alma from "Captive Dreams" makes a brief appearance, as does old Doc Wilkes. Rann's neighbor, Jamie Shaw, was mentioned briefly in "Hopeful Monsters" and, along with his cousin Sandra Locke, was the protagonist in another story, "The Longford Collector."

AFTERWORD TO THE AFTERWORDS

So why isn't "The Longford Collector" in this collection? Three reasons. First, it had not been originally written with that intention. Second, it treated a theme already used in one of the other stories. But most decisively, it was just too light-hearted in tone.

These stories share more than a neighborhood. They share a common ambiance of deep melancholy and terrible ambiguity. Even when a good does obtain—a treatment for progeria, a revival of space travel, a woman saved from the streets and cleansed of insanity—it is like a ray of light piercing a sky otherwise packed with dull gray lint. How often were people used without their consent, as if they were mere objects or "resources"? Mae Holloway (at least for a while), Ethan Seakirt, Sadie the Lady, Rachel Brusco. How many of their users acted from their own sense of despair? Dr. Wilkes, Alma, Henry, Karen. And is it so much different if the user and the used are the same person, as were Kyle and Rann? We are as capable of treating ourselves as objects as we are others.

I have sometimes contended that hope is the queen of virtues since without it none of the others can come into play. Despair is the one sin that is never forgiven, because it is the one that never asks forgiveness. These stories can be read as various changes on the theme of hope and despair: the hope of Dr. Wilkes, the hope of Rann Velkran, even the hopes of Kyle Buskirk or Karen Brusco. Hope fulfilled, hope mishandled, hope misplaced, hopes dashed. And with hope, faith: in nanotech; in AI; in genetic engineering. These will save us. Or not.

I've also noticed retrospectively little acts of cowardice here and there. Characters who could have said something or done something, or who could have thrown away their masks. I'll mention only Brenda in "Melodies of the Heart," Charlie and Jessie in "Hopeful Monsters," and Rann and his captain in "Buried Hopes." You may have your own list. Courage, too, is a casualty of the failure of hope.

None of this was intentional, and I don't claim all of it runs through every story. The points came to mind in retrospect, in the course of writing these Afterwords. But I am not one to suppose conscious intentions are all there are. In any case, I am not a critic, least of all of my own stories, of whose merits I may have a prejudiced view. You may see other themes. In the end, either the stories moved you in some way or other; or they did not. Against that, all analysis is futile.

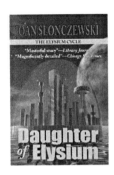

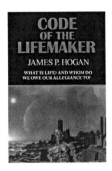

CPSIA information can be obtained at www.ICGtesting.com
Printed in the USA
BVOW031041250712

296084BV00003B/1/P